The Wager

A Unit 1 Novel

Allen Kent

AllenPearce Publishers © ©

Library of Congress Cataloging-in-Publication Data
Allen Kent
The Wager
Kent, Allen
ISBN: 0996403604
Cover Design: Jillian Farnsworth

To my Soulmate

For your love, support,

and willingness to be part of the adventure.

ACKNOWLEDGMENTS

A number of years ago a good friend, Lori Marble, suggested the general plot idea of this book as one she thought would make a great novel. I tucked it away at the time in my 'great ideas' memory bank and pulled it out when looking for the next Unit 1 idea. Lori gave me permission to use it and though I suspect it is quite different than she had envisioned, I am most grateful for both the idea and the permission.

Thanks also to my great editing team: Richard and Anne Clement, Holly Farnsworth, Diane Andris, Marilyn Jenson and Maryruth Farnsworth. As always, their help has been invaluable, both in terms of shaping the story and in minimizing errors. My appreciation also to my friends and travel agents, Karol and Bart Mayer, who helped find a fun and creative way for me to get to Budapest to research setting. Kevin and Christine McGreevy were great companions as we explored the city and visited sites mentioned in the book. And thank you to Jillian Farnsworth for her creative and attractive cover. This book would not have been possible without you all.

COVER DESIGN: JILLIAN FARNSWORTH

PART ONE

ONE

The assignment had first been given to another agent, a man Adam had never met. He knew him only as the guy who had been found buck naked, sprawled on top of an eiderdown in a small rented cottage in England's Yorkshire Dales. A thousand milligrams of heroin were on the bedside table and enough had been pumped into the man's veins to kill him three times over. In the suicide note found by the cleaning woman, the dead man described an elaborate plot to abduct American tourists throughout Europe and sell them to agents of the Iranian government to be used as hostages. He claimed to have taken more than thirty from various cities across the continent and to have received hundreds of thousands of pounds for delivering them to agents of the Islamic state to be used as some kind of human shield. But his conscience got the best of him, the note read. He had rented the picturesque little cottage out of some unexplained nostalgic urge, stripped off his clothes, and gone to bed with the white lady. Which was, of course, nothing close to the truth.

The man had never kidnapped American tourists and, even if he had, was without enough conscience to let it get the best of him. He was an agent of the Unit and had committed the cardinal sin. As Fisher put it, "He had become involved with a woman and let his dick do his thinking for him." Adam knew all this because Fisher had managed them both and had contacted Adam about getting the man's Washington apartment sanitized before anyone else could find it and look it over.

Adam had also never met Fisher. His control was just an aged, smoke-stained voice on the phone who handed out assignments and was able, on a moment's notice, to provide any support his operatives needed. Adam assumed the old man had also once been one of the skilled, loyal, but unacceptably insubordinate members of a military branch or of one of the country's legitimate security agencies. Those seemed to be the people who were pulled into Unit 1 because of their fierce independence, a belief that official channels weren't always the best way to get things done, and comfort with legal ambiguity. That, and an unshakable obsession with finishing whatever they started.

After the call from Fisher, Adam took a red-eye from Phoenix to D.C. and drove a rental from Dulles into the city. He arrived at the Georgetown brownstone in the wee hours of the morning when the city was catching the few hours of sleep it managed every night. Ninety minutes later, he walked away with everything but the man's furniture, clothing, and assorted personal items: toiletries, half a dozen biographies of early presidents, two photographs of a rocky stretch of seashore with grey, cold-looking ocean. He also left behind a large map of the United States with thirty multi-colored stickpins indicating the cities from which the tourists presumably had disappeared. Just enough evidence to convince federal investigators that the man's suicide story was legit and to keep their noses out of his real business—which had been trying to figure out what actually happened to these people.

There was something both sobering and eerily fascinating about being in the apartment of another person who, in any identifiable way, didn't exist. Someone from the Unit whom he had never heard of and who had never heard of him. Two ghost ships that didn't even pass in the night. The apartment was as blank as the man's identity. No mail. No photos of friends or family or of recognizable places. Nothing in the small refrigerator that showed where he shopped or in drawers or pockets that put any face on the man. It was as if the dead agent had sanitized the place himself before he left—which was probably the case.

The man's one act of carelessness in the apartment had been the envelope in a small black floor safe in the corner of his tiny clothes closet: a safe that would have been no more than a minor inconvenience to any skilled thief. It was obviously there for burglars looking for drug money whose synapses were already a bit fried. Adam pressured his thumbs up under the edge of the electronic key pad and lifted it off, revealing the two AA batteries that powered the code mechanism. He pushed a clip aside on the right side of the battery holder and it fell forward, dangling on its red and black wires. Behind it, a half-inch slot accepted what Adam knew to be a long, double-headed skeleton key, the manual backup if something went haywire within the electronic pad. It was not the kind of key his picks were designed to attack. The keys were far too large and cumbersome to be carried on a ring, and he knew one must be concealed somewhere in the apartment. Not in the obvious places—under a welcome mat, taped to the bottom of a drawer, or sitting on top of a door lintel. There were too few books to use as hiding places and no joints in the maple flooring beneath the throw rugs that indicated a lift-out board. Ten minutes later, Adam found the key. It was secured behind a short section of baseboard that Adam's observant eye noticed wasn't nailed into place but was held in a corner behind a bedroom nightstand only by its beveled edges.

The safe contained a single manila envelope, a stack of twenty-five one hundred dollar bills, and four cheap pre-paid cell phones, two still in their sealed plastic packaging. Adam guessed there would be prints on the money and the unpackaged phones, the same prints that would be found all over the apartment. They were the prints of the dead man and presented no risk. But they would drive investigators to distraction. They wouldn't show up in any database.

Adam glanced into the envelope, saw that it contained the photos he had been asked to retrieve, and slipped it into his briefcase. The two phones that had been activated and may contain call information went in after the pictures, but the money stayed in the safe. He used the key to snap the bolts that secured the safe door back into place and returned it to its hiding place behind the baseboard. The Feds would have their own lock expert who wouldn't need its help. He picked up his briefcase and a larger suitcase found in a hall closet that now held the dead man's laptop, a plastic bag stuffed with the contents of a shredder, and a notepad that had been left on the bedside table. An imprint on the yellow surface was deep enough that Adam could clearly read "Kate," along with a ten-digit phone number. Another indication of the carelessness that had killed the man.

Adam gave the apartment a quick final walk-through and paused for a moment at the door. In his hands he held the remnants of a solitary life—one very much like his own. He felt the need to offer some kind of benediction but could think of nothing to say. Stepping quietly into the hallway, he locked the door and walked out into the first pink blush of an early Washington morning.

At a rest stop along the Dulles Access Road on his way to the airport, Adam handed off the suitcase to another of Fisher's sanitizers. The man would do whatever Phase II sanitizers do with the effects of a man whose lack of identity needs to become permanent. The briefcase and photos remained with Adam. By 10:15 a.m. local time, he was back in Phoenix, having spent most of the flight ruminating over how absolutely dispensable the agents of Unit 1 were and how quickly a man whose identity had already been completely reinvented could lose what little was left of himself. Who was this Georgetown agent and where had he gone wrong? They were supposed to be the best and the brightest—stronger, quicker, better trained, and more disciplined. By the time his flight touched down in Phoenix, Adam realized that he was probably no smarter or better trained than the best of the enemy. He just had to depend on making fewer mistakes—and having better luck. Some might say he had the advantage of God and right on his side, which was a load of bull. One man's god and truth were another man's idols and blasphemy. Adam didn't put a lot of stock in God delivering him from evil. He had seen too many lives lost on both sides of the God-Evil equation. But he did have *his own* sense of right, and that would have to do. He had absolutely nothing else.

* * *

Adam's induction into Unit 1 had followed three distinguished years as an Air Force instructor pilot that ended suddenly when a sandhill crane smashed through the canopy of his T-38 at three hundred knots. The shattering collision instantly killed the student in the front seat and sent a bullet-sized piece of Plexiglas through Adam's visor and into his left eye. Under most circumstances the accident would have ended his military career with an honorable discharge with disability. But when Adam managed to land the crippled jet trainer with the canopy largely blown away and the left side of his face blind and bloodied, he had become something of a superstar—the kind the military likes to keep around to trot out on ceremonial occasions. In his case, they chose to showcase him to their finest officer candidates by placing him in a classroom at the Air Force Academy in Colorado Springs. A master's in engineering from MIT made him perfect for the Academy's math and sciences-based curriculum, a match seemingly made in heaven. But the groom immediately found that he loathed the arranged bride, the be-on-display expectations of the new in-laws, and a kind of regimentation that was against his basic nature. Within three years of leaving the cockpit, his other marriage had disintegrated. His nights were haunted by flashbacks of trying to focus on the instrument panel through a spray of blood as he struggled to line the aircraft up on his last final approach. Days among the Academy cadets served as constant reminders of the opportunities awaiting those who could both see and do. When the time came to re-up, he knew that he couldn't ride this disaster all the way to the ground, and he chose to bail out.

The initial contact from the Unit had come when he was standing on the balcony of his apartment overlooking Gleneagle Golf Course, gazing across the valley at the spires of the Air Force Academy chapel rising against the backdrop of the foothills of the Rockies. His furniture was already gone, sold with the red '85 Mustang convertible to buy a van. His name at the time had been Tom Mercomes and all he had to show for his life was in the boxes stacked on the living room floor behind him. As soon as the apartment manager came to check the place over, he was history.

Behind him through the open patio doors, the phone buzzed loudly against the granite countertop. The apartment manager must have been delayed. Tom walked across the empty room and snatched the receiver from its cradle.

"Mercomes," he answered.

"Captain Mercomes, I understand you are a person who enjoys interesting assignments and likes to do things your own way."

"Who is this?"

"I represent a group that might have an attractive employment opportunity for you." The voice at the other end was a raspy baritone.

"What kind of job are we talking about?"

"It has many of the same enticements as your old flying position. I can't say more about it now, other than that it's not Air Force but is involved in maintaining the nation's security. If you're interested, you will find another phone in your mailbox. I'll call you in exactly ten minutes."

"What the …?"

There was silence at the other end of the line.

Tom tested the connection. "What makes you think I'll be interested?"

"If you're not at least curious, you aren't the person we're looking for…." And the line went dead.

He had been curious enough to go to his mailbox, retrieve the phone, and take the call. And he had been intrigued enough to accept the assignment. But the man sent by Fisher to clean up after an agent found naked in the Yorkshire Dales was no longer recognizable as Tom Mercomes. The face was essentially the same shape: long and chiseled with a lop-sided grin that lifted the left side of his mouth more than the right, and the same engaging hazel eyes. But Tom Mercomes had been balding, with only a thin peninsula of brown hair that ran from his crown to the center of a high forehead. This man had a full head of hair so expertly grafted that there were no visible rows or patches, just thick brown waves that he combed straight back. Tom Mercomes' nose had been broken as a teenager and allowed to heal with a visible leeward tilt. This man's nose was straight and narrower at the bridge, his ears set more tightly against his head.

Mercomes had almost always worn a black eye patch over his left eye, finding it less disconcerting to others than his less-than-convincing prosthetic. But with a new prosthesis, even when standing a few yards from the former instructor pilot, it was difficult to tell that one eye was artificial. And though he still often chose to wear the patch, this man called himself Adam Zak.

* * *

Though the flight from Dulles to Phoenix took just under five hours, Adam gained three back as he flew west. By noon he was comfortably tucked away in a small second bedroom that served as the den in his ground-floor apartment. He had picked a place on Main Street in the heart of Old Town Scottsdale in what was called the Arts District, no more than a hundred steps from at least ten upscale galleries. Here a man wearing a black eye patch, heavy beard, and long brown ponytail looked completely at home. In fact, his appearance gave the area a certain air of authenticity for the pink-legged tourists and sagging, halter-topped snow bunnies who window-shopped the street and filled the trendy restaurants. Bronze statuary crowded the narrow paved walk that separated his apartment building from the Xanadu Gallery next door and a few feet toward the street, a small pergola with a dome the color of raw adobe provided daytime art seekers a brief respite from the relentless Arizona sun. To other residents of Main Street Plaza, Adam was a thirty-something escapee from Silicon Valley who had made enough by selling his startup to PayPal to live the life of a man of leisure in the Valley of the Sun.

"We did the same thing PayPal did and had enough of the market share that we were worth buying," was all the explanation that seemed necessary. Residents of Old Town were used to the story.

Comfortably settled in beside a rustic barnwood table that served as a desk, Adam slipped the photographs from the envelope he had retrieved from the Georgetown safe and spread them across the varnished surface. Five beautiful women and an attractive young man—all professionally photographed. One of the women was in evening wear that was clearly designed to showcase her ample cleavage. Two wore bikinis that did the same for their entire bodies, and three waist-up shots were nude. Adam studied the bodies for a moment, noting that all of the women looked skillfully augmented, then turned his attention to the faces. These were not your run-of-the-mill prostitutes and not even a reasonable cross section of Washington's high-end escort stable. There wasn't a sultry, seductive, pouty-lipped beauty among them. They had been chosen for their alluring look of innocence—the Mary Anns that he remembered from watching old *Gilligan's Island* reruns as a kid. Not a Ginger in the bunch. Even the guy, though sculpted from neck to navel, had the face of a country club valet. And that, he guessed, was not accidental.

He turned to a message from Fisher that accompanied the file and learned that the assignment had nothing to do with the missing tourists. That, apparently, had either been passed on to another member of the Unit or resolved to Fisher's satisfaction. The message read:

A number of high-ranking government officials are being blackmailed after being compromised by partners they met through seemingly "chance" encounters. The partners disappear immediately after the brief affairs, even in cases in which the official was interested in continuing the relationship. The clients include a cabinet member and powerful legislators, several of whom claim there was no relationship and they have no idea how the pictures were taken or "created."

Shortly after the affair is broken off, hand-delivered packages show up containing photos, videos, and taped conversations of a seriously compromising nature. No requests for money—just for key votes, committee decisions, or public statements supporting or opposing important positions contrary to the officials' known political views. Three senators and the cabinet member took this to the Director since they had been close Senate colleagues before the Director came to the CIA. He views it as being too messy for the FBI to handle, but reaching crisis proportion due to its scale and sophistication. Director wants us to track and stop.

Hand-written notes on two pieces of yellow legal paper outlined what Adam's colleague from the Unit had discovered before being lured to the English cottage and pumped full of heroin. He had met privately with a number of the compromised officials. From a binder created using internet photos of expensive East Coast escorts, they had identified the six whose pictures were in the envelope. The agent had managed to track down three before his death. Women with faces and occupations like these couldn't afford to keep them hidden. One had shown up working with an expensive escort service in New Orleans, one in LA, and a third in Miami. New Orleans and LA had claimed ignorance and said they'd never been on the East Coast. Miami was the only one on the sheet with a name—Brandy Wingate. She had admitted to the liaison but denied she knew they were being photographed. She was aware, she said, that she had been hired to seduce a prominent senator. The woman who contacted by phone had guaranteed $50,000 if she could get him in bed and "doing some crazy shit."

Adam slid his chair down the table to his laptop and plugged "Brandy Wingate" into the search engine. May as well start with the one who had admitted being involved. If he could reach her again, she might remember something more about the woman who had called her. Young voice or old? Accent? Did this Brandy have a phone number for the woman?

The first five search entries under the name were for a Texas attorney, but number six found Brandy Wingate in Miami and told Adam there was no need to try to meet with the woman. It was a front page article from the *Herald* with a headline "Grisly Penthouse Murder." Brandy Wingate, pricey Miami call girl, had been found in the penthouse bedroom of a Miami Beach waterfront high-rise with all ten digits cut from her feet and hands by garden pruners that were conspicuously left at the scene. Her throat had been slashed and her tongue severed and removed, then pushed backward into her gaping mouth. When found, the girl's mutilated hands were resting on her chest, her toeless feet tucked up against her pelvis with soles together. The Miami Beach chief of police speculated she had been tortured for information, then murdered and carefully arranged to fit into a photograph.

"Gangland or mob killing," he told the media. "And meant to be a message to someone—or several someones." When asked what the message was, the chief said simply, "You'd better keep your mouth shut."

TWO

Security cameras at the Downtown Berkeley BART station would eventually identify Joshua Shallenburger boarding the southbound Richmond-Daly City Line just before 7:00 a.m. on Tuesday morning—though not by name. He looked like any of a hundred other graduate students at UC Berkeley, a serious face partially hidden by a healthy dark beard, round sunglasses, jeans and a faded UC sweatshirt. A green Oakland A's baseball cap was pulled low over what authorities would later guess to be a shaggy brown wig. He was pulling a mid-sized roller bag and carried a backpack loosely slung over one shoulder. The train was packed with morning commuters and as he stepped into the car, he tucked the roller bag against the stainless steel partition just inside the door and stood holding the overhead rail. The train was crowded enough that despite warnings, after two more stops no one was paying attention to who got on when or where, or who was carrying what.

What the cameras didn't reveal was that Joshua was not a UC student at all. But for the past two weeks he had been a serious student of BART. He knew that the 3.6 mile tube that went under the Bay between San Francisco and Oakland had not been constructed by drilling a tunnel. It had been built in sections on land, hauled out into the bay on barges, and sunk to the bottom, then stabilized with sand and gravel. The tunnel opened in 1974 but had recently been refurbished, its deepest section 135 feet below the surface.

Joshua had also carefully read an online case study that described a threat analysis and response plan for the massive system and knew that the roller bag would be the problem. But he had also learned that during the 7:00 a.m. rush hour, though security was heavier than normal, the crush of passengers through the gates and a desire to maintain a high level of customer service led to only cursory screenings. He had carefully timed his arrival to be able to move through ticket control and directly onto the train, minimizing the chance of passing a canine patrol with a particularly sensitive nose.

Images from on-board cameras relayed to BART's Operations Central Control at the Lake Merritt headquarters in Oakland showed that he appeared to be playing a game on his smartphone while the train absorbed more passengers at the Ashby, McArthur, and 19th Street stations. Just before the doors closed at the West Oakland stop he stepped off, carrying the backpack but leaving the suitcase behind. Continuous BART warnings to passengers caution them to watch for unattended bags and to notify authorities immediately if a suspicious package is discovered. But in the crush of the morning commute, few passengers paid attention to anything other than keeping their cups of coffee upright or avoiding the elbows of the person crammed tightly beside them. The system's cars were designed to comfortably carry sixty but accommodate two hundred during the morning rush. The train started the descent into the tunnel under the Bay with a capacity load.

Two minutes out of the West Oakland Station, when beneath the deepest part of the Bay, an igniter in the black roller bag detonated forty pounds of C4 explosive—a homemade version of two M183 military demolition kits designed to bring down major hardened obstructions. Joshua had not manufactured the explosive, though he could have found instructions using the same internet search tools that had educated him about BART.

The forty pounds of C4 blew the third car on the Richmond-Daly City Red Line and a passing car on the Blue Line to Dublin Station to smithereens and ruptured the tube one hundred feet below the surface of the Bay. Joshua felt the explosion and heard a rumble somewhere out beneath the Bay Bridge. He knew that tons of water were flooding the steel tube in both directions. But he did not know until late the next day that 1,487 people had been in the two trains and that he had created the worst transit disaster in the nation's history. By then he was 900 miles away.

* * *

Adam had waited until eight to call Fisher. The man was always available no matter what the hour. But it seemed decent somehow to wait until later in the morning, even though he suspected his control was in the Eastern Time zone.

"I'm feeling some need to get this extortion thing wrapped up," he said when the old man answered. "One of the girls was murdered in Miami and I suspect it was because she talked to whoever had this case before it came to me."

He had learned during his first months working for Unit 1 that there were three cardinal rules when calling Fisher: always use the secure phone and number; no formalities, just get to the point; and never assume there was something the old man couldn't get done.

"What do you need?" the voice rasped into the phone.

"I'd like copies of the actual blackmail photos, tapes, or recordings. Some of these people claim they don't remember it happening and I'd like to either put that to bed—so to speak—or see if these pictures are being doctored in some way we can't detect. And maybe I can learn something from the settings. Won't know 'til I can inspect them."

"I'll see what I can do," Fisher said. "And you may have another candidate. This morning's *Washington Post* said Senator Von Holten has come out in favor of significant gun control measures."

"Idaho's Von Holten?" Adam's tone smacked of skepticism.

"Yes. Our Mr. Fire-Ready-Aim. He published an opinion piece in which he says he's come to recognize the wisdom in Senator Mehrens' position that we're seeing far too many gun deaths in the U.S. He's now advocating a ban on assault rifles, mandatory background checks before all sales, and some culpability by manufacturers when a sale through an approved distributor is made without proper backgrounding."

Adam sniffed. "You're right. Either hell's freezing over or someone has pictures of the good senator with his gun out of the holster. I think I'd better pay him a visit."

Fisher's gravelly chuckle was cut suddenly short and for a moment Adam thought the line had gone dead. Then the voice was back, quieted almost to a whisper. "Do you have the news on?"

Adam glanced through the door of the study at the flat screen mounted on the wall on the other side of the living room. "You mean now? Am I watching the news now?"

"Yes. Turn it on."

"What's going on? Sounds ominous."

"Someone's just bombed the BART tunnel under the San Francisco Bay with casualties estimated at 1500."

"*My God*!" Adam jumped from the chair, searching for the remote. "Any claims of responsibility?"

"They're talking about that now.... Apparently the networks have received a tweet that says 'BART is just the beginning. Allah is Great. Beware the Warriors of WIS.'"

"World Islamic State," Adam murmured. "The crazy bastards are here. Tomorrow Von Holten will be calling for every American to carry rocket-mounted grenades!"

"If he doesn't," Fisher said, "we'll know someone really has him by the short hairs."

THREE

If Dan Triplett were to credit one individual with having influenced his decision to become a professional soldier, it would have been James Brewer—though he suspected he had been born with a love for combat coded somewhere deep within his DNA. But Mr. Brewer seemed to have recognized the latent need within the perpetually sullen tenth grader in his first period English class. After the bell one morning, the teacher handed Dan a book of American short fiction with a yellow post-it note stuck between two pages.

"I'd like you to look at this one story," he said. "Then tell me what you think."

Dan paused long enough to say, "Why don't you ask someone else," but couldn't get out of the room before Brewer had a chance to follow up.

"There's no one else in the class whose opinion I'd like to hear as much as yours," he said.

Dan swept the book from the man's hand but left it unopened on his dresser for the rest of the week. On the weekend when a torrential spring thunderstorm swept across the Camas Prairie and brought everything in the small Idaho town of Grangeville to a soggy standstill, the teen's curiosity got the best of him. Without the downpour, he would have been stalking through the nearby Gospel Hump Wilderness with a .410 shotgun tucked under his arm, looking for pine hens—or making a solo descent into Hells Canyon in search of Indian artifacts. Since his father's death in a logging accident the summer he turned eleven, Dan had grown to prefer his own company. With the rain sloshing over the eaves of the family's white-framed two-story, he slouched on the bed against a pile of pillows in his second floor bedroom, glowering at the weather. The yellow bookmark caught his eye and he retrieved the book from the dresser, slid a thumbnail in beside the tab, and looked at the story's first page. "The Most Dangerous Game." Cool title!

He read the first few lines.

"Off there to the right--somewhere--is a large island," said

Whitney. "It's rather a mystery--"

"What island is it," Rainsford asked.

"The old charts call it 'Ship-Trap Island,'" Whitney replied. "A suggestive name, isn't it? Sailors have a curious dread of the place. I don't know why. Some superstition--"

An hour later Dan Triplett closed the book and leaned back against his rough pine headboard. He had read, then re-read Richard Connell's classic short story about a big game hunter marooned on an island inhabited by a mad Cossack who rescued shipwrecked sailors, then used them as quarry for his own solitary hunts. By the time Dan finished the second reading he knew what he wanted to do with his life. He didn't bother with any of the other stories but delivered the book into his teacher's hands at the beginning of the hour on Monday.

"What did you think?" Mr. Brewer asked.

"I liked it," Dan said.

"Was there anything in particular you took away from it?" the teacher asked.

"Yeah," Dan said. "The greatest sport in the world is hunting other men."

* * *

As Triplett now leaned back in a rustic pine rocker and lifted his booted feet onto the rail of the porch that stretched across the front of his log home, he was the product of what his English teacher would eventually refer to grimly as "Brewer's Folly." Triplett called the place his "cabin in the woods," but it was neither a cabin nor in the woods. The multi-gabled mountain lodge perched at the timber's edge on a hillside above two hundred acres of meadow that surrounded a clear alpine lake. Beyond the meadow more timber stretched to the horizon and Triplett owned the land for as far as he could see.

The voice on the other end of the phone was a rich, sonorous baritone but the words were clipped with rage. "Our deal was to create a scare—not kill half the damn Bay Area!"

"Our deal," Triplett said testily, "was to put the fear of God into these toads so they'd start acting like patriots. I'd say we did a pretty damn good job!"

"But fifteen hundred people! My God! We killed our own citizens!"

"If I remember your exact words," Triplett said, "they were 'This may be the worst enemy we've ever faced and the country's asleep. We've got to wake them up! This is war!' And in war, there's going to be collateral damage."

"If I recall my words," the icy voice said, "I told you we needed a Pearl Harbor, but without the casualties. I wasn't talking about this kind of action. Nothing close to it! I'm out as of now…."

"I don't think so," Triplett said quietly, watching two bull elk move out of the trees along one edge of the meadow and walk cautiously toward the lake. The rest of the herd would follow when the leaders' posture relaxed, signaling all was safe.

"You financed this little project and we already have two others ready to go—paid for by your money," he said.

"It wasn't my money—just money I found for you. And those people had no idea this kind of thing would happen! *I'm out!*" The man at the other end was shouting.

"Follow the money," Triplett said. "You're in—and will be to the end."

"No more killing then…."

"The wheels are in motion. It's out of my control at this point. Has to be—to ensure plausible deniability."

"Speaking of 'out of control,' what happened to your man Von Holten? I thought you had him bought and delivered."

"I'll deal with Von Holten," Triplett said, his own voice rising. "You just take care of your end of this business."

"I never intended this…. It's already gone way too far."

"It's just beginning," Triplett said. "We're going to do just what you contacted us about. We're going to save America."

FOUR

He had never seen Washington this quiet. The Mall in front of the Capitol was a no-man's land, the usual flood of tourists avoiding the Metro and any public place that might be next on the terrorist target list. An occasional car moved cautiously along Constitution Avenue. Federal employees who couldn't reach a destination using the vast network of underground tunnels that connected government buildings scurried furtively from one to another without so much as a nod to passers-by.

A lanky six-two gentleman with a short beard, shoulder-length hair pulled into a ponytail, and black eye patch seemed to be just what security at the Russell Senate Office Building had been watching for—even when wearing a blue blazer over neatly pressed gray pants and a crisp, button-down shirt. Adam allowed them to pull him aside for a quick wanding and pat-down without comment, even though he had stepped through the metal detector fully in the green. Then he showed them the personal invitation card from Senator Von Holten.

"Our apologies, sir," one of the guards said when he produced the card. "We have to be particularly cautious after the BART incident."

"Understood," Adam said, then added, "though I noticed you didn't wand and pat down the two young ladies who passed through just in front of me." The guard's jaw tightened but he said nothing.

On the second floor Adam found the office with "Charles Von Holten—Idaho" on a bronze plaque beside the door and entered the small anteroom. A young, dark-suited aide stood to greet him.

"Mr. Zak?" the aide asked, showing the same tight-lipped suspicion Adam had seen on the faces of the security guards. He had barely nodded before the young man guided him to the senator's door and ushered him into the office. The senator was apparently anxious to see him.

Von Holten stood stone-faced behind his spacious desk and didn't step forward to offer Adam his hand. Around him the office was a museum of Western art, interspersed with photos of the silver-haired majority leader in boots and faded jeans sitting astride a sorrel mare. In an 8x10 beside the door as Adam entered, the senator squatted beside a downed elk, a vintage 30-06 rifle propped against one knee and his hands holding the majestic set of antlers aloft for the photograph. One side of the desk was covered with framed photos of his wife and three daughters, all looking blissfully happy somewhere on Von Holten's 2000-acre Idaho ranch. The photos were carefully arranged to be visible both to the senator and to visitors sitting in front of the desk. He was a "family values" man, and the desk screamed both family and values.

Adam scanned the office quickly, recognizing on a tabletop a Remington bronze of four cowboys riding side-by-side with six shooters raised to the sky. To the left of the desk hung a Charles Russell painting of a grizzly stalking menacingly through the timber, a wolf skulking in the background. If he were a visiting constituent, Adam knew that there would be a ten minute walk-around as the senator chatted about his collection, how much he loved the West, and what a down-home guy he really was. Then there would be the "What can I do for you?" But today, he skipped right past the chit-chat and without inviting Adam to sit, waited until the door was closed and said sharply, "What is it you want?"

Adam indicated four leather-backed chairs grouped around the dark, cherrywood table that held the Remington bronze.

"Can we sit? I have a few questions."

Von Holten didn't move. "You contacted the office and said you wanted to talk about some pictures. Let's start by you telling me what this is all about?" He faced Adam directly but his eyes studied him up and down as if scanning him for a wire or wondering what kind of long-haired liberal had come to make the next outrageous demand.

Adam again gestured toward the chairs. "You responded pretty quickly for not knowing what I wanted to talk about. But I'm not going to just stand here in the middle of the office. Come take a seat." He moved to the table and settled into one of the chairs. The senator paused for a moment, looked again toward the office door, then frowned in resignation and moved around the desk to sit opposite him.

"What is it you want?" he asked again.

"I want to help you out of this jam," Adam said evenly. "First of all, you aren't in it alone. There are at least a half-dozen others in a similar mess. I would guess more. But I need to know what happened, when, and with whom."

The muscles in the senator's jaw tightened, then relaxed and he leaned back, lifting one booted foot over a knee and resting his hands in his lap. His gray eyes examined Adam's face with intense suspicion.

"What makes you think I'm involved in something?"

"Your vote on gun control, for one thing. And your immediate scheduling of this appointment when all I said to your appointment secretary was that I needed to talk to you about the pictures."

The senator tilted his head slightly to one side, his brow furrowing just enough to be noticed. "Who are you?" he asked.

"A person who's been asked to give you some help with this."

"From one of the agencies?"

"No. This isn't being handled by the agencies."

"What do you know about it?" The senator again glanced toward the door.

"I know that a number of you are being blackmailed by someone for your votes and that the extortion is being done with photos or videos of you in some very compromising situations. Situations that don't exactly smack of family values, God, and country."

The senator flushed but his face remained an expressionless mask. "I don't need the sarcasm," he said flatly. "What do you mean when you say you've been asked to help?"

"I'm trying to assess the extent of the extortion, collect all the information I can, minimize the damage, and make it disappear."

"By yourself?"

"By myself."

And you think you can do all that alone?"

"Would you like more people involved?"

Von Holten lifted one hand from his knee, rested the elbow on the chair arm, and rubbed the crease between his chin and lower lip with the tip of a finger. "I'll repeat my question. What do you want from me?"

"I want the pictures or videos to study and I want you to tell me everything you can remember about the circumstances that produced them."

"And if I destroyed them…?"

"I don't think you did. You needed them in case someone like me came along and you thought you could get some help."

"I'm still a little uneasy about this man with no credentials who wants to take copies of what he describes as career-ending photographs. How can I know you're who you say you are?"

Adam reached into the inside pocket of his blazer and produced a business card. It bore the seal of the Central Intelligence Agency and a name the senator recognized.

"Call and ask," Adam said, leaning back in his chair. "That's a direct number."

"I thought you weren't Agency."

"I'm not. But he can assure you I'm legit."

"This number might just go to some phony person who's expecting the call and will tell me you're the real thing…."

"You're on the Intelligence Committee. I'm sure you have his number somewhere. Call whatever number you like."

The senator pushed abruptly from the chair, strode to the desk, and thumbed through an ancient Rolodex. He punched in a number and watched Adam intently until his call was answered.

"Steve? Von Holten here. I've got a man sitting in my office who tells me…." The man at the other end interrupted and the senator listened for a full minute.

"Why isn't the FBI investigating this?" he asked finally, then listened again.

"I guess you're right," he said. "I know the press watches those people pretty closely to see what they're up to. But I can't say I like the looks of this guy. Could be some damn extra from a pirate movie." He listened for another minute, his face again reddening across the temples.

"Well, you oughta at least insist that they cut their hair and look professional," he finished and hung up the phone. "So," he said, returning to the chair. "What do I have to tell you?"

FIVE

The screen in front of Dreu Sason displayed a dizzying array of words, letters and symbols—cryptic code written in C that constructed the security system for one of the nation's largest federal agencies. As she scrolled slowly down through the lines, insuring that her staffer had followed all of the appropriate protocols, her assistant rapped twice on the half-open door and poked her head in.

"Call for you, Dreu. Some guy who sounds pretty insistent."

"Can you get a number? I'm almost through with this...."

"He said to tell you it's Randall Murch...."

Dreu was working at a standing desk beside the window of her single-story company building in West Chandler, Arizona, and immediately stepped back from the desk. She turned away from the woman to gaze out at the small artificial lake that curled behind the complex of office buildings.

"You okay?" the assistant asked.

Dreu nodded without turning, then sucked in a deep breath and walked over to the table that held her office phone. "Transfer it in," she said. "I guess I'm ready for this."

"Well," she said when the line connected. "If it isn't Jason Bourne!"

"Somehow I didn't take you as a Ludlum reader," the caller said.

"I don't read Ludlum. I watch Matt Damon. And I thought I was supposed to call you first."

"Would you have called?" he asked.

"To be honest, I've been thinking about it. But I was a little afraid you wouldn't still have that phone."

"I keep it with me all the time—just waiting for the call."

"But decided you couldn't wait any longer, I gather."

"Actually, I need your help. I'm looking for a great computer analyst and you're the best I know."

"How did you know where to call me? Oh, wait! I forgot! You can find out anything!"

"You told me when FedTegrity closed down in Dallas that

you were moving out here and planned to stay in program security for federal agencies. That didn't make you too hard to find. But you don't seem to advertise."

"No need," she said. "I have all the business I can handle with eleven people and don't want to expand beyond that. And we're unlisted…which means you did get some help."

"I confess. Does your company have a name? I drove by the address I was given and didn't see any signage."

"You came by here? When was this?"

"Earlier today. Nice, innocuous location. Dentist office, psychiatrist, some kind of entertainment business in your little complex of buildings. And one no-name generic. Very nice, though."

"I don't know whether to be flattered or frightened," she said, glancing out across the small lake at what was still a vacant lot in the east Phoenix suburb. She wouldn't have been surprised to see him standing in the scraped patch of dirt across the lake, giving her a playful wave.

Her introduction to the caller had come when she was working as senior analyst for a Dallas firm that had become a major player in a national security breach and he had used her to get to her boss. She had once been certain she loved him.

After a pause that was becoming uncomfortably long she asked, "Why did you come by?"

"I've been resisting the impulse for a long time but decided if I was going to call, I'd like to have some feel for where you are. It helps me place you in my brain."

"You know my last stalking experience didn't turn out well," she said, hoping that her tone was light enough that he realized she was partly teasing.

"It can only be stalking if I keep it up," he said. "And I'd rather meet on your terms. I really do need your help."

"And that's why you called…?"

"I've been looking for a reason. But this is, in fact, a real one. Can we meet for dinner tonight?"

She had been feeling the lightness that came from just hearing his voice but at the thought of meeting, her pulse quickened. She wasn't certain if it was anxiety or excitement.

"I'm not sure…."

"Which means you're free if you want to be."

She was silent for several seconds and he waited without prodding.

"I've missed you more than I ever wanted to allow myself to," she said finally. "I'm a little afraid to get together again."

"As I told you when I spoke to you last, where this goes needs to be your decision. I know what I want—and can assure you I've missed you just as much."

She dropped down into the chair beside the table that held the phone. "And you say you could use my help. Can you elaborate?"

"I'd rather not. You know. Jason Bourne and all that. I'd prefer to meet and talk."

She paused for another moment. "What are you going by nowadays? Are you using that Mr. Murch all the time or are you back to Zak?"

"No. It's Adam Zak. I just knew Murch would get your attention without giving your assistant my real name."

"Do I even know your real name?"

"As much as anyone does. Can we meet?"

Dreu thought about their last meeting at Sandi Cooperman's ranch north of Dallas and how angry she had been. He had just saved her from the stalker they were joking about. But at the same time, it had become clear that after convincing herself there was finally some man she could let back into her life, someone she could trust with her closely guarded affection, she really didn't know him at all. He had used her to get to her boss—and though he claimed to have developed a genuine affection for her, he admitted the deception. Even so, since that day there hadn't been another that she didn't wonder where he was and want to make the call she had said she might someday make.

"You told me you were moving to Scottsdale and I assume you have," she said finally. "There's a place up there called Brio Tuscan Grill. Do you remember Brio? The girl I worked with when I was in New York? When she came out here for a visit we thought it would be a fun place to try. Food's good. Quiet. Do you know it?"

"Up in the north part of town in the Quarter," he said.

"That's it. Can you meet me there at seven?"

"I can—and thank you."

"Do I need to bring anything but myself?"

"Maybe a vivid imagination," he said.

* * *

The exit from Interstate 435 onto State Highway D was marked with a one mile warning and Dwayne Cargile signaled and eased the Forester into the right lane. He had been on the road for just over twenty-four hours, breaking the drive into eight-hour days to keep him fresh and alert. He couldn't afford a traffic mistake and he needed to be at his best tomorrow morning. The GPS indicated he was less than ten minutes from his destination and he began to relax—feeling a bit like he did when he drove into the return lot with a rental car and there were no bumps or scratches.

His drive had taken him through Missoula and Bozeman, Montana, then down to Gillette in Wyoming and across into South Dakota for a tedious 380 miles to Sioux Falls. On the eastern edge of the Dakotas he picked up I-29 south through Nebraska into Missouri. He had driven during the latter part of the week—Wednesday, Thursday, Friday—and traffic was light across I-90 and south until he hit Omaha. Then it started to pour rain and he was sloshing along in the wake and spray of a steady stream of eighteen wheelers that kept his wipers drumming at a rapid cadence. There seemed to be patrolmen every twenty miles—possibly because of the downpour, possibly to slow Friday traffic. He was trying to be a model citizen and with this cargo, he couldn't afford even a minor fender-bender. Missouri County Road D looked like a farm road and would mean lighter traffic, no heavy trucks, and no cops.

He exited right, turning back over the interstate and west for a hundred yards on D, then south on Brightwell Road. A white pickup passed and the man gestured a friendly salute by raising two fingers from the steering wheel. Dwayne signaled back but the truck was past. Two miles south he turned again west and drove another mile to a crossroad, blocked in front and to his left by yellow pipe gates. Beyond was a high chain link fence that forced him south onto what the sign said was NW Hampton. He knew that a short distance ahead behind another metal gate, a gravel drive led to two storage barns surrounded by cornfields. He slowed to a crawl as he passed the gate, checking the chain and padlock that secured it and reaffirming that both barns had large open bays facing the road. The rain had lightened to a drizzle and he pulled onto the gravel that separated the road from the gate and climbed out, looking behind the Forester. The rock surface had been packed hard by farm machinery and there were no tread marks.

As he made the trip east, Dwayne had spent his nights camping, stopping in organized campgrounds to avoid being questioned by curious authorities. Tonight he had a spot reserved at Weston Bend State Park, fifteen miles north of the storage barns along a sweeping bend of the Missouri River. By daybreak tomorrow, he would be back at the cornfield with the padlock cut and the car secreted inside one the barns. He would have his cargo unloaded, and he would be ready. He was exactly a half mile off the end of Kansas City International Airport's runway 19R.

SIX

She was even more stunning than he remembered, looking much more the woman who had spent six years walking the runways of Manhattan's Fifth Avenue than one of the country's most respected computer security experts. He made it a practice in his business never to keep photos and he was reminded that the images in his memory never seemed quite as vivid as the real thing. She wore trim black pants that accentuated her long, slender legs and a loose, long-tailed shirt in cobalt blue that fell below her hips, the sleeves rolled loosely to her elbows. Her ebony hair, usually kept in a single braid in his memory, fell in loose curls behind her ears. Her dark eyes and caramel-brown skin, blessings of mixed Indian-Spanish European ancestry, had a radiance that suggested she had spent extra time getting ready. As she approached, patrons at the other tables glanced up at the tall, statuesque woman and a general hush fell over the room, followed by quiet murmurs as guests bent toward each other to ask if she was someone they should recognize.

As the waiter brought her to the booth Adam rose and gave her a light hug, then stepped back and looked at her with what he hoped wasn't transparent adoration.

"My God, you are beautiful," he said, and she smiled in a way that welcomed the greeting.

"And you have hair again," she said. "I like you better that way." The last time they had been together he had not only been traveling as Randall Murch, but had shaved his head and beard and removed the black patch to match his travel documents.

"Back to my old self," he said, inviting her into the seat opposite him as the waiter brought water. He sat for a moment without speaking, etching her image into his brain until certain he wouldn't lose the detail again.

She broke the awkward silence. "I was surprised to get your call. I honestly wasn't sure whether I'd been more than an access point to my boss during that Weavers investigation."

"And I wasn't sure you would take the call. I know you felt betrayed—but my feelings were always genuine and still are.

I've missed you."

She spread her napkin on her lap and looked absently at the menu. "But you called because you need my help…."

He heard again in her voice a fleeting echo of the deep-seated insecurity that had surprised him so much about her when they first met. She was classically beautiful and had been offered what most young women would view as a dream career, modeling for one of New York's best known agencies. But she had been born into a family of Stanford physicists for whom neither beauty nor the fame it could bring were measures of legitimate success.

Imitating her mother's clipped Indo-British accent she had once told him, "Mother would tell me over and over, 'So you are a pretty girl. What does that say about you? Nothing! You must show that you are an *intelligent* girl! Then you will have respect." She had returned from New York for a master's degree in computer science from Stanford with areas of specialization in both network security and information management and analytics, but as she looked at him across the table at Brio's, she still seemed to be grasping for that needed ounce of respect.

"I called because needing your help gave me an excuse," he said. "As you know, I have other sources of information. But I saw this as a chance to come to you." He paused as the waiter took their orders: a strawberry chicken salad for Dreu, Shrimp Mediterranean for Adam. He selected a bottle of the house Della Venezie Pinot Grigio and kept conversation light until each had a full glass.

"Tell me about your new business," he said as they waited for their entrees.

"We're doing much of the same kind of federal security work we did at FedTegrity and have added custom requests from a few business clients—some of whom you've heard about in the news. When a company has a huge security breach, they often come to us for solutions. Our client list is classified but you can guess who's on it."

"I assume your federal work requires pretty high levels of security clearance…."

"Everyone in the firm is thoroughly vetted and has top secret clearances. And I have them randomly reviewed on an ongoing basis."

"When we were together last, you weren't sure you could trust me," he said, smiling thinly. "And ironically, I now have to ask for your absolute trust. I'm not sure I can say this has quite the catastrophic potential of the Weavers' affair you helped with, but it does have some significant national security implications. Is that something you even want to consider getting mixed up in again?"

"Does it have anything to do with the BART attack?"

"No. I'm sure the FBI's investigating that. All that work can be done with public knowledge."

"It's frightening," she said. "Most of my employees who were using mass transit are now choosing to drive. But I'm afraid I can't commit until I know what your issue is." She looked at him with dark, serious eyes. "And if it involves you seducing other women while I provide you with support, no thanks."

"Nothing quite so tame, I'm afraid. There does happen to be a lot of sex involved—but I'm not in the mix."

Dreu continued to study his face thoughtfully. "Will your contact person—whoever it is you check in with when you need information—approve of this liaison?"

"He did before. But you didn't want in. And to be honest, I don't plan to ask this time."

She smiled and took a sip of her wine. "That sounds even more like Jason Bourne. But I do have to admit you have me intrigued. What is it you need help with?"

"No details until you swear absolute confidentiality—even if you decide not to join me."

The waiter arrived with their meals and she stirred the small silver dish of balsamic dressing into her salad. "What kind of danger's involved? I don't want to have to deal with another steely-eyed Chinese assassin…."

The photo Adam had been sent of Brandy Wingate flashed through his mind, her toes and fingers sheared away and her severed tongue protruding from the gaping mouth. The lesson was "You'd better keep your mouth shut." And Brandy had talked about exactly what he wanted Dreu to investigate.

"I don't see this putting you in any danger," he said truthfully. "You'll just be feeding me information and no one will know you're the source."

Dreu took a bite of salad, continued to stir the dish while she ate, then placed her fork back on her plate. "Okay, I'm in. But for now, this will be a business arrangement. You hire my firm to do whatever work you need to have done."

"It can't be your firm. It needs to be you. No one else involved, period."

"Understood. What's the job?"

Adam leaned back from his own meal and smiled sheepishly across the table. "I'm afraid I lured you to dinner under slightly false pretenses. I can't show you here for reasons you'll immediately understand. We need to go to my place."

Dreu had been wiping her lips with her napkin and dropped her hands into her lap. "Is this for real at all?" she said quietly. "I was hoping…."

"Cross my heart, Dreu. I'm dead serious about everything I've said. I just can't show you what I need to have analyzed in a public place."

"Okay," she said with a note of skepticism, returning to her salad. "But for now, strictly business."

They finished dinner without speaking again about the job. Adam asked about family—if her brother was still racing with an Italian cycling team and how her parents felt about her new business venture.

"Oh, they're completely disgusted with Arun. His team does very well but as you know, cycling is a team sport and he's not the star—the one who gets to wear the yellow jersey." She slipped back into her mother's accent. "And what is this cycling? What does it say about you? That you have strong legs? A girl from a good family will want an *intelligent* man. Someone who will bring her respect!"

She flashed him an embarrassed smile. "With me? They're pleased. They hated the modeling stint so much I think any respectable computing job is a major relief. And my own company? What more could two obsessive achievers want for their kid?"

* * *

After dinner she followed him south on Scottsdale Road across the canal and into old Scottsdale. They turned right on Main and swung around a roundabout that displayed a statue of a bronc rider. He took her another block south and into an alley and parking lot that backed his apartment. When she climbed from the car, she stood and surveyed the surrounding buildings.

"I know exactly where we are," she said partly to herself. "All the art galleries are out on the street in front."

"Welcome to my part of the world," he said with his lopsided grin. "The independently wealthy Bohemian."

"Very clever," she muttered. "Lost in the Arts District among all the other Bohemians."

He led her through a walkway to his door and, once inside, she again stood and critiqued his decor. "You don't decorate like an independently wealthy Bohemian," she laughed. "More like a starving artist."

"That just shows you I haven't been luring women to my apartment. No one would believe my cover." He flipped on the television as they passed through the living room into his den. "I'd like to catch the late news if you don't mind. See what they know about the BART attack."

Two leather-backed bar stools were pushed up to his barnwood table and he drew one back for her to sit, then went to his floor safe in the closet and withdrew a DVD and the large envelope he had retrieved from Georgetown. Back at the table, he emptied the envelope onto the varnished gray surface in front of Dreu.

"Here's where we begin," he said, spreading the photos across the tabletop.

"You're investigating *Penthouse*," she joked.

"Not a bad guess. These professional escorts have been paid handsomely to lure some of our more prominent Washington politicians into very compromising situations, then film and blackmail them into changing key votes. My guess is that there are quite a few more than I have here."

"I've wondered about some of the really crazy political antics I've seen lately. This would explain a lot. But it must have been pretty damning to get some of these people to compromise their principles."

"Principles!" Adam scoffed cynically. "I prefer to use 'positions.' I think most politicians' principles are shaped by whatever gets them re-elected. And you're right. They did get themselves into some real damning situations." He slipped the DVD into the slot in his computer and sat back while it booted up. The film had been edited and opened with a man's face planted firmly between a woman's naked thighs, his head bobbing rhythmically.

"Ohhh," Dreu murmured. "I'm not sure I'm old enough for this."

"Don't worry," Adam said. "You'll age while you watch."

The man lifted his white head and leered up at his partner, who was moaning plaintively off-screen.

"*My God!*" Dreu exclaimed. "It's Senator Von Holten!" Adam remained silent as the senator rose and encouraged his partner through one acrobatic position after another.

"The old guy's got stamina. I'll say that for him," Dreu muttered. "And this certainly explains how someone could get him to change his vote on the gun laws. Mr. Family Values and God-is-my-copilot."

"You see the problem. And why I couldn't spread these on the table at the restaurant. You can also imagine why they're keeping the FBI out of it."

"Yeah. Even the agencies have leaks, it seems," Dreu observed. "What do you know about when and where this happened?"

"This one? Budapest," Adam said. "I met with the senator yesterday and talked him into giving me a copy of the disk and telling me his story. There was a week-long meeting of NATO powers in Europe a month ago to discuss Russian aggression in the old Soviet bloc countries. Hungary hosted the conference and the U.S. sent a six-person delegation. The woman involved was one of several hostesses for the American group and immediately showed a liking for our dapper senator. By the fourth day he was having dinner with her and on day five, she invited him back to her flat for drinks. The rest, as they say, is history. Recorded history."

"So this is an international conspiracy. Some foreign power trying to get leverage like the North Koreans did with the Sony Studios hack?"

"My initial guess is no. The changes in political position the extortionists are asking for seem more in line with some kind of domestic agenda. But whoever's organized it obviously has an international reach."

"She's a beautiful woman. I can see the attraction," Dreu admitted. "But I'm not sure what help I can give. Are you trying to locate her?"

"Her and some of the others. And even more importantly, I need some expert film analysis. Both still and video. Several of our victims claim they were never with the girls they're filmed with. They admit to having met the women and say there were efforts to seduce. But two men claim there was no private rendezvous and no sex. One is pretty convincing. I need someone to help me determine if some of these pictures and videos have been doctored."

Dreu reached over and picked up the photo of the buff young man. "And they're working on some of our women legislators as well, I see."

"No," Adam smiled. "Just men of divergent tastes. My guess is that they see women politicians as too inclined to resist—and possibly too genuinely principled, with the exception of several that come to mind."

Dreu nodded her agreement. "I'm afraid film analysis is hardly my area of expertise. But I have a great person in the office…."

"Can't bring anyone in," Adam insisted. "These faces are too recognizable and I can't take the risk. Can your person tutor you through it?"

"I suppose so. It depends on how much of it is training and how much is an innate knack for noticing small changes—like your ability to see everything that's happening in the room around you."

"I don't think I know a person who's brighter and more naturally observant than you are," Adam said. "Can you give it a try?"

"What do we have to look at?"

"I have a batch of photos and four video disks, including my most insistent innocent. Others will trickle in as I identify new victims and convince people to share their files."

"Let me see what kind of equipment's needed and I may choose to do this at home."

"Or we could set up here…," Adam suggested.

Dreu cocked her head to one side and smiled. "Or we could do that," she agreed.

In the living room the late news began and Adam swiveled on his stool to catch the headlines. The evening anchor was Grant Huston, one of those newscaster faces that is television perfect: full head of hair combed perfectly back, serious creases in his brow that convey concern and credibility, riveting eyes that look through the camera into the minds of every viewer, and a voice that sounds like Harry Connick Jr. singing "Who Can I Turn To."

"In our lead story tonight, a surprise announcement out of Washington. Just weeks before the Iowa caucuses and the major democratic primaries, Vice President Alan Carradine has announced that he is withdrawing as a candidate for the presidency and is throwing his support to Delaware senator Clayton Mehrens. Carradine, who has been an active and seemingly successful campaigner in the early polling, was running slightly ahead of Mehrens. In a formally prepared statement, he said that family concerns have convinced him that this was not the right time to consider the nation's top office."

Adam turned to Dreu who was listening with rapt attention.

"I think we can add another to our list," he said. "Carradine was the senior member of the delegation to Budapest."

SEVEN

The 6:00 a.m. flight of InterState Airlines between Kansas City and Dallas was normally a commuter run—day travelers with ten o'clock appointments in the Texas metropolis and plans to be back in Kansas City by evening. But it was early August and students were beginning the return migration to Texas' dizzying array of colleges and universities. With the airport's unusual concourse arrangement where once through security there were no shops or restaurants, most students lingered in the circular corridor outside of the screening checkpoints until 5:30, then crowded to the gate with backpacks and carry-ons in hand. A mother with two toddlers guided them through the scanning booth, heading home from a visit with grandparents in Overland Park, Kansas, across the river. Even those with a nagging fear of flying had no premonition that the plane would never reach cruising altitude.

By 5:15 a.m. Dwayne Cargile had cut the lock on the farm gate, hidden the Forester in the open bay of the first of the metal storage sheds, and unpacked his cargo. He had practiced the limited assembly a hundred times and within minutes had the FIM-92 Stinger missile ready to fire. It was classified by the military as a MANPADS, a Man-Portable Air Defense System, and was a thirty-two pound, shoulder-fired weapon that could bring down an aircraft flying as high as 15,000 feet. Dwayne's target would be no higher than 1,500 feet with a closing speed of 1600 miles per hour, and he needed his targeting to be exact. The morning weather report confirmed winds from the south, making 19 Right the primary runway. By 5:50 he was waiting under the eaves of the barn for the 6:00 a.m. departure of Flight 839 for Dallas. He knew it was an MD 80 and would be carrying approximately 160 passengers and crew.

Though Dwayne knew the operation of this FIM-92 like he knew the engine of his Dodge RAM pickup, he had practically no knowledge of how it had come into his hands. Should any fragments of the missile be traceable, investigators would find that it had been manufactured by Roketsan in Turkey under license from the American company Raytheon. It had been smuggled by the Turkish military across the border into northwest Syria to support anti-Assad forces, where any records of the Stinger ended. Three days later, Afghan arms dealers who were profiteering from the Syrian uprising had loaded it into the bed of a returning aid truck and secreted it back into southern Turkey. From there it traveled overland across Turkey, Bulgaria, Serbia, and Bosnia to the Croatian shipyards at Kraljevica. There it was smuggled aboard a luxury yacht, the fifty meter *Last Patriot*, built in the Balkan port on commission for American billionaire Dan Triplett. With a crew of eleven flown into Italy and ferried across to Croatia, the *Last Patriot* left the Adriatic and Mediterranean and made its maiden trans-Atlantic crossing with the Stinger aboard. After passing through the Isthmus of Panama, the yacht made port in Seattle—anchoring long enough in route to send a motorized dingy carrying the Stinger ashore a hundred miles south along the Oregon coast. Dwayne Cargile first saw the missile at King's Mountain, Triplett's secluded Idaho training camp. But every bit of evidence would indicate it had come from Syria, with no traces of its circuitous route to reach American soil.

At 6:10 he heard the roar of engines accelerating to take-off speed, stepped out of the storage barn, and rested the launch tube securely on his right shoulder. As the jetliner lifted off and began its climb-out to the south, he picked it up in the barrel-mounted sight and tracked it as it rose toward him. He was surprisingly calm—a soldier on special assignment with a carefully designed plan. When the jet was forty-five degrees to the horizon, Dwayne fired. The rocket streaked skyward, its infrared guidance system locking onto the climbing aircraft. Within seconds, the missile detonated between the left engine and the fuselage, ripping the side of the plane open and igniting fuel in the left wing. The jet rolled up and to the left, smoke and flames pouring from the ruptured body. But Dwayne saw little of the death roll. In the fifteen seconds it took the airliner to loop and nosedive into the ground with an earth-shattering explosion, he had replaced the launcher in its case and backed the Forester out of the barn. By the time airfield emergency crews were on their way to the crash site, he was back on I-435 headed south toward the maze of overpasses where four major interstate highways came together. He would lose the Forester at a salvage yard north of Lawrence, Kansas, and make the rest of the drive back to King's Mountain in a blue Taurus. By late morning, the launcher, case, and Forester would be crushed into a metal block the size of a small dumpster.

At the first rest stop in Kansas, he pulled into a parking spot long enough to send an innocuous one-sentence text: "*Should make it home for dinner*." Three minutes later, a twitter message that originated in Boston reached the major network newsrooms. "*No infidel will escape the swift justice of Allah. The Warriors of WIS*."

* * *

They decided to meet the evening after their dinner at Brios at Dreu's Chandler apartment. It was a short fifteen minute walk from her office and backed the Ocotillo Golf Resort, a luxury she had selected more for location than for any interest in the sport. Adam noted that her greeting embrace was a little longer and firmer and he hoped it meant he was on the road to being forgiven.

Her place was simply but tastefully furnished, something he wouldn't normally notice had he not still been smarting a little from her assessment of his own basic furnishings. She led him into a combination living-dining area with laminated wood floors and area rugs, urban contemporary, but still in the earth tones he remembered from her place in McKinney, Texas. She had a knack for creating a space that was immediately intimate and relaxing without seeming quaint. Three pictures were grouped around the base of a lamp on an end table beside the sofa and he picked up the one of the woman he judged to be Dreu's mother.

"May I?" he asked.

"Sure. Meet the Sasons. That's my mother—Tanvi."

"I guessed as much," he said, studying the face of the regal

Indian woman in an iridescent blue sari. Her raven hair, large dark eyes and wide mouth had been copied into her daughter, while Dreu had inherited the narrower chin and nose of her father.

"Beautiful woman," Adam said, placing the photo back on the table and picking up the one of the older man.

"Not a compliment she would appreciate," Dreu said with a wry smile. "She spends her summers back in India working with women's groups and campaigning for equality. Sort of the ultimate feminist. Any comment about appearances is viewed as demeaning. Something you wouldn't say to a man, and ignoring the real essence of the woman's value."

"I was just going to say that your dad's a handsome guy," Adam said with a grin, glancing down at the picture in his hand. "Sason. Where does the name come from?"

Dreu lifted two wide flat bowls from a cupboard above the sink. "More story than you want to hear. His family were Sephardic Jews and were Sassoons when they came to the U.S. I think his grandfather intentionally decided to separate himself from the image of wealth and Jewishness that was associated with the Sassoon name. So he changed it. You could say I'm a child of the 'you deserve only what you earn for yourself in the world' school of child rearing. That third picture is of one of the family failures."

Adam placed the photo of Dreu's father back beside the lamp and picked up the one of a young man with the same dark hair and large, brown eyes. It was a head-on photo of him leaning forward over the handlebars of an expensive racing cycle, a short-billed blue and yellow cap on his head and "Festina" emblazoned across the chest of his matching shirt.

"He raced for Festina?" Adam asked. "I thought the team was disbanded after a doping scandal years ago."

"It's just a workout shirt—and part of the rebel image," she said. "He actually rides for Bardiani-CSF."

"He looks happy," Adam said, placing the picture back beside the others.

Dreu had been rinsing the bowls and wiped them absently

with a checkered towel as she turned to him with a smile that this time looked more wistful.

"He is very happy," she said. "In fact, I think in this family you can only be truly happy when you can finally break away from the peloton and ride on your own."

Adam eased away from the table and the obvious source of her discomfort and stepped across to a tiled hearth that held a large flat-screen TV rather than a fireplace. Above it on the wall, three frames held ornate, heavy silver necklaces that were designed to be bent into place around the wearer's neck.

"Well, it's a very nice and comfortable place," he said. "Are these African?"

"Nepalese," she corrected, "and from a shop near where you live. I just liked them. And I can't say I'm feeling too nice and comfortable right now. This airline disaster in Kansas City really has me shaken. They've come right into our heartland."

He nodded grimly. "Meeting today of the National Security Council and all of the legislative leadership. The president's trying to be reassuring and at the same time do everything possible to keep people from demonstrating and gathering in large public groups. There was one in Washington today anyway—just spontaneous. People are beginning to panic." He guided her toward the sofa but she redirected him to the chairs at the dining table.

"I have dinner ready and thought you might want to get right to work. We can talk while I get things on the table. Grab that salad bowl and give it a stir and maybe you can help me understand what's going on."

He tossed the salad with a pair of tongs, thinking how comfortable he felt working beside her.

"Pretty unnerving," he agreed, "and masterfully planned from what I can tell. Kansas City International is about as isolated as any urban airport in the country with mile-long stretches of farmland off the ends of both runways. A perfect place to set up an attack like that without being seen. And then it's only another mile to the junction of most of the major interstates in the central Midwest. The attacker was able to disappear in minutes into a mass of traffic going in any direction."

"Do you think this was really a ground-to-air missile?" she asked, stirring a pan of roasting vegetables.

"They're pretty certain. People traveling on I-29, a half-mile west of the suspected launch site, saw the trail."

"How would this World Islamic State bunch get something like that smuggled into the country?" she asked.

"You'd be amazed. Remember that guy who brought a Stinger missile launcher to a gun buy-back in Seattle a few years ago? Said he bought it from some other man in town for a hundred dollars. People bring grenade launchers and all kinds of things to those buy-backs. We're a no-holds-barred, gun-loving society and shouldn't be surprised when some of the most destructive weapons show up in the hands of the enemy inside the country."

"You know what it's doing," she said, carrying the bowl of vegetables to the table. "It's playing right into the hands of Carter Graves' campaign people."

During the drive over, Adam had been mulling over the same thought. The Oklahoma governor was on the noon news railing against the current administration for not reacting quickly enough and with enough force. "When I become president," he assured the interviewer, "we will stop this aggression with an immediate and overwhelming show of force that hits them where they live." He had closed with what was becoming his campaign slogan. "A strong America is a safe America."

"He's convincing a lot of people that our only salvation is to respond with an aggressive attack," Adam said. "The rest of the candidates are scrambling to keep up with his hawkishness."

"Let's eat," she said, setting a platter with the main dish in front of him. "We can do more worrying later. And I think I have some information you'll find interesting."

She had prepared cedar-plank salmon, another nod to reconciliation. Though he prodded, she wouldn't give even a hint about her findings until they had finished a tantalizingly small slice of a bourbon-pecan tart and collectively cleared the dishes. Then she led him into her own second-bedroom-turned-study and pointed toward a barstool-height roller chair. Unlike his own den, which was mainly open table space, Dreu's had wrap-around, waist-high counters on three sides. They were covered with a mind-boggling collection of computers and monitors, printers, modems and routers. The wall to the left of the door as he entered displayed two thirty-four inch screens, one already showing digital images of the still photos he had given her of the escorts.

"My playroom," she said with a light laugh. "I like to stand while I work, but feel free to sit." She punched a key on one of her computers and three of the photos appeared in highlighted frames. "We've already been able to locate these women. Two are still on the East Coast and one in California. They're still working for expensive escort services but not in the D.C. area. So it shouldn't be hard to get exact addresses. Now—as for whether some of the photos were doctored…."

She turned to the other screen and three pictures of Damion Rutledge appeared: the conservative house majority whip from Arizona who had insisted convincingly that he had never been with one of the call girls. One photo, like Von Holten's, showed him with his face wedged between the thighs of his partner, eyes closed and her hands wrapped behind his head, pulling him inward. In the other photos the woman was astride him, sitting upright in one pose and in the other with hands on his shoulders and head thrown back in apparent ecstasy. She was a short, pretty brunette with a sculpted, athletic body.

Adam studied them for a moment without either speaking, then turned to Dreu.

"They look genuine—but not quite right to me. What did you discover?"

"Pretty astute of you to think they look genuine, but not quite right. My best assessment is that they're legit and our man from Arizona was actually with this woman."

"Hmmm," Adam muttered. "When I talked to the guy I would have sworn he was telling the truth."

"Well, yes—that's the really interesting part. If a photo's been doctored, there are three or four ways to tell that it's been manipulated. One is that any digital image contains metadata called EXIF data that's specific to the type of camera and settings used. If something is plugged into a photo from another picture, the metadata generally won't match."

"And in these cases?"

"In the cases of both your men who insisted they weren't involved, it did. So at least the same camera type and settings were used—which seems highly unlikely if two photos were being integrated with subjects this different. But even if the camera and settings were the same, you can look for tool marks. By enhancing an image, you'll often see a halo effect around sections that have been inserted or overlaid."

"And…?"

"None here. But the giveaway—the thing even the best pros have trouble with—is getting shadows just right. It's very difficult to get light sources so they're perfectly aligned in two merged images. A man named Farid has done some really great work on triangulating light reflection off faces, for example, to determine if it comes from slightly different angles. And in this case, see how in the two pictures with him lying on his back…?" She turned to Adam, who was chuckling softly to himself. "So—what's so funny?"

"I should have remembered you wouldn't be willing to give me some simple 'yes' or 'no' answer. But are we getting there?"

"I'm assuming," she said with a trace of testiness, "that you might want to be able to explain this to someone else, if needed."

He raised his hands in surrender. "Proceed! I'm taking this all in."

"Well—the long and the short of it is that both men you said claimed not to have been involved were originally in the pictures. No doctoring in either case."

"But you agreed when we started that the photos didn't look quite right."

"I *do* agree. Look away, then back at them closely and without trying to be too analytical. Just give me a first reaction. And try not to fixate on the woman's boobs."

He glanced down at the countertop, worked to clear his mind

of images of the lithe brunette, then looked back at the photos. "My first impression is that I can't tell whether the congressman is enjoying himself or in pain—although I guess it could be both."

"Or maybe isn't even conscious," Dreu suggested. "His eyes are always closed, mouth agape, and head supported. We can't even be sure he's awake."

Adam studied Rutledge's face. In each case his head was in a position that, even if unconscious, left his jaw slack and mouth open.

"And I'll bet that if you check the hotel where this woman was coming on to him and he thought he'd resisted, you'll find these bedspreads on the beds." She ran a laser dot over the spread beneath the two bodies. "My guess is that when he showed he was going to be difficult, they drugged him, then went into his room and set these pictures up. And did you notice anything else?

Adam studied the pictures again and shook his head.

"Come on, Mr. Observant. These three shots are from different angles. Do you think a room would have been set up with three hidden cameras? The photographer was moving around the subjects."

Adam nodded slowly. "You're right. I should have seen that. It's pretty obvious when you point it out."

"And I suspect our congressman would have noticed a roving photographer. I'll bet if you ask him, he'll remember waking up the next morning with a killer hangover." Dreu looked over and smiled. "Better yet, ask the woman. She's the one we found in San Francisco."

He was gazing absently at the pictures, lips pursed and brow furrowed and she could tell his mind was on something else.

"So…what are you thinking?"

"Let's play a variation of your little game," he said, examining the photos on both screens. "Think about what you've learned about this whole situation from when I told you about it yesterday until this evening. And clear your mind of the fat, pale congressmen. Any overall impressions?"

She didn't need to consider the question. "In fact, I thought about that all morning. All very conservative politicians—except Carradine. All have made public statements moderating their positions on some contentious social or political issue—gun control for Von Holten, immigration for Rutledge, healthcare for Tennessee's Wyrick. And each has either implicitly or directly supported the positions being taken by Senator Mehrens. Then Caraddine drops out and throws his support behind the gentleman from Delaware. People are starting to talk about him being the man for our time."

"Exactly," Adam agreed. "But has Mehrens ever struck you as the kind of man who'd engineer some kind of massive extortion like this?"

"You never know. Power corrupts," Dreu reminded him. "And he has a campaign apparatus. Even if he's pretty clean, some of his people might not be."

"This is more than just an ethical violation," Adam said. "I'm sure whoever's behind this murdered that woman in Miami Beach."

Dreu shuddered as she switched off the images on the two screens. "Speaking of murders, these terrorist acts are having just the opposite effect. People are terrified and fear is driving them toward Governor Graves and his 'Reclaim America' campaign. As conservative and aggressive as he is, I'd have placed him a distant fourth on the Republican side. But this is starting to turn into a two-horse race."

Adam nodded. "I think I'd better have a talk with Carradine and see what changed the VP's mind—then fly out to California to visit our brunette. We need to find out who's pushing these buttons."

EIGHT

Getting an appointment with the vice president turned out to be no more challenging than it had been with Von Holten. Adam simply told the appointments secretary the meeting involved getting the VP's help with "identifying some of the people in the informal photos that were taken in Budapest." Her initial reaction had been, "I'm sorry, but the vice president is a very busy man. I'm sure someone else can help you with the photos."

"If he's in, ask him," Adam suggested. "If he isn't in, call and ask. I think he'll want to do the identifications himself."

Carradine made time for him the next day and suggested that rather than meeting at his office in the Eisenhower Executive Office Building, they have lunch in the Senate Dining Room.

"The vice president will have an aide meet you inside the west entrance of the Capitol at 11:15 and bring you to the dining room," the secretary said, and Adam again made reservations to fly to Washington.

He had met with Von Holten as Adam Zak but made this reservation on Southwest as James Roszell. He shaved the beard and got an afternoon appointment at Salon Tru near his apartment where he had his hair shortened, styled and lightened to what the stylist called light ash—close enough to the photo he used on the Roszell license to pass muster. If for any reason Capitol security was monitoring visitor activity, he didn't want the same ponytailed man with an eye patch to enter again, only days apart. He also chose to fly into Baltimore-Washington and take the train into the District. Whoever was watching the prostitutes could also be watching their clients.

Security at the west entrance was intense with full body scans of every visitor. He passed through without the patch and wearing a dark blue suit, white shirt, and conservative tie. The same guards who had checked him so thoroughly a week earlier seemed mainly concerned with what could be hidden under his clothing and didn't give his face a second glance.

The aide recognized him from the forwarded photo and met him just beyond security with an enthusiastic "Welcome to the

Capitol, Mr. Roszell!" then directed him to a small elevator that took them to the lower level. At the door to the Senate Dining Room the aide spoke briefly to an attendant, then hurried away. Adam was led across the spacious room beneath the massive central chandelier to a side table beside one of the high draped windows.

As Adam approached, Carradine stood beside the table visiting with Rosalind Cowen, senior senator from Massachusetts. She had been prepped for his arrival and immediately excused herself with a polite nod. The vice president indicated one of the seats at the white-clothed table and took the other without bothering with further introductions.

"Thank you for meeting me here," he said without a trace of thanks in his voice. "I have use of the dining room because of my status as Senate president and it's a place where protocol provides as much privacy as the diner wishes. We should be able to speak very openly here." His own quiet tone indicated that he still preferred 'open' to mean pianissimo. "Let's order and we can talk."

He beckoned a waiter to the table. "You probably know that bean soup is the famous standard here, but I recommend the steamed lobster salad."

"I'll take the recommendation," Adam said to the waiter and Carradine ordered the same.

"Now," he said when the attendant left with the menus, "I don't have a lot of time. As you can imagine, things are pretty tense and hectic around here. But I'm anxious to hear what you wanted to see me about."

"Your decision to withdraw from the campaign," Adam said directly.

"You seem to know the reason. I'm very curious as to how you know."

"To be honest," Adam said with a thin smile, "it was just a guess." Carradine's jaw tightened visibly and he leaned intently forward.

"I hope you aren't here to add to this outrage in some way," he hissed, glancing about the largely empty dining room. "I've about reached the point of sucking it up and going public."

Adam adjusted the linen napkin on his lap and tried to look reassuring. "Quite the opposite. I'm here to see what I can do to make this go away."

The vice president sat back, hands in his lap, and studied Adam with intense brown eyes. "And who are you that you can do this?" he asked. "I'd think that if the FBI were aware this had happened, the Director would have called me directly."

"I'm not with the Bureau—or with any of the other agencies in any formal way. I work on problems that need to be dealt with outside the formal organization. Can you accept that?"

Carradine nodded slowly. "I've heard rumors."

"Do you think you're alone in this?" Adam asked.

"My guess is that I'm not. No one has said anything to me, but I see behavior on the other side of the aisle that doesn't make sense unless there are other victims."

Adam nodded. "Some of them have recognized the same thing and have spoken to each other. But as you say, they're all on the other side. You people don't seem to be speaking to each other about anything across party line."

"Not something like this," Carradine muttered. "They would have found a way to make it public and destroy my candidacy."

"Which happened anyway," Adam reminded him. "Though I think you're wise to have taken the quiet approach. Explain to me how this compromise occurred."

The vice president's eyes showed his surprise. "I thought from your call that you must know more about this than you apparently do."

Adam drew a photograph from his inside jacket pocket and handed it across the table. It was a cropped copy of the face of the woman in Von Holten's video.

"Was this the woman?"

Carradine looked carefully at the picture. "I know this woman," he said. "She was one of the hostesses at the conference. Was she involved?"

Adam nodded. "But apparently not with you."

Carradine shook his head with obvious remorse. "I was such a fool! You get away from home and some pretty young thing comes into your room as the housekeeper and seems to show up each evening when you're working to relax. Turns down the bed and leaves some chocolates. You know the routine. So you get to talking. She said she was a student at the Franz Liszt Academy of Music—a cellist who dreamed someday of playing with the Budapest Symphony Orchestra and touring in America. She was working as a night maid to pay for her schooling and we spent a lot of time talking about her aspirations. I said I might be able to help her a little financially and at first she objected. But then she suggested maybe there was some way she could repay me for my generosity. Before I knew it, there we were."

"There weren't Secret Service around?"

He shrugged dismissively. "They secure the floor and then try not to be too intrusive. I suspect some of them noticed she was spending quite a bit of time in the room, but they also try to be discreet."

"Do you have the film?"

"No. I destroyed it immediately."

"Honestly? It would make a big difference if I could study it."

"Honestly. Once I made the decision to withdraw, the last thing I wanted was someone 'studying it.'"

"Not helpful," Adam said as the waiter delivered their salads. "I'm not sure who's behind this, but I need to be able to talk to as many of the girls as I can. Someone's trying to quiet the escorts here in the States, so I may have to go abroad."

Carradine shook his head. "I didn't want the thing anywhere around. It's pretty graphic, I'm afraid."

"These women are pros," Adam agreed. "You don't, by chance, have some other picture of her? An informal shot you took with your phone or something like that?"

He again shook his head, then paused. "Wait!" He pulled a long wallet from his inside breast pocket, thumbed through it quickly and found a wallet-sized photo that he handed to Adam. It was of a string quartet, all formally posed with their instruments. "She's the one on the right," he said. Adam didn't need the instruction. The cellist, a young woman who he guessed to be eighteen to twenty, had soft brown shoulder-length hair that framed an angelic face. She looked innocently at the camera with eyes and a soft smile that said "Take me under your wing."

"Brilliant," Adam muttered. "I wonder if she can really play?"

"Oh, I think so," Carradine said. "One of my daughters is a violinist and I noticed that Reka had the same callouses on her left hand fingertips."

"Reka?"

The vice president flushed. "Yes. Reka. Funny thing is, as embarrassed and betrayed as I feel, I still feel like she was telling me the truth. Maybe she didn't know we were being filmed?"

"It's possible," Adam said, not wishing to burst the final bubble. "May I keep this?"

"By all means! What do I need to do from here?"

"I'd keep a low profile on controversial issues," Adam suggested. "But one other thing. You chose to endorse Senator Mehrens when you withdrew. Was that part of the instruction?"

Carradine shook his head decisively. "I was just told that if I didn't drop out, the film would go public. They gave me a date but no other instructions."

"How did you get them—the instructions I mean?"

"A phone call. On my private cell number. They know a lot about me. Not many people have been given that number."

"Can you get me a list?"

"Not exactly. But it will be close. I don't give the number to many people."

"Write down those you remember and text it to this number." He gave the vice president the number of a recently purchased disposable.

"What would be your reaction if I suggested Mehrens' people might be behind this?" Adam asked.

"Absolute shock!" Carradine's face and voice reflected his conviction. "I've known Clayton since we were at Yale. He's the real deal. My sense is that he not only wouldn't do anything like this himself but has made it clear to his staff that he won't tolerate any shenanigans. One of his weaknesses, in fact, is that he's too damn nice. And too passive. But he's a standup guy."

Adam couldn't help but wonder if there was anyone in Washington who was that 'standup,' unaware that as he was pondering the thought over a bite of lobster salad, Senator Clayton Mehrens was having a similar conversation immediately across the street.

* * *

The group that crowded the office of Delaware senator Clayton Mehrens looked like a well-dressed version of the Harvard College Democrats—a dozen twenty-somethings, racially diverse, and clearly among the smartest people in the Russell Building. The man who faced them, leaning awkwardly against the corner of his desk, looked just as bright but wasn't the image most people had of a front-running presidential hopeful. He was of average height, a little on the heavy side, with close-cropped gray hair that circled his otherwise bald head like a Roman civic crown. Though he used one of northern Virginia's best tailors, his suits never seemed to fit well. This was a reflection, his wife insisted, of his habit of eating little during the week and far too much on weekends.

Mehrens had initially been elected state attorney general in Delaware as an Independent, but by the time he decided to make a run for a vacated Senate seat, he had politically defined himself much more clearly as a Democrat. Unlike most of his staffers, though he had attended Yale as an undergraduate, he was a graduate of the Widener University School of Law and was a Delawarean through and through. Generally thought of as a quiet, thoughtful man, Mehrens was a feisty floor debater. His Senate colleagues appreciatively called him the Little Blue Hen, a reference to the fighting cocks that had given Delaware one of its state nicknames. He had been coaxed into the primary by some in the party who viewed Carradine as too much of a Washington insider. They saw in the sixty-year-old Mehrens a savvy, solid liberal who had been untainted by life inside the Beltway.

"The past two weeks have taken some interesting turns," the

senator said, surveying the half-circle of eager staffers. His face and voice gave no indication of his views of the current developments. "The vice president's withdrawal and endorsement were unexpected, to say the least. And for some reason our worthy opponents across the aisle seem to be rushing to endorse some of our positions."

"Congressman Fahnestock announced this morning that he's moderating his position on climate change," a young woman seated in one of the office's few chairs volunteered. "He claims to have been swayed by growing evidence from the scientific community and believes Congress should reexamine its position relative to Kyoto."

Mehrens raised a surprised brow. Fahnestock was a senior Republican congressman and a stalwart Kansas conservative. "This must have just happened," he said.

"I heard it in the halls on the way over," the woman said. "He didn't hold a press conference. Just sent out a brief release."

The Delaware senator studied the young faces, his mouth a tight line and hands fidgeting against the edges of the desk. The group that had been all smiles when they assembled in the room quickly sobered uneasily to reflect his mood.

"What do you think's going on here?" he asked, directing the question to no one in particular. The staffers glanced at each other uncertainly, surprised at his grim response to their apparent good fortune.

"Carradine's been painted by the media as a career politician and a big spender with no real fiscal sense. That makes the public nervous," one of the young African-American men offered. "They're looking for someone new and fresh, and I suspect he saw the writing on the wall."

"When he was leading in the polls? And when for some reason all the major conservatives have had a 'Come to Jesus' moment?" Mehrens retorted. He paused and again scanned the faces. "Doesn't this make any of the rest of you a bit suspicious?"

"It's moving a lot of Independents in our direction," another of the women said. "What's your assessment, Senator?"

"I have this very uncomfortable feeling that someone's manipulating all this," he said pointedly. Holding each of their eyes for a moment, he looked around the circle. "We can't afford a Watergate. I need to know that no one in this room is involved in something that could blow up in our faces. Jared?" He began with the aide to his left and worked his way around the room, calling each out as he went and waiting for a "No, Sir." When each had firmly denied any involvement, he pushed away from the desk and scratched thoughtfully at the fringe of hair above his left ear.

"What else are you hearing in the halls?" he asked, knowing that news moved through the staffer community much faster than through official channels.

"The fear factor's growing," Traci Ruzic, a UC-Berkeley product from Santa Clara, observed. "Though I'm hearing this more from home. Some of my parents' really liberal friends are starting to talk about the need for a more militant response to these terrorists. BART scared them—and Kansas City terrified them. Some are even leaning toward Carter Graves. His numbers are skyrocketing."

Mehrens nodded. "Another of these attacks and we'll see a major stampede to the Graves camp. But he must be puzzled that a number of the party establishment seem to be jumping ship and moving in our direction. There is a chance, I'm afraid, that this is being done to set us up as the candidate the Republicans would prefer to run against. Have any of you considered that possibility?"

From their expressions it appeared that several had.

"Any of you tight with staffers in one of the offices where there's been a dramatic position change?"

A thin, sharply dressed young Asian named Thomas Lee raised his hand in quick acknowledgement. "I'm pretty good friends with one of Von Holten's aides."

"See if you can learn anything about why these people are changing positions," the senator said. "I don't believe we're seeing genuine changes of heart among these gentlemen. And I don't want to be another month down the road and get blindsided. I also don't want to be anybody's patsy."

It wouldn't take another month for Mehrens to know he was in trouble.

NINE

The PGA Championship—or more accurately the U.S. PGA Championship—moves annually around the country to some of America's most celebrated golf courses. The venues are selected in part for their visual beauty for the television audience but primarily for the challenge they afford the 156 players the tournament's complicated selection system puts on the roster. On this particular Sunday, Quail Hollow Country Club in suburban Charlotte, South Carolina, was hosting the tournament. Public interest among golf fans was especially high, with a nostalgic American favorite tied going into the final eighteen holes with a young South African who had already won two of the year's majors. It was a beautiful August day with light winds and temperatures expected to be in the low eighties. Despite the paranoia that was sweeping the country, the public had arrived early in record numbers to stake out positions on a favorite tee or around one of the perfectly manicured greens.

LeAnn Gillming had been following the favorites since the opening round. She leapfrogged ahead every few holes to give herself time to find an ideal spot to set up the Nikon that best suited the shots she wanted. Bringing her specially designed roller cart through security with cases for both her cameras and assorted lenses had been a hassle the first two days. At the press gate checkpoint the same security guard stopped her both mornings to open each case and examine its expensive cargo nestled in custom-formed Styrofoam beds. But on the third morning he gave her a smile of recognition, took a quick peek inside, and ushered her through. On day four with the popular matchup of leaders, press was streaming in from all over the country and she found herself ten back when she arrived at the gate. As she had expected, screening of familiar faces was cursory and when she reached security, the guard opened the long aluminum tube that held her tripod, gave her a quick smile and "good morning," and waved the person behind her up to the table.

LeAnn again followed the final pair from their opening tee

shots and was pleased to see that they not only retained the lead, but swapped it back and forth. Coming into the final three holes—a stretch the commentators referred to as "The Green Mile"—they were tied at twelve under par. She hurried ahead and claimed a spot between the two grandstands that framed the back and one side of the eighteenth green, setting up her tripod with the D800 and a Nikkor 200 mm zoom lens.

Number Eighteen at Quail Hollow is a 493-yard par four. Both leaders skillfully drew their tee shots into the left-sloping fairway just beyond the single bunker, avoiding the stream that guarded the left side. Through the lens, LeAnn could see them as if they were standing twenty feet in front of her. She snapped shots as each studied his yardage book, the 36-million pixel resolution of the D800 recording them more accurately than the human eye.

Spectators who had been clustered beside earlier greens and fairways scrambled toward the grandstands to see the final shots into eighteen. LeAnn tucked her cart in beneath the metal superstructure of the central stands and checked again through her viewfinder. She snapped a dozen images of the second shot of the American veteran as he addressed the ball, paused for a millisecond, then swept through his effortless, left-handed swing. The ball landed five feet beyond the pin to a deafening roar, biting and spinning backward off of the green's upper tier as the crowd followed with a disappointed groan. LeAnn swiveled the camera to frame the South African, then grabbed suddenly at her stomach and bent forward.

"Ohhh," she groaned softly, turning to two equally equipped photographers who crouched beside her. "I think I'm going to be sick!" She lurched away from the stands toward restrooms that backed the seating area, continuing past them to the parking lots at the front of the majestic white clubhouse. When her case exploded, taking most of both grandstands with it, she was already in her car and pulling out onto Gleneagles Road, headed back into the city.

It was 4:35 in the afternoon on the East Coast and 26 million viewers were watching the final round of the Championship. By the end of the evening news, the migration of voters to the Graves camp had indeed become a frenzied stampede.

* * *

Shockwaves from the blast at Quail Hollow were felt three thousand miles away at the Tunnel Top lounge and bar, just off San Francisco's Union Square. Adam had visited the bar a year earlier during a Bay Area visit and liked the ambiance of the place. It showed a touch of the grit of a dive bar but had a coziness that made it comfortable without being "new trendy." Plus, the rough wooden tabletops reminded him of his own laid-back den. He had called the escort service that listed Selina Kyle and arranged to meet her there at 1:00 p.m. for a late lunch.

"I've got most of the day in the city and a friend recommended her as great company," he offered, wondering as he did so why he felt the need to explain.

"You'll be very pleased," the woman on the phone said.

His first thirty minutes with Selina showed why the congressman had been impressed. She was pretty but not beautiful. Large dark eyes that were more playful than seductive and a small, firm body that promised exercise as much as ecstasy. She arrived wearing tight designer jeans and a snug sky-blue T-shirt. He guessed she had been schooled to meet a man for lunch looking more like a fashionable date than a paid companion. Adam had arranged for a table on the Tunnel Top's upper balcony where he could see the door, and recognized her when she entered. She looked up and seemed to know that he was her appointment, smiling as he walked to the top of the stairs to greet her.

"Brandon Lewis," he said, giving her a light kiss on the cheek. Her smile showed either genuine pleasure at her good fortune for the day or a much practiced ability to look impressed.

"Selina Kyle," she said as he led her to the table.

"That's Catwoman's name, isn't it?" Adam chuckled. "I like that."

She sat and studied him pleasantly, transferring a cell phone from her hip pocket to a brown and tan-checked Louis Vuitton shoulder bag that she placed on the tabletop. It seemed heavy and she laid it down gently enough that Adam guessed it contained a small handgun.

"Actually, my name really *is* Selina," she said. "But Selina Alvarez. I find that Kyle attracts more interest." She said it with the same matter-of-fact genuineness that matched the rest of her. "So—you'd like to see a little of the city and spend some time together before you leave town? My agent said a friend had recommended me. I wondered who, since I haven't been out here that long."

"I lied," Adam grinned. "I found you online and liked your name and picture."

"I guess it works, then," she laughed lightly.

They ordered lunch and talked about how the city was healing from the BART disaster and the effects the panic was having on tourism in the Bay Area.

"I know San Francisco has a reputation as being a pretty relaxed place," she said. "But people here are amazingly resilient. You can't live on a fault line and be squeamish. But that and the Kansas City thing have pretty well stopped the tourists. People aren't traveling."

Adam nodded, smiling to himself that "resilient" and "squeamish" were words he was hearing from a call girl. They were just finishing a common plate of onion rings when the shockwave hit. Two men seated toward the front of the balcony beneath a large flat-screen TV lurched back from their table, spilling their chairs over onto the wooden floor as a general gasp rose from the bar below.

"My God!" one of the men shouted. "They've bombed the PGA!"

The screen had been showing the tournament with the sound turned low, allowing those who wished to follow the visuals without disturbing others who wanted a quiet lunch. A camera from somewhere down the eighteenth fairway was broadcasting the scene live. As Adam looked up, tangled pieces of metal and fragments of body parts were raining down on what had once been the final green. The principal broadcast team had apparently been in a tower not far from the center of the blast. One of the color commentators, a veteran from the LPGA, was trying her best to control her voice and describe the mayhem around her. In the Tunnel Top, the only sound came from a woman sobbing on the floor below.

"The seating area is completely gone," the commentator said, her voice bordering on hysteria. "And the tower has collapsed. I don't know what's happened to our team…." The camera caught the American pro struggling onto his knees midway up the fairway, then swept to the young South African who stood with both hands wrapped around his head. He was looking straight down at what appeared to be a woman's dismembered leg that lay on the ground in front of him.

"Oh, my God!" Selina sobbed. "They've done it again—and right on TV!" She lowered her chin into her hands but continued to stare transfixed at the screen.

Adam dropped three twenties on the table and took her arm. "Let's go," he said and she let him lead her down the stairs and out onto the walk. Like the bar, the street had become eerily quiet. Word of the attack had swept across the city like a tremor, and pedestrians were scurrying into buildings to find a television set.

They walked to Union Square and stopped at the edge of the open plaza. The few who remained on the square were huddled around tablet computers that streamed the news, and a silence lay over the city as if everyone had suddenly been sucked up into some alien vortex. Vendors' booths, easels displaying street art, and even the grocery cart of a homeless person stood unattended. As if on command, their owners had disappeared into department stores and hotels that lined the plaza in search of the broadcast. An occasional car crept along the street, drivers peering nervously out at the vacant square, wondering what new calamity had befallen the city.

Adam pulled Selina more closely beside him and guided her toward the square's high central column that supported a statue of Victory. "There's some serious shit happening in the country," he said, wanting to immediately regain her attention, "and I need your help with some of it."

She balked and pulled away, seeming to know instantly what he meant. "Who are you?" she asked, trying to twist from Adam's grip that had tightened around her arm.

"I was referred to you," he said, turning her again toward him, "by Congressman Rutledge. He said you spent a little time together in Washington. I need to know who arranged the meeting."

She bent forward, trying again to pull free. "You're going to get me killed," she hissed. Adam swung his hips hard to the side as she tried to fire a knee into his groin.

"The thing that will get you killed is if this doesn't get stopped," he said. She was holding the purse in her left hand—the arm he had in his unyielding grip—but fumbled at the flap with her right.

"I wouldn't be pulling anything out of there," he said, jerking the arm downward. "I'm about the only chance you have to get out of this without getting hurt. Just tell me who set you up with the congressman and I'll make sure you get protection."

"I don't know who it was," she said, relaxing the arm. "But if it's who I think it is, you can't do anything to protect me. They're too big.... And I wasn't reaching for my gun—though I do have one in here. I need to show you something."

They were standing alone in the middle of the plaza and he released her arm and watched cautiously as she raised the flap on her handbag. She slipped two fingers into one of the side pockets and withdrew a creased photo, handing it to him.

"That's what will happen if I talk to you," she said quietly as he unfolded the picture. It was the brutalized body of Brandy Wingate, eyes bulging and severed tongue protruding from her mouth.

"I've seen this," he said, trying to reassure her that he knew more about the case than he did. "And I can protect you from this if you'll just trust me. Let's find a place where we can talk and...."

A dull 'thump' sounded behind him from the direction of the

Stockton Street entrance and Selina pitched backward against the base of the column. A crimson spray of blood and pink matter painted the granite behind her and spurted from her shattered head. She slumped to the pavement as Adam spun to see a gray sedan with heavily tinted windows accelerate down the street and take a right on Post.

He dropped to his knees beside the woman he had just vowed to protect, knowing that he didn't need to feel for a pulse. A dozen thoughts flashed through Adam's mind in the split second it took to process them. Selina was dead. He could never catch the fleeing sedan. He couldn't explain his way out of this murder without a flood of complications. He was probably being recorded by cameras from three or four different vantage points at that very moment. He had to leave her lying there and was disgusted with himself and the responsibilities that required it of him and with his part in getting her killed.

He knew that when Selina was found, patrons at the Tunnel Top would describe the tall, clean-shaven man with medium-length, light-brown hair, black-rimmed glasses, and a reservation made under the name Brandon Lewis. The escort service would confirm the name. He had driven to the city from Phoenix and his car was parked along the wharf near the Ferry Building. Without looking around, Adam left the plaza moving quickly toward the corner of Geary and Market Streets and the steep hike down the hill. As he passed an abandon vendor's stand, he grabbed a black Giants ball cap from a hook and pulled it tightly down over the top of his glasses. If he was lucky, cameras covering the square had recorded the murder and would see that he was not the shooter. But he was certain other cameras along Market would pick him up, and the man who had reserved an afternoon with Catwoman needed to disappear.

* * *

South of Bakersfield Adam pulled into a truck stop and placed a call to Fisher. The voice that answered was not the aged, gravelly rasp but the soft alto of a woman.

"I'm calling for Fisher," he said.

"He isn't able to take calls today," she said. "I can help you, Mr. Zak." She had the distinct accent of a native Spanish speaker and he felt like he had heard the voice before.

"I just met with one of the escorts in San Francisco. Do you know what I'm referring to?"

"Yes. I'm very familiar with it."

"Things took a bad turn. She was shot and killed while I was talking to her in Union Square."

"It's already on the news. And you were picked up on several cameras—nothing very clear that I've seen yet. They do seem to know that you didn't do the shooting, but Brandon Lewis is being listed as a 'person of interest.'"

"Did they track me to the car? If they have me in the lot on the wharf, I'll need to ditch this car and get something else."

"The report just described you in general terms. Be sure to get rid of the cap. That was specifically mentioned. I don't think they have anything up close and no description was given of a vehicle. Where are you?"

"At a Renegade Truck Stop on 99 south of Bakersfield. And the cap's in a dumpster in Daly City."

There was silence for a few seconds at the other end.

"You still with me?" he asked.

"Yes—the Renegade on the Mettler Frontage Road?"

"That's the one."

"If you want to wait there, I can have another car delivered from LA in two hours. It will be a rental in the name of Adam Zak, to be dropped off in Phoenix."

Adam surveyed the lot. He needed to stay out of sight as much as possible and the parking area had about forty cars and half as many eighteen wheelers. Better to be tucked in among them for a few hours than stopped at a checkpoint somewhere out in the Mojave Desert with no escape route.

"I'll wait here for your car," he said. "Call when the driver gets close with the make and model and I'll be watching for him. And there's something else I need. Check to see who runs high-end prostitution in the D.C. area. I need to know who might be keeping tabs on these girls after they leave the East Coast."

"I can tell you that without checking," the woman said. "It's the Levanzo family. Gio and his son Tony."

"Send me what you can about them, would you please? To my box in Scottsdale."

"Right away. Anything else?"

"Everything okay with Fisher?"

"I can't comment on that," she said, but her voice seemed to tremble.

"Well, I hope he's okay," Adam said. "And I have to say—your voice sounds familiar."

"We met once. At a little gas station in Remington, Virginia."

"Ah, yes." He could picture the plump Latina with the gray-streaked hair who delivered a set of listening devices. "Before I went to the Compton house."

"That was me," she said. "Call me Nita."

"Nice to meet you, Nita. Tell Fisher I hope he's back soon."

"Thank you," she said, which didn't sound to Adam like an answer.

TEN

Dan Triplett's camp for patriots had been named to honor the Battle of King's Mountain, a conflict that in Triplett's mind had been a turning point in the southern campaign of the War of Independence. Since his tenth grade epiphany in Brewer's English class, he had become an obsessive student of American military history, particularly those battles where the strategy of a capable leader played a decisive role. The Battle of King's Mountain had been fought near present-day Blacksburg in rural South Carolina. It was here that British Major Patrick Ferguson, assigned to protect the flank of the main Loyalist force commanded by Lord Cornwallis, had issued an ultimatum to the rebel militia to lay down its arms or suffer the consequences. When the rebels refused, Ferguson began to withdraw to the safety of the main army. But after riding for much of two days through a pelting rain, the Patriots surrounded and ambushed Ferguson at King's Mountain, soundly defeating his Loyalist troops. Though outnumbered, the rebels lost only twenty-nine soldiers to the Loyalists' 290. Patriot forces captured 668. Before this battle, Cornwallis had been routing the rebel army but the King's Mountain victory boosted rebel morale to the point that they were able to turn back an attempt by Cornwallis to move north into North Carolina.

For Triplett the battle was a case study in the 3G's of patriotism--God, guns and guts. He fully believed that America was now in full retreat from all three. The country had belatedly accepted the British major's demand to capitulate, and two and a half centuries later was laying down its arms. Only a return to the 3G's could save the nation. If Triplett were pressed to add a fourth G, it would be *guerilla*. America wasn't going to be won back by some frontal assault on a hidden enemy, but by the ambush kind of action that had turned back Ferguson and Cornwallis at King's Mountain.

From the air, or even to a backpacker wandering into the collection of log buildings in the Idaho mountains, Triplett's camp at King's Mountain looked like a comfortable, newly completed recreation resort. There were ten log cottages surrounding a central lodge, an outdoor tennis court with basketball hoop on one side, and riding stables tucked back under the shadow of the pines. Triplett had developed it with nothing more in mind than bringing a group of like-minded patriots together where they could survive if the Union became completely derailed. But after the call, he began to rethink the group with greater intent and formally created the Order.

The call had come two weeks to the day after his interview aired with Chase Rayborn, the weekday evening anchor for PAX News. Someone on the PAX news team had learned that Triplett was the money behind a series of large PAC contributions to the presidential bid of Oklahoma Governor Carter Graves. Rayborn had come out to learn why the Idaho businessman and former Special Forces officer was so willing to commit a fortune to the conservative governor—and so early.

Triplett spent most of the interview explaining why he thought Graves was the only man who would ask something of Americans—demand that they step up and accept some responsibility rather than just expect more and more from the government.

"We need someone who will restore our desire to show respect," he said. "To make and keep commitments, to work harder than the rest of the world and demand the same from every neighbor who wants to enjoy the benefits of citizenship."

"You can't show me a single place in the Good Book where the Lord tells us we should be taking care of the able-bodied," Triplett told the newsman. "The halt and the lame. The sick and the afflicted. Sure. But 'afflicted' was never meant to mean 'too damn lazy to work and too cocksure of yourself to go to school.' I say, to every man according to his own labors. We need to get back to that place as a nation, and Graves is the only man with the guts to get us there."

"But be honest, Dan," Rayborn had chided while the cameras rolled, "Graves is such a long shot. What could realistically happen to make him a viable candidate?" It was Triplett's reply that had prompted the call.

"Fear," he said sharply. "Americans need a big dose of reality therapy. They need to get their heads out of their… out of the sand and see what's going on in the world. We're facing the greatest threats to our freedoms *ever*! I don't give a tinker's damn whether this WIS group is representative of the rest of Islam or not. They're the ones who are speaking with the loudest voice and raising all the hell. These fanatics are organized, well equipped, and not afraid to die. That should scare the hell out of us, and it's not. We need a big dose of fear—of being afraid that if we don't act, and act *soon*, we're going to lose everything."

The man who called following the broadcast of the interview identified himself only as a fellow patriot who was intrigued by what Triplett had said about fear.

"I've had exactly the same belief—and the same realization that we don't have much time and that Graves may be our only hope. I'm also giving him money, but I'm pretty sure that's not going to do it. What do you think it would take to create the kind of fear among Americans that you talked about in the interview?"

"I'm sorry," Triplett said, "but I don't think this is the kind of conversation we should be having over the phone. If you're serious about discussing it, we need to get together face-to-face."

"That's not possible," the caller said. "My professional position—and what I would stand to lose from what I want to discuss with you—require that I stay out of the picture. I'm not even willing to work through an intermediary."

Triplett was silent for a moment. "Why don't you tell me what you think it might take to create the support we would need for our man? Then I can decide whether it's worth talking further."

"An incident within our borders," the caller said immediately. "Something that leads people to believe that there's no security inside the United States without stronger leadership at the top."

"What kind of incident?"

"It would need to appear to be an attack on our soil against the people of the United States by a foreign enemy. A Pearl Harbor of some sort, but without all the casualties."

Triplett again was silent, then said, "I've had exactly the same belief. But it won't happen."

"Not unless it's created," the caller said.

"This is a conversation that needs to happen face-to-face," Triplett said again.

"Can't happen."

"You're sounding like you'd like to ask a lot of me and have the advantage of knowing who I am, but don't want any risk yourself. Not acceptable. If we can't have at least the level of trust that allows us to talk man-to-man, we have nothing to discuss."

The caller thought for a long moment, then agreed. "Alright. But just the two of us."

So they met at Triplett's home overlooking the lake and talked about fear and how to generate it. The deal had been sealed with a handshake and they had not met since. That week Triplett began to pull together the King's Mountain team by contacting two former Special Forces buddies. By the end of the following week, five families and three singles inhabited the ring of cabins. There was no camo, no paramilitary training, and no huge stockpile of weapons. Team members were officially the Order of King's Mountain but referred to themselves simply as "The Order." There was no racial purification agenda, no vision of an isolated America. The Order's sole function was to bring to the White House American leadership that would restore the nation's historic preeminence as a military power and God-centered nation. They would do what was necessary to support the candidacy of Carter Graves, the only man they believed would champion the principles of a free society they saw so clearly enumerated in the Constitution. The America they had come to despise was fat, lazy, undisciplined, and far too willing to mortgage its freedoms for the promise of a free lunch. And they knew there were no free lunches.

Triplett had carefully recruited each member: a weapons specialist, an explosives expert, a strange little fellow who had once been an operations planner with Central Intelligence, a mechanic who could repair anything with a combustion engine, and a multi-lingual smuggler—the man who arranged to bring the Stinger out of Syria. All the Order lacked now was an expert hacker: a computer genius whose political philosophy and love for America matched Triplett's. He had feelers out and was getting some response. When the hacker was in place, they would be ready for a final push to the primaries.

PART TWO

ELEVEN

It began innocently enough. Though long before the two men met at the NoMad Bar in midtown Manhattan, they had shared a loathing for each other that was almost palpable. The hatred sprang in part from their diametrically opposed political views—as disparate as two positions could be for men who were supposedly in the business of being professionally objective. At the heart of the disdain was a deep, consuming jealousy that arose from each having a consciously repressed admiration for the other's talents—and lingering self-doubts about his own. All of this bubbled to the surface when Chase Rayborn happened to pass Grant Huston sitting at lunch with two young female interns from the NBS News studio at a table at the NoMad. Rayborn paused beside the green leather-upholstered booth and smiled at the interns. They reddened as if they had just been caught sneaking back into their dorm after a night at the Kappa House.

"Good afternoon, ladies," he said with a disarming Chase Rayborn smile. "I see you've found your way over to the shadier side of Manhattan." Then to Grant Huston, "Getting a little oil on the machinery so you can spin out some of that liberal pap NBS passes off as news?"

Huston lowered his cocktail glass to the polished wood tabletop and wiped his lips with a cloth napkin.

"We were just having a conversation about whether a network like PAX should even be allowed to call what it dishes out 'news,'" he said, also smiling at the interns. "When you rudely interrupted, we were debating between whether it's propaganda or just plain bullshit." The interns deepened another shade of crimson.

"Based on the level of vocabulary, I'd guess you were leaning toward bullshit," Rayborn said. "And please do excuse the interruption. I just thought your friends here might want to meet a real broadcast journalist." He walked to the end of the stylish hotel bar and took a seat at the last booth where he ordered his own favorite pre-broadcast drink: what the menu called "Gingered-Ale."

Twenty minutes later as 1:00 p.m. approached, the interns pushed themselves from the booth and hurried out toward Broadway. Grant Huston watched them go, then also slid from the bench and walked to where Rayborn sat.

"When it's just the two of us, I don't mind you being an asshole," he said, softly enough that those seated nearby couldn't hear. "But when I'm eating with guests, maybe you could at least limit it to just being an ass."

Rayborn grinned up at him. "I was serious. Those girls need to think about the gatekeeping that goes on at a place like NBS. If a news item doesn't include, 'And in today's news, President Britton performed even greater miracles to make America heaven on earth,' you people don't report it."

"Hogwash," Huston said. "But even if it were true, it couldn't come close to balancing the 'Today President Britton moved us one step closer to becoming a socialist state' tripe that you redneck hacks dish out."

"*Hogwash*? *Tripe*? More of that impressive vocabulary! You must write your own copy…."

"Well, Britton will be gone in another eighteen months and you'll have some new person to demonize who's just trying to do his or her best to serve the country."

"*His*," Rayborn said. "This is going to be our year."

"Not a chance," Huston laughed. "Since we're being candid, your conservative friends have managed to gerrymander congressional districts to the point that they can manipulate House and Senate elections. But when the public votes as a whole, even with our archaic electoral college, the nation stays center-left. Too many people depend on government to solve their problems."

"Wanna bet?" Rayborn grinned. "Here. Have a seat. Let's make a little gentleman's wager on this next election. Just between the two of us. No one else need know about it. You win—I treat you and your favorite intern to dinner at the Manhattan restaurant of your choice. And I publically announce on PAX Nightly News that a year before the election, the fabled Grant Huston called this one right."

Huston slid loosely into the seat opposite Chase Rayborn, his face reflecting his complete contempt. "I'd be embarrassed. Like taking candy from a baby. You may not be willing to admit it, Rayborn, but America comes to me for its news. If I wanted to, I could subtly shape reporting over the next year to the point I could pick my candidate and put him in the White House."

Rayborn's smile twisted. "Now it's my turn to say 'bullshit.' You may have the numbers in the ratings, but your numbers don't show up at the polls. And it will be the events of the next year that choose our president. Not Huston the Magnificent."

"As you said," Huston arrogantly reminded him, "*we* are the gatekeepers. We decide what's news and what isn't. Events take on meaning to the degree we give them time and attention. They don't refer to the media as the Fourth Estate for nothing."

"Well! Listen to you, Mr. I-Set-the-Agenda!" Rayborn sneered. "I'm the one who has the ear of the people who actually go to the polls. You ever been in a motel lobby in the Midwest? It isn't NBS News they have on." He leaned forward over the table. "If I chose to, I could put someone like… like Carter Graves in the White House. He's formed an exploratory committee and will probably run."

Huston scoffed loudly enough that several patrons turned to look at the pair. "That's like saying you could get Yosemite Sam elected. The governor's a wild man! A nut case! If you could get him elected, I'd not only treat you and…are you still married? Well, you and whoever your squeeze-du-jour might be to dinner, announce your impeccable judgment on the air, and step down as NBS news anchor."

Rayborn sat back and looked in amusement at his nemesis. "Now, that's worth serious consideration," he said.

"I *am* serious! Carter Graves in the White House and I'm gone!"

"So who do you see instead? Of those who are showing interest."

Huston thought for a long minute. "Who would I *like* to see? Clayton Mehrens. He's about the most decent and thoughtful man in Congress."

It was Rayborn's turn to scoff. "Yosemite Sam versus Elmer Fudd. I'd take that bet in a heartbeat!"

"You pompous sonofabitch," Huston muttered. "If I thought you were foolish enough to do it, I just might take you up on this."

"Oh, I'm serious," Rayborn said. "I could get Graves elected."

"Only by eliminating everybody else in the race!"

"No. The rules would be that we can't directly attack any of the other primary competitors. They'll be doing enough of that themselves. We can just generate support for our own man."

"Add a provision that we can't directly attack or smear the other person's candidate and I might take your bet. Mehrens will be a much easier sell than Yosemite! And if neither's elected, we call it a draw and just go right on thinking the other's a sonofabitch."

"You're on," Rayborn said, reaching across the table. "No elimination of other competition in the primaries. Just support for our guy. And no direct smears or attacks on the other person's candidate. And we both remain sonofabitches. Any other rules?"

"This is strictly between us," Huston said. "If we involve anyone else, they can't have any idea about this wager."

"Fair enough," Rayborn said. "Start saving your pennies. I'm going to want to go somewhere expensive and bring my whole bevy of squeezes-du-jour. Then, when you have to resign, you'll be broke."

* * *

The bet was, of course, an absurdity. It ran against every letter of Huston's professional code of ethics and every ounce of good judgment. He'd determined within minutes of leaving the NoMad Bar to forget it. But it wouldn't go away. He'd love to show that half-witted excuse for a journalist what kind of influence the real kings of the profession had. There hadn't been many over the years. Murrow. Cronkite. Koppel. Russert. These were the people who shaped how America thought, and he liked to imagine that Grant Huston was among them. Yet as he prepped for his evening broadcast, he couldn't help thinking about how the stories might be sequenced, spun, or deleted to influence how the public felt about Clayton Mehrens and his candidacy.

There was another mass shooting at a mall in upstate New York. If he were supporting Mehrens, that should get top billing, followed by an interview with a father of a child lost in one of the earlier school shootings, imploring the public to do something about gun violence. He would move the story about a new wave of illegal immigrants to the end. By that time people would assume they had heard the top stories and would be tuning out or channel-checking. He might be able to convince the news editors that they had run enough on illegal immigration and should drop the story altogether. But then, he would hate to be seen inside the newsroom as someone who was manipulating the news.

It would be much simpler, he decided, if the right stories arrived on his desk in the first place. He had always liked Mehrens. Thought the Delaware senator made more sense than anyone currently in Washington. And though the man didn't look presidential, he seemed to be ethical, tough-minded, open to reasonable compromise, and widely respected. And the fact that he didn't appear presidential? Well, that would make the challenge all the more interesting. What Huston would need was a string of stories that built support for the senator's policies, especially if that support came from unlikely places and couldn't be ignored by Rayborn and his pack of PAX lapdogs. NBS could roll out a valid news item every week that Grant could milk for a few days to say to the country, "This man makes sense for America."

To the few who knew him well enough to be aware of his personal politics, Grant Huston was something of an enigma. He was the oldest son of an Illinois Full Gospel preacher and had thought fleetingly about following his father into the ministry. He saw something magical about standing in front of an enthralled congregation, with waves of "*Amen*" sweeping back at him as he proclaimed the will of the Lord. But he had made the mistake of accepting a scholarship to the University of Chicago, then compounded the mistake by enrolling in a comparative religions course taught by the fabled H. Eugene Heidrick. Heidrick's courses were as much sociology, political science and ethics as they were religious studies. The man started every discussion by throwing out a question such as "Suppose you are the Indian Emperor Ashoka in the third century BCE. You have just conquered most of the Indian subcontinent at the cost of hundreds of thousands of lives. Even more people have been forced into exile. Why might the relatively new tenets of the man his followers called the Buddha appeal to you as the basis for establishing a state religion?"

From Heidrick's courses Grant had come to believe that religion was essentially a manifestation of culture. It became deeply engrained over the centuries not only because it met important needs of the spirit, but because it could be circumstantially pragmatic, socially healing, and politically malleable. As a result, it was often the ideal vehicle and justification for promoting great justice and great injustice—and both were going on in the world all the time. His Heidrick education convinced him that his father's pulpit was too conservative, too judgmental, and far too confining. He set his eye on a grander pulpit, the pulpit of network news, and worked his way from the news desk at WGN in Chicago to the major anchor position for NBS News. For the last six years he had been the news voice for much of America.

Yet as hard as he struggled to remain the dispassionate objective newsman, there were two groups that Grant Huston despised. In his memoirs, being written in secret as he lived them, he referred to them as the Pharisees, drawing his inspiration from one of his father's favorite warnings to his congregation from the Gospel of Luke. "Woe unto you, scribes and Pharisees, hypocrites!" The first group was the ultra-wealthy tele-evangelists who preached a gospel of blessed entitlement. "We all have a right to be rich," they insisted. "This is simply a manifestation of God's outpouring of blessings upon those who serve him faithfully!" They seemed, Grant thought, to overlook the parable of the rich man and the camel—and most of the rest of Jesus' teaching, for that matter.

Group two included the sanctimonious family-values conservative lawmakers who had built their political careers on the unequivocal sanctity of life. Grant had been raised with the same sense for life's sacred value, but Heidrick's courses had convinced him that a life is a life. The politicians he despised saw nothing wrong with sending a drone-guided missile into a village in the Hindu Kush because some suspected enemy of the Republic might be hiding in one of the mud huts. So what if twenty-seven women and children were killed as collateral damage. But aborting a single fetus was an abomination. And these same SOBs didn't care whether that fetus left the womb on some fly-infested garbage dump in Calcutta or from a sixteen year-old crackhead in the Detroit projects who insisted on hanging onto the kid because it meant a bump in her monthly welfare check. Once those fertilized embryos were assured their sacred right to be born, it didn't matter if they were consigned to a life of suffering. That was tough shit. They were now sentient beings with free will and were damn well on their own. Though Grant acknowledged that some social and religious conservatives were good people of solid principle—principles with which he disagreed, but could respect—when given power, many showed themselves to be what his father called "whited sepulchers." They were shiny bright on the outside but festering with corruption and greed within.

Huston's experience with the Washington elite had convinced him that things weren't much better on the other side of the political spectrum. Didn't these liberal yahoos ever have to manage a personal budget? One thing Grant *had* retained from his conservative father was a belief that if you spend more money than you make, you're going to have to answer for it someday, especially if you keep borrowing from people who aren't your best friends. Unlike most of his NBS colleagues, he detested the ultra-liberals who didn't seem to see the inherent danger in developing an electorate that was fully cared for by the state—and from whom nothing was expected. As this election season shifted into high gear, the Democratic National Committee had launched a major campaign to identify, register, and mobilize those in the twenty-something age group who were receiving some form of public assistance, but rarely voted. The mobilization effort grated against every residual grain of Huston's evangelical upbringing. If the DNC could get them to vote en masse, they were a segment of the population that could control any election. Though he kept the view very much to himself, he feared that a society that actively cultivated an electorate consisting of fewer and fewer producers was destined to collapse.

He had once been invited to guest-host one of the Sunday morning Washington Week in Review programs and had wrapped up the hour convinced that the whole Capitol Hill bunch were no more than Tickle-Me-Elmo dolls. Pull the string, the lips moved, and out came one of four or five scripted messages. If you were lucky, the platitude related to the question in some remote way. More often, the response ignored the question altogether and simply fired another random volley at the opposition.

Grant had come away from that tedious Sunday morning wondering how much longer he could do the job. If only these political hacks could be exposed for what they were—desperately insecure men and women whose political futures were far more important to them than any public policy issue. While he was still in the position to do so—while he still had influence—did he have the personal courage to do what was right for America? Chase Rayborn may have just given him the chance to find out.

TWELVE

Had there been no PAX News with its willingness to openly espouse conservative values and principles, there could have been no Chase Rayborn. He was too angry to fit into what he and his circle called the "mainstream media." Chase had been raised a military brat, born in Omaha when his father was stationed at Offutt Air Force Base with the Strategic Air Command. He spent his high school years at Incirlik Air Base, fifty-six kilometers off the Mediterranean coast near Adana, Turkey. His father, a bird colonel, was Air Force liaison to the 10th Air Wing of Turkey's Second Air Force Command. It was from this perch on the western edge of the Middle East that Chase witnessed the decline of the West.

He and his classmates at the DOD-administered Incirlik High School had been given strict orders to avoid confrontation with the locals. This meant that virtually every day as they walked through the streets of Adana they endured the taunts of young men who loitered on street corners and the muttering glares of old men who sat under the shade of faded canvas awnings puffing blue smoke rings from their hookahs. Turkish girls were off limits, rarely out on their own and never approachable. Across the Turkish frontier to the east, the best of Chase's generation were losing their lives in an attempt to bring some semblance of order and opportunity to a dysfunctional tribal world. Yet two-thirds of the population in the warring countries wanted to be left alone to wallow in their own corrupt and repressive mire. His own country was no longer the envy of the world and no one wanted U.S. troops on their soil as long as American aid kept their economies precariously afloat. But they all wanted American boots, weapons and supplies if they got their asses caught in a ringer.

To those who argued that the United States could no longer be policeman to the world, Chase simply asked, "Who do you want it to be then? Are you going to assume no more Hitlers? No more Holocausts? And when they arise, what other country do you want to trust with the power to stop these maniacs before they make it onto our soil? Do you want to give that power to Russia? To China? Give me a break!"

He had enrolled after high school at the University of Wyoming in both News Media and Air Force ROTC with one goal in mind: to work for Armed Forces Radio and Television Services. He wanted to be in a position to reassure American troops on a daily basis that they were appreciated and that the future of the democracy depended on their courageous service. By the time he completed a four-year stint in the military, he was anchoring the DOD News from the Pentagon Channel News Center and when he separated from the service, PAX News snapped him up.

Chase had taken the bet seriously from the moment he shook Grant Huston's hand. The man was a Marxist and was kept in check only by his phony commitment to journalistic objectivity. Though Chase had been taught as a journalism student all about news objectivity, he saw it as no more than a principle that made the purveyors of news feel good about themselves. But it never really existed in practice. News didn't just happen. It was created. And that creation began with decisions about which of the literally thousands of consequential happenings that occurred in the world each day the media chose to cover. When a Malaysian jetliner disappeared over the Indian Ocean on March 8 of 2014, it filled the news for weeks thereafter. Was that any more important than the fact that on that same day, Russian troops gained control of a military office and armory in the Crimea? Or that a small German anti-virus firm called G Data announced that it had uncovered a piece of spyware that had been inserted into hundreds of government computers in the United States? Both of these events had major long-term implications for the security of the United States but if asked the following week, most Americans would have had no idea either event had happened. The media didn't tell America what to think, but it sure as hell told it what to think about. And over time, that created public perception.

The challenge as Chase Rayborn saw it was one of determining how to shape that perception to favor the only candidate he really believed could rescue a failing America—Carter Graves. The Oklahoma governor had two imposing primary opponents: a former governor from New York with a law-and-order reputation, and a Latino U.S. senator from Orange County, California, who was promising to deliver the Hispanic vote to the GOP if chosen to lead the ticket. By agreement, Chase couldn't try to discredit these men directly. He had to find a way to give Graves greater appeal. His answer came during the interview with Dan Triplett.

Chase had become interested in the man when he saw his name atop a list of major contributors to the Carter Graves Exploratory Committee. It had been Rayborn who suggested to the news director that Triplett would make a great human interest story. "Human interest" turned out to be an understatement. Triplett was in his mid-fifties but looked ten years younger: clean-shaven but with a constant shadow of dark beard, square jaw, and thick wavy hair that left the impression he had just stepped out of a commercial for Jamaican rum. He had enlisted in the army out of high school, completed a degree through the University of Maryland while on active duty, and been accepted into Officers' Candidate School. His eight year record, five with Special Forces in Iraq, was a case study in how to become a highly decorated soldier: Distinguished Service Cross, Bronze Star, Purple Heart, Presidential Unit Citation. His reasons for leaving the service hadn't been discussed in any of the information Rayborn was able to dig up before the interview. After his discharge he had returned to Iraq with his own company, Iron Shield, that contracted with both American civilian and governmental operations and their employees for personal security. When Iron Shield was forced out of Iraq after a series of incidents in which Iraqi citizens were killed, Triplett returned to the U.S. and after thirty-seven years of bachelorhood, finally married. His bride was a woman five years his senior and sole heiress to a North Dakota oil fortune.

"We met at a fundraiser for Bill Von Holten," he explained when Chase met him in the living room of his sprawling Idaho ranch house. The room was larger than Chase's entire apartment on Central Park West, with heavy dark leather furniture and a stone fireplace that filled half of one wall. The stonework was a primer in western geology and anthropology, studded with chunks of petrified wood, dinosaur bone, Native American metates and manos, and at least two impressive stone axe heads. Sliced geodes, their blue diamond interiors open to the room, sparkled in the late afternoon light. The opposite wall, all glass, displayed a breathtaking view of a quarter mile of high grass pasture that dropped away to a cobalt blue lake, its surface mirroring the Bitterroot Mountains that rose beyond to the east.

Chase had come by himself, packing his own equipment. He set up two static cameras, one focusing on the rancher who was dressed in a slate gray long-sleeved shirt and blue jeans that fell over a pair of black Lucchese cowboy boots. The other camera pointed at Chase, looking professionally relaxed in a deep leather armchair.

"Sandra and I found we both liked the same things—the mountains, trail riding, guns, good beer, and the rest is history," Triplett said with a disarming smile. "I learned later that she also enjoys Fifth Avenue in your hometown, King Street in Charleston, and Newbury Street in Boston. She's at one of those places right now or I'd introduce you."

Chase had the distinct impression that the two didn't keep very close tabs on each other. With her out of the house, the rancher seemed completely at ease and he and Chase talked about the price of cattle, the mess the Middle East had devolved into since Iron Shield left Iraq, and finally Carter Graves.

"He's a real patriot," Triplett said. "The only man I can think of in Washington who will stand up in front of a crowd and call them out for their lack of courage and commitment. If I'd had some commanders like him in Iraq, I'd still be over there working to clean that mess up."

"Why did you leave the service?" Rayborn asked.

"They thought I was getting 'too intense' was the way they put it. We were doing house-to-house in villages in Anbar Province—you know, over on the west side of the country? By Syria? God, I loved that part of the work! That's when you feel like a soldier. A warrior! And we were digging the insurgents out a few at a time. But hundreds of them…." He trailed off and Rayborn brought him back on task.

"Speaking of Graves," he said. "What would make him a serious contender?"

It was Triplett's final statement that remained indelibly etched into Chase's consciousness. "We need a big dose of fear—of being afraid that if we don't act collectively, we're going to lose it all." The statement prompted the call two weeks later and the second meeting at the Idaho ranch.

* * *

Grant Huston had also gone to one of his old interview contacts. The possibility of actually stripping away the plastic veneer that coated some of Washington's most sanctimonious politicians was more than he could resist. Especially if at the same time he could advance the possibility of putting a rational man in the White House. The thought had tugged at his ego until he succumbed to the same failing that drove the monstrous egos of the men he was hoping to destroy: he started to believe that he was invincible. He was Grant Huston, the most recognized and trusted face in American news. He could get this done. And he knew where he had an unlikely ally—in the man who controlled the world of organized crime in Washington and on the East Coast between Philadelphia and Atlanta—Giordano Levanzo.

Though it was no secret to anyone in Washington that Gio Levanzo was the godfather of the Beltway, he moved very openly and comfortably through Washington society. Layers of underlings insulated the don from the drugs, prostitution and racketeering networks that annually netted him tens of millions of dollars. These foot soldiers were not only sworn to oaths of secrecy but had witnessed the consequences of violating those oaths. When new muscle entered the ranks of the Levanzo organization, the first duty was often to eliminate the man who was being replaced—a traitor who had in some way broken the covenant.

The top echelon was all family, all descended from immigrants of a tiny fishing village on an island of only 450 inhabitants that guards the entrance to the port of Trapini on the west coast of Sicily. The first Levanzos were transplanted to the United States by the U.S. Army after playing a vital role in the Italian underground prior to the Sicily invasion during World War II. When Allied bombers struck Axis military targets in Trapini as they moved across the Mediterranean into Italy, it had been Levanzo spotters who called in the air strikes from the heights of nearby Monte San Giuliano.

Though the family had been fishermen by trade, their new homeland showed its appreciation by setting them up with a small grocery and fish market business to serve the burgeoning Italian community in Baltimore's Little Italy, just east of the city's inner harbor. By the end of the decade the Levanzos were running numbers from the back door of the stock room, moving quickly into becoming the distribution center for the growing drug trade in Baltimore and nearby Washington. When they took over the lucrative prostitution business that flourished in the expensive hotel districts around the nation's capital, organized crime in the greater Washington area belonged to the Levanzos.

Huston's first interview with the crime boss had occurred six years earlier when Grant was still working as senior Washington correspondent for NBS. Though the District of Columbia has an elected mayor and a district council of thirteen locally-elected members, the Congress of the United States remains its supreme legal authority and can override any local decision. Following the election of a new group of young conservative congressmen, the U.S. House of Representatives threatened to tighten down on prostitution in the District—particularly the high-end variety that was such a part of entertaining foreign dignitaries. To get his take on the new congressional obsession with decency from the Capitol's purveyors of pleasure, Grant Huston had wrangled a rare interview with Gio Levanzo.

Three of the five richest neighborhoods in America are in Maryland, just on the northwest fringe of the Washington Beltway. The senior Levanzo lived in the wealthiest of the three, the Bradley Manor-Longwood neighborhood of Bethesda. This enclave of multi-million dollar homes sits just on the edge of the District where I-495 meets the I-270 spur, but the heavily-wooded suburb is virtually invisible from the highways. From his office in downtown Washington, Huston was able to reach the don's sprawling Mediterranean villa in thirty minutes. Its paved, circular drive led to an arched entryway that extended upward through both floors of the impressive white stucco mansion.

Grant rang the bell and while he waited, admired the beautifully manicured lawn and gardens that surrounded the home. It sat with five others on a cul-de-sac, much less secluded than he had imagined. Though the front of the estate was guarded by a shoulder-high wrought iron fence, there was little other evidence of security and he wondered if the other homes on the street were also family and if security took care of itself. No one was stupid enough to consider breaking into a house on Levanzo Street.

The aging don answered the door himself, greeted Huston warmly, and ushered him into an intimate sitting room to the left of the high entryway. As soon as he was seated, a black-uniformed maid appeared and asked if she could get the newsman something to drink. Grant accepted coffee and asked if he could record the interview.

"Just with your written notes," Levanzo said with a wry smile, seating himself in a comfortable blue and white print armchair while Grant sat on the heavily-cushioned blue sofa. "I'll be quite happy to answer any of your questions. But I would like to remember the answers as I believe I gave them rather than as you have them on tape." He was thinner than Grant remembered when he had seen him in public, with a long narrow face and arched nose set under dark, attentive eyes and heavy gray brows. His hair was also a mottled gray and his skin looked as if he had just climbed ashore from one of the fishing boats that sustained his family in the old country. Grant had the impression the don was the kind of man who was neither used to small talk nor appreciated it, and the newsman moved directly to his question.

"As you are aware," he said, "the new Congress is pressuring the council in the District to crack down on the sex trade, particularly in parts of the city frequented by tourists. I was curious about your reaction to this effort."

He had been mistaken about Levanzo's sense of hospitality.

"Questions so soon?" the Sicilian said with the same smile. "We haven't even had a chance to get acquainted. Tell me about yourself. Family? How long you've been in D.C.? I've set aside the morning for you and we might as well take advantage of it."

Grant shared a little about growing up in rural Illinois, getting into the news business and working the Washington desk, then listened attentively as he learned about the Levanzo's American tale. The story failed to mention the expansion opportunities that followed establishment of the Baltimore fish and grocery business.

"You've obviously done very well," Grant prodded. "But did this all come from developing the family markets?"

Levanzo nodded. "Indirectly," he said. "Commodities. One of the things you learn very quickly if you are going to succeed in the family grocery business is what is happening in the commodities market. Your supply to your customers must remain steady, even if source opportunities do not. So you're anticipating, watching trends, seeking new sources of perishables you can't stockpile or store for long. And you get pretty good at knowing what's coming your way in terms of supply and demand. That's essentially the commodities market and my family has become very skilled at anticipating."

"You're aware, I'm sure, that many accuse you of being the major supplier of a number of illegal commodities—including the one affected by the D.C. controversy. Has that been part of your success?"

Levanzo chuckled softly but remained relaxed in his chair. "We're back to the interview, I see. Good enough. People say all kinds of things about me and few of them are true. I have my views about the congressional pressure on the district council, but they are no more informed or worthwhile than the views of any citizen of the area."

"I'd be interested in knowing what they are anyway," Grant

said. "You're a man of considerable influence in the region."

Levanzo nodded a modest acknowledgment. "Then I'll share my thoughts, for what they are worth. But you're an observant man. Let me ask you this. If you were to stop a hundred visitors to the District and ask them what they think of the prostitution problem in the popular tourist areas, what do you think they would say?"

Grant shrugged. "Unless they had sought it out, I suspect they'd say they saw no evidence of it."

"Exactly. So it isn't its visible presence that's at issue. Wouldn't you agree?"

Grant had the feeling that he had somehow become the subject of the interview but offered an assenting nod.

"So seeing working girls wandering around the hotels isn't the problem," the Sicilian said. "In fact, many of these congressmen come from districts where prostitution is both more prevalent and more visible, and I can't find evidence that any has made a fuss about it at home." He leaned forward and took his own coffee cup from its coaster, cradling it in both hands. "I can only assume, then, that they are posturing. They have a new national stage—and your hungry cameras—and they've latched onto an issue that makes them look morally righteous but doesn't really require any action on their part. They can play around with District policy with no risk of political fallout. There are much more serious moral issues facing the nation and the world right now. Starvation in Somalia. Endemic disease in other parts of Africa. Children being killed in school shootings here in our own country every year. And I don't see a single piece of legislation being given serious consideration that addresses any of these issues. These men—and a few women—are performers. To paraphrase the Bard, they strut and fret their hour upon the stage in fear that they will be heard no more. They're getting their fifteen minutes of fame and are playing it for all it's worth." He took a sip of his coffee, his eyes gleaming at Grant across the top of the cup and seeming to ask "Well, newsman. What are you going to do with that?"

Grant tried his best to appear unruffled. "I gather you don't see prostitution as a serious moral issue, then," he said.

Levanzo lowered the cup with a furrowed frown. "In some cases, yes. Trafficking in children. Forced involvement. But most of the women these congressmen are worried about are successful professionals, making a very good living by choice. Of course, there are the druggies who work 14th Street. That's different. But that isn't what I've heard these congressmen raising a fuss about."

"What's the difference?" Grant asked.

"There are people in the world who are going to make bad choices and screw up their lives. They are people who thrive on drama and personal crisis and, frankly, you can't do much to salvage them. They want to be train wrecks." Levanzo again sipped at his coffee, studying Grant for a reaction. When he saw none, he continued.

"Then there are the true professionals. These men and women are really no different than professional dancers or athletes. They see their bodies as ways to make a living—a very comfortable living."

"At some considerable risk to themselves," Grant offered.

Levanzo raised a questioning brow. "More so than a professional football player? Than someone involved in this cage fighting that's become so popular? Where is the outcry about that?"

"But what about the social damage? The cost in terms of shattered relationships and feelings of betrayal?"

"That," the Sicilian suggested, "is damage of choice and not the fault of the woman. If the john didn't have her, he'd go to some other woman—possibly a married woman. Would that be better? I know from our earlier conversation that you are no longer married but when you were, if your wife learned you had a massage at the spa in the Ritz, would she have felt betrayed? But if she learned you spent the same hour having sex with a prostitute, she would. The intimacy of the physical contact isn't a lot different."

"The degree of physical and emotional response is certainly different," Grant objected. "And we've determined as a society that certain levels of intimacy should remain sacrosanct."

"Exactly," Levanzo said. "But if for the participants they aren't, where is the harm? It shouldn't be the role of government to legislate personal morality." He paused and swirled the remaining coffee in the bottom of his cup, studying the rings in the dark liquid.

"There is a great irony in all of this," he said, looking back up at the newsman. "These Victorians who want to put a chastity belt around the District are the same libertarians who don't want government messing in their lives, telling them what they can own and not own, imposing zoning restrictions on their property, or regulating their financial transactions. But they sure as hell want to be able to tell me who I can go to bed with and who I can't. And my guess is they'd jump in the sack with one of these high-priced beauties in a second if they thought they could get away with it."

This was the comment Grant Huston remembered when he decided to get Clayton Mehrens elected to the presidency.

THIRTEEN

Arranging a second meeting with Giordano Levanzo was considerably more complicated than simply showing up at his front door with a notepad. Grant was now living in New York and was certain the man's movements must be monitored on a minute-by-minute basis. And Huston couldn't afford to be seen with the don.

A chance encounter at the opening of a traveling exhibit of works of the Dutch Masters at the National Gallery in Washington put them together for a brief private moment in a corner of the Sculpture Garden. Grant learned quickly that the Sicilian was used to dealing with such challenges.

"It's been some time!" Levanzo said, greeting the newsman warmly. "I've never thanked you for being kind to me in your report on our interview. When was that? Five years ago?"

"Six, if I remember correctly," Grant said, momentarily unsure whether he should try to take advantage of this extraordinary piece of serendipity. But it may never come again. "I'm so glad I ran into you! I was wondering if I could arrange to meet with you on a very private matter—preferably not at your home."

Levanzo studied him with an amused smile. "Or in New York at your home or office, I assume. How private is private?"

"*Very* private," Grant said, knowing that he wasn't disguising his nervousness.

Levanzo nodded. "These things come up." He pulled a card from a thin wallet he carried in an inside pocket of his dress jacket. "When you have a morning free and are going to be in the area, call this number and tell my assistant the day you would like to meet with Mr. G. Come in one of the cars from DCLimo you can hire at Reagan National—one that has a privacy window. Be in the parking lot of the Woods Academy near my home at 8:30 in the morning. If this is a *very* private talk, I suggest you disguise yourself as well as you can. You're a recognizable face and people will be watching. Pay cash for the car and don't reserve it in advance. There are almost always some at the curb and if you give us a few days' notice, we can have one waiting." His smile broadened. "Very *Levanzo*, don't you think?"

He left Grant standing alone beside a statue of a giant hare sitting on a boulder doing its best to imitate Rodin's *The Thinker*. It did strike Huston as being *very* Levanzo and he wondered if he were being toyed with by the crime boss. But hc arranged to have an open day two weeks later, called the number, and told the woman at the other end that he had talked to Mr. G at a social gathering and was asked to set up an appointment through her. A week from Wednesday morning would work, and he would be at the requested place.

"A week from Wednesday morning," she said, as if she had expected the call. "Fly into Reagan and there will be a limo waiting at Ground Transportation. Check with the attendant at the DCLimo desk."

Huston caught a 6:00 a.m. flight from LaGuardia to Reagan National, unconcerned that a number of passengers looked at him with open curiosity. He heard their whispers, was used to the recognition, and enjoyed it. The flight landed a few minutes after 7:00 and he slipped into a stall in a restroom just outside the arrival gate, glued on a thick, drooping mustache purchased earlier from a costume shop on New York's 25th Street, and donned a pair of heavy-rimmed dark glasses. With a plaid Scottish cap pulled low over his forehead, he followed the signs to Ground Transportation and found the desk for DCLimo. The attendant had a car at the curb.

"Your drive is only about twenty-five minutes when traffic is light," she said. "But at 8:00 a.m.? You should give yourself another fifteen minutes."

Grant slipped into the rear seat, noting the Plexiglas privacy screen. This *did* feel very Levanzo. Without asking for a destination, the driver headed into the city toward the Beltway.

The Sicilian was waiting in the parking lot at the Woods Academy when the car arrived and climbed in beside Huston, signaling the driver to leave immediately. Again, the chauffeur seemed to have his instructions and wove through the streets of suburban Bethesda until he could blend into traffic moving north and east on I-475.

Levanzo was dressed in casual twill slacks, a comfortable long-sleeved cashmere pullover in a deep maroon, and brown loafers. As he entered the limo, he smiled and nodded at Grant's disguise, an acknowledgment that he thought it sufficiently effective.

"I have grandchildren at the school," he said as they pulled away. "I walk them here every morning, rain or shine. It gives me a little exercise and some time for the kids with Papa.... And this," he said, patting the seat of the black Chrysler, "is how I find privacy. DCLimo is one of my companies and I know I can trust the drivers—who can't hear us anyway. So, how can I be of service?"

Grant had rehearsed what he would say almost hourly for a week and it had never come out the same. There was no teleprompter. No notes in front of him on the desk. No scripted way to sell one's soul to the devil. He had finally decided not to practice but to tell the truth as the truth came to him at the moment. He was certain the crime boss didn't tolerate lies and he didn't have time to try to keep a lie straight anyway.

"I'm going to be very forthright with you and hope I don't offend," he began, watching the dark face for cues. Levanzo remained expressionless.

"I'm assuming that most of the rumors about your profession are accurate. Which means that you are extremely skilled at distancing yourself from actions that may advance your interests, but also potentially get you into trouble." The weathered face still showed nothing.

Grant drew a deep, slow breath, hoping he wasn't conveying too much of his uneasiness. "I'd like to hire you to do the same for me," he said. "Advance some of my interests in ways that could definitely get me into trouble, but keep me distanced from the actions it will take to get the job done."

Levanzo's face finally folded into a thoughtful frown. "Most of my business I conduct very much in the open," he said. "But if I were involved in the kind of affairs you refer to, I suspect there would be a number of people who would like me to admit to it. Having me talk to some trusted figure like yourself would be a clever way to do that."

Grant had anticipated the concern. "If you're worried that I'm wired or something, you can check me over. I assure you, I'm here to ask for your help with something I wouldn't want those same others to know about."

"I know you aren't wired," Levanzo said. "The car checked you when you got in. But just your testimony would have a very powerful effect."

Grant nodded. "What can I do to assure you I'm on the level?"

Levanzo had been sitting half-turned toward his visitor and shifted back to gaze out the window on his side. They were driving east across the north edge of the District, had crossed the Old Georgetown Road, and were into the wooded area that bordered the junction with 270.

"Tell me what it is you want to do and perhaps that will help," he said finally, turning back to Grant to study his face as the newsman explained his request. Levanzo's eyes conveyed the distinct impression that the don would know if he were being lied to.

"When I interviewed you at your home years ago, you said that you believed that some of our more self-righteous politicians, if given the chance, would succumb to the temptations of the flesh. I would like to see if that's true."

Levanzo's face gradually softened into an amused smile, followed by a soft chuckle. "What an interesting idea! You want to create the situations that would test them then, I gather?"

"Exactly."

"Why, if I might ask?"

"I believe that for most of them, the one thing that is more important to them than their political position is their job—which depends on their moral reputation. I'd like to leverage that reputation to be able to persuade them to change some of those positions."

"You want to blackmail them into changing their politics?"

the don said bluntly, his smile curling cynically. "I thought you were supposed to be above politics."

""I'm reaching the point that because of all of the partisanship and political wrangling, I'm beginning to fear for our future," Grant said grimly. "I don't want to be in a position to have to report on the decline and fall of the empire."

"And what's the endgame here?" Levanzo asked.

"I want to get Clayton Mehrens elected president."

The Sicilian had shown no sign of surprise up to that moment, but Grant noted the quick blink and look to the side that signaled the unexpected.

"Why Mehrens? He's a dark horse in this race."

"He's the only horse I see that might promise four to eight years of honest, rational government. And I'm not sure we have another eight years to waste."

"You start messing with this and get caught and you're committing professional suicide."

They had crossed Connecticut Avenue and the six gold spires of the Washington Mormon Temple rose into view in front of them above the treetops. Grant watched them pass without answering, then nodded his agreement. "I'm willing to take that risk but hope you can minimize it significantly."

They rode in silence for three or four minutes while Levanzo digested what he was hearing. They passed the junction with 95 and the Beltway turned south toward Virginia.

"I couldn't agree to something that might compromise my own interests," he said as they reached the midpoint of their transit around the sixty-four mile highway loop. "I do see Mehrens as being principled but not a moralist, and that appeals to me. But I'm not sure I see how forcing political change among some of Washington's Januses would get him elected."

Huston smiled at Levanzo's reference to the two-faced Roman god, wondering if he was also using the name because Janus ruled over passages and transitions. Ancient mythology and Shakespeare. The man had more substance than Grant had given him credit for.

"I have a list of ten targets, one of whom will be Mehrens'

major primary opponent. The others are the vocal conservatives who rail against key positions Mehrens supports—gun control, immigration reform, climate change. I'll try to use the dirt we get on them to force a re-thinking of their positions to more closely align with Mehrens as the election approaches. In the case of the vice president, I'll just encourage him to withdraw." As Huston said it, he knew that he was violating one of Rayborn's rules of engagement—but he was ransoming his honor at the moment anyway, so what would it matter if he added another few pieces of silver?

They were now on I-95 just north of the runways for Andrews Air Force Base, turning back toward the west.

"So we're even going to set up the vice president," Levanzo muttered, giving the first indication that he was considering a partnership.

"Would you like to see him president?" Grant asked. The VP was an unpredictable grandstander and Grant guessed Levanzo favored predictability over politics.

"Low on my list," the Sicilian answered. "But so is almost everyone."

They drove in silence until they crossed the river into Alexandria, then Levanzo asked, "What were you thinking this would be worth to you?"

"I have some money from my mother's estate," Grant said. "I was thinking a hundred thousand per…what would we call this? Compromise? Well, a hundred thousand per video record of a significant indiscretion. But it would have to be hard evidence and graphic."

Levanzo chuckled. "You don't have much sense for the kinds of money that flow through the underworld, do you? A hundred thousand is change."

Grant reddened but said, "That's about what I can afford."

The crime boss studied the drab, industrial side of Alexandria that passed them on the right, rubbing the top of his prominent nose with the middle finger of his right hand. When he turned back to Huston, there was no smile and no trace of indecision.

"Let me suggest this," he said firmly. "I'll give you a PO box number. You send your list there, then call the contact number I gave you earlier and give her a post office box address that you, and you alone, know about. If a file should show up in that box, send fifty thousand in cash back to the box I've given you if you find the evidence satisfactory. If not, return the file."

"Only fifty thousand?" Grant was unable to veil his surprise.

"Only fifty thousand—and an understanding that whoever acquired the file information will also be keeping a copy of it for his own use."

Grant thought for a moment. "Agreed," he said. "As long as that use doesn't precede my own. And I may need help delivering the files and my requests to the victims."

Levanzo returned to rubbing his nose, then said, "Send an instruction of what you want delivered with the file to the same PO box, and when. Then when it's apparent the file and request have been delivered, send the other fifty thousand."

They had been on the road for an hour and were approaching the turn back into Bethesda.

"I'm comfortable with this arrangement," Grant said. "Is there anything else you need from me?"

"No more visits," the Sicilian said. "Though this one has been most interesting."

FOURTEEN

When Chase Rayborn met again with Dan Triplett, the log mansion seemed less imposing, diminished by low, moody clouds that shrouded the valley below in a misty drizzle. And Chase was too nervous to be awed. The rancher's wife was again away and the men pulled two of the heavy leather chairs closer to the fire.

Triplett fingered a cold Coors wrapped in a blue foam jacket. "I know you wanted to remain anonymous," he said, "but I wasn't about to negotiate any arrangement of the kind you were hinting at unless we were face-to-face. *Mano a mano*. And I knew who you were anyway."

Chase raised a surprised brow. He wondered if Triplett knew that *mano a mano* didn't mean man-to-man. But given the circumstances, it really didn't make any difference.

"I listen to that voice every evening," the rancher said. "And when you came to interview me, I remember thinking how much you sounded like you do on TV. When you called, you hadn't said two words and I knew it was Chase Rayborn. So tell me—how serious are you about creating some kind of national crisis? Something that will generate the kind of fear to drive people into the Carter Graves' camp?"

"Dead serious," Chase said.

"I thought you news people tried to stay above all that."

"On the surface," Chase agreed. "We joke around with each other on the air, but you should hear the conversations that go on off camera. We're all scared shitless."

"About…?"

"WIS. Growing Chinese influence. The tipping point," Chase said. "And I don't mean that book by Malcom Gladwell. I mean the tipping point in the electorate at which the number of active voters who are being supported by the government exceeds the number who are contributing to state and federal coffers. The point at which the voting population can control more entitlements, more tax burden on the declining number of workers, and more regulation."

"I shouldn't have to tell you this, but we're there," Triplett said.

"We're there in numbers but not in active voters—yet! But the DNC's working at it. Thank God congressional districts have been arranged to protect the interests of some of the taxpayers or we'd already be a socialist state."

"And you think fear will trump the desire for handouts, when push comes to shove?"

"The so-called poor in America have no idea what poverty really is," Chase said with a note of bitterness. "You and I have both seen poverty, and there's nothing close to it in the U.S. I ran across some data recently that showed that the bottom five percent of Americans in terms of income are still richer than seventy percent of the rest of the world. They're completely taken care of at the most basic levels. So if we want to get Maslowian about it, yes. Fear and personal safety will trump other basic needs."

Chase tilted his own beer, found it empty, and gazed into the fire. "Most of us have never had to live with real insecurity," he continued, "and the thought of it worries the hell out of us. The reality of it would terrify us. If we want to grab America's attention, we'd need to create real insecurity at the survival level."

Triplett called back over his shoulder to an unseen person deeper in the massive lodge. "LeAnn? Could you bring us a couple more beers?" He turned back to Rayborn. "And why have you come to me?"

"Because you're smart," Chase said. "I think the most frightening thing about our major terrorist enemies right now is that they're led by smart, well-educated men. If we're going to respond by duplicating their threat, it has to be with similar thought and planning. It can't be through some backwoods supremacy group that's been pulled together by a couple of high school dropouts whose only status in life is that they think they've been born into some superior race." He glanced over at a door that exited the living room to their left. "You showed me your library when I was here last and I know you're a serious student of our history. You also have a sterling military record. That's the kind of person we need leading what I guess I would call a 'covert' effort to get Graves in the White House."

A pretty brunette in tight jeans and a loose flannel shirt carried two cold beers in and placed them on coasters on the table.

"Thanks, Lee," Triplett said. "We're going to be talking privately." The woman looked up at Rayborn, smiled with apparent recognition, and left the men to their conversation, brushing Triplett's shoulder lightly with her hand as she passed. He glanced back at her, his face reflecting a trace of embarrassed irritation, then returned his attention to Rayborn.

"I think we could play on people's basic patriotism and get some support. But I wouldn't try to appeal to Americans on the basis of any sense of historic duty," Triplett said. "For one thing, we've reached the point that most Americans can't trace their ancestry to our founding generation. And even those who can have developed some fantasized vision of the Founding Fathers and their Constitutional intent that's pure bullshit." He grinned at Chase. "How many signers of the Declaration were there?"

Chase ran some quick calculations in his head. Thirteen colonies and maybe four signers per colony. "I'd guess about fifty-two," he offered.

Triplett raised a surprised brow. "Closer than most! Fifty-six. Now—name ten."

Chase leaned back in the deep chair and gazed at the timbered ceiling. "Let's see. Jefferson." He ticked off the guesses by raising fingers on the hand that wasn't supporting his beer. "Franklin, Adams, Washington…and John Hancock, of course."

"Not Washington," Triplett corrected and Chase folded a finger back into his hand.

"Madison? How about Madison?"

Triplett shook his head.

"Hamilton or John Jay?"

Another shake.

"You've got me," Chase said, smiling thinly and making a mental note to look them up when he got back to New York. "I know I should know more, but they aren't coming to me."

"For those who can name any, you got the common four," Triplett said. "And I'll give you credit for five. There were two Adams: John and Samuel. But do the names Gerry, Ellery, Paca and Hart ring a bell?"

Rayborn frowned and shook his head.

"You and nobody else. But think about what that means for those of our persuasion. We make a big fuss about Constitutional purity and intent but can't name one out of four of the men who gave us our freedom—and don't know anything about what they thought or believed. And I can assure you, they weren't all men of great Christian values or impeccable character. We seem to gloss over the fact that Jefferson and Paca had children with slave women." He gazed distantly into the fire and his jaw tightened. "But they did all have one thing that most of us have lost. *Courage*. If a few little skirmishes with the British had gone the other way, they all knew they were signing their death warrants. They'd have been publically hanged, just for having their names on that document. But they signed anyway."

"I need someone with that kind of courage to help me get Carter Graves elected," Chase said, leaning forward again in his chair. "Is that something you can do?"

Triplett sat quietly long enough that Chase thought he would decline.

"As you know, I spent five years with Special Forces," Triplett said finally. "I've seen the kind of fear we're talking about. Been in the middle of it more times than I like to remember and know what makes it happen." He looked up at the man from PAX News. "To be honest, I've thought almost daily about trying to do more than just give money to Graves since he looked like he might have a shot at the presidency—even if it's a long shot. He's just what the country needs."

"But you chose not to."

Triplett laughed cynically. "That kind of thing takes money and I'm a billionaire with no money. What I made with Iron Shield went mainly into legal fees." He glanced up at Rayborn, then stared again into the fire. "You know we were accused of killing some Iraqis. Got in a firefight when some embassy staff we were guarding got ambushed in the middle of a village. There were a bunch of people in the square and some women and children got killed. Who knows who shot 'em. All hell had broken loose and there were rounds coming from everywhere. But it's a pretty damned sorry state of affairs when a man ends up defending himself against the government he was trying to protect." He was quiet and Chase let it remain that way. After a long moment Triplett looked back up, his face reflecting mild surprise that he was sitting there in the room with Rayborn.

"You were talking about not having money," Chase reminded him.

"Oh, yeah. It belongs to my wife through her first husband, and we have a pretty ironclad pre-nup. She's semi-sympathetic to the cause but would never go for something like we're talking about. She doesn't pay a lot of attention to what I do, but she does to what I spend. I couldn't bankroll this kind of action."

"I know some heavy hitters who are solidly in the Graves camp," Chase said. "You set up a fund under some innocuous name—nothing to do with electing Carter Graves—and I'll get money into it. I think within a month I can have twenty million dollars."

Triplett's nod showed he was impressed. "That should do the job.... But we start this under one condition. We do it my way, and your job's to get the money into the account."

Chase shrugged his agreement. "I can't ask for more than that," he said.

But that was before BART, Kansas City, and Quail Hollow. Before he realized Triplett was a man without conscience. For the leader of the Order, American lives were no different than the dozen women and children Iron Shield had gunned down in the Iraqi square. Collateral damage in the name of the greater good. Now Chase wanted to ask for much more! Things were way out of control and he had to get them stopped.

PART THREE

FIFTEEN

Since his divorce, Grant Huston had developed a reputation as a womanizer, a condition that existed long before the split-up and accounted for a good part of it. He was also known as a loner. When he wasn't at a mandatory function or escorting an attractive woman to a social event somewhere in the city, he made it known that he preferred his own company. This was particularly the case following his evening broadcast when, after taking care of wrap-up responsibilities at the studio, he headed for a privately held table at the Rum House on West 47th Street. Though not a jazz fan, the jazz piano kept the bar quieter than Johnny Utah's a few blocks north. At Johnny's, the main source of entertainment was a mechanical bull and Huston sometimes liked to take a date there because it meant less conversation. But after his broadcast, it was the Rum House where the regulars knew not to disturb him. Any out-of-towner who happened to recognize him in the shadowy corner where he insisted on hiding with only the light from the central candle, received a less than cool reception if they approached. Unless, of course, it was a particularly pretty and unaccompanied young woman. But when his newscast was over, Grant wanted the hour to decompress, think of as little as possible and, of late, try to calculate his chances of getting Clayton Mehrens through the primaries as the Democratic nominee.

With each of the terrorist attacks that were rocking the country and turning Americans into panicked, mindless reactionaries, support was growing for Carter Graves. Even the Democratic leadership was beginning to murmur about finding their own take-the-war-to-the-enemy alternative. Domestic policy was slipping so far onto the back burner that it wasn't even simmering, while hatred, suspicion and a growing sense of national helplessness were at full boil. Without some kind of miraculous return to a belief that the country was again secure, Yosemite Sam looked like he was on a bullet train to the White House. When Grant made his wager with Chase Rayborn, who could have guessed that the GQ poster child from PAX News would get this kind of horrifying support?

The moody cloud of his depression added enough to the dimness of his corner table that he was initially unaware of the figure standing slightly behind him. The man shuffled uneasily, but enough to draw Grant's attention back to the room. He looked up to see one of the last people he had expected to intrude.

"Well!" he said, leaning back carefully on his light, spindle-backed chair. "If it isn't the kingmaker!"

Rayborn tilted his head slightly to acknowledge that he was also a little surprised to be in this dark corner of the Rum House. Grant noted immediately that there was none of the brash snarkiness that always seemed part of a Chase Rayborn drive-by.

"May I sit?" Rayborn asked, looking around to ensure that his presence wasn't attracting too much attention to the corner. The regulars, already in the habit of leaving Huston alone, seemed even more aware of the need to ignore the pair.

Grant indicated the chair opposite with a loose wave. "As a matter of fact, I was just thinking about you and your man. It's hard for me to imagine a worse set of circumstances for the country—and a better set for a man who thrives on division and conflict."

Rayborn sat stiffly opposite him, his handsome face creased with what Grant could easily have mistaken for fear. Casting another quick glance around the room, the PAX anchor leaned forward on his elbows. "That's just what I came to talk to you about," he said quietly. "As much as it pains me to have to say this...we're in deep shit and I need your help."

Huston rocked his chair forward again onto four legs and studied his nemesis with a suspicious frown. "I can't imagine that you've had a crisis of conscience, so I have to assume you're here to ask me to capitulate—to acknowledge that we need your madman to get us out of this terrorist mess."

Rayborn returned the look directly but with no sign that he had come to gloat.

"Actually, it's almost the opposite" he said cryptically. "I've come to ask for your help to stop these terrorist attacks, but not necessarily to advance the interests of my candidate."

Grant's eyes continued to bore into the candle-lit face across from him. There was nothing about this man that he trusted, but his nerve at coming onto Huston's turf to even mention the wager intrigued him. And Rayborn looked genuinely frightened.

"I'm listening," he said.

Rayborn again glanced about nervously, leaned farther over the small round table and raised an index finger pointedly toward his rival.

"First of all, I've got to have your word that this conversation stays right here. Just between the two of us."

"Does it relate to the wager?"

Rayborn nodded. "But it would be one helluva news story and you need to promise that we're totally off the record—that it stays *right here*." He drummed his fingertips against the tabletop for emphasis. The man's expression told Grant he needed to know about this and better agree.

"Alright," he said. "Completely off the record."

Rayborn sat silently for a moment, studying Grant in an effort to gauge his sincerity, then said, "Suppose I were to tell you that these terrorist attacks are not foreign at all. That they're the work of a domestic militant group that sees them as a way to ensure Graves' selection as the Republican nominee."

Huston's mind had been racing through possible explanations for Rayborn's intrusion and hadn't even approached the edges of this possibility. His stare became rapid blinking as his mind shifted gears and tried to engage with what it had just heard.

"I can't imagine such a thing," he said finally. "Internal terrorists have always been anarchist—out to destroy the government. Why would a group that's trying to support the political process, albeit in a deranged way, be willing to murder our own citizens?"

Chase Rayborn shook his head slowly, the muscles in his jaw flexing involuntarily. "It's hard for me to imagine either," he said. "But I know that's what's happening."

"What is this group?" Grant asked.

"They call themselves the Order of King's Mountain."

"Never heard of them. I'd think the name would ring a bell if it were a domestic militant group."

"It was formed specifically with this end in mind," Chase said, his eyes diverting and forcing the inevitable question from Grant.

"And you know about this because…?"

Rayborn didn't reply and Grant's mind began to connect the dots that had just been thrown up on his mental screen.

"Are you involved in this somehow?" he asked, his tone showing that even as much as he despised the PAX news anchor, he didn't want to hear the answer.

Rayborn drew a deep breath. "Does the name Dan Triplett mean anything to you?"

Huston nodded. "I listened to your interview."

"Then you might remember the very end—the part in which he suggested that the only way to salvage this country was to create a great enough sense of fear that people would turn to a strong, security-minded leader. Someone like Carter Graves."

Huston nodded, sensing where this was headed. "So you think this Triplett is behind these attacks in an effort to build support for Graves."

"I know he is," Rayborn muttered.

"And how do you know this?"

Rayborn looked nervously into the tabletop, speaking in a low whisper. "After our little bet, I got back in touch with him. Asked him how serious he was about that statement. And when he said 'very serious,' I asked if he thought there was a way to generate that kind of fear. He said that with the right support, he believed he could do it." Rayborn looked back up at Grant. "The support he wanted was financial and I helped him find it. I essentially helped him create the Order of King's Mountain. I had no idea the man was a lunatic and would do this kind of thing."

"My God!" Huston murmured, pushing back the chair and standing as if the revelation had jerked him onto his feet. He turned and gazed vacantly across the dimly lit bar, then back at Rayborn and whispered down at him. "They carried out all three of these attacks?"

The anchor from PAX waved across the table at Grant's chair. "Sit back down. You're attracting attention." He waited until Huston dropped back into his seat.

"Yes, I believe they carried out all three attacks," he said quietly. "I called Triplett after I read about BART and he as much as admitted it—and said other attacks were already in the works and couldn't be stopped. I think that meant he had no intention of stopping them. But I swear, I had no idea he had this kind of scare tactic in mind. I was thinking more like blowing up a vacant building or wiping out a section of rail line hours before a train was scheduled to come through…."

"But you're complicit…" Huston said.

Even in the dim light, Rayborn's face darkened visibly. "*We're* complicit," he said acidly.

Huston raised a brow. "Even if our wager were to come to light, none of this could be laid back on me."

Rayborn's eyes sparked. "Damn it, Grant. Are you listening to what I'm telling you here? Our little wager has resulted in thousands of people dying and you're trying to play 'I didn't know nothing about it!' For Christ's sake, can't you see that a plan by two news anchors to manipulate an election would implicate you in this as much as anyone?"

"All I'm hearing," Huston hissed back in a loud whisper, "is that you were stupid enough to climb into bed with some psycho and are now just figuring out that you got screwed. I wasn't even in the bedroom."

Rayborn leaned so far across the table that Grant could smell the man's breath and felt a light, beery spray as his rival spit the words at him.

"Listen, you pompous asshole. It hasn't escaped me that a number of top Republicans seem to have suddenly adopted political positions that are a one-eighty from their earlier points of view—and surprisingly in line with Clayton Mehrens. Something—or should I say, someone—has found a way to exert irresistible pressure on these men. Even getting the vice president to step down, which wasn't part of our deal. How was all that done?"

Huston shrugged impassively. "They must have had a change of heart."

"*Bull shit*!" Rayborn spat. "I wonder why?" Several of the bar's patrons looked their way, then huddled again over their drinks.

"With the mess the country's in, maybe these men decided to become rational," Huston said.

"While the rest of the country's going to hell in a hand basket and people are beating a path to Graves' door? I don't think so."

"Then what would be your explanation?"

Rayborn reached into the inside pocket of his jacket and pulled out two photographs, dropping them onto the table in front of the anchor from NBS. Both were morgue shots, one of a pasty gray woman with her throat slashed wide open and a fleshy lump protruding from her mouth. The other, another young women with a single bullet hole in her forehead. Rayborn tapped the two photos.

"One of the values of working in a newsroom is that odd bits of information cross your desk because they have some morbidly alluring news interest. I read both of these when they came in, after I was already wondering how you were getting these guys on Capitol Hill to come out with radical changes of position. You know what these two ladies had in common?" He adjusted the photos in front of Grant so he could see them clearly. The chill in Huston's spine reached his brain before the answer began to form, but he shook his head.

"They were both murdered in what appeared to be mob-style executions. And they had both been high-priced hookers in the Washington area before they beat it out of town."

"I don't see what that's got to do with your mess," Huston said, pushing the photos back across the table."

"Strange little coincidence here," Rayborn said grimly. "I knew one of these girls." He tapped the photo of the dead Brandy Wingate. "I used to visit her a couple of times a month. But when I called her one afternoon, she was in Miami. Said she'd had to leave town in a hurry and you want to know why? She wasn't specific, but I got the impression she got paid a lot to get something on an important politician and then was told to split."

"Coincidence," Grant said, knowing his own uncertainty was beginning to show.

Rayborn snorted. "Suppose they get to Triplett on these attacks and he tells them about me. I'm going to spill my guts about this wager but insist I had no idea Triplett was a crazy sonofabitch. Those federal guys aren't idiots and will start putting two-and-two together. They're going to wonder why Mehrens started getting all this support after our little bet. One of the politicians will admit he got blackmailed and they'll start looking for the girls. Are you confident enough that these deaths are coincidence to want a federal investigator looking into these murders, knowing you made a bet to try to get Mehrens elected?"

Huston knew there was a possibility Rayborn was right—that the girls *had* been part of the blackmail. He also knew the worst thing he could do was ask Gio Levanzo if the deaths were more than coincidence.

"No," he said finally. "I wouldn't want that kind of investigation. Though I can honestly say I don't know there's any connection. Let's just say I've made some third-party inquiries myself, and I'm not sure exactly what's happened as a result."

"But you're pretty sure some of these politicians are being blackmailed," Rayborn said.

Huston answered with his silence.

Rayborn leaned back in his chair. "So you're pretty much where I am. We both got others involved and lost control. And I don't know about you, but I'm feeling guilty as hell and have got to do something to get this all stopped. Which brings me to the reason I came looking for you here. To use an old Wyoming expression, we're both up shit creek without a paddle and it's time we figured out how to get out of the canoe."

Huston leaned forward onto his hands, his fingers combing through his heavily sprayed hair. He'd known he was taking a serious risk when he approached Gio Levanzo—but one he thought he and the crime boss could control. It hadn't occurred to him that risk control to the don might mean eliminating those who knew about the blackmail, without worrying about whether it would ever come back on Huston. Grant had sent his names to an anonymous PO box and had received the photo files at another. His payments had gone back to the same box, one he was certain Levanzo would deny knowing about.

And Grant hadn't even begun to imagine that Rayborn had done something even more disastrous. How could the guy have been that stupid! But then, climbing into bed with Washington's major crime family hadn't been the brightest move on the board. He sat upright and looked through the dim flicker of candlelight at Rayborn.

"You got any ideas?"

Rayborn tipped forward again with both hands on the table and looked intently into the distinguished face of Grant Huston. "The way I see it," he said, "is that I have a loose cannon who needs to be screwed down. And you seem to have found a way to get powerful men to change their minds about what they say they believed with all their hearts. Can we do the same thing to Dan Triplett?"

Huston thought for a long moment, wondering how willing he was to scratch at a sore that was already a festering boil. "The problem I see," he said finally, "is that before a man will change his position, there has to be something he wants to preserve more than he does that position. For the people we've been talking about, that something's been what little vestige of respect and reputation they have. If it's stripped away, they're nothing. What does Triplett have to lose?"

"His fortune," Rayborn said quickly. "Triplett has no money of his own. It all comes through his wife. And they have a very strict pre-nup that if he goes, none of the money follows. And he knows the money is the basis of all his power and influence."

"And she'd cut him off if he betrayed her?"

"My impression is they don't care for each other that much. And I'm pretty sure she wouldn't tolerate being publicly humiliated. You're the master of public embarrassment. Is there a way we can get to him like you have with these politicians?"

Huston chewed thoughtfully on the inside of his cheek. "It would mean making a contact I was told not to make again—by someone who doesn't take ignoring his instructions lightly." He nodded toward the photos that were back in Rayborn's pocket. "I'm not sure I dare do that."

"How have you been getting the information to him?"

"PO box."

"Can't you just send another name, or whatever you do?"

Huston considered that for a moment. "Possibly. Let me think about it. If I decide we can—and decide I want to take the risk—I'll call you after it's done and let you know. I'll just say, 'It looks like it might work out,' or 'We can forget that idea.' Then you'll know. But this could be pretty dangerous."

Again Rayborn snorted. "The way I see it, we're both drowning. Is it going to make any difference if the water's deeper? And we've got to do something to stop this guy. If he keeps this up and gets caught, we're both screwed. Plus, I can't live with letting anything else happen. Haven't slept in days as it is."

"Does Triplett have something else planned?"

"I have no idea. But I'd stay off the subway, cancel your Knicks tickets, and try not to fly. I suspect he does and it scares the hell out of me. My guess is that it's going to be something big."

SIXTEEN

"I need to go to Hungary," Adam said, turning from the wall map of the United States that displayed stickpins in each of the states from which he knew there was a compromised public official. The map idea had come to him from seeing the one on the wall of the Georgetown apartment of the agent who had initiated the work on this extortion case—a map that was unrelated to the prostitutes but showed the home cities of American tourists missing abroad. Adam had been struck by how much the visual display instantly stimulated his thinking. He had found himself standing in front of that map looking for patterns when he should have been moving quickly through his cleanup routine.

On his new map, at least one pattern was immediately apparent. Eight of the nine pins were red. The one blue pin represented the vice president. A set of white pins indicated the cities in which they had located the call girls who had fled Washington, with black pins in Miami and San Francisco where the girls had been killed.

Dreu Sason was standing in front of a waist-high desk Adam had added to his scanty decor to accommodate her compulsion to stand while she worked. The screen in front of her displayed her latest find—a pretty, fresh-faced blond from the video of a congressman from Nevada. The girl was now in New York City and was a redhead.

"You don't think after San Francisco any of these American girls are going to talk?" she asked, still facing the screen, then answered her own question. "Not if they got the warnings."

Adam's answer was heavy with remorse. "I'm afraid even approaching them will put their lives in danger." He shifted his gaze back to the black dot that covered most of the Bay Area. "Selina didn't tell me anything, and I'm not sure she would have. But she'd been approached and that was good enough for whoever's watching the girls. Both of the women in the U.S. who were contacted in person are dead."

"And you think the European girls might not be monitored?"

"I don't know. I just know the ones here are and I don't want to put any more of them at risk if there's an option."

Dreu turned from the computer and looked him up and down critically.

"The European women won't talk to you," she said.

Adam frowned and twisted to study himself in the window, its surface mirrored by the deepening dusk beyond. His hair was again a dark brown, matched by the thickening shadow of a two-week beard. The black patch again covered his prosthetic left eye.

"I think I look like the picture of trust and discretion," he said.

Dreu snorted. "You look like you should be swinging aboard from the yardarm with a cutlass between your teeth."

"That's the new casual chic," he defended.

She laughed. "I think you're a notch or two below casual chic. If you came up to me in a Budapest bar, I'd signal the bouncers."

He continued to examine himself in the window. "The Hungarian women are our next best shot and I can shave again after I get out of the country. Those California photos of Brandon Lewis haven't been circulating for a few days and they're pretty grainy. I don't think I'm at high risk anymore."

"The girls still won't talk to you about this, even if you look like the best of casual chic. My guess is that even if they aren't being watched, they were sent the picture of Brandy Wingate."

"It's still our next best move. We have to get to someone who can link us to the next person in this extortion chain."

"Agreed," she said. "But I'm the one who needs to go."

Adam's face tightened into a scowl and he turned and raised both hands as if warding her off.

"Not a chance! I got you into one mess before and barely saved you from that."

"But since then, you've pulled me into the middle of *this* mess and I've known we were at the point we needed to get to the Europeans. I've been thinking about it the last few days and I'm pretty sure I can get them to talk to me."

"Because you're a woman?"

"Partly. But more because I can convince them I'm one of

them."

Adam arched a brow. "You're going to take a crash course in Hungarian?"

"No. I mean one of the girls who was part of this whole extortion thing."

"And why would you be coming to them?"

"To warn them. To tell them to disappear."

"And how would you explain that you know who they are?"

"I don't have that worked out yet. You'll need to help me with that."

Adam shook his head. "Way too dangerous. And I'm supposed to work solo."

Dreu looked around the room, then back at her desk and computer. "This doesn't look solo to me. You seem to be a little hesitant to contact your head office or whatever you call it, now that this woman's answering. And as for dangerous, I told you when we separated before that one of the reasons I was hesitant to get back together is that you'd be going off on one of your mysterious missions and I wouldn't know if you'd ever come back. Maybe you need to be on the other end of that for a change. Plus, the thing that frightens me most right now is being here at home—getting on an airplane or going to a concert in *this* country. They said this morning on the news that air travel is down by fifty percent and a lot of major concerts and sports events are being cancelled, partly because crowds are down so much and partly because they don't want to be targets. That's what scares me!"

"Yeah," Adam said. "We say we won't be intimidated by all this stuff, but we are. See? Even you're nervous. But if that's scaring you, you don't want to be standing in a park with one of our girls when someone puts a bullet in her head. You're not trained for this." But his voice was beginning to show less conviction.

"You've been struggling with that girl's death every minute since you got back, so don't lecture me about being able to take the pressure." The conviction had transferred to Dreu. "And you're trained for convincing prostitutes to talk to you?" She looked him over again critically. "The ones we're talking about aren't your average street hookers. The time I spent in the fashion business in New York taught me how these high-priced girls live and dress. I know the look and I can convince them I'm one of them."

As he looked at her now, he knew she was right. Dreu was exactly the kind of woman the extortionists had been using—a stunningly lithe body with an innocently beautiful face. When he was out with her, every man she passed looked at her as though thinking how wonderful it must be to be with her. And each secretly believed she might find within him that something he knew made him special.

She straightened behind her standing desk, brows arched and mouth a hard, resolute line. "You don't think I can do this?"

"It's got nothing to do with your ability.... I'd just be worried every minute you were out of my sight."

"And I'm not supposed to worry while you're out doing your thing? Let's be honest with each other here. You either believe I can do it or you don't. Which is it?"

"Again it's not a matter of 'can or can't do,' Dreu, but of training. I've spent hours drilling for in-flight emergencies. They put me through Special Forces training just to learn how to react, and react quickly, if someone threatened me. Those things matter if something goes wrong."

"Well then, if you were going to be flying with these girls, or fighting them, you'd be ready. But I still haven't heard anything that convinces me you can sit down with a terrified woman and convince her she needs to tell you who she thinks might be trying to kill her. And I admit I probably can't fight my way out of a tight spot, but I've spent my life solving complex problems. I'm never going to know how I'll do when my back's against the wall until I get there. Just like you didn't know. You pulled me back in and I think you owe me a chance."

He looked at her challenging face, waiting for a hint of doubt or hesitation. She refused to flinch.

"You sure about this?" he said after a moment.

"Absolutely. It's our best chance at getting one of these girls to tell us who recruited her. And if they're being watched, if another woman approaches them it may not be seen as suspicious."

"Then we're going together."

"The only way I'd go," she said. "But when we're there, I'll need to make the contacts on my own."

"Understood." He pulled two chairs together beside his barnwood table. "Okay—let's work out an explanation for why you might be coming to find them."

SEVENTEEN

Joshua Shallenburger stood awkwardly in the doorway of Triplett's den, hands thrust deep in his pocket, and waited until his commander looked up.

"Talked to my sister Janna," he said without elaboration.

"And…?" Triplett coaxed.

"Well, she got out of Aliceville about the time this woman you was asking about come in. She knew *about* her, but didn't really know her."

Triplett twisted in his chair to face his explosives specialist. "So? Was your sister able to get in touch with anyone who knew this Nims woman?"

"Yeah. Jan called an old cellmate who just go out this month. Name's Felicia. She knew the woman better than Jan did." When he didn't continue, Triplett rose from behind his desk, walked around to its front, and perched on a corner. The application for the computer position from an Amber Nims indicated that she had recently done time in the Aliceville Federal Correctional Institution, and the Order's leader knew Joshua's sister had been there on a counterfeiting rap—for making bogus hundreds, if he remembered right. But Shallenburger didn't seem in a talkative mood.

"I've gotta make a decision on this woman, Josh. What were you able to find out about her?"

"The word was, she was some kind of computer genius. That's what got her sent up. Hacked into the government somehow and got caught. But she couldn't use computers inside, so no one really knew for sure how good she was. Not supposed to get near 'em, now she's out."

"That's it? That's all you were able to find out?"

"That's about it," Joshua said. "That's what you asked me to find out about."

"I wanted to know whatever you could learn about her," Triplett said, knowing that he hadn't picked his most communicative soldier when he gave Josh the assignment.

"Well, Janna's friend did say that inside, they called her the Badger," Joshua offered. "And said she wasn't a person to mess with. Got pretty tight with her own cellmate, a woman named Marzilli who's connected somehow with the Washington mob. Marzilli came to pick her up when she got out of Alice."

"This Marzilli have another name?" Triplett asked.

"Guess so. I didn't ask. But she was in when Jan was there. I'll ask her."

"Do that. And see what else you can find out about them both," Triplett said. "And about what kind of relationship this Marzilli had with Nims while they were inside."

"Yeah. Okay. I can do that," Joshua said and left Triplett propped against the desk, staring thoughtfully down at the application.

This Nims was a whiz with computers, just out of prison, and willing to break parole. Sounded perfect.

EIGHTEEN

On a September evening when the scattered aspens were turning gold and the sun dropped earlier each evening below the peaks to the west, he lit a fire in the camp's central lodge and called the Order together. It was time to celebrate their victories, meet their new member, and outline the plan for what might be their final action. They sat in a semi-circle on one side of the massive central fire pit with its suspended brass hood. The rustic pine chairs and couches created a comfortable air of campfire story-telling rather than one of nurturing the seeds of fear.

Triplett stood beside the circular stone pit for a few moments and let them talk. Many had just heard on the evening news about a proposed delay in opening the regular NBA season. According to the report, unattributed threats had been received by front offices of the Bulls, Spurs and Thunder. Most members of the Order listened to Chase Rayborn on PAX News and knew there had been another poll swing toward the candidacy of Carter Graves. Even those who tuned into other networks were talking about reports of a rising tide in favor of the conservative governor and his "Restore Strength to America" campaign.

"Excellent work, my fellow patriots," Triplett finally interrupted. "This has gone about as well as we possibly could have planned. Support for Graves is soaring and tonight we'll get a briefing on our next, and possibly final, campaign. But first, there's a new member of the Order I want you to meet."

He turned slightly to his left where a young woman who looked like she was just breaking out of her teens curled comfortably beneath a blanket in one of the oversized lounge chairs like a tawny cat. She was plump without being heavy, with a pretty pixie face framed by shaggy orange hair that hung over her forehead to partly shade two emerald-green eyes. She uncurled as she was introduced, revealing a cascade of floral tattoos that began high on each bare shoulder and flowed over her upper arms. She wore a high-necked, sleeveless T-shirt and a heavy pendant necklace—a circular yin-yang with a dark eye in the center, hanging from what looked like tightly woven black human hair.

"This is the Badger," he said, giving her a quick nod.

"*Badger?*" Dwayne Cargile snorted from the other end of the semi-circle. "What the hell kind of…."

The green eyes fixed on him like two lasers, freezing him in mid-sentence.

"The Badger comes to us from Alabama," Triplett continued. "A place called Aliceville. She just completed an eighteen-month stint being boarded by Uncle Sam. Apparently she couldn't resist working her way into some of the country's most secure computer systems and leaving little love notes. Her references say she's one of the very best in the business."

"But she got caught," Dwayne said defensively, still smarting from the stare down.

"Got ratted out," the Badger said, speaking to Triplett rather than Dwayne. "By someone I should have been able to trust." Triplett understood the message in her comment and dismissed it with a wave.

"As you'll hear in just a minute, none of us, including Dwayne, can afford to be ratting out anyone. So welcome to the Order."

He turned to the rest of the assembled members. "Technically the Badger's still on parole, but she's chosen not to check in each month with her officer in New Orleans. She doubts they'll be looking hard, but please, no announcements to anyone that she's come to stay with us." He paused and looked appreciatively at each of his three recent project leaders. "And now, we've got some outstanding work to recognize."

He had ordered three replica Revolution-era flintlocks from a company called ReplicaGuns that specialized in quality reproductions—beautiful pieces with burled walnut stocks and silver inlay. It would take the gun maker several more weeks to craft the pieces but Triplett had their design proofs, complete with inscribed names, to present to Dwayne, LeAnn and Joshua. They had carried out their assignments with honor and distinction and were the new Patriots, heroes of the new America. With all members of the Order standing, including the

Badger, he called each of the three forward and presented them with the artist's rendering, assuring them that there would be even greater ceremony when the actual weapons arrived.

When the three were again seated, Triplett paced slowly across the front of the blazing fire. It was being fed with pine logs that crackled nosily, spitting occasional sparks up towards the metal hood.

"Because of the fine actions of these three, we have the nation's attention," he said. "Sumler has strategically planned our attacks to let every part of the country know that as our national security now stands, no one's safe. But we've made the public believe that by hunkering down and staying off public transit and away from major events, they'll be okay." He stopped pacing and faced the group directly. "We need to change that perception. This one involves every one of you. Wade, talk us through it."

Wade Sumler was one of the singles in the camp, a gaunt spider of a man who was in constant motion. When he sat, one foot beat a rhythm across his knee that only he could hear, but the beat sparked his arms and head into motion at unpredictable moments. He spent most of his time alone in the last cabin in the row: a silent, curtained place that the few children in the camp gave wide berth. Wade was an obsessive planner and all three of his operations had gone off without a hitch.

He perched on the edge of a gray granite hearth that surrounded the pit, no part of him completely still, and eyed the rest of the Order with a look that seemed to bounce between manic and delighted.

"As Trip said," he began, "this one will involve every one of you—all in different parts of the country, but at the same moment. When it's over, every American will be clamoring for leadership that promises protection—that can secure our neighborhoods." For the next thirty minutes he outlined his design, one that left even the most committed members of the Order wondering if they were stepping too far across the line.

* * *

Carter Graves paused, surveying the group of men and women who surrounded the round, white-draped tables that filled the front of the Minneapolis Convention Center's Ballroom. They were the nation's Republican governors, assembled a final time before the national primaries to talk strategy and consolidate bases of support. Graves waited until those who were still deciding whether to eat all of the generous slice of caramel swirl cheesecake lowered their forks in surrender and turned their attention to their luncheon speaker.

"I know we have some good men on our side of the ticket," he said when all eyes were in his direction. "And I know some of you have pledged support to others in the party. But at this pivotal moment in our history—that pressure point on the balance that will either tip us toward a future of secure stability or one of chaos and anarchy—we cannot afford to be divided." His eyes swept the faces of his fellow governors to ensure each would hear what he was about to say. He continued with a slow, deliberate cadence, his jaw firmly set, hand raised with index finger pointed above their heads.

"If this terrorist activity in the United States continues unabated…" he said solemnly, then repeated "…if this terrorist activity continues unabated, we will enter a new era of vigilante justice—of 'every man for himself' solutions to public crises. Communities will form militias, lacking confidence in state and federal law enforcement to keep them safe. We won't be able to go to the grocery store without a security check, and all of those recreational enjoyments—our theaters, our zoos and public parks, our Friday nights at a high school football game—will become things of a desperately longed-for past."

The message passed through the ballroom like a gray winter fog and he watched as faces hardened and men and women involuntarily pulled their jackets more tightly about their shoulders.

"Now I know," he continued, "that my worthy opponent from New York has a reputation for law and order. But he has spoken openly about his opposition to increasing our involvement abroad. And we will not defeat this enemy unless we take the fight *to* him. This cannot be a defensive battle! It *will* take boots on the ground. We *must* strike hard, and as often as is necessary until he has neither the will nor the resources to respond." At the front tables there was a smattering of affirming nods while others tucked their chins against their chests and gazed soberly at the floor, unable to dismiss what they were hearing but knowing it would mean hundreds of American lives. But they were already seeing theaters and parks close in their home states, and hate crimes were on the rise, seemingly average citizens attacking anyone who appeared remotely foreign.

"And my esteemed congressional colleague from Orange County whose major pledge is that he can woo the Latino community to our ranks?" Graves continued. "The polls show that the shift is occurring anyway, but to my campaign. Like every other American, our Hispanic citizens are afraid and they want action."

"My fellow governors," he concluded. "I will bring you action. I will not shrink nor shun the fight. We are constitutionally guaranteed life, liberty, and the pursuit of happiness, all of which are now in great peril. I ask your support to help me restore our security, our liberty, and our honor as a great nation."

Graves turned purposefully from the podium as the applause grew. It was not boisterous and not enthusiastic, but it was what he had hoped for. It was deliberate. If he had waited to again survey the crowd he may have noticed that at a back table one of the senior Republican governors who, two years before, had been elected to his third consecutive term, was showing much greater restraint. Douglas Donnel, governor of Iowa, had received a hand-delivered packet to his room that morning. He had been number ten on the Grant Huston list. The governor had just been placed on notice that some of his activities during a recent economic development trip to the Netherlands had not remained secret. They involved an encounter with a young Dutch developer who had invited him to his home on the outskirts of

Amsterdam for a late-night drink. The price of the photos? Endorse no one in the presidential primaries.

NINETEEN

One sentence of Graves' speech to the assembled governors was about to become prophetic in ways he could not possibly have imagined. As the state leaders met in Minneapolis, nine self-proclaimed patriots from the Order of King's Mountain scattered across the country to carefully selected locations. Community size was not a factor. Geographic distribution was. Some had departed the camp three days earlier to reach New England and the Southeast. Some, two days before, to be in position by noon Saturday in mid-America and the Southwest. The Badger left Saturday morning, making the two-hour drive south to Pullman, Washington. Each drove a vehicle that had been purchased from salvage yards across the Northwest and was virtually untraceable. VIN numbers had been removed, engines replaced, bodies repainted and misleading bits of information pushed under and behind seats. The cars would all be abandoned within fifty miles of their target cities where another untraceable rebuilt vehicle awaited its Patriot.

Each member of the Order had been altered as well—skin darkened, hair covered with black wigs, faces hidden behind heavy sunglasses, and women wearing head scarves. The other piece of common equipment was a mid-sized dehumidifier in its original box with a sales slip stapled to the cardboard flap. All of the items were on their way to be returned.

Triplett had intentionally kept the Badger close to home. She had spent the previous week maneuvering her way through a labyrinth of internet links until deep inside a server managed by one of the Middle East's most dangerous and unpredictable jihadist groups. Within the server's intricate circuitry, she had buried a message that would come to life and broadcast on Saturday at exactly 11:15 U.S. Mountain Daylight Time. She had managed to back out of the system, erasing every trace of her entry. When the message reached the major news outlets in the United States, it would easily be traceable to its apparent source in northern Syria and not beyond. But although the claim of responsibility was designed to auto-send at a precise moment,

Triplett wanted the Badger back at the camp as quickly as possible in case, for some unexpected reason, the message was discovered or failed to release. Plus, Triplett saw the day with all of the other Patriots on the road as an opportunity to get better acquainted with the feisty little redhead.

During her two weeks with the Order, the Badger had shown herself to be the only member of the group who was not intimidated by its charismatic leader. If anything, she flaunted her independence and needled him about his need for obedience.

"You need to chill a little, Danny Boy," she teased when she found him alone one evening in the lodge's assembly room, hunched forward in deep thought. She moved behind his chair and, without invitation, placed her hands on his shoulders and began to gently knead the knots from them with her thumbs. "You're carrying too much of the weight of this whole thing on these pretty impressive shoulders," she murmured.

He didn't resist but leaned back slightly into her hands, twisting his neck to release more of the tension. "Someone has to be carrying the weight," he said with a trace of irritation. "I don't think you can imagine me passing it along to the rest of this lot."

The Badger laughed softly. "I've seen it's your way or the highway."

"Discipline's the guiding principle in a place like this," Triplett said. "We don't call this an Order for nothing."

"I've lived a life of imposed order for the last two years," she muttered. "And I'm through with that." She leaned forward until her lips were only a few inches from his ear. "So now I do what I want, when I want, and with whoever I want. Those are my rules."

Triplett pulled forward enough to loosen her hands. "That will work as long as we both want the same things," he said seriously.

She reached again for his shoulders and drew him back into the chair.

"I think we both want the same things," she said. "And you won't find anyone who does what I do better than I do it." She leaned again beside his ear, whispering. "Remember that if you decide you want to explore the web. I have everything I need in my cabin."

When she left for Pullman that morning, he walked with her to the car.

"You'll be the first back," he said. "When you get here, I'll meet you in your cabin and we can make sure the message went out as planned. And maybe we can celebrate a little."

"I'd like that," she said, giving his arm a light squeeze.

She's not a badger, he thought as she pulled away. The woman's a little minx!

* * *

As they sat in the transfer lounge in the Brussels airport, Dreu's nervousness was beginning to make Adam uneasy. They had rehearsed to the point that he thought she could comfortably slip into the role, but when they boarded their international connection in Newark, she clutched his arm as they approached passport control. During the overnight flight to Belgium, she slept fitfully. He found an isolated corner of the Brussels airport lounge and pulled her close in beside him on the hard metal seats.

"It will be fine with me if when we get to Budapest, you tour the city and I find our lady and see what I can learn," he said. "You don't need to do this."

She pushed in tighter, enjoying the closeness. "I'll be okay," she said with enough conviction that he began to feel better. "This traveling under an alias bothers me more than I expected. I keep thinking someone's going to walk up to me and say, 'Hey, I know you! You aren't Tanvi Russell! So what are you really up to?' But so far, no one's even looked at my passport twice, so I'm starting to get a little more comfortable with it."

"I find it easiest," Adam said, "to approach these assignments as an actor would—by not even thinking about it as an alias. Assume the new identity as completely as you can. Don't worry about someone thinking you're not Tanvi. *Be* Tanvi. You were smart to use your mother's name and one that's a little unique. If someone calls you Tanvi, you'll instinctively turn. Now just take the next step and become Mrs. Russell."

"I'm enjoying that part, Mr. Russell. But I have to stop and think about calling you Brian—even after we've been using the names all week. I'm afraid I'm going to slip and call you Adam at the wrong time."

"If you do, don't get flustered. That's why I picked A as a middle initial on the passport. If pressed, we can say my middle name's Adam and I use it at home. The key to lying well is to assume that people normally expect you to be telling the truth. So we shape our identities into a new truth."

They had done little to change their appearances. Dreu's long black hair was pulled into a loose knot, held with a mother-of-pearl comb that actually had belonged to Tanvi. She wore clear-lens glasses with fashionable black frames. Adam's face sported a three-week beard, and an expensive human-hair weave added a foot of ponytail to his own dark hair. The distinctive eye patch covered his left eye, an element of appearance that he found distinguished him to the point that observers often couldn't recall any other features.

"I know I'll be really nervous when I meet the girl at the Academy," Dreu admitted. "But I want to do this. I know it will work better if I'm the contact. And I just need to prove to myself that I can do something like this."

"Just be the frightened prostitute," Adam said with his half-smile. "The rest will fall into place."

Their flight was called and as their boarding numbers were announced, Dreu stood and pulled Adam to his feet. "Time to board, Brian."

At the ticket control station the gray-uniformed attendant glanced at her passport, then back up into the beautiful brown face.

"Tanvi," she said. "I have a friend from India named Tanvi."

"My mother's Indian," Dreu said truthfully. "Father's not, but they gave us all Indian names."

"Very pretty," the woman said, swiping the ticket. "Enjoy your flight, Mrs. Russell."

TWENTY

Galen Lanear pulled into the acre of parking that fronted the BestMart in Marietta, Georgia. He drove to the front of the block-long store, cruised slowly beside the array of grills, hunting wear, and end-of-the-season garden products displayed along the walk, and turned back down one of the exit lanes. Two-thirds of the way toward the back of the lot on an outside row he found a parking spot and nosed the green Camry in next to a cart collection rack. Popping the trunk, he pulled one of the discarded carts to the back of the car and loaded a boxed Frigidaire dehumidifier. It was 12:50 in the Eastern time zone and he was right on schedule. He knew that in eight other BestMart lots from Flagstaff, Arizona, to Bangor, Maine, fellow patriots were loading their carts and starting toward one of the entrances. The men wore hoodies over their dark glasses, their bronzed hands and beards all that showed to the cameras that constantly scanned the parking areas. Federal investigators studying the digital feed from the camera recording Galen's section of the lot in Marietta would later note that he struggled with the box, as if it were considerably heavier than the standard fifty-five pound shipping weight for the unit.

He entered through the doors on his right as he approached the store. An elderly woman in a green BestMart vest cheerfully stamped his sales receipt and asked if he knew where the return counter was. He nodded and turned left across the front of the row of checkout counters that disappeared toward some vanishing point into a swarm of Saturday shoppers. Lines of seven or eight stood at each counter where checkers, like so many automatons, swiped items across digital readers, adding a staccato of electronic beeps to the general murmur of human conversation. Deeper into the gigantic store, patrons on motorized scooters wove through the mass of shoppers pushing carts, half on cell phones attempting to locate other family members who had wandered off into the labyrinth of display racks.

Galen took it all in with a quick visual sweep of the store. At precisely 12:54 he parked his return item against the wall outside of the restrooms, stepped five paces away and turned to ensure that no one was showing any interest in the unattended cart. Seeing none, he walked leisurely to the doors at the opposite end and crossed the lot to the Camry. By 12:58 he was back on the street in front of the BestMart where he pulled to the curb and fished a cell phone from the zipper pocket of his hoodie. With a ten-digit number punched into the keypad, he donned a woodcutter's safety helmet with visor and ear protectors, watched the small clock in the bottom corner of the phone display until it clicked over to 1:00 p.m., and pushed the call button.

At nine BestMarts across the United States at precisely 11:00 a.m. Mountain Time, the front half of the giant supermarkets disintegrated in massive balls of orange flame. Pulverized concrete, wood, human flesh, and chunks of shattered counters and display goods shot through the rest of the store like volleys from a thousand cannons. In a block-wide radius around the stores every window shattered, including those on the passenger side of the green Camry that sat a quarter mile from the lot in Marietta.

Galen crouched low in the driver's seat, the helmet pulled tightly down over his head. The car rocked hard up onto its street-side wheels, then bounced back into place. He remained curled beneath the steering wheel until the hailstorm of smaller pieces of the store subsided. When he could no longer feel the jarring blows against the top of the car or hear the thunderous rain of debris, he pushed the helmet onto the floor in front of the passenger seat and struggled up behind the wheel.

Damn! he thought dizzily. Wade had sure as hell underestimated the size of the blast zone! They should have been given another three or four minutes to get farther out. Despite the protection of the helmet, Galen could barely hear the cars that now rushed toward the blast site, and the inside of his skull felt like it had been churned by an eggbeater. He struggled to focus, knowing that he needed to start the fifty-mile drive toward the west side of Cedartown before emergency response crews began to arrive. His escape car, a red Mini Cooper, waited there in a rented storage unit.

Three weeks later after sorting through the rubble, fielding calls from frantic Georgians with lost loved ones, and following up on license plate numbers salvaged from the pile of twisted automobiles where the front half of the BestMart parking lot had been, authorities would determine that 573 people lost their lives in the Marietta bombing. Another 217 were injured. With the exception of Pullman, Washington, where 417 died, it was the lowest fatality count among the chain's nine demolished superstores.

* * *

In his second-floor office in the Russell Senate Office Building, Clayton Mehrens' staff clustered soberly around the wall-mounted television set. The subdued voice of Grant Huston was describing what was being learned about the BestMart attacks as the studio switched from one scene of devastation to another. One of Mehrens' aides, a fresh-out-of-college novice from Middlebury, Vermont, wiped self-consciously at his eyes and others hunched forward in office chairs, hands clutched prayer-like against tightly pressed lips.

"The attacks were obviously carefully coordinated and part of a combined action," Huston was saying as the camera swept across an aerial shot of the blackened remains of a BestMart in Pueblo, Colorado. "Federal investigators have determined that all nine blasts occurred within two seconds of each other, a precision that almost defies explanation. There is speculation that they all may have been triggered by a single signal and authorities are trying to identify a call to all nine cities at that precise moment. Within fifteen minutes of the attacks, an email message was received by each of the major television networks, attributing responsibility to the jihadist World Islamic State. Jessica Layton of our NBS affiliate in southern Illinois is on the scene in Carbondale where state police have been able to recover video from an office in the rear of the store. Authorities believe they may have identified one of the suspects. Jessica, what are Illinois police telling you?"

The shot turned to a young blond reporter in a blue quilted jacket with NBS News emblazoned above the left pocket. She glanced quickly at her notes, then back into the eyes of the mesmerized audience.

"Grant, an employee who was working in a back office where the video feed for all of the store's cameras is housed survived the blast and immediately led state policemen to the recorded files. Since power is out in what is left of the store, police took the disks to a nearby rental shop in a strip mall just down the street from the BestMart. Although what you are about to see was recorded by one of our news cameras shooting images on a screen in the store, it clearly shows what appears to be a woman unloading a heavy box from the back of a red pickup truck and wheeling it on a cart into the store."

The screen switched to a grainy video feed and Mehrens' staff leaned forward in unison, focusing on the woman in the dark head scarf and large, round-rimmed sunglasses. Jessica's voice continued to describe what they were seeing. "Cameras inside the store show her checking the item with the door greeter, then leaving it beside the restrooms while she exits. Outside cameras again pick her up and show her driving away in the small truck. Police have issued an all-points bulletin for a late-model GMC Sierra pickup. The plates appear to have intentionally been smeared with mud but are thought to be Illinois plates."

The camera returned to Jessica Layton, who again consulted her notes. "State police have also requested help from authorities in Missouri and Kentucky, since Carbondale sits right down here in the bottom of Illinois. It's within a few miles of these adjoining states, and really isn't that far from Arkansas and Tennessee. They are hoping someone will spot the pickup and give them a lead on who may have been responsible for this horrendous act. This is Jessica Layton, reporting live from the scene of the terrorist attack on the BestMart in Carbondale, Illinois. Now, back to you, Grant."

Clayton Mehrens' senior campaign advisor, a battle-scarred

veteran of two previous presidential campaigns, turned to his boss who leaned soberly against the front of his wide oak desk. Mehrens had been completely silent since the broadcast began and now stood with arms folded, watching the studio transition back to Grant Huston.

"We need to ramp up our message about taking the fight to the enemy," the aide said grimly. "The country's going to be shouting for blood."

"We don't have a message about taking the fight to the enemy," Mehrens said quietly. "That hasn't been my message, and it still isn't. Since World War Two, we've never defeated an enemy by directly going to war with them, and we won't with this one." As he spoke, he could see the doubt and desperation on the circle of young faces.

"The public will expect a swift and bold reaction," the advisor said. "I'm not sure we will get one from the president, but I can assure you Carter Graves will be promising one. We'll see another ten point swing in the polls."

"This is a global threat," Mehrens said resolutely. "And the response has to be global. France, Belgium, Britain and Australia have all suffered similar attacks at one time or another. We need to come together around some collaborative strategy that turns opinion so completely against these fanatics, particularly within the broader Muslim community, that they can't buy a loaf of bread, let alone explosives. Going to war against them simply creates more martyrs and solidifies regional opinion against us. The collateral damage we do in the places they're hiding is their best recruiting tool."

The advisor threw up his hands in desperation as the television screen again swept over the pile of rubble that only hours earlier had been a BestMart in Texarkana, Texas.

"We've got to do *something*," he sputtered. "Talk has already begun about staging a solidarity rally, but there's a very real fear that no one will venture out into a large crowd like that. They have us paralyzed!"

"We come forward again with our message," Mehrens said, exhibiting the calm he was hoping to re-engender in his staff.

"This will serve to bring the world together and we can provide that leadership as well as we can provide arms and destruction."

"By tomorrow," the advisor said prophetically, "one of the other contenders on our side will be calling for counter attacks. We won't even be a footnote in the *Times*."

TWENTY-ONE

Dan Triplett was waiting in the Badger's cabin when her Honda Fit pulled into the King's Mountain camp. She had used a Toyota Tacoma for her delivery and after the explosion, left town heading north, swapping the truck for the Honda in Colfax before turning back into Idaho on State Highway 272. Like all of the Patriots, she had been instructed to uncover her head, wipe off the dark makeup, and remove the wig and glasses as soon as she left the attack site. But she was to keep everything with her when she changed vehicles and bring the disguise back to the camp for disposal. She walked into the cabin to find Triplett sitting back in a worn chocolate corduroy easy chair with boots off and feet crossed loosely on a matching ottoman. He didn't rise when she pushed through the door, locking it behind her.

"Nice work," he said, turning from the television set that stood on a narrow desk opposite the curtained window. "Any problems?"

On the screen, rescuers picked through the rubble of a store in Cedar Rapids, Iowa.

"According to script," she smiled, throwing a small duffle with head gear and loose black pullover onto one of the other chairs.

"Any problem getting the makeup off?"

She raised her hands to frame her impish face and turned from side to side like a young girl displaying her first attempt at lipstick and eye shadow. "That cold cream took it right off. Pretty good stuff!" Dropping her hands to her hips, she stood and watched the news coverage for a few moments, then asked, "Any problems anywhere else?"

Triplett shook his head. "Not that I can see. We'll know in a few hours." His instructions had been that no one call until at least two hours from the bomb site, concerned that some giant computer in a federal agency would look for phone messages originating from the nine cities, going to a common location. Even with that precaution, he had the eight remaining Patriots calling into three different numbers.

The Badger walked to the desk and punched the "on" button on her laptop. "Let's see what the liberal media are saying about all this." She plugged CNC.com into the address line. When the news website appeared, she enlarged the live streaming box and they watched as Carl Murray, senior reporter for CNC's "RapidFire," fussed and fumbled his way from one on-site reporter to another.

"The guy at PAX was having a hard time with this too," Triplett said.

"That Chase Rayborn? Yeah. If he thinks this is foreign terrorists on our turf, he'll be shitting bullets," the Badger said. "Don't know many men who could plan something like this and sit through it as calm as you are." She turned the sound down on the computer, adjusted it slightly on the desk, and turned back to Triplett, eyeing him with a suggestive smile.

"You feel like doing some celebrating?"

Under her pullover she had been wearing a gray, high-necked T-shirt that clung to her like a wetsuit, accentuating her high, full breasts. Triplett began to push himself up out of the deep chair.

"Why don't we move on into…."

She caught him halfway up with a hand to his chest and pushed him backwards, stepping over the padded arms of the chair and straddling him with her pelvis planted firmly across his lap.

"No reason we can't celebrate right here," she said, rocking back and forth to settle deeper onto his hips.

"I think I'm starting to celebrate already," he murmured, adjusting himself beneath her.

"Want to know why they call me the Badger?"

As Triplett began to choke out a reply, she grasped the bottom of her shirt with crossed hands and effortlessly stripped it up over her head. Triplett couldn't contain a startled intake of breath. From just below the indentation at the bottom of her throat, a life-sized badger snarled out at him, the hairs of its black and white face so perfectly rendered by the artist that they appeared to bristle at being exposed. The trailing vines he had seen on her bare shoulders the night he introduced her to the Patriots tangled in about the beast, giving the impression that it was bursting out of some thicket deep within her chest. Its heavy front legs wrapped down across the sides of her breasts, the tips of the inch-long claws pointing to silver studs that pierced her brown nipples.

She leaned forward, pulling his hands up into the badger's grasping arms. "If you don't pamper the badger, she might just eat you alive," she purred. "Or maybe she will anyway. Would you like that?"

He didn't answer but pulled her tightly against his chest, biting his mouth hard against her own and thrusting a hand down the back of her black, terrorist pants. She twisted away long enough to say, "Ohhh! I think you *like* the badger," and to rip the buttons open across his chest.

"You are such a *bad* girl," Triplett groaned, leaning again into her.

On the desk, the black eye of the computer stared unblinking. You have no idea, she thought as she pulled his hungry face between the outreached arms of the badger.

* * *

Budapest's Ferenc Liszt International Airport is small even by European standards but welcomes arriving visitors with a bright, contemporary interior, immediately serving notice that the new Hungary has assumed a comfortable position in modern Europe. Dreu and Adam stepped forward together when the officer at passport control signaled them across the yellow holding line. Adam noted with some relief that Dreu handed the young man her book and customs document without the least sign of nervousness. The officer swiped the data strips through his reader and placed the passports side-by-side on the counter as he reviewed their profile information on his screen.

"You are here for pleasure?" he asked. Adam thought he saw a light blush tint Dreu's cheeks and neck.

"Yes. Vacation," he said. "We will be here three or four days, then plan to drive out of the country." He had scheduled their return flight from Vienna, knowing that if for any reason they should have to leave the country under duress, the airport in Budapest would be a natural choke point.

"Hungary is surrounded by seven other nations," the officer said pleasantly. "Those that are members of the EU can be entered with no visa. For Ukraine and Serbia, no visa for U.S. citizens if you are staying less than ninety days."

Adam nodded. "I think that should cover us."

The officer stamped their passports and slid them back across the counter to Dreu, giving the tall woman with the striking dark features an appreciative glance.

"I am so sorry for the bombings in your country," he said, his expression reflecting his sincerity. "We are all of the same world in our fight against these terrorists."

"Thank you," Dreu nodded. "We are holding our breath that something doesn't happen while we're away."

The officer's face darkened. "I'm sorry. Then you do not know what has happened today?"

They had begun to turn away from the counter and stepped back to face the young official.

"What happened today?" Adam asked.

"Nine of your very big market," he said. "They were bombed at exactly the same moment in different place in your country. They think over five thousand people have died."

Adam instinctively wrapped an arm about Dreu's waist and felt her body slump, then tense again as a wave of anger swept through her.

"We weren't aware…," he muttered. "Thank you for your thoughts." He eased Dreu past the booth into the corridor that led to the baggage claim area. They walked in silence to the carousel that displayed a sign for the Brussels arrival.

"My God," Dreu murmured as they stepped into the crowd beside the long stainless conveyor. "What's happening to our country?"

"I feel like I'm spending my time on the wrong things," Adam said quietly. "I don't know if the Director has asked Fisher for help, but this sure seems a lot more serious than a bunch of randy politicians who can't keep their dicks in their pants."

"If these girls weren't getting murdered…," Dreu reminded him. "There are lives to be saved there too."

Bags were beginning to drop from the conveyor and Adam stepped forward as he saw Dreu's silver Samsonite slide from the chute. He knew he could stop the murders of the women simply by leaving them alonc. Was spcnding his time protecting the reputations of a group of men who were choosing to be disreputable a good use of energies that could be focused on protecting the home front? He was certain the terrorist activity was being orchestrated from inside the country—that there was a control center somewhere on American soil. And with Fisher's seemingly inexhaustible access to resources and information, he believed he could find it. If they could quickly get what they needed from the girl at the conservatory….

While they waited for his bag he stepped to the back of the claim area and phoned Fisher on the secure number. Again, the woman answered.

"Fisher's still unavailable?" he asked.

"At the moment, yes."

"I just arrived in Hungary and heard about the store bombings. Have we been asked to provide any help with this?"

"No. The agencies are handling it internally."

"Are you hearing about any progress?"

"Since we haven't been approached, we're not in that loop."

"I'm here trying to close in on the blackmailers," he said. "But this seems relatively unimportant…."

"It's hard to judge its importance until we know who's involved and where it's coming from," the woman said. "You need to stay with it."

"Understood. But when we get this wrapped up, I'd like permission to see what I can find out about this terrorist cell."

"I'll give it some thought," she said. "Let me know when you're at that point."

He hung up, noting that she'd said "*I'll* give it some thought." What had happened to Fisher?

* * *

They took a cab from the airport to the Sofitel Budapest Chain Bridge, a five-star hotel overlooking the river in the heart of the city. It was majestically perched along the Danube above the Szechenyi or Chain Bridge, an engineering marvel of the mid-nineteenth century. The bridge had been the first permanent span to connect the two sides of the Hungarian capital, Buda and Pest, forming a single city in the late 1800s.

The ride brought them into the city through a drab industrial zone on the flatter Pest side of the river, then into an area of colorless Soviet-era flats, and finally along broad, tree-line avenues bordered by buildings whose architecture modeled periods from the Renaissance to the modern. Both passengers sat in silence, his hand cupped loosely over hers on the seat as they stared absently at picturesque squares that lined the riverbank, bustling with busy shops and quaint open air cafes. Few of the buildings were more than four or five stories high and even with the rush of afternoon traffic, the city seemed to exude a quiet somberness that added to their personal malaise.

Walking into the Sofitel pulled them abruptly back into the present. Just beyond a central column of elevators, the hotel's glittering atrium soared eight stories above them, with a replica vintage airplane floating high above the polished parqueted floors and sumptuous paneled interior. A wide, brightly lit staircase in polished mahogany rose from the lobby to a spa and eateries that overlooked the central atrium. Their sixth-floor suite, tastefully furnished in Danish Modern, looked across the Danube at the Buda Castle, an eighteenth century palace and fortress that stretched for a quarter mile along the opposing hilltop.

They ignored the view and before the porter could arrive with their bags, Dreu found CNC on the television and they hunched at the foot of the king-sized bed and watched rescuers work their way through the rubble of the destroyed BestMarts. A small box in the corner of the screen displayed a running total of confirmed casualties and was already above 3,000. Dreu cupped her hands in front of her face, elbows braced against her knees, and eyes peering over the top of her fingertips. Adam rose and stood stiffly with arms folded, too supercharged to remain on the bed.

The porter knocked and entered without invitation, carrying a bag in each hand. He glanced at the set, frowned solemnly and offered a sympathetic nod as Adam reached into his pocket for a tip.

"It is very sad for you," the man said and held the five dollar bill back toward Adam—his small gesture of support and healing.

Adam wrapped the bill back in the man's hand and gave it a firm squeeze.

"Thank you," he said. "We will be okay."

Dreu pushed herself from the bed and walked to the wide plate glass window, inspecting the riverscape below. The bridge, guarded at both ends by a pair of reclining stone lions, was a stream of activity across the wide placid river. Each end of the span was supported by massive arches that reminded her of miniature Arcs de Triomphe. On the opposite bank, the old Royal Palace filled the hilltop like some version of the American Capitol whose builders had run amok, adding one wing after another to the central domed edifice. Though almost too much to absorb, the view was breathtaking.

"I feel like I should be awestruck, but all I feel is numb," she said, leaning her forehead against the expanse of glass. He moved to stand beside her, slipping an arm about her waist.

"I don't want to sound heartless, but there's nothing we can do from here but try to get this other mess straightened out. Let's try to make the most of being here."

She lifted her head and tucked it against the side of Adam's neck. "I can see you've done what you can to make that happen," she said. "This room must have cost a fortune. No wonder our government's in debt."

He chuckled softly against her ear. "I'm picking up most of the tab. Part of my plan to seduce you."

"You mean re-seduce. I think the first time was during your last assignment when I thought you were just an ordinary nice guy."

He pulled her more tightly against him. "And now that you know that I'm an extraordinarily nice guy, it should be easier. And this is supposed to be a romantic city…."

She looked again at the broad river separating them from the Buda side of the capital. "The Danube isn't too blue here," she said. "That might have helped with the romantic atmosphere."

"And we're both depressed and completely beat—and have a long day ahead of us. That's not going to contribute much either."

"Romance doesn't need to be exhausting," she said, nuzzling against his neck. "The restaurant looked nice. Let's get some dinner and talk through again what I need to do tomorrow. Then we can plan some not-too-exhausting romance."

"Mind if we take a little side trip first? The rental car was delivered to the hotel and I'd like to run by the Academy of Music this afternoon before you go on your own in the morning. Just so we're familiar with the layout. It's not far from here."

She nodded. "That would make me feel better, too. The more I know, the less nervous I'll be. But I need to warn you, if we're up too much longer, I'll be out cold before my head hits the pillow."

"Then I'll just have to cuddle with your cold still body for a while," he said. "Let's run by the Academy, then get some dinner. We need to make sure you know exactly what you're going to say when you meet Reka Bator."

* * *

The courier had insisted on delivering her package directly into the hands of Grant Huston. And she demanded a signature. Anything less and she'd miss out on a promised bonus. The news anchor's assistant had been told to watch for the delivery and to call him wherever he was—which in this case was on the set, seated behind the NBS broadcast desk recapping the evening news. The BestMart bombings had filled twenty of the thirty minutes. Huston was wrapping up the half hour with a brief feel-good piece to keep the report from being a complete night of disaster and tragedy. A man in Stuttgart, Arkansas, after being tested as a potential kidney donor for his brother and proving negative, had learned through the donor bank that he was a perfect match for a young girl in Halifax, England. He was flying to Britain the next day to give the girl a kidney. With as much conviction as he could muster, Huston was talking about how, even during the darkest hours, rays of humanity pierced the gloom, bringing promise of a brighter tomorrow.

When his assistant stepped onto the edge of the set and waited expectantly for his wrap-up, millions of viewers saw him hesitate for a brief moment. Beneath a thick layer of makeup, his iconic face had drained to a pallid shade of gray. Then his professional training kicked back in. He finished with his hallmark "Goodnight, good people" and stared resolutely into the camera until certain the control room had switched to a commercial, then waved her over.

"Your delivery's here but the girl won't give it to me," she said testily. "Says it must go directly into your hands, with your signature. She's waiting at my desk."

Huston pushed past her, brushing aside a production staffer who wanted to ask about running an extended version of one of the bomb site stories on the NBS web edition. He hastily signed for the package, gave the girl a twenty, and without comment to the flustered assistant, closed himself in his office and locked the door behind him.

The small parcel contained only an eight gigabyte thumb drive. No note and no return address. He hastily inserted it into an open USB port and turned down the sound on his computer. If it contained what he thought it did, the outer office didn't need to hear the grunts, moans and expletives that had been the soundtrack for the other videos. But the image that initially filled his screen wasn't of Chase Rayborn's Idaho rancher putting his brand on some young heifer. Instead, it showed the leader of the Order of King's Mountain standing beside a blazing stone fire pit while another member of the group spoke to a small assembly. It looked as if it had been shot using a camera strapped to one of the participant's chests or foreheads. Huston watched with rapt attention as the camera turned to frame the face of each member of the Order as the man spoke.

Huston turned the sound back up until the voice was clearly intelligible and leaned closer into his screen. As he listened, his pulse accelerated and the pallor became a temple-pounding flush. The speaker was outlining in graphic detail an attack on nine BestMart stores across the United States and making individual assignments. When the planner finished, Dan Triplett stepped to the front of the fireplace for a final admonition. Huston's lips had become chalky dry and he licked at them nervously as he eased the sound up another notch.

"This is our last one," the Order's commander said. "Our final and finest moment. This is the one that will crystalize the fear that's already driving people to Carter Graves. By the convention, he'll be confirmed by acclamation." He paused and held the gaze of each of his soldiers for an affirming moment. "It's in your able hands, my fellow Patriots. No wavering and no mistakes. Nothing that indicates this is anything but a hostile attack by a foreign enemy. Like our kinsmen at King's Mountain, no surrender! On Saturday we mount our final ambush on the complacent and the cowardly. Godspeed!"

It was so much more than Huston had expected that he sat motionless as the video segment ended, his newsman's mind thinking nothing but 'biggest story of the century!" and "Peabody or Cronkite Award!" But his wagering lesser self immediately began to elbow his ego aside and shout, "If you break this, you'll be implicated—and it will lead to the dead prostitutes…." He reached for "replay" but the darkened screen was again blinking to life.

Grant's fingers fumbled at the keyboard to again lower the sound. A young, full-bodied redhead, her intricately tattooed torso on full display, straddled a sturdy armchair where the naked Dan Triplett sprawled beneath her. His head was thrown back in pained ecstasy while she twisted and ground across his hips. For the next fifteen minutes, the couple struggled in unrestrained desperation from one position to another, the girl consciously maneuvering her partner to keep his lecherous face in full view of the camera. As the film ended, she collapsed onto him and murmured, "What do you think your skinny-assed wife would think of *this*!"

His laugh sounded of exhausted disdain. "The bitch wouldn't even know that half of this was possible," he said. Pulling his face between the paws of a badger that was inked in life-like detail across her chest, the woman looked into the dark eye of the camera and winked.

TWENTY-TWO

With everyone safely back in camp and no indication in the media that federal investigators were looking for anyone other than a domestic cell of WIS extremists, Triplett called the Order together in the lodge's central commons room in the late hours of morning. The weather had turned colder and the fire in the round stone pit spit and popped, filling the room with the scent of freshly cut pine. In front of it, a plain wooden table held replica flintlocks that the commander had ordered for his virgin soldiers, plus three beautifully engraved powder horns to add to the rifles that had arrived for his returning veterans.

Like the fire, the room crackled nervously, the bombers supercharged by both the enormity and horror of what they had done. Triplett quieted them with raised arms, sweeping the half-circle with an admiring gaze.

"You are the true patriots," he began when the room was silent. "The day will come when…." He paused and scanned the room behind the seated members of the Order, then asked, "Where's the Badger?" His voice betraying its first notes of suspicion.

The others looked about in confusion.

LeAnn spoke first. "I haven't seen her at all today. I'll run over and see if she's okay."

Triplett nodded and paced across the front of the fireplace with head down and lips curled into a thoughtful frown until she returned. She pushed breathlessly back through the high, yellow pine door.

"She gone," she gasped. "Everything's gone. Her place is empty."

Triplett stopped his pacing but continued to stare soberly into the plank flooring. When he looked again into the faces of his followers, his expression was urgent and resolved.

"Go back to your cabins and pack up," he said. "We need to close the camp by dark."

"That little…," Dwayne began but Triplett silenced him with a glare.

"What's going on?" Wade Sumler demanded, his head and arms jerking nervously. "She can't have turned on us. She was as involved as anyone."

"More involved," Triplett muttered, heading for the doors and beckoning the others to follow. "She was much more involved."

* * *

The cream limestone façade of the Ferenc Liszt Academy of Music was enough to overwhelm a first-time visitor without the additional pressure of finding a free-spirited cellist and convincing her to betray the people who were blackmailing American congressmen. The building was tucked into a quiet corner of the old Jewish Quarter between Király Street and Andrássy Avenue and had been virtually invisible until standing right in front of it. Dreu paused on the steps of the four-story neo-Renaissance building and gazed up at the bronze statue of its namesake, majestically enthroned above the arched entryway. The seated figure rested on the bowed backs of four beautifully carved male figures, an ornate contrast to the collection of non-descript shops and apartments that surrounded the Academy.

On this Sunday morning there was little car or foot traffic, the only activity on the small plaza in front of the academy a young boy on a rickety bicycle who rode circles on the gray pavers. Farther along the closed walking street, a woman in a traditional embroidered apron swept the front step of a small shop.

Reka Bator would be easy to identify. The intelligence from Fisher's partner assured them that the musician came to the Academy every Sunday at eleven when the shops began to open and students were admitted into the building to practice. She would arrive on the metro at a stop on Andrássy Avenue, spend two hours in one of the revered conservatory's small, second-story recital rooms, then take the subway back to her apartment east of the city center in District XIV. Dreu was on the steps in front of the barred doors of the Academy half an hour early, anxious to be waiting when Reka entered the building.

At precisely eleven o'clock, a woman who appeared to be a

cleaning attendant unlocked the double set of doors from the inside and quickly retreated back into the dim interior. Dreu waited until two young women carrying instrument cases arrived and pushed through the high wooden doors, talking excitedly and passing with only a brief glance. They were tall blonds, both pleasant looking but without the quiet, innocent beauty of Reka Bator. Dreu followed them into the ornate entryway of the main-level concert hall.

The floor of the central foyer was a polished white marble, centered above by a wide circular chandelier that remained off on this weekend morning, the foyer lighted by rows of wall sconces that surrounded the lobby. Opposite the entrance, finely carved gold paneling framed two sets of double doors that opened into the rear of the building and the main performance hall. Corinthian columns in green marble supported the high ceiling and Dreu positioned herself beside one with a clear view of the entrance.

She had chosen to wear a gray wool skirt that fell just above the knee, a white silk blouse and short matching gray jacket, wanting to look successfully professional. Her heart thumped so loudly she feared it must echo in the stillness of the vaulted ante-room and she begged for the woman to arrive. Once she was in action, she knew the nervousness would disappear.

The third woman to enter the foyer was even more attractive than her photo and Dreu's heart surged a beat faster, then slowed as she stepped forward.

"Reka?" she asked and the young woman looked up at her tall, attractive visitor with a curious smile.

"*Igen*," the woman said, pronouncing the Hungarian word *ee-gan*.

"Do you speak English?" Dreu asked.

"I do. Yes."

Dreu extended her hand. "My name is Tanvi. I wonder if we could find a private place to talk?"

A shadow passed across the woman's delicate face and she glanced nervously about the empty foyer. "What do you want to talk to me about?" Her English showed only a trace of accent. An older man with a head of unkempt, shoulder-length white hair entered the building and nodded politely at the women.

"*Jo reggelt, Reka,*" he greeted.

"*Jo reggelt, egyetemi tanar,*" she said with a slight bow. "One of my professors. Many people come in on Sunday morning," she said, reminding Dreu that they were not alone.

"That's why I would prefer to visit with you privately," Dreu said. "I assure you, there is no reason to be afraid of me. But you may be in danger and I'm here to help."

The young woman's eyes widened slightly and she hesitated, then nodded for Dreu to follow as she climbed a set of stairs that left the foyer to the right. "I have a practice room reserved. We can talk there," she said.

The second floor recital room moved the ornate decor of the foyer another step toward Baroque. The windows were heavily draped in fringed red satin, a massive gold chandelier centering a gold-tiled ceiling, and beautifully parqueted floors partially covered by rich Persian rugs. Every corner and every niche between windows displayed the bust of a famous European composer on intricately carved pedestals: Mozart, Beethoven, Brahms, Schubert, Bach, Haydn and Wagner. A grand piano commanded a quarter of the floor space, the remainder filled with armless, green-upholstered Queen Ann chairs that faced the piano in neat rows. Half of one green-papered wall displayed a life-sized portrait of the young Franz Liszt standing regally beside a bust of his musical muse, Gioachino Rossini.

"My!" Dreu murmured as they entered the room. "This doesn't look like the practice rooms where I attended college!"

"Or at Indiana," Reka Bator said with a nervous smile. "That's where I did my undergraduate study. But we have the same here—tiny little rooms with a single stool. On Sundays you can often schedule one of these recital rooms. The sound is so much better in here. And the surroundings so much more inspiring." She sat on the piano bench and looked nervously at her American guest.

"Tell me what you mean…that I am in danger," she said directly.

Dreu pulled one of the plush single chairs over to face the young musician.

"You work part-time at the Four Seasons Gresham Palace Hotel as a night maid, I believe," Dreu began, following their rehearsed script.

Reka shrugged defensively. "I am a student and have to eat. And it is a very nice hotel. But how did you know this?" Her eyes betrayed her growing suspicion.

"Yes. It's very nice," Dreu agreed, staying with the script. "And I am aware that earlier this year, you entertained a very important American politician there."

Reka had begun to relax as they talked about college and cell-like practice rooms but immediately stiffened. "Who are you and what do you want?" she insisted.

Dreu raised a calming hand. "I'm not judging you. I've had some experience in the profession myself." She paused and watched Reka's face. The woman stared resolutely at the floor, nibbling nervously on her lower lip.

"As I said," she muttered quietly. "I am a student and must find a way to live. Here in Europe we do not have the obsessive sense of sexual morality that consumes you Americans. Some of these extra jobs are not viewed as negatively as you wish to judge them." She looked up directly at Dreu. "And your politicians didn't seem to mind the attention."

Dreu nodded and said again, "I'm not here to judge. But there were a number of women—here and in the United States—who were hired to entertain our political elite. I work for a man who indirectly arranged for these connections. His name is Gio Levanzo. Is that name familiar to you?"

Reka stared again into the floor, working the lip. After a moment she shook her head.

"No, I don't know of this man. But what does he want with me?"

"Were you aware that you were filmed when you were with the vice president?"

Reka jerked upright on the bench and shook her head vigorously. "*No*! There was no filming!"

"There was filming and I have seen the video."

The pretty face flushed deeply and she shifted her gaze to the side of the room.

"Is this on the Internet?" she asked.

Dreu suppressed a smile at the unexpected concern. "No. This involved our vice president. Very few people have seen it." She paused and let Reka process the information, then asked, "What were you asked to do when you were contacted about this?"

The young woman shrugged. "What I am always asked to do. To be sure some important guest has a very good time while here. This time, they said they would pay me very well if he had an especially good time."

"You mean let him fulfill all of his fantasies…."

She nodded. "And what happened to this film?" she asked quietly.

"Along with others, it was used to pressure officials to change some of their political positions. In the case of the vice president, to withdraw from the presidential campaign."

"And that's why I am in danger?" she asked, returning her eyes to Dreu.

"We don't know by whom, but some of the women in America who were involved have been murdered," Dreu said, holding the cellist's gaze. "Since the vice president was one of the most important men involved, we feared that you might be on this list to eliminate."

The flush on the lovely thin face drained to a gray pallor. "I don't believe you," she said, but she was gripping the edge of the wooden bench as if she might pitch forward if she loosened her hold.

Dreu opened the small clutch she had carried with her to the Academy and drew out the autopsy photographs of Brandy Wingate and Selina Kyle, leaning forward to place them on the bench beside Reka. The woman glanced down at them, diverting her eyes and squeezing them closed as she released the bench to clasp her hands over her mouth, muffling a cry.

"Who contacts you about these jobs," Dreu asked while the woman was still reeling.

Reka looked back at her dumbly, still grappling with the horror of the photographs.

"I need to talk to whoever recruited you for the job," Dreu repeated. "That person may also be in great danger and we are trying to warn everyone in the chain."

"Who do you think is doing this?" Reka asked, pushing the photos away. "Your government? Your country is so violent!"

"No. We think the men involved have privately hired people to make the problem go away. I'm sure you have people like that in this country."

Reka seemed not to hear. "How do I know you are who you say you are—and not some person who has come to find me?"

"If I had come to kill you, I wouldn't have come to the Academy. And I can assure you, I know the terrors of being hunted by men like this." She removed her jacket and as Reka watched with widening eyes, unbuttoned her blouse. "I am loyal to Mr. Levanzo because he rescued me when this was happening," she said, lifting her bra and showing the cellist the thick scar that ran horizontally the full width of her right breast. "I have a similar scar that runs here." She replaced the bra and traced a line with a finger across her lower abdomen. "When Mr. Levanzo saved me, I was barely alive. I don't want that to happen to you, or to anyone else here. I think you might want to go visit relatives somewhere until we can get this cleared up. But I need to know who contacted you about meeting with the vice president."

Reka's frightened eyes continued to stare at the buttons of Dreu's blouse. "You need to talk to Katalin," she said finally. "She is the one who sets up these jobs. I'll call her for you and arrange a meeting. What should I tell her?"

"Tell her there is a woman here who needs to talk to her about the escorts she arranged for the American politicians. That her life may be in danger."

"How can she call you?"

Dreu gave her a cell number. "When you have talked to her, leave the city and don't tell anyone where you are going—not even Katalin."

Reka nodded. “How will I know when I am safe?”

“I’ll send a note to you here. Call every few days and ask if there is a message from Tanvi.”

The cellist stared again at Dreu’s chest. “Why did they cut you?” she asked.

“Because I knew too much,” she said.

TWENTY-THREE

The throng that packed the Iowa Events Center in Des Moines was three times the number Carter Graves' planners had anticipated. They operated from the premise that you never want more seating than the expected crowd, creating the impression of a packed house. Based on best estimates, they had initially scheduled the 4,500 seat Hall C on the Exhibition Level. At 7:00 p.m., an hour before Graves was to appear, they expanded into Hall B, rolling back the partition and scurrying to unfold and position another 4,000 chairs. By 7:30 they were negotiating permission to position remote screens in the foyers in front of the halls. Estimates the following day placed the crowd at just over 11,000.

Graves' handlers were also unprepared for the crowd's dark energy. The staff huddled in a planning room debating whether to attempt to quell bands of marchers who rumbled like storm troopers through the foyer and down the aisles. The main hall echoed with shouts of "Take the war to WIS" and supporters carried placards showing bodies strewn across the remains of supermarket parking lots. As seats filled, a number of Marine veterans in the crowd began to yell "*Hoo-ha*" after each "Take the war to WIS." Soon the entire center echoed with stomping feet and ear-splitting *Hoo-ha*. The consensus of the staff was to let them go. The media were loving it and no one seemed in imminent danger.

Outside the massive complex on 3rd Street, a smaller collection of demonstrators paraded along the walk carrying signs declaring that "Guns don't kill people. People with guns kill people," and "We Created WIS." As three young men approached the hall, their hair military short, they stopped and shouted across at the demonstrators, "You couldn't even protest like that if you lived in I-raq, you dumbshits." One of the protesters raised a middle finger and shouted back, "We wouldn't even have gone to Iraq in the first place if we weren't such dumbshits." A brief scuffle ensued, quickly broken up by the Des Moines police who surrounded the center in heavy numbers.

With a late change of heart, Iowa's Governor Donnel had chosen not to endorse his conservative colleague from Oklahoma and was visibly absent from the rally. But at precisely 8:00 p.m., Iowa's Republican congressman from Davenport stepped to the mic and began a ten-minute introduction. Remarkably, his own "take it to the enemy" philosophy aligned perfectly with the conservative wing's favorite son and rising star.

"And now, it is my distinct honor..." he concluded, and the hall erupted in what had become the multi-layered chant of the boomer generation who made up the core of the Carter Graves faithful. "*We Dig Graves*! *We Dig Graves*!" the crowd thundered, drowning out announcement of the name that needed no formal introduction.

The handsome governor, dressed in his signature dark blue suit, red tie, starched white shirt and flag lapel pin, stepped to the podium and embraced the booming chant. Holding his arms aloft until the crowd had quieted enough that he could be heard, he shouted, "Is America ready to give WIS the Graves they deserve?" The throng surged to its feet. "*We Dig Graves*! *We Dig Graves*!"

For the next hour, pausing every few minutes to bask in thunderous applause and shouted slogans, Carter Graves pledged in unequivocal generalities to rid America of the demons who now rained fear and terror on the beloved of God.

"We will root them out wherever they hide," he shouted above the standing mass as he brought his speech to a crescendo, his voice rising steadily. "We will rebuild the tunnel beneath the Bay. We will defend our skies against all enemies. And we will show the jihadist horde that we cannot be frightened away from our schools and our shopping centers. We will stand in the breach! We will put on the full armor of God! And with our voices mingling with those of our forefathers, a hymn will again be heard across this great land—'*Onward, Christian soldiers, Marching as to war!*'"

Eleven thousand strong, the congregation of the elect of God took up the refrain with a single voice, "...*With the cross of*

Jesus, Going on before!" Many hadn't sung the anthem in years, their churches troubled by its strident and divisive message. But like anything forbidden, there was an excitement in feeling it again on the tongue and in breathing it in as it filled the hall.

"*Forward into battle, See his banners go…*," the masses sang, and Carter Graves stood centered in a spotlight on the podium, arms stretched wide as if he were the personification of the cross of Jesus.

* * *

As the chorus mounted in the Des Moines Event Center, eight Patriots of the Order of King's Mountain scattered across the land they had just brutalized, some going further into the woods to hidden retreats, others scurrying for the borders of Canada and Mexico, hoping to disappear into another wilderness.

With Dwayne Cargile seated beside him, Dan Triplett watched the Graves rally on PAX in his home overlooking the alpine lake and the distant snow-capped spires of the Sawtooth Mountains—and waited. He didn't expect the authorities to come after him. It would be a personal delivery of some kind, a data drop into one of his computer files with an accompanying text telling him where to look. Or a personally delivered package by a messenger who had no idea what he was carrying. Triplett would look at the video, boil with rage that the little vixen had deceived him and that he'd fallen for it, then begin to plan with Dwayne how they could get to the Badger. And what to do with the man he knew had released her from her cage.

* * *

Just beyond the end of the Liszt Academy's ornate front, the paved plaza widened into a pedestrian greenspace with brick walks skirting a central tree-shaded garden. On both sides of the elongated square, small shops and eateries filled the ground floor of mustard-colored buildings. As Adam entered the greenway from the end opposite the Academy, waiters scurried to extend orange awnings over wrought iron tables and chairs that lined the walks.

He positioned himself with a cup of strong coffee at a table that allowed an unobstructed view of the Academy's entrance, dressed in the faded jeans and loose, high-necked charcoal sweater of a student. As he waited, he absently scrolled through files on a computer tablet and watched the nearby shops slowly come to life. Dreu entered the building minutes after it opened and he recognized the cellist when she arrived, then sat nursing the coffee until both again left the Academy. Dreu exited first. The Hungarian musician ten minutes later. By the time he returned to his rental and made the short drive back to the hotel, Dreu was in the room standing at the window that overlooked the river. A line of long, triple-decked cruise boats were moored along the near bank and she watched as their passengers filed ashore to gather around waiting guides for their early afternoon tours. She turned as he entered, a thin smile creasing her lips. He waited for her to speak, letting her say what she felt needed to be said before he smothered her with questions.

"The lying doesn't come easily," she said. "Maybe it gets better with practice."

"I'm afraid it does," he conceded. "Was she convinced?"

"I'm pretty sure she was. I showed her the scars and that seemed to do the trick."

"Who would have thought something positive could come from that stalker attack when you were working in New York," Adam muttered.

Dreu nodded silently, then said "...and I'm almost certain she's an innocent pawn in this whole affair. I don't think she even knew she was being recorded."

"So she was just contacted about entertaining the vice president while he was in the city?"

"Yes. Encouraged to show him an especially good time—for a special bonus."

"And what did she say when you told her some of the girls had been killed?"

"She was shocked. Genuinely frightened. I think she'll leave town and try to stay in hiding."

Adam had moved up beside her at the window, an arm about her waist, and together they watched the tourists start off along the pier behind their energetic guides. "Did she tell you who'd contacted her?" he asked.

"Yes. And she's calling the woman to arrange a meeting with me. Someone named Katalin."

"Katalin Dulay," Adam said, and she immediately remembered the connection.

"Another area where I need practice," she said. "I should have put two-and-two together."

"We've been saying Kat-a-lin and as you heard, they pronounce it more like Kat-leen," he said. "Easy to miss. But she's the woman Fisher's information showed was with Von Holten—the official government 'hostess-with-the-mostest.' If she's linked with the state in some way, she's probably more than just an on-call escort like Reka. We need to be careful with this woman."

The phone on the night stand jangled as if on cue and Dreu jumped involuntarily. "That can't be her. I gave Reka my cell number, not the hotel."

Adam stepped quickly across the room to the open bathroom door where another phone hung just inside on the wall beside the stool. "On three," he said and began to raise fingers. One. Two. On three they both lifted the receivers.

"Hello," Dreu answered. She was learning quickly. Her voice didn't waiver.

"Mrs. Russell?" a woman asked.

"Yes."

"This is Katalin Dulay. Reka Bator called and said you would like to meet with me." The woman's English was also excellent but more heavily accented than the younger Reka.

"Yes! Thank you for calling so quickly. I thought I had given Reka my cell number."

"I learned that you and Mr. Russell are staying at the Sofitel and thought I would call directly. Reka said she thought you would want to meet privately."

"Yes. As soon as possible. This is quite an urgent matter."

There was a moment's pause at the other end and Dreu glanced over at Adam who stood in the bathroom door, his left hand pressed tightly over the mouthpiece.

"I know you arrived in Budapest just yesterday," Katalin said, apparently wishing to impress on Mrs. Russell that there were no secrets. "But have you been here long enough to know of the Cave Church?"

She saw Adam nod.

"Yes, I know where it is." Her lying was also improving.

"Today will be very busy there. Tomorrow, not at all busy at eight o'clock in the morning. I will meet you inside at eight o'clock."

"I will be there,"Dreu said. "Eight o'clock."

"Will Mr. Russell be coming?" Katalin asked.

"No. I will be alone."

"Tomorrow, then," the woman said, and hung up.

Adam returned the phone to its cradle. "We need to wire you this time," he said. "I don't have a good feeling about this."

TWENTY-FOUR

The file arrived on Triplett's computer by data-drop, reaffirming what an accomplished little bitch the Badger really was. In a way, that took away a bit of the sting. She really was the quality hacker he'd needed for the final project and her talents had kept the federal investigation centered on groups in the Middle East. If he guessed right, the file would tell him to cease and desist, but not threaten to expose him. Both the Badger and the sonofabitch who had hired her had too much at stake themselves.

A text message told him where to look. In the privacy of his study, surrounded more by glass-eyed moose and elk heads than by books, he opened the file named "You've been Badgered." Very cute, he thought, as he clicked on the round central "play" button. This time as a spectator, Triplett watched as the agile little nymph performed her magic. At the end of the twenty minute video she pulled his head tightly between her breasts, smiled and winked at the camera. The screen blackened except for a white printed message in large block letters.

"STOP THE KILLING NOW, TRIPLETT. ONE MORE DEATH AND YOUR WIFE GETS THESE FILES."

He knew his prickly, self-righteous spouse would die of shame if she knew he had planned and carried out the four terrorist attacks. But if she were to see this film and know others had seen it, she would resist death with every fiber of her being, just to be able to heap as much misery as she could on her penniless, loathsome worm of an ex-husband. Not because he had been unfaithful. But because he had humiliated her publically with his sexual antics. He could tolerate life in federal prison while his lawyers argued that an act couldn't be considered treasonous if its intent was to strengthen and protect the future of the nation. Jail would be a cakewalk compared to living an un-incarcerated year with the betrayed bitch from hell nipping constantly at his heels.

He re-started the video and watched transfixed as the Badger skillfully braced herself against the arm of a chair so that he was positioned to look directly into the lens of the camera. There must be a number of copies of this thing out there. But his face was not well-known and unless the video was linked to him in some way, it would appear to be no more than a poorly shot amateur porn movie. Rayborn, he guessed, would have some kind of message stored with his copy—one of those "in case of my untimely death" kinds of things. The Badger—probably not. She was a tool. Not the machinery. He and Dwayne would find and quietly eliminate the threat from Rayborn, then get rid of the bitch. Triplett had interrogated men like Rayborn when he was in Iraq. Not battle-hardened tribesmen with a constitution of iron and no fear of death. But soft politicians who had sold their souls to the enemy. Rayborn would break and would tell him where his copies of the video were kept, and they could make a deal. The newsman would bring the files to him and they would be destroyed, and in return Triplett would stop all attacks. And Triplett would agree not to slowly torture the life out of the sniveling anchor from PAX and everyone he loved.

TWENTY-FIVE

Amber Nims had been born into money in the Woodland Heights neighborhood of Richmond, Virginia. Though an only child, her family's Riverside Drive colonial overlooking the James River boasted six bedrooms and as many baths, just in case extended family, of which there were also few, happened to stop in. To her mother, size mattered. And though her father was viewed as a hard-nosed and occasionally ruthless negotiator who had made a fortune as a lobbyist representing some of the state's most powerful interests in the state capital, he acquiesced to his wife's every wish. The *Times-Dispatch* had once labeled him the most powerful man in Virginia state government. But in his own home, he was no more than the tired-sounding voice of agreement from behind the closed door of his office.

From the time she entered adolescence and began to think seriously about how she fit into the grand cycle of existence, Amber had loathed four things: money, politics, spineless men, and Patricia Nims. She hated the latter because as long as her mother had her colonial with a view of the river, a Latina cook and maid to keep things tidy and meet friends at the door, and a large enough sunroom to host her weekly bridge club, she had no interest whatsoever in what the other two members of her household did. No children Amber's age lived in the other extravagant homes that lined Riverside Drive. No one seemed to have time to take her to visit the few friends she made at school. In fact, Amber couldn't remember a single conversation with either parent that she would consider "personal." Patricia Nims spent more time talking in intimate whispers to her two white Pomeranians than she had ever dedicated to her daughter. While the Poms were constantly being groomed and stroked, Amber couldn't recall ever receiving a caressing touch from her mother.

As she became more solitary, she found companionship through social media. At fifteen she met a man in Forest Hill Park who had driven his van up from South Carolina to meet the girl he knew only as Nims. They spent the day in the van, the man a heavy, awkward thing whose sex with her had been loud, messy, and over almost before it began. But he had wanted time to lie close to her and stroke her body and tell her how beautiful and sexy she was. It had been the most disgusting and affirming day of Amber's young life.

From that first encounter, Amber learned that she could manipulate at least parts of the world using two talents. The first was a very responsive body that some men seemed to find enthralling to the point of complete distraction. The second, a natural understanding of computers and the vast networks that linked them together and shielded them from each other. She manipulated her way through George Wythe High School and the University of Virginia, honing her skills in both. During one unforgettable night in Alexandria with a Saudi diplomat, she learned that there was a thin and dangerous line between passion, anger, and violence. Once she mended from her battle with the Saudi, she became much more discriminating about who benefited from either of her talents.

The week she graduated from Virginia, she received a call from the family's minister, a man she had met only when her mother entertained the elite of the congregation with Sunday evening coffee. He called to tell Amber that the lobbyist had been found dead in his study. His heart had apparently been crushed by the pressures of Capitol Hill from which he received no respite at home. Patricia Nims had been too distraught to make the call to her daughter. But by the time Amber reached the white colonial, her mother seemed to have made a miraculous recovery.

Much to Patricia's chagrin, the compliant Chester Nims had done in death what he had never managed in life. He had made some independent judgments about his fortune. Years before, he had established a trust for Amber into which he directed the considerable assets he brought into the marriage from his father's estate. Arthur Nims had accumulated a sizable fortune as founder and developer of Nims Furniture, the manufacturer of metal office furnishings and the largest producer of filing cabinets in America. Patricia vigorously contested the will and did her best to shame Amber into relinquishing at least part of her inheritance. She contended that the girl's shameless life had been a major factor in Chester's death and that his daughter was entitled to nothing. But the will proved iron-clad. Patricia was able to keep the house and support her domestics on Chester's informed investments as a lobbyist, but overnight Amber became the wealthier of the two. It was all she needed to sever any ties with the woman she loathed and to do whatever she wished. And what Amber wished was to become a principal force within the loosely confederated hacktivist community that called itself "Anonymous" and wreak havoc on establishment computer systems.

She found an apartment in an equally anonymous high rise in the Bunker Hill section of downtown LA as far from Patricia as she could get without leaving the continental United States. She spent her days haunting the back alleys of the Internet and her nights ceasing to be Amber Nims. At a tattoo parlor called Unbreakable, she shed the last of her Virginia sheen, had her hacker nom de plume tattooed in vivid detail across her chest, and officially became the Badger.

It was as the Badger that she met the Raptor, a man (or so she was led to believe) who was the most talented hacker her considerable experience had exposed her to. She decided that if you could describe a man by the imprint left by his elusive movements through the cyber world, the Raptor had to be dark with piercing black eyes. Agile. Ripped like one of those climbers who scale sheer cliffs using only his toes and fingertips. And brighter than Stephen Hawking. She followed as he led an Anonymous attack on one of the nation's largest credit card companies. He was able to find ingenious ways into its vast system of records and personal data with such a fine but passionate touch that it made her body flush and tremble. And once there, he simply sent a message to each card holder giving notice that their identity and personal account information had been hacked by Anonymous. If cyber spies could do it, he told the customer base, others could too. He warned them to get new cards, change any personal access information for the company who had issued it, and insist that the vendor abandon the archaic magnetic strip and convert to the chip and PIN system being used elsewhere in the world.

When she learned that he was personally aware of her, it took her breath away as no sexually-provoked touch had ever done. It came in a brief two-line text that said, "*Badger—impressed with your work. You have a great intuitive sense. The Raptor.*"

She read the message through a dozen times, wondering if it could truly be from the dark-eyed scaler of cliffs. She walked away from it, sat across the room from it and nervously shelled a handful of pistachios, then returned to the computer and read it again. Then she wrote, "*Thanx. Love your work too. Best I've seen.*" She held her breath for a brief moment before firing off the response.

For twenty minutes her return message box remained empty, then blinked with, "*I see you're in LA. Got any projects in mind?*"

She knew it had to be the real Raptor. Though on the surface most of her messages were completely innocuous, every bit of data that left her computer was veiled and protected in as many ways as her considerable skill could manage to hide its point of origin. Over time she had been able to gain access to a host of personal computers around the globe that were left on 24/7. A program of her own design routed every item she sent through at least five of these surrogates in different countries, randomly changing the sequence so that the selected computers and the order of their use changed continuously. Yet he had been able to trace her.

"*Why do you think LA?*" she responded.

He replied within seconds. "*Found you by pure coincidence. We use some of the same surrogates. Tagged your messages as they came through and tracked the common computer in each sequence.*"

"*You must have thousands of surrogates then....*"

"*Tens of thousands. Even so, once I received a message I knew was from you, I was able to tag characteristics and watch for messages with that signature to pass through. Been trying for months to find you.*"

"Why?"

"I'd guess you're self-trained but no cracker. You don't think like others. You're a unique problem-solver. Not many of you around."

"I'm flattered—and embarrassed. Should have been harder to find."

"You should know as well as I do, no one's impossible to find. That's why we always get to our marks."

"Still embarrassing. And no. No current projects."

"Too bad. I was hoping for a twosome."

Again the message touched her like a warm fingertip running up the inside of her thigh. She backed away from the machine, considering how much she wanted her response to convey.

"I like twosomes," she finally entered. *"Sounds fun. You got something?"*

"Nothing working. Been toying with IRS. Getting copies of tax records of the 1000 wealthiest Americans and making them public. Let the world know how little these people pay in taxes."

"I like the idea! If you decide to go, I'm in."

"Was thinking of it as solo. Could bring down some serious shit."

"Not afraid of that. Been in deep before."

"You ever work in real space? Always liked the idea of working with a partner where I can be talking ideas while storming the barricades."

"Never do. Pretty much a loner."

"Gottcha. Just a fantasy thought. Seemed like yours would be a fun brain to pick. Be talkin' to you." And the Raptor was gone.

As the screen stilled, the Badger felt the first small window she had welcomed onto the world close. She had fired off her *"Never do. Pretty much a loner"* out of protective habit when his question about "working in real space" had ignited a very small flame in a heart that she was beginning to fear was stone cold.

She gazed at the final line. It offered a promise of re-connection that kept that weak spark from completely extinguishing. She left the words on the screen for several minutes before closing down her machine.

It was early afternoon and she pulled on a long-sleeved plaid shirt over her sports bra, donned a baseball cap and sunglasses, and descended from her fifth story den to walk in Grand Park. Children splashed noisily on the mirrored surface of the black granite membrane pool that surrounded the memorial fountain. All around her, couples stretched side-by-side on the sun-drenched lawn, reading to each other, nuzzling, or sprawled on their backs gazing into a cloudless sky. She walked the park's length to the Cathedral of Our Lady of Angels, then back toward the imposing white tower of City Hall. At a bright pink outdoor café she stopped for an espresso, feeling that it connected her in some small way with the variegated crowd of Angelinos that passed her table. She sat until afraid that if she remained longer, someone might ask to sit with her. As the afternoon began to cool, she walked back to her high-rise and took the narrow, echoing stairs to her apartment. She sat in front of her computer, reconsidered what she was about to do for only a moment, and called up the Raptor's message, clicking on "reply."

"Been thinking about your side-by-side suggestion," she wrote. *"If we were to do this, where would it happen?"*

She sat for fifteen minutes with no response, the warmth of her walk and climb up the stairs gradually cooling to a lonely chill. She had closed the door too hard, possibly catching a finger. She walked into the bathroom to wash the film of perspiration from her face and jerked visibly at the distant "ping" from her workroom.

"No one comes to my place," the Raptor said. *"And my guess is that no one comes to yours. Do you fly?"*

"Don't like it, but can," she entered.

"Denver is about halfway. Willing to meet there? The downtown library is ugly as hell but has private space with mega-speed connections."

"How soon?"

"I like to fly on Tuesdays. Not as many people. How about next Wednesday morning?"

"I'll need to check flights. May be full this late."

"Probably not on a Tuesday," he said. *"If you want to meet*

and can get a flight, let me know. I'll be in the main reading room at ten when it opens."

"How will I know you?"

"Do you have a shirt or something with your totem?"

"Yes. A sweatshirt."

"I'll find you," he said and was again gone.

As she sat in silence she felt strangely like the morning she had walked from the colonial to meet the stranger from South Carolina in the park. She was frightened. Excited. Determined to hold onto some control of her life but test its boundaries. Though a lively presence on the web, she had been gradually disappearing in every other way. On particularly lonely nights, she feared going to sleep, afraid that she might disappear altogether. She found herself obsessing about the sci-fi cyber classic *The Matrix*. Was she really a creation of some omniscient programmer who constructed a reality so convincing that its avatars didn't realize they were no more than electronically-generated consciousness? Was she simply a plug-in who with a single key stroke would be gone? If that were the case, what she did didn't matter. So she may as well make the walk to the van, take the flight to Denver, and come face-to-face with the Raptor.

* * *

He had been right about the library. It was one of the ugliest buildings she remembered seeing. It looked like the creation of three first-year architecture students who had been assigned to design individual projects, then had their novice plans cobbled together to form the final structure. The central foyer and desk area were a step up architecturally but a bit disorienting. A central atrium rose to a vaulted ceiling four levels above, with the third-floor façade reflecting an abstract panorama of the Denver skyline and surrounding mountains. She glanced up, then quickly back at the floor to regain her equilibrium as the space above seemed to tilt backward. At an entry turnstile she checked her backpack but was allowed to carry her laptop and notepad into the vast open hall.

She paused a few steps onto the tiled floor and studied the signs over archways that led into side galleries housing the permanent collections: Children's Library, Periodicals, Western History, Genealogy. Nothing that said Reading Room. As she approached the information desk, she saw him seated at a table along the rail of the second floor balcony at the far end of the atrium. She knew instinctively that it was the Raptor. He was indeed dark. In fact, his skin was almost ebony black, and he had the close-cropped hair and the thin, agile-looking body she had imagined. As she looked up and caught his eye, he smiled faintly and nodded towards the stairs that rose to the second level.

As she approached the small table, she saw that he was a little older, possibly thirty, with skin as smooth as poured dark chocolate and irises made darker by the pure ivory of the whites that surrounded them. He wore a gray hoodie, pulled back with the drawstrings draped across his chest. An MSI Ghost Pro sat in front of him on the desk. He stood as she approached.

"So—the Badger's a woman!"

"Does that disappoint you?" she said self-consciously.

"Not at all! And you're not hard to identify with that shirt," he said, his smile broadening to show an even set of pearl white teeth. Her sweatshirt displayed an exact replica of the snarling badger that adorned her chest.

"You look pretty much like I thought you would," she said, sliding into the seat opposite.

"I've been a great admirer," he said.

"Mutual admiration."

He leaned back in his chair and studied her face with an intense fascination that raised the blood in her cheeks. "I tried to get into the Pentagon records to see if I could find accurate casualty data on Iraq and Afghanistan. The same stuff you were able to get to and publish. But I couldn't get through," he said. "That was masterful."

"How did you know that was me?" she asked, the flush deepening.

"As I said in my message, I found some signature characteristics and have been following your work. It's pretty amazing. Did you make that penetration on your own?"

"Like I told you, I work pretty much alone."

"I have a partnership proposal for you," he said, reaching down into the side pocket of his hoodie.

She also leaned back, trying to decide where she now found herself in the Matrix. Was he Morpheus or Cypher? Or even Smith?

"It would have to be a pretty attractive opportunity," she said.

"Very attractive," he said, lifting a brown leather wallet onto the table and flipping it open to display a gold shield. "I'm Special Agent Davies with the FBI's cyber-crime division and you're under arrest for crimes against the United States Government. Everything you say…."

She shut out the rest of his Miranda monologue and searched desperately for an escape among the stacks that led away from the balcony. But now that she was aware, she easily identified two other agents at nearby tables, one male and one female, guarding the staircases. Both were poised to move if she even flinched in her seat.

"You lying sonofabitch," she murmured, feeling the last small glimmer of blue flame sputter and go out, leaving her insides completely cold.

Davies reached across the table and pulled her computer to him. "Let's get up quietly and walk outside," he said. "Our Denver office is just a quarter mile up Broadway and we can talk there. I actually do have a proposal for you."

The car was a heavily tinted black SUV just as she had imagined. She rode sandwiched between Davies and the female agent, a stony-faced woman in a dark pantsuit who didn't say a word during the ten-minute drive. In a bare interrogation room with the obligatory mirrored window, Davies faced her across a metal tabletop and made his offer.

"I was telling you the truth when I said I admire your abilities," he said. "You're perhaps the most skilled hacker on our list and you do have this unorthodox style that makes you unpredictable and imaginative. You're probably looking at three to five years in federal prison for what we know we can pin on you. But because of your talents, I've been authorized to offer you a deal."

The Badger stared sullenly at the mirrored wall wondering who else was watching the negotiation.

"We need the best talent we can find working on our side," Davies continued. "If you come and work for us, I can arrange to get you placed on probation and working with a pretty good salary for the Bureau. You can even work out of the LA offices if you choose. We're out in Westwood by the National Cemetery."

From that moment, and for the next four months, the Badger remained as silent as a tomb. While her case moved through federal court, she refused to speak to her court-appointed attorney and ignored instructions in court. Until the second day in her cell at the Federal Correctional Institution in Aliceville, Alabama, the Badger didn't utter a word. On that second afternoon she turned to her cellmate, a petite brunette who had been introduced as Gabriella Marzilli, and asked, "And what are you getting screwed for?"

TWENTY-SIX

The entrance to the Cave Church in Budapest's Gellert Hill is a perfect half circle, chiseled out of the stone cliff above the Danube in the 1920s by a group of Pauline monks. Access to the sanctuary is guarded by an ornate grillwork of gray steel that slides across inner glass doors. Once called St. Ivan's Cave after a legendary hermit who lived in the cavern, it served for a time during World War II as a field hospital for Nazi soldiers.

Dreu took a cab south along the river's east bank, a bright morning sun warming the city and glowing in soft yellows off the Buda Palace on the opposite bank. On the crest of Gellert Hill, the statue of Liberty stretched her arms skyward, holding a palm leaf above a city that had been battered by both Nazi and Allied troops during World War II and had risen resolutely from the ashes. Even the river, dark and moody in the afternoon shadows when they arrived, reflected hints of the blue that gave it its famous name. The sun on her shoulder warmed the deeper blue of her light jacket and the city seemed much more familiar and alive on this new day. For the first time during their travels, she was feeling completely Tanvi Russell.

The taxi crossed the Szababsag Bridge and immediately turned right along a short drive. At its end, an open terrace overlooked the river and served as a drop-off for the church and an ancient monastery that had been constructed beside it against the steep hillside. On a smaller stone platform a few steps below the terrace, a stylized statue of St. Stephen stood beside his horse, his back to the Danube and the morning bustle of traffic that hurried along the river road below.

Though it was still ten minutes before the hour when Dreu climbed from the cab, the metal grillwork was pulled back and the church doors stood open. She turned slowly in a full arc, examining the terrace and speaking softly into a miniature microphone that had skillfully been worked into her dangling earrings. After she dressed, she and Adam had spent half an hour weaving the small transmitter into the thick, loose braid of black hair that fell midway down her back.

"I'm at the church," she said quietly when her back was to the cave entrance. "There's a man standing in front who looks like he's guarding the door—but no one else is on the terrace."

Their preparation for her arrival had taken most of the previous afternoon. When Katalin Dulay named the Cave Church as their rendezvous, Adam found the shrine on Google Earth and guessed the upper floors of the historic Gellert Hotel immediately across the street would be slightly above the level of the cave entrance and a good observation point. The reservation clerk at the Gellert informed him that there was an available fourth-floor room facing the street. It was booked for Monday evening and if he reserved it, he would have to vacate by 11:00 that morning. Adam made the reservation and together they slipped out of the Sofitel through a back employee entrance. They walked until certain they were not being followed, then crossed the Szababsag Bridge on foot and checked into the Gellert.

The hotel is one of Europe's most celebrated, built during the First World War in the popular Art Nouveau style of the day. When Allied bombers leveled a good part of Budapest during World War II, the hotel was miraculously spared and remains a monument to the city's resilience and glorious past. Dreu insisted they take advantage of their afternoon of historic luxury to see the hotel's magnificent, naturally heated baths, their vast two-story atrium supported by marble columns and covered by an arched glass ceiling. They ate in a stately dining room where high-backed white chairs surrounded tables laid with white china and centered with bouquets of white lilies, draped to the floor in starched white linen.

"Has something of a celestial feel to it, don't you think?" she said as they waited for their soup to arrive in wide white bowls.

"As long as it's not a harbinger of some kind," he said. "We have dangerous work ahead of us."

"So we need to enjoy a relaxed moment beforehand," she said. "You were so worried someone might follow us. If they see us eating here, they'll assume we really are the vacationing Mr. and Mrs. Russell."

"Dreu," he said seriously, "with this Katalin, the ante goes up a couple of notches. She obviously has ties to the government. If she isn't the Hungarian connection for whoever's running this extortion scheme, she's probably only a step below. Tomorrow we need to be on top of our game. No mistakes."

She had ordered ***pörkölt,*** a meat dish with onions and a heavy dose of Hungarian paprika, with a side of fried goose livers called *libamáj.* As the dish was placed in front of her, she sat for a few moments to admire the presentation.

"I was nervous when the day started," she said, poking at the livers with her fork, "but the meeting with Reka went about as well as we could hope. I'm going to be fine."

"You need to be wired," he repeated. "We'll use the earrings we got from Fisher. There's a good sightline from our room into the front of the church and I should be able to hear you. But you won't be able to hear me." He had ordered a stuffed cabbage dish called *töltött káposzta* and quieted while the waitress placed the plate in front of him and re-filled their wine glasses.

"I would think," she said, "that the choice of the church is good for us. It's secluded, but from the hotel window it looks like there's only one way out—for them as well as for me."

"Not the same," he said, peeling back cabbage leaves with his fork. "We're guests. She's government. Even in the new Hungary, that makes a big difference."

They had returned to the Sofitel for a night that limited its romance to sleeping wrapped in each other's arms. Adam left again in the morning through the rear workers' exit, drawing a few quizzical stares as he traipsed in mock confusion through a kitchen storage area and out into one of the back corridors. He had parked the rental on the street a few blocks from the hotel and left thirty minutes before Dreu's cab was scheduled to arrive. He wanted to again ensure that he wasn't followed and be in position on the fourth floor of the Gellert when she reached the church. He wished that he could somehow signal that he was picking up her voice.

* * *

As she approached the metal grating of the outer doors, the solitary man stepped forward barring her path. The guard pointed brusquely at a sign beside the glass door that announced opening time to be 9:00 a.m. He was a thick, neckless block of a man in a heavy, tightly-fitted suit that strained against his shoulders and upper arms. He looked the picture of a bodyguard: solid, imposing, moving with that stiff gait that suggested he worked out a little too much, and completely without expression.

"Church is not yet open," he said in broken English. It struck her that he had not chosen to speak Hungarian. With her dark complexion and hair she was often mistaken for Indian or Latin American. But he had addressed her in English.

"I'm scheduled to meet someone here at eight," she said, trying to look past him into the glazed interior. The cavernous church was dimly lighted and she couldn't see beyond the reflecting face of the glass.

"Who you are meeting?" he asked.

"Dulay Katalin," she said, reversing the names in what Adam had told her was Hungarian custom. Her pulse had quickened but she looked steadily into the deep-set eyes of the guard. She was taller than the man and he looked nervously away—a fleeting display of uncertainty, but one that bolstered her confidence.

"She is here for you," he said awkwardly and stepped only slightly aside so that she had to push past him to reach the glass doors.

The entrance to the church was what had been the original cave, still natural rock arching above a poured and tiled floor that offered room only for a small ticket counter, a raised central altar, and a souvenir stand displaying an assortment of religious trinkets. In the rear wall to Dreu's left, a narrow tunnel sloped gradually downward into the hillside where a failed attempt had been made to blast a pathway through the rock to the riverside.

Dreu paused, glanced back at the upper floors of the hotel across the street, and judged that she could still maintain line-of-sight contact if she followed what she could see of the tunnel. She descended slowly until it widened into a larger cavern, then looked back again to confirm that the Gellert was still in view. In front of her, thick stone columns divided a larger chamber into small chapels and when she entered she saw no one. But she was only a step into the cool, dim interior when a woman stepped from a dark side passage immediately to her left.

"Mrs. Russell?" she asked, her voice echoing in the hollow of the cavern. Dreu recognized her immediately as the woman who had been with Senator Von Holten in the video. She was older than the other escorts and an exception to the profile, with an earthy sensuous face and full figure.

"Yes—and you must be Katalin. Please call me Tanvi," Dreu said.

"Tanvi," the woman repeated, smiling comfortably. "That is not a name I have heard before."

"It's Indian," Dreu said. "My mother was from Bangalore."

"Ah," Katalin said. "But Mr. Russell must not be Indian."

"Mr. Russell is not Mr. Russell," Dreu admitted, a decision she and Adam had made over pork and cabbage at the Gellert. "He is what you might call my bodyguard."

Katalin raised a surprised brow—probably, Dreu decided, not because the woman didn't already know, but at this unexpected display of candor.

"But your bodyguard didn't accompany you to this meeting?"

"No. He is nearby, but is here mainly to protect me from those I have come to talk to you about."

Katalin nodded. "Reka said you had come to warn me." She turned and beckoned Dreu to follow her back into the side chapel. "Though the church does not open for an hour, come with me in here where we can speak more quietly. I do not like the echo of the sanctuary."

Dreu looked hesitantly at the narrow side chamber, afraid that if she moved out of the main cavern she would lose her connection to Adam.

"I'd be more comfortable remaining here," she said.

Katalin's smile tightened. "You have come to warn me but don't trust speaking with me privately?" she asked. "The monks will be coming soon to open for other visitors. I think they would prefer that we not be speaking here in the center of the church. It is a place of silence."

Dreu glanced back up the tunnel where the face of the Gellert Hotel was barely visible through the grated front and tried to decide what Adam would advise. "It's not a matter of trust," she said. "I am never completely certain I'm not being followed and don't want us to be in a difficult place if someone were to come in after us."

The Hungarian tossed her head dismissively. "We have Kolos at the door. He will keep anyone but the monks from disturbing us." She turned and walked back into the narrow side chamber.

"As long as you're feeling safe," Dreu said uneasily, and followed.

The side passage was more a tunnel that connected three tiny chambers, joined by low arched passageways that had been blasted between them. Icons of saints filled shallow niches in the rock walls and at the far end, a larger arched alcove carved into the rock face displayed a chi rho cross, the symbolic X across its stem and elongated P at the top etched into the stone above a narrow wooden table. Plain, straight-backed oak chairs lined the sides of the gray limestone chambers and the women's footsteps clicked noisily against the tiled floor as Dreu followed Katalin deeper into the hillside.

In the final chamber the woman indicated one of the chairs and pulled another around to partially face her.

"This will be much more private," She said. "Do you know of our Saint Stephen?" She was apparently in no hurry to hear about the danger Reka had warned her about. "You saw his statue as you entered the church. He was the first king of the Hungarians, unifying our country a thousand years ago. And the first in his family to become a devout Christian. He did many things for our country. Unified it. Chased out the Romans and separated from the Roman Church." She paused and looked up at the cross emblazoned above them in the alcove. "He was known as a good man, but was insistent that everyone follow Christian customs. And he could be ruthless with those who betrayed him." She returned her gaze to Dreu and said, "Now—what is it you have come to tell me?"

The message of Katalin's brief lesson in Hungarian history was not lost on her visitor. Dreu wondered again if her transmitter was penetrating the yards of rock that separated her from her safety net on the fourth floor of the Gellert. Her inexperience was showing. She should have found some way to insist they stay in the main sanctuary and again felt the pounding in her chest. She fought the urge to suck in a slow, deep breath to calm it, aware that every gesture and expression was being carefully watched.

"You were part of a plan to get incriminating videos of some of our country's most important politicians," she said evenly, channeling Adam's advice to *be* the person she wished to project. "Several of the women who were involved have since been murdered. I'm here to warn you that your life may be in danger."

"And you were sent by Mr. Levanzo?"

Dreu refused to blink, though every impulse was to react to hearing the name of the American crime boss come unsolicited from Katalin Dulay.

"Yes. To warn you and Reka."

"Why didn't he just call the Russian directly?"

The Russian? Another surprise! Dreu again struggled to appear unruffled. *Be* the person you wish to project, she thought frantically, hoping this conversation was getting to Adam.

"You and Reka both did a great service and this danger seems immediate. Mr. Levanzo thought you deserved to be warned personally."

"And you are going to meet with Gizi as well?"

Oh, God, Dreu thought. There's a third! Is Gizi male or female? *Be* the person….

"Yes. But I don't have contact information for Gizi. I was hoping you could help me with that."

Katalin's brow tightened slightly and she looked more intently at Dreu. "As far as I know, she's still working at the club not far from your hotel."

Ah. Female. "I'll check there tonight," Dreu said. "But I need to let you know that the man you were with is powerful and ruthless. You may want to drop out of sight until he can be silenced in a way that protects you."

"Surely you can't be planning to eliminate one of your major politicians!" Katalin smiled cynically. "Here that might happen. But in America? I don't think so."

"We plan to make it clear that should anything else happen to our girls, his reputation will be ruined," Dreu said, reflecting the smile. "In America, that's about the same as being eliminated. I'm sure you feel the Russian can give you protection, but these men are powerful and clever."

"He will do what is necessary. But we are grateful for your warning." Katalin looked up as the massive guard in the tight suit filled the arch that led back to the sanctuary. He raised a cell phone and jerked his head toward the outer chamber. The Hungarian woman rose and apologetically excused herself.

"Call for me and there is no reception back here. I will just be a moment."

"I'll come with you," Dreu suggested. "I should call my partner and get him to see if Gizi is working this evening."

The guard gave his head a quick shake and Katalin stopped and looked back at Dreu, any sign of friendliness wiped from her attractive face. "I think Kolos wants you to stay," she said. "I will only be a moment…."

"I think I should come," Dreu insisted, moving toward the big man. He planted himself beneath the narrow arch, arms folded menacingly across his chest.

"You will stay here," he ordered, spreading his feet until he filled the entire space.

Dreu shrugged and sat back on the hard wooden chair. Despite the cold of the cave room, she felt her forehead moisten and mouth dry. Time for a rescue, she thought, wondering what bit of damning information might have called Katalin out in the middle of their meeting. Before she could work through the possibilities, the Hungarian woman tapped the guard's shoulder and pushed past him back into the small chapel.

"I am most sorry for the interruption," she said, her face again relaxed. But she remained standing. "I'm afraid there is some confusion here. That was the Russian on the phone and he has been talking to Mr. Levanzo…."

The perspiration on Dreu's forehead couldn't be hidden and she swallowed visibly. Come on, Adam. Time to show up!

"Very good," she forced through her parched lips. "I'm sure he confirmed our concern for you."

Katalin's laugh was hard and brief. "You are not a good liar, Ms. Tanvi—or whoever you are. We can't be sure because Mr. Levanzo has never heard of you."

Dreu was freelancing, her planning with Adam having failed to anticipate Katalin's recognition of Levanzo and the appearance in the equation of the Russian.

"You're right," she said with a resigned smile. "I'm not here representing Levanzo. But I am here with a group that wants to save the lives of the women who are being killed. We're trying to protect you."

"The women who died weren't killed by these politicians," Katalin said grimly. "And I am certain you know that. They forgot the rule of Saint Stephen. You do not betray those who have placed their trust in you."

"Be that as it may," Dreu said, finally able to speak the truth. "I'm here to keep other women from being killed."

"Please stand," Katalin said, nodding to the guard and making it clear that it was not just a polite request. As Dreu rose, the man stepped forward and drew a small black wand from his jacket pocket. He ran it quickly over Dreu's body, beginning just below the neckline and sweeping the navy pants and jacket she wore over a white silk shell.

He shook his head and said something in Hungarian, stepping away.

Katalin pointed at Dreu's earrings. "Do the head," she said in English, and the man lifted the wand to the side of her face where it buzzed urgently.

"Please remove your earrings," the Hungarian woman ordered. Dreu twisted them from her ears and laid them on the chair. The guard swept them to the tile floor, ground them under a thick heel, then retrieved the pieces and slipped them into his jacket pocket.

"Kolos," the woman said, turning to her guard, "we will need to take Ms. Tanvi into the back chamber."

Without responding, he stepped across the chapel to the alcove that displayed the cross, appeared to slide a small panel on the underside of the wooden tabletop and trip a release, then pushed against the rock wall with his shoulder. Slowly the section displaying the stylized cross moved backward and to the left as part of a massive door, opening into a black tunnel that plunged deeper into the cliff. He groped along the right side of the wall until he found a switch, illuminating the passage with a single dim bulb.

Dreu glanced desperately back along the passage that ran into the main chapel.

"He won't be coming," Katalin said, matter-of-factly. "The doors are locked and he is on the outside. Now—please, you go first," she said with mock politeness, indicating the tunnel. "It's time for you to meet the Russian."

TWENTY-SEVEN

Gabriella Marzilli wore her orange Aliceville jumpsuit the way starlets on the red carpet wear a Jovani: expertly tucked and fitted in all the right places to accentuate the perfectly shaped body beneath. There was major debate on the cellblock over why she decided to take the Badger under her wing. Some argued it was because her new cellmate talked so little while Marzilli was an infomercial on steroids. Others believed Gabriella liked the look of the fresh new body and wanted it all to herself. Still others maintained that taking care of the Badger simply gave the high-energy Italian something new to do. Even when enrolled in every possible class and every therapy group, time in Aliceville crept forward like mange on a dog's back and Gabbi Marzilli liked action. The truth be known, all of the speculation had truth to it. The Badger was quiet, looked good enough in her own orange suit to deserve Marzilli's attention, and seemed like an interesting project.

Word of her muteness preceded the Badger to the lockup and as she passed through processing and what seemed like endless sliding steel gates, whispers of "She's the one who don't talk" followed her through the cellblock. So Marzilli viewed it as a personal triumph when the Badger asked what she was getting screwed for.

"So I guess you do talk sometimes," Gabbi said, folding her legs beneath her on the bunk and inspecting her project.

"When I've got something to say," the Badger said bluntly.

"What am I in for?"

The Badger nodded.

"Ever heard of an SBS?"

"Don't think so."

"Stands for Short Barreled Shotgun. Under federal law, you can't be carrying around a shotgun with a smooth barrel under twenty-six inches long." She said it as if reading from an ATF manual, but with a distinct New York accent.

"And you were carrying one," the Badger guessed.

"Well—two, actually. We got stopped with 'em in the trunk.

And had a couple of suppressors, too. You can't have silencers for your guns."

"I didn't think shotguns had silencers."

"Well, yeah. There was other guns in the trunk, too."

"You say 'we' got stopped?"

"Yeah. Me and my boyfriend."

"And the guns belonged to you?"

"Of course they did. Otherwise he'd be in here—well, up in Leavenworth or somewhere like that."

"And it was better you came here," the Badger guessed.

Marzilli smiled. "You ever heard of Gio Levanzo?"

The Badger shook her head.

"Yeah. You're West Coast. You live up around D.C., you know about Gio Levanzo. Well, Tony—that's his youngest son. Tony's my guy."

"So you took the rap for Tony…."

"Hell no! They was my guns. That's the way it was." She leaned further back into the bunk. "This your first time down?"

"You mean first time in prison? Yeah. First time."

"For bustin' into federal computers, the way I hear it."

The Badger nodded.

"You didn't fight it, so I guess you did it."

"Every chance I got," the Badger said grimly. "And they know that when I get out of here, I'll be back after them, the lying sonsabitches."

"That," Marzilli said, pushing forward and leaning toward her project, "is the last time you're gonna say that. You get outta here when they think you're no longer a threat to society. And I can have you out in eighteen months. Guaranteed."

The Badger looked skeptically at her cellmate but said nothing.

"You're a lucky girl," Marzilli said.

"How's that?"

"Tony takes good care of me here and everybody knows it. You stay close to me, you'll be okay."

"I can take care of myself."

"I'm walkin' in about twelve months," Marzilli said. "Maybe

you'll need to take care of yourself then. But 'til then, you stay close to old Gabbi here and that will be good enough."

* * *

By the time Gabbi Marzilli was paroled, she was the closest to a friend the Badger had ever known. And the only real lover. Marzilli was right. Even after her release, the Badger was protected property while in Aliceville. It had been made clear that Tony Levanzo and his people would be watching after her. No one messed with the Badger.

When the Badger left the gates of Aliceville on her final morning as ward of the federal government, a white Cadillac limo sat in the "no parking" area in front of the administrative building and Gabbi climbed out to meet her. They had written or called every week since Gabbi's release so there was little catching up to do. The prison was north of town and rather than going into Aliceville, the limo turned the other way toward Pickensville, then east on Highway 86 toward Tuscaloosa. For the first twenty minutes Gabbi sat quietly holding the Badger's hand, letting her soak in the greenery that had been hidden behind the high, razor-wired walls and again feel openness around her. When they turned east from Pickensville, the Badger broke the silence.

"Something wrong? You're never this quiet."

"Lettin' you get used to bein' out," Marzilli said.

"That took about two minutes," the Badger said. "Thanks for picking me up."

"That's what friends are for." She gave her hand a long squeeze. "…and maybe I got something for you. How current you feelin' about what you can do with computers?"

The Badger shrugged. "Haven't been on one, of course. And a condition of my parole is that I stay off. But the dumbshits subscribed to all of the best computer magazines in the library and I've been reading them cover-to-cover. Probably know a helluva lot more than I did when I went in."

"You interested in a job that will make you some good

money, but means you gotta break parole?"

"Is that all? I figure if it's one you have for me, it means more than breaking parole."

Gabbi laughed. "Yeah. Well, that too. We want you to get laid in a video. But you've also gotta be really smart with the computer thing. When Tony asked if I knew anyone who could hack their way into anywhere and make a born-again Christian's balls ache, I said I knew just the woman."

"And just getting out of Alice isn't going to matter?"

"Might be a plus."

"You serious about getting laid in a video?"

"Yeah. That's the main part of the job."

"What for?"

"Don't know for sure. I think Tony wants to bring some guy down, and this is how he wants to do it."

The Badger shrugged. "If you want me to do it, I'll do it. Tell me about the job."

A week later she was in Triplett's den being interviewed. Four weeks later, she was straddling him on the chair in her cabin with the computer sending a direct feed to a desktop in New York that the Badger had known better than to ask about. After Triplett left her room, she waited through the second day for those with east coast assignments to reach the camp. Then she packed her few belongings and, just after midnight, hiked two miles through the pines to a car Gabbi arranged to be left at a campground in Idaho's Panhandle National Forest. By daybreak she was halfway across Montana and when Triplett sent LeAnn to check her room, was well into South Dakota.

Gio Levanzo had a retreat of his own in the Blue Ridge Mountains south of Luray, Virginia, bordering Shenandoah National Park. When the Badger arrived, Gabbi was again waiting to welcome her and share the night.

"He'll come looking for me," the Badger said. "He's not a man who's going to take something like this lying down." Gabbi began to giggle, then laugh until the Badger was laughing uncontrollably with her, tears streaking both of their faces. Gabbi pinned her beneath her on the thick cushions of the woven bamboo sofa.

"He'll have to come through me if he plans to get to you," she gasped, and they both dissolved again into side-cramping laughter.

*   *   *

Five minutes after Dreu entered the Cave Church, Adam lost her signal. He heard her greet Katalin Dulay, heard the Hungarian woman suggest they move into a side chapel, and heard Dreu's objection. Then nothing. A hulk of a man who bulged beneath a dark suit stood beside the outer door and slid high metal bars back across the opening after Dreu entered, then planted himself like the stone statue beside the terrace, arms folded across his chest. Adam couldn't enter now even if he crossed to the church, and what had seemed the perfect listening post now began to reveal its shortcomings and the differences in strategy that came with working with a partner.

He ran through the possibilities she may be facing, considering how he would respond if he were the one in the church. Katalin may be cooperating, accepting Dreu's story and naming the next person in the chain of conspiracy. In that case, Dreu would soon walk out with what she needed and all was well. Or the Hungarian may be feigning ignorance, in which case Dreu had been instructed not to push, but to regroup. They would formulate another plan of attack. But worst case scenario, she had been discovered for what she was: someone sent to expose the Hungarians' involvement and identify the connection. In that case, they would remove her from the church and, he guessed, try to discover who she was and what she already knew. Then—well, he wasn't yet willing to think about the "then." But he needed to be ready for that possibility and the room in the Gellert wasn't the right place to do it.

Leaving the hotel to cross to the terrace in front of the church would take five to seven minutes. That would give those inside the cave time to leave unseen and mount the paved path that ascended the hill twenty yards along the drive to the left of the entrance. They could be far enough up the slope to be out of sight when he reached a new vantage point—though if Dreu still had the mic, he should be able to follow once she was out in the open. That was assuming the mic was now dead because of the thick rock and not because it had been discovered.

If he stayed at the window, a car could pull onto the terrace, pick up Dreu and Katalin, and be back on the street before he reached the walk. One way or the other, the hotel was a trap and he took a final quick glance across at the barred church entrance and dashed across the room, out the door and to the stairwell at the far end of the hall. The ancient elevators had been agonizingly slow coming up.

He was in the street in two minutes and though from street level the terrace was above view, he was able to watch the mouth of the church drive as he sprinted to it and turned up the lane. His soles slapped noisily against the pavement and he stopped briefly and slipped off his loafers, padding up the drive in stocking feet. As Adam approached the terrace he slowed to a brisk walk, listening for the barred door to slide along its track.

A clump of spirea filled the side of the drive where it joined the terrace, long past the flowering stage but thick with fall-tinted foliage. Adam stopped behind it and peered through at the guard. The man had taken a few steps away from the door and was listening intently to his cell phone, his stern expression folding into a furrowed frown. He nodded abruptly, pocketed the phone, and with what seemed an effortless motion, pushed the steel gate aside and entered the church.

To follow was too risky—but so was standing in stocking feet beside the drive. Adam slipped on his shoes and walked briskly across the terrace to the steps that descended to the statue of St. Stephen, moving quickly to an edge of the lower circle that was hidden from the church doorway. The door scraped open again and he heard the voice of Katalin Dulay. The conversation in Hungarian was animated and Adam eased along the waist-high wall until he could see her veiled figure through the bushes.

"*Igen...igen,*" she said firmly into a phone, listening for another moment. Then she muttered a terse "*viszlát*" and tucked the cell into her handbag, disappearing back into the church. As she entered, she pulled the steel barricade across the glass front and Adam heard it lock into place. He leapt the five stairs to the main terrace in a single bound and rushed the front of the church, reaching the barred entryway as she was locking the inner glass doors a yard behind the metal barrier. She looked up at him through the thick glass, a tight smile creasing her lips, then turned and vanished into the shadows of the church cavern.

Adam shook impotently at the grating, stepping back and scanning the church's arched front. The bars filled the entire half-circle, deeply embedded into a false concrete stonework that had been used to shape the edging around the grate. He had been in places before where he knew he was in mortal danger and his entire system had been super-charged, every nerve firing as he fought to save himself. But he didn't ever remember being this afraid. He had ignored every rule of his training—every condition of his assignment—and brought in a partner. Someone he deeply cared about. And now she was the one in danger and the thought terrified him.

For a few brief seconds the fear was paralyzing, inserting tiny insulators into the circuitry of his brain and disrupting every effort to think, edging him toward panic. He shook it off, reminding himself that panic was the enemy of considered action and he needed to act, and quickly.

There appeared to be no cameras monitoring the front of the cavern. Adam scanned the area for a rock or something that could be thrown between the bars into the window, potentially setting off an alarm. The terrace was swept clean of every leaf and twig and he ran toward the drive where the rocky hillside rose to the top of the cliff. As he reached the clump of spirea, a hooded man in monk's robes sputtered up the narrow lane on an ancient motorbike and Adam turned and chased after him to the front of the church.

"Do you speak English?" he asked breathlessly.

The monk dismounted far too slowly, parked the scooter beside the steel gate, and pulled back his hood. His wizened face and wisps of gray hair made Adam wonder how the ancient figure managed to balance on the scooter.

"Yes. How can I help you?"

"My friend is locked in the church," Adam said, knowing as he said it that he wouldn't be believed. "I need to get to her very quickly."

"She was closed in last night?" the old monk asked, looking skeptically at the barred entrance. "We inspect the church very carefully…."

"No. This morning. She met a woman here this morning and they are closed inside."

The monk looked around nervously for help. "I am here to open the church," he said. "No one can go in until I open it."

"They had it unlocked," Adam insisted. "A Hungarian woman named Katalin and a big man. And they met my friend here."

The monk fumbled beneath his robes and pulled a ring of keys out of a hidden pocket, showing them to Adam as if it settled any argument. He moved stiffly to the sliding grillwork. "You may come in with me and see if she is here," he said. "But I am the one who opens the church each morning."

Adam followed him along the descending passage into the cool shadows of the inner chamber and looked immediately for the side chapels. The three-chambered passage disappeared into the dark immediately to his left.

"Where are the lights?" he asked, stepping toward the first stone archway. The monk shuffled to a bank of switches just inside the main cavern and dim yellow light radiated across the interior. Adam searched the side chamber to the alcove that displayed the chi rho cross, working his way along the rock surface, feeling and prodding for anything that might release a hidden door. In the center of the back chamber he stooped to examine a spot on the floor where it appeared some hard object had recently been ground against the slate tile. Finding nothing, he returned to the main sanctuary and moved systematically among the massive stone pillars, probing into every cavity large enough to hold even a small icon or contribution box while the monk followed, looking increasingly nervous. A round window, large enough for the passage of either of the women, opened out towards the river but was covered with thick, fixed glass. At the back of the main chapel, another tunnel led to a locked iron gate and beyond it, a heavy wooden door.

"They must have gone out through here," Adam insisted, but the monk shrugged off the suggestion.

"This goes into the monastery," he said. "The gate is always locked and my brothers rise early in the morning to study just beyond that door. No one has come through."

"Could you check?"

"I have no need to check. I was there from six o'clock until I left to come open the church. Others are still there."

Adam grasped the iron grate and gave it a frustrated shake. "There are no other ways out of here?" he asked the ancient monk.

"Only the door through which we entered," the old man said.

"No secret doors or passages?"

The monk smiled a wet, toothless smile. "Only in legend. I have been unlocking this church since it reopened in 1989 and know every crevice in the rock. There are no secret passages."

Adam collapsed backward onto one of the straight wooden chairs. He believed the old man was being honest, but it was the wrong truth. Dreu had gone somewhere back into that hillside. He needed to find someone who knew where.

TWENTY-EIGHT

The small grotto that backed the alcove with the chi rho cross had once been part of the larger chamber and extended another six feet into the limestone cliff. The movable wall filled what had been a narrow waist in the hourglass-shaped cave. It had been skillfully constructed in such a way that what appeared from the front to be a solid rock wall swung backward into the cavern behind it to allow tight passage into the rear cavity. The gap was narrow enough that the thick bodyguard had been forced to slip sideways into the opening to grope for the light switch. Once into the rear grotto, a tunnel blasted into the rock went straight back into the cliff for another six feet, turned sharply right for eight or ten paces, then turned again left where, after another few steps, it was blocked by a heavy plank door.

The passage was less than two yards high and half as wide and Dreu had to hunch forward, prodded by the pressure of Katalin's hand on her back as she inched along in the dim light. They halted before the wooden door. Keys rattled behind her and Kolos, who had followed them into the grotto, pushed up beside her, flattening her against the damp wall as he inserted a long skeleton key into a sturdy mortise lock. A bolt snapped back behind a metal plate. Dreu expected the door to squeak ominously as it was pushed inward, but it swung silently on well-oiled hinges into a natural chamber the size of the small single garage that served her Chandler apartment.

The guard stepped back and Katalin pushed her through into the cave, lit only by a dim bare bulb that hung from a looped rod screwed into the ceiling five feet above her head. As she was ushered into the room, Dreu noticed that the light switch was on the tunnel side of the door. An insulated wire ran up the timber frame and through a small hole bored through the lintel.

As they penetrated deeper into the hillside, the temperature began to climb and this new chamber was uncomfortably warm with a stifling sulfurous smell, the air almost too thick to breathe. Heavy vapor drifted from a dark pool the size of an old wash tub that punctured the floor on the far side of the grotto, steam rising into the still air as the thermal waters met the cooler rush from the tunnel. It was as if she had stepped from the sanctuary of God's house through the gates of hell and she raised her hand across her nose to block the acrid fumes. Another faint odor tinted the chemical vapors—heavier and darker against the back of her nostrils. But it didn't fit with the infernal images that filled her brain and she pushed it aside.

To Dreu's right a second plank door indicated another passageway, but the trio stopped in the steaming grotto.

"We wait here," Katalin said.

The room was completely bare, the high damp ceiling draped with the broken remnants of what had once been stalactites. The two Hungarians stood in nervous silence, the massive guard with his back against the door through which they had entered and the woman pacing back and forth across the close chamber. For the first time since Katalin had confronted her about Levanzo, Dreu had a moment to bring order to her racing thoughts. They had vaulted from calm confidence to sudden terror as she realized she had been discovered and was probably where Adam couldn't hear her—even before her transmitter was destroyed. Then there had been a surprising moment of calm, an echo of his voice in her subconscious saying, "Never react to what you think might happen. Anticipate what could, and be ready. But don't let the fear of what hasn't yet happened keep you from preparing for what will." In that moment of calm, she realized that they now knew with certainty that Gio Levanzo was involved with the women and the blackmail, and was probably the one who had ordered the girls murdered. That same realization meant that Katalin Dulay was connected with Levanzo in some way, a way that didn't make the Hungarian woman vulnerable but numbered Dreu among those who could expose them, placing her in mortal danger. And that danger came from someone called "the Russian" who must be the Washington mobster's counterpart in Hungary. She knew she was about to meet him and what she said would mean the difference between whether she made it out of this little piece of hell or died here in the hidden caverns beneath Budapest. It may be that what she said wouldn't make any difference, but she needed her wits about her if she had any chance of survival.

A key scraped in the lock of the other door and both of the Hungarians stiffened and turned to face it. Dreu had formed a mental image of the man, but the figure who stepped into the chamber was a far cry from the burly, grizzled Russian of her imagination. He reminded her instead of the central figure in a popular beer commercial that invited drinkers to join "the most interesting man in the world:" a suave, handsome, intelligent-looking man with a short gray beard and mysterious smile. The Russian closed the door behind him and stood looking at her with the same mild amusement.

"Katalin said that you were a beautiful woman," he said evenly, holding her eyes. It was what Dreu guessed to be an intentional effort to demonstrate that he could appreciate her without the usual full-body scan she got from lesser men.

"But she failed to do you justice," the Russian continued. His accent seemed more central European than Russian.

"Thank you," she said as calmly as she could muster.

"And you have come to Budapest to warn our women that they are in danger."

"Yes."

"From whom?"

"I don't know from whom."

"But you said you worked for my friend Gio Levanzo—which is not true."

"Yes. I said that because I wanted them to take me seriously."

The Russian's smile widened and his eyes laughed at her. "And his name just came to you as one that might mean something to Reka and Katalin?"

"I knew he had arranged for the girls in the States and assumed there would be some connection here."

Dreu's eyes were beginning to sting and beads of perspiration trickled down her back. The Russian looked completely at ease and unaffected by the stifling heat, his well-tailored gray suit hanging perfectly on his slender frame. He walked slowly around her to his right, pausing beside the vaporous pool. She turned with him, not wanting the man to be at her back.

"And how did you determine that Mr. Levanzo was managing the girls you speak of?" he asked in the same even tone.

"You might say that I'm quite a talented computer analyst," Dreu said. "There's very little that I can't learn if I put my mind to it."

The Russian nodded as if he liked her answer, then stooped and dipped a finger into the thermal pool, drawing it back quickly and shaking it in the thick air.

"But you must have a reason for wanting to know," he said, blowing on the digit.

Dreu followed him as he continued to circle her.

"Do you know the name Selina Kyle?" Dreu asked, watching the Russian's face but seeing no ruffle on the still surface. "She was the woman killed in San Francisco. Selina was my half-sister."

The Russian stopped and arched a carefully trimmed gray brow. "Ah," he said. "So you are trying to avenge your sister! That's something I can understand—and admire in a beautiful woman."

He folded his hands behind his hips and rocked slowly forward and back in his expensive black Italian shoes. "Who do you think killed Selina?" he asked.

"I don't know. She was involved, I think at Mr. Levanzo's request, with some very powerful people in our government. I think they may be trying to clean up their mess."

"These politicians?"

"Yes. I think they are being blackmailed with videos that were made of them having sex with Selina and others."

"And how did you track these 'others' to Reka and Katalin?" the Russian asked, appearing to be genuinely curious.

"I watched political behavior and when I saw unexplained changes in position, looked for common denominators. The vice president and a senator named Von Holten led me here. They had little in common but the Budapest conference and it wasn't difficult, just from the press information, to tie Von Holten to Katalin. She was his escort and a very attractive and appealing woman."

"And Reka? I don't think photos of a hotel maid appeared in the press."

Dreu offered the Russian her own amused smile. "I went to Washington and found an aide who had traveled with the vice president," she said. "Asked her what pretty women had given Mr. Carradine special attention during his time here. I think the aide is a little fond of the vice president herself, and she was already suspicious of Reka. Women are that way…."

The Russian's mouth turned down slightly and she read it as an indication he was mulling over her story and feeling some angst that if true, it had been this easy to find the women involved. A thin line of perspiration was collecting along the back of Dreu's waistband and she wanted to reach back and tug it away, but she kept her hands folded in front of her.

"Brilliant," he muttered. "And that's why you didn't know about Gizi. You didn't know she was involved…."

"No. I didn't," Dreu admitted. "Not until Katalin mentioned her."

The Russian continued another quarter around the circle with Dreu turning to follow. Near the door where she had entered the cave, he stopped and turned again to her, raising an inquiring finger. "There's still one thing I'm uncertain about," he said with the same amused smile. The smile and tone said, "You are very good, but you haven't told me everything."

"And what is that?" she asked, holding his eyes steadily.

"It's about the man who is traveling with you. Your 'Mr. Russell.'"

"He's a friend and private investigator," she offered before he could ask. "He came to lend his support and try to keep me from getting into a mess like this." She smiled in what she hoped was a disarming expression of candor.

The Russian laughed softly. "Not a very good bodyguard," he said. "Did he know your sister?"

"They met a few times. Social events. Family gatherings."

The Russian reached into his breast pocket and pulled out a photo, looked at it briefly, and handed it to Dreu. "And on Union

Square in San Francisco, just before she was shot?"

The photo showed Selina Kyle standing beside the column in San Francisco, talking seriously with a man who was clearly Mr. Russell with shorter hair and black-rimmed glasses.

"Yes. He was with her when she was shot," Dreu said but heard the choke in her voice. "She told us she was in trouble, and we were worried about her…."

"And he felt some need to disguise himself…."

"Actually, he disguised himself for this trip. We didn't know who might be watching for us."

"And what did *you* do to disguise yourself?" he asked, looking her over more critically.

"I didn't need a disguise," she said. "I wasn't caught on film when Selina was murdered."

The Russian nodded slowly. "I'll tell you what I am going to do," he said, his own voice showing an edge she had not heard earlier. "I'm going to let you have the night to think about this story—if you make it through the night." The amused smile again drifted across his face. "I like your story. It is very convincing. But I know your mister Russell made an appointment with your 'half-sister.' Not what I would expect from a friend. We're going to let you stay right here and think about it. And you'll quickly learn some things about this little room." He looked about him as if deciding which of its many features to describe first.

"For one thing, very little air comes in here. It becomes hotter and hotter, and the gases fill up the room. From the bottom, I should warn you, so if you want to make it until tomorrow morning, I would remain standing. And have you ever been deep in a cave when the lights are turned off?" He looked back at her with an inquiring tilt to his head. "It becomes completely dark. I don't mean *very* dark. I mean *completely* dark. Your eyes never adjust. And there is no sound. Only the sound of your own breathing and of your heart. You will hear it get louder and faster as you feel yourself starting to get dizzy. And though there is not much air, I am told there *is* some rare variety of centipede that lives here in the dark. They are six centimeters long." He held up two fingers, spread about two inches apart. "And they have a very painful sting. Some of my overnight guests don't survive long enough to be bitten and feel the sting. But for those who do, they drop into the sulfurous gas just to stop the pain."

The Russian completed his circuit of the floor and stood again by the door where he had entered. "Do you want to start again with your story, Mrs. Russell?"

"I've told you why I'm here," she said quietly, her legs already feeling as though they might collapse beneath her. "There's nothing more I can add."

"So be it," he said and nodded to his underlings. He held the door while they exited in front of him, then turned to her a final time.

"I will come again in the morning. If you have survived the night, we will talk again and see if you have new things to tell us—or would like another night in the cave." His frown was disconsolate. "I'm afraid no one has ever survived two nights, and most don't make it through the first. What a shame! You truly are a very beautiful woman." He pulled the door tightly closed behind him, and she heard the bolt snap into place.

The dark was as thick and total as he had described. She widened her eyes and turned her head as much as her neck would allow in both directions without shifting her feet, wanting to remain oriented in the closed space. After a few moments, she realized the chamber would remain completely black. The acrid bite of the sulfur was already heavier in the air and floating on its vaporous surface, the other odor that had escaped her when she entered. She recognized it now. It was the smell of death.

TWENTY-NINE

The start time for Chase Rayborn's morning run in Central Park was as precise as for the PAX evening news broadcast. He crossed 8th Avenue at West 65th Street early enough that he could take his first steps south onto West Drive at exactly 6:30, as if cued by some studio producer who stood atop the huge gray slab of rock just inside the park entrance. Six miles and fifty-eight minutes later he returned to the same spot, used the walk back across 8th Avenue to his apartment as cool-down, and by 8:00 a.m. was showered and dressed. That was assuming his run had no interruptions.

On this Monday morning he was fifteen minutes into his routine and approaching Terrace Drive on the east side of the park when a runner pulled up beside him. When Chase glanced over he had to catch himself to keep from stumbling forward onto his face.

"What are you doing here?" he muttered brusquely, looking again at the road in front of him.

"You don't sound happy to see me," Triplett said, adjusting his pace to stay beside the PAX news anchor.

"I didn't expect us to ever meet again," Rayborn said. "Our business is finished."

"Apparently not," Triplett said. "Turn left here on Terrace."

"I run the full circuit," Rayborn said, checking traffic at the approaching intersection.

"Not today. We're headed back to your place." Triplett stayed on his right, guiding him back towards the west side of the park. "We have a final business transaction to complete."

"Like I said, our business is finished. You went way beyond anything we'd discussed."

"We did exactly what we discussed," Triplett said. "Except for your last little bit of bullshit."

Chase cast him a quick glance. "I don't know what you're talking about."

"Well, let's start with the assumption that you didn't tell anyone about our plan and I didn't tell anyone—but my team, of course. So when a member of the Order disappears and I get pictures of her sitting on my face, what am I supposed to think? That she just showed up on her own and decided she didn't like the work she was hired to do, so she decided to break my balls and get it on tape?"

"I still don't know what you're talking about," Rayborn said. "Sounds like she might have decided you're as wacko as I think you are—and needed some insurance."

"She knew way too much for that," Triplett said, ignoring the insult. "She'd obviously been sent—by you, or someone you've talked to."

Rayborn didn't reply and they jogged side-by-side in silence until Triplett said, "Here's the deal. I know you have copies of the video. You want to use them to get me to stop, but you know that if you go public with them, you're screwed along with me."

Rayborn remained silent.

"You want the attacks stopped? I'm through with them. No more. Unless I don't get your copies of the video. If I leave town without them, there's more to come and there may be some evidence that points right back in your direction." He paused and watched Chase's eyes narrow and jaw tighten, then continued. "We've sort of got each other by the balls, I'd say. So I'm offering a truce. You give me your copies and everything quits. No attacks, no implicating evidence, nothing."

"We can't undo what's been done," Chase said.

"Just my point," Triplett agreed. "If any of this gets out, we're both screwed for sure. But we can't have one of us holding a hand that falls outside of the deal—like messing with my wife's crazy head."

They passed the statue of Daniel Webster and the path leading to Strawberry Fields and turned south again onto West Drive.

"So, supposing I have these video copies and give them to you. That would be it? No more contact between us? No more attacks?"

"I guess I'd have to believe I had all of the copies," Triplett said. "Maybe the girl kept one."

"The girl didn't even know what was going on," Rayborn

said, deciding his safety now depended on agreeing to Triplett's terms but giving him as little information as possible. "She was just a high-dollar whore with some pretty good computer skills. I learned about the job you were trying to fill and knew someone who could fill it and do what I wanted done. I offered her a lot to make the video. She did the job. End of story, as far as she's concerned."

"Where is she?" Triplett asked.

"No idea. She streamed the video live and I recorded it. Don't know what happened to her."

"She got a name?"

"I knew her as Traci. She was just out of prison and I knew she was a first rate hacker—and was available for some pretty good sex. I called her a few times when I wanted a no-commitments night. But when I tried to get hold of her after she sent the stream, the number was no good. I guess you had her do some stuff that could get her sent back to prison for a long time."

"Guess we've all got each other by the balls, so to speak," Triplett said. "Where are the copies?"

"I've got them in a safe deposit box at a branch of Chase on Columbus and Seventy-second."

"We go to your place, get the key, and I go to the box with you."

They slowed to a walk and Triplett followed Rayborn across 8th Avenue and up to his tenth-floor apartment that looked out over the top of St. Vincent Church onto the park.

"Nice setup," Triplett said, taking in the view from an east window. "Where's your home safe? Or are you going to make me hunt for it?"

Rayborn led him to the bedroom closet where a small floor safe was bolted solidly into whatever lay beneath the carpet.

"Open it," Triplett ordered and Rayborn showed him that it held only a small metal box with emergency cash and an envelope with a living will and the title to his apartment.

Triplett sat near the door while Rayborn showered and changed into a pair of gray sweats and tennis shoes. "The bank won't be open 'til nine," he said. "I'm going to fix some eggs benedict. You want some?"

He added sliced bananas and strawberries and they ate without conversation, then walked the ten blocks to the bank. Two copies of the video on DVDs topped the bundle of folded papers and envelopes that filled the metal box. Triplett put them aside then sorted through the stack until confident there were no loose pictures or hidden thumb drives.

Once back on the street, Triplett turned and nodded but didn't offer his hand. "No more contact, no more jobs," he said, and Rayborn grimly returned the nod. Triplett watched him walk back down Columbus until confident the newsman would not see which way he left the bank. He sent a brief text, then turned away from the park on 72nd Street toward the metro station two blocks west. He would have a three-hour wait at Times Square. Then he and Dwayne would begin to make their way through the maze that was the New York subway system across the river into Queens and on to JFK. By evening, they should be back in the Idaho mountains where they could begin their search for the woman. Triplett was certain her name wasn't Traci and that she wasn't just some former Rayborn lay. She was cute and sexy, but no high-priced hooker. But the PAX news anchor had been right about one thing. She had killed five hundred people and would be keeping her mouth shut until they could silence her permanently.

* * *

Chase Rayborn was thinking about Triplett and the woman as he sorted through the day's stories and started to work with the news team on piecing together an evening broadcast. He knew practically nothing about her. She was Huston's find and he had arranged for the video stream.

Chase had watched the video a dozen times—first to ensure that Triplett was clearly identifiable, later to marvel at the savage badger leaping from the woman's chest and fantasize at being under attack. He knew from a brief note from Huston that she'd been in prison but beyond that, had no idea where she'd come from. He knew even less about where she'd gone. But from watching her perform, he had every confidence the woman could take care of herself—and they had the result they wanted. Triplett was through.

An intern brought in sandwiches someone had delivered for the news staff—subs from the shop down the street wrapped in heavy green paper and labeled with the choices: tuna salad on wheat, turkey and avocado panini, corned beef on rye with spicy mustard. Chase took the thick corned beef, balanced it jokingly on one hand, and glanced around the room.

"This is one helluva sandwich! Who ordered the corned beef with mustard? Am I that predictable? Anyway, thanks for knowing my favorite." He peeled back the tape that secured the heavy paper wrap. In a floor-shattering blast that sent window glass and pieces of furniture across the plaza below, the news team and hapless intern who had unwittingly delivered the explosives were shredded by embedded shrapnel as, within a single heartbeat, all six wrapped bundles detonated.

THIRTY

Dreu Sason had grown up largely without phobias. Even on the darkest nights, the secure neighborhood in Palo Alto where she spent her childhood years glowed with the soft yellow light of ornate wrought-iron streetlamps that lined every street. Few crawly creatures breached the redwood fences that surrounded the manicured yards or invaded the heavily chlorinated pools. She had been a child of privilege and one of the benefits had been learning about the things nightmares are made of largely from books and movies. She and her friends had their lists of things to act squeamish about. Giant slugs that showed up on the bottom of hosta leaves. Baiting a hook or removing a fish when one of the fathers took them fishing off the coast. Finding a neighborhood cat dead in the street. But none of them had ever experienced the messy underside of the world in any visceral way.

When modeling in New York she had first experienced real terror when an obsessed psychopath, convinced that God had anointed her to be his bride, stalked her relentlessly. When finally convinced the divine union wasn't going to happen, he broke into her apartment and mutilated parts of her body to try to make her sexually unattractive to anyone else. She had found since that she didn't have any great fear of death, knowing that she had stared it in the face and turned it away. And later, when confronted by a Chinese assassin across a shallow creek in east Texas, she had felt more resigned than afraid—a resignation Adam had saved her from.

All of those thoughts flitted though her mind as she stood in the absolute blackness of the cave beneath Budapest's Gellert Hill. She was afraid to move, more because she wanted to avoid the hot pool than from any fear of attracting some poisonous centipede. When the door first closed she remained stone still, wanting to be certain she could locate both of the doors if the Russian was telling the truth—that not even the slightest glimmer of light penetrated the vault. She closed her eyes tight to help them adjust, opened them wide as if she could somehow expand the pupils to better absorb any tiny ray, and lifted a hand to her face until her palm brushed her nose. Nothing.

It occurred to her that the Russian might leave her there for thirty minutes, maybe an hour, before returning to see if she was beginning to break. See if she couldn't stand the absolute darkness and choking gas. And though she was losing any sense of time, after what seemed an eternity she realized he had been telling the truth about that too. He wasn't coming back until morning.

As she stood in the smothering heat, the blackness seemed to thicken, to become liquid against her exposed skin. What had first seemed to be complete quiet began to echo back to her as a soft whistle, the sound of air being drawn through her nose. Then the muted, double-beat metronome of her heart. The sounds amplified as she became aware of them and she imagined that she could hear the soft *shushing* of blood through her veins with each beat.

She had no idea what lay beyond the door through which the Russian had entered. The passage beyond had been dimly lit like the one she had been forced through, but if she had any sense of direction at all, it led deeper into the hillside. She did know that tourists were browsing through the church beyond the door to her right and guessed Adam might be among them. She took two sidesteps in that direction, arm extended, but felt nothing. She was certain she hadn't moved since being left, but suddenly had the terrifying feeling of being in a limitless void, one that extended endlessly in every direction. There was the sense that she was standing on a suspended disk that would end if she moved too far from its center and she would tumble into the blackness. Beyond the liquid press of the air against her skin, the only sensation was of solid rock beneath her feet and she wanted desperately to drop to her knees and feel about with her hands. But the sulfurous sting in her nose convinced her the Russian was speaking truth about the gases as well. They were heavier than any breathable air that remained in her cell and to drop to her knees increased the chance of losing consciousness. And by feeling her way across the floor, she feared that she might lose any sense of direction and become the child lost in the forest, turning in an endless circle.

She again closed her eyes and extended both arms straight to the sides, seeking balance more than direction. Hushing her breath to focus every sensory impulse into her fingertips, she eased another half-step to her right, then another. Her right hand impacted the wall with startling force and she pulled back, then inched the hand outward again until her fingers touched the damp rock. She had not found the door.

Keeping the hand firmly pressed against the stone, Dreu slowly eased herself around until facing the wall, both arms extended in front of her with palms against the slick rock. There was an overwhelming comfort in feeling something solid in two directions and the suspended disk again became a room. But was she left or right of the door? Intuition told her that the door was to her right so she decided to slide right two steps and, if no door, back to her left four steps. It had to be somewhere within that arc.

With the first step to the right her hand found the edge of the frame and she shuffled sideways until the door was immediately in front of her. She leaned an ear against the thick planking and trapped her breath, begging her heart to quiet its rhythmic '*lub-dub*' so that she could pick up the slightest sound from the church beyond. She heard nothing but knew visitors would be moving through the chambers in respectful silence and may simply not be making noise. Bracing her left elbow against the frame, she pounded with all her might against the boards with both hands. The sound that reverberated back through the chamber was both startling and deflating. Each thump strained to reach even the far walls of the cavern before being sucked up in the moist air like the muted bumping of a water-soaked log against the side of a wooden dinghy. Swollen and softened by heat, humidity, and sulfurous lime, the planks were soft against her touch. She knew that beyond the turn in the tunnel and the heavy blocks of the statue wall, even an attentive listener would hear nothing. She wondered for a moment if she could scrape or scratch her way through the damp planking. But she had seen nothing in the bare cell to use as a tool and as she thrust a fingernail into the wood, it became firm a few millimeters beneath the surface.

Dreu stripped off her jacket, used it to wipe her forehead and the back of her neck, and dropped it to the floor beside the frame where she could find it if needed. The white shell beneath clung like plastic wrap to her chest and back and she tugged it away, fanning it against her dripping skin. From Katalin's comment, she guessed Adam had reached the church door as it was being closed and had to be aware she was inside. He would search the building and decide there must be another exit—one hidden somewhere behind the rock. The curators might know about the door behind the cross, but she doubted the Russian would have left her there if the cave were known to many. Budapest was famous for its underground caverns and Adam would begin to look for someone who knew the vast labyrinth of passageways that honeycombed the hill. She could think of no way to break out. While he tried to break in, she had to find a way to survive until she could again face her enemies and convince them to let her go.

When the Russian had opened the opposite door, he had released some of the heavier air. But it was beginning to rise, creeping up toward her elbows through the inky blackness like wet fog over a night swamp. She felt it dampen the fine hairs on her arms as it rose and knew she had only a few hours before it invaded her mouth and nose.

As the thicker gas reached her elbows, she felt it whisper against her skin, a tiny swirl that would have gone unnoticed had other senses not been so depressed by the acrid smell and complete blackness. She moved her right hand to the spot where she felt the tingle on the back of her arm and froze in place, sensing it again against her hand. The wooden door was still inches in front of her and she eased the hand forward until it hit a metal surface—the inner side of the mortise lock. Turning her palm toward the lock, she felt across its warm steel until her fingers found the keyhole. A tiny stream of air brushed against her fingertips and breathed hope into her body. She dropped to her knees before the door and pressed her lips against the steel lock, sucking stale, warm air through from the chamber beyond. Though the section of movable wall in the church fit snuggly against its stone frame, it was not airtight. If she could kneel upright until morning....

A white-hot needle suddenly punctured her left ankle as tiny spines latched onto her where her shin stretched along the wet floor. She pulled reflexively away from the lock, sucking in a mouthful of the gas, and immediately felt her mind fog and limbs weaken. The creature wriggled forward until forty tiny legs gripped her skin and slithered forward inside her pant leg. She felt again with her lips for the keyhole, sucking desperately for a lungful of the cleaner air. She expelled it with a choking cough, locked her mouth again against the tiny vent, and fought a spasm that started at the top of her chest and struggled downward.

She hadn't believed the Russian about the centipede. But like the darkness without light and the air without breath, everything he said was true, including the likelihood that she would not live to see morning. Her one chance was to remain immobile, appearing to the poisonous creature like another piece of the cavern wall. If it stung her again and its venom cramped her over, she would fall from her tiny platform into the endless blackness, and when Adam or the Russian came wouldn't matter. Her lips groped again for the keyhole and she shifted slightly against the stone floor. Instantly the tiny pincers again pierced her leg and molten liquid poured into her veins, moving with crippling speed toward her knee. She cried out against the slippery face of the door, slammed her fist hard against the crawling insect, and dug her nails into the soft wood to keep from slipping downward.

I must do this, she thought. I must survive this night. But for a brief moment she imagined that she was her brother who had broken away from the peloton, only to turn and find that no one was behind him. She quickly pushed the thought aside.

"I can do this," she murmured, then found herself whispering, "Oh, Adam, where are you?"

* * *

As soon as Adam realized she was no longer inside the Cave Church, his thought turned to who might know the system of caverns and fissures that lay beneath Gellert Hill. The wizened monk had followed him out onto the terrace, suspecting the American might be delusional and need help.

"She may have slipped out while I was distracted," Adam said to allay the old man's concerns. "I'll check back at the hotel. I'm sure she'll be waiting."

As the monk tottered back towards the glass doors, Adam turned with him and asked, "But just for my own information, who knows the underground caves in this area better than anyone else?"

The old man turned again and studied him with a sympathetic frown, then apparently decided to humor his visitor. "That would be Hamli Andris," he said. "He and his father have explored every cavern that can be reached."

"Where would I find him?"

The monk pointed across the terrace at the front of the Gellert Hotel. "He has a small shop up the first street past the hotel. It is called Bela Bartok Street. On the right side. He guides tourists who want to go into the caves."

Adam pulled two ten thousand forint notes from his pocket and handed them to the monk. "For you and the church," he said and the man bowed deeply and pulled the bills to his chest.

"*Köszönöm,*" he said gratefully. "Thank you!"

Seventy dollars well spent if this Andris can help, Adam thought.

* * *

The shop was not hard to find, with "Cave Tours" displayed in large red letters across the top of the main window. Photos of smiling people in spelunking gear covered the glass. The interior was divided into two sections: a front reception where a woman Adam guessed to be in her mid-thirties sat behind a simple desk, and a rear room through an open archway where helmets, lamps and assorted caving gear filled metal racks and hung from the walls. A thin older man with brown leather skin, rheumy eyes, and hair the color of dusty cotton sat in a corner against the windows, chewing contentedly on the long stem of a burl pipe. Adam had seen men like him before: old fishermen who could no longer go to sea but sat each afternoon on the pier in Northeastern fishing villages, waiting for the lobster boats to return with the day's catch.

Adam glanced quickly around the shop. "Is Mr. Halmi Andris here this morning?" he asked the woman behind the desk.

She smiled apologetically. "No. Andris has taken a group into the caves today." Her English was excellent, but heavy with the deep throatiness of Eastern Europe. "You are interested in a tour?"

"Actually, I'm interested in learning what I can about the caves," he said, fighting the urge to show his desperation. He couldn't afford another Hungarian who thought he was just a confused or delusional tourist. "Is there someone else who knows them well that I could talk to this morning?"

The woman nodded at the old man in the corner. "Andris is my husband. This is Andris' father. He is Hamli Vilmos. He knows the caves very well—maybe better than Andris. There are places we do not go now."

Adam turned to the old man, who continued to lean into the corner chewing on his pipe.

"May I ask you some questions about the caves?" Adam asked and the man looked questioningly at the woman behind the desk.

"He speak only English only when he wishes," she said, moving around the desk and bringing her chair with her. "But he understands very well." She was a plain, sturdy woman with short brown hair, dressed in canvas pants and a long-sleeved working shirt.

"I am Emese," she said, "and I will help you." She translated Adam's request while she planted the chair in front of Vilmos for Adam and pulled another from across the small room for herself.

Old Vilmos said something in Hungarian, a shine in his watery eyes showing that he had been waiting all morning for just this moment.

"He would like to tell you about the caves," she said. "What do you wish to know?"

As Adam had climbed the street to the shop, he had decided that if he found Halmi Andris, he would tell him directly about Dreu's disappearance and of his suspicion that there were hidden passages inside the Cave Church. Being vague would cost time, and time was something he didn't have. If they thought him crazy, he would be no worse off than he was now.

"I have a strange story to tell you, Mr. Halmi," he said. "This morning a friend went into the Cave Church to meet a woman from the government. The church was unlocked at eight o'clock for the meeting and I waited outside." He paused to let Emese translate but the old man nodded that he understood.

"The woman from the government locked the church from inside while I was watching," Adam continued. "But when an old monk came to open the church at nine for visitors, I went in with him and the church was empty."

The shine in the old man's eyes dimmed and his jaw locked more tightly around the pipe stem.

"I asked the monk if there was another door from the church and he said there was none. He also assured me there were no hidden doors or rooms inside the church. I came to ask you if you know of any caves that might have hidden entrances into the church."

Emese began an explanation but the senior Hamli held up a hand, removed his pipe, scraped vigorously at the bowl with what looked like a small, flat-head screwdriver, and banged it against the edge of a large brass bowl that sat beside his chair. He drew a pouch of tobacco from his shirt pocket, tamped a wad of moist strands into the bowl with the back of the scraper, and puffed quietly without lighting it. After a few moments he asked in clear English, "The woman who was meeting—she was with the government?"

"Yes. She sometimes works as a hostess for visiting officials from other countries."

"And was your friend speaking to her about the government?" Emese sat back and let the old man talk.

"No," Adam said. "But about a meeting the woman had with an American official who was recently in Budapest."

"And the woman and your friend did not come out from the church?"

"No. And a man was with them. He looked like he might be a guard for the government woman."

Halmi Vilmos rocked thoughtfully in his chair, then spoke in Hungarian and Emese shook her head, indicating she didn't like the question. Vilmos tossed his head and turned toward Adam, leaving her out of the conversation.

"What did the woman do for the American official?" he asked.

Adam smiled thinly. "She entertained him in his room. Now he is being blackmailed."

"Blackmailed?" He shook his head, indicating he didn't understand the word.

"*Zsarolásnak!*" Emese explained and her father-in-law sat again in silence, his face becoming more agitated. Then he spit into the container beside the chair and growled "Do you know of the Russian?"

"The Russian? Or of the Russians?" Adam asked.

"No—a man we call 'the Russian.'"

Adam shook his head.

"He is a very bad man in Budapest. Maybe the worst criminal," Vilmos said, spitting again into the spittoon.

"Why do you ask about the Russian?" Adam asked, the urgent tension in his chest tightening another degree.

Emese inserted herself back into the conversation while Vilmos nodded to show agreement.

"During the war, the Germans used the cave for the sick soldiers. They made a—what do you call it? To go from one room to another?"

"Door?"

"No--longer than a door."

"Hallway? Passage?"

"*Igen*! A passage to another small cave. Then to the outside. When the church was made, the passage was closed."

"What does this have to do with the Russian?"

She nodded. "Many of the workers who closed the…the passage when the church was made were men who worked for the Russian. He made them make a way into the other cave for him to use. Then he made the workmen disappear. Only the Russian knows the door. When someone here disappears, they say he has gone to the cave of the Russian."

"And the passage to the outside? Does anyone know where it is?"

Vilmos answered. "No one knows where the passage is. Perhaps it goes first through other caves."

"And there is no way into these caves—other than through these hidden doors?" Adam was feeling time slip away and was no closer to getting to Dreu, but the old man wouldn't be hurried. He sat expressionless, his red eyes fixed on Adam. Then he asked, "Who is this friend who went to the church?"

"She is trying to solve a crime of women who are being killed," Adam said, beginning to show his impatience. "I work with her and she is my friend. A very good friend."

Vilmos again sat without speaking, drawing long breaths of tobacco-flavored air through the pipe, then asked, "Do you work for the American government?"

"Indirectly. We try to help solve problems for the government. But we do not work for them officially."

Vilmos nodded at the explanation. "The Russian is a very dangerous man," he said. "One of our own officials—a good man—he tried to stop what the Russian does. Last week…" the old man threw both hands up in a gesture of resignation, "…he disappeared."

Adam sat back in his chair, feeling the need to move—to do *something*. "If I go to the police…?"

Vilmos smiled cynically. "Some police might help. Some will give you to the Russian."

"Is there any other way into the chamber?"

Vilmos chewed resolutely on the pipe stem. “Do you ever go into caves?” he asked finally.

Adam smiled nervously. “No. I used to be a pilot. I prefer to be above the ground.”

“There is a way,” Vilmos said and Adam again leaned toward the old man. “But it is very dangerous. Only one man I know has gone.”

“Through the caves?”

“Yes. And through the water.”

Adam’s pulse drummed an extra beat. When he’d taken swimming lessons as a boy in Nebraska, he’d learned that he had the buoyancy of a suit of armor and always felt like he was wearing one when in the water. He had finally learned to stay afloat, but for as short a time as absolutely necessary. When the Unit sent him through Special Forces training before putting him in the field, he was sure they’d given him an unearned pass on swimming.

“Like cave diving?” he asked. “With scuba?”

“Scuba?” Emese asked and Adam held one hand to his face and patted his back to represent a mask and tanks.

Vilmos shook his head. “*Nem, nem*!” He drew a deep breath and appeared to dive forward in the chair, arms in front of him.

“You just hold your breath and swim?” Adam asked, feeling the chill he knew the answer would bring.

“*Igen*!” Vilmos nodded, taking another deep breath and holding his nose.

“For how long?”

Vilmos shrugged. “*Tiz masodperc*. Ten seconds.”

“Just ten seconds?”

The old man nodded and held his hands up in front of him, explaining in Hungarian.

“Maybe more than that, but it is very narrow,” Emese said. “No more than a meter wide.”

“Three feet,” Adam muttered, the chill descending his spine. With the loss of his eye, he had learned to compensate by developing an exaggerated turn of the head, practicing a lesson he had tried to drum into the heads of student pilots when he was instructing. “Be aware of everything around you. Always keep your head on a swivel.” Two conditions compromised that ability—limited light and tight spaces. Despite his efforts to resist, he had become mildly claustrophobic.

“Why has only one man done this?” he asked.

The old man frowned and shook his head, speaking through tightened lips.

“My friend found a room with locked doors. No good air and the smell of death. He knew he found the room of the Russian.”

“Can someone take me to the place? To where the water goes through?”

The old Hungarian again sucked for a few moments on his pipe without answering. Then he pushed forward out of the chair and stood stiffly.

“I will take you,” he said. “To get to the water is not hard. To get into the cave is hard. To come back from the cave?” He shrugged dramatically. “Who can say?”

THIRTY-ONE

Emese did her best to dissuade the old man from taking Adam into the caves. He was now seventy, she said, and arthritic from a life spent in the damp underground. He hadn't been back into the caverns for ten years and she reminded him of the physical strain that had forced him permanently to the surface. But when the old Hungarian wouldn't be moved and assured her he remembered his way beneath Gellert Hill as well as he did through his own home, she relented. With Adam's impatient urging, she helped him gather the needed supplies: a long coil of white, nine millimeter rope; helmets with head lamps; leather gloves; a small oxygen canister that looked like an aluminum water bottle with a snap-on rubber tube; and swimmer's goggles and short fins.

"For the water," Vilmos said, holding up the goggles. "It is hot. You will want these for your eyes." He inspected Adam's shirt, jeans and loafers and found a pair of red and blue coveralls in the back of the shop. "We will sometimes crawl and there is mud," he said. "But when you swim, only your—" He didn't know the word for underwear and turned to Emese, but Adam filled in the blank and the old man nodded.

Emese also changed into coveralls, closed the shop and insisted on being part of the expedition. They followed Vilmos through a narrow alley that ran along the side of the Gellert Hotel, a high grated fence separating them from the outdoor baths that filled the rear gardens. At its end, they turned back down the gradual slope of the main road toward the Cave Church. The old Hungarian tottered forward like an aging tortoise and Adam had the urge to lift him bodily and carry him toward the shrine. He had been in Vilmos' shop for less than thirty minutes but it seemed like an eternity. If Dreu was trapped somewhere beneath that hill....

Before meeting the lane that had taken Adam to the church terrace, the old man turned up concrete steps to a paved path that mounted the hill through a heavily wooded park. With Emese holding one arm, he led them halfway up the slope and stopped long enough to ensure they were alone, then left the path and struggled up the rocky side of the hill into thick brush. Just out of view of the path he paused beside a gray stone outcropping and pushed aside a tangled pile of dead branches, uncovering the opening of a pit the size of a manhole.

Adam stepped cautiously to the edge and looked down into the blackness.

"We go in here?" he asked, looking skeptically at Vilmos.

"Not too far down. Seven meters."

"How do we get out?"

"We come out another way," the old man said. "But it is one kilometer to get out. If we go in here, we are close to where we want to be."

Vilmos fixed on a head lamp and nodded for Adam to do the same.

"I will go first," Emese said. "Then you will have some light. You will be second. Then Vilmos." Her father-in-law ran the rope around a nearby tree, looped it about the woman's chest with a bowline, and she scrambled backward into the darkness. Adam followed the white circle of her lamp against the side of the pit as she descended and saw it stop twenty feet below. The old man had planted himself like a stubborn bulldog and lowered her downward with surprising strength. At the bottom, she gave the rope three quick tugs and Vilmos pulled it back up. As he circled Adam with the rope and swiftly tied the knot, Adam looked questioningly down at Emese's distant lamp.

"How do you get down?" he asked. The Hungarian pointed at the tree, held up the rope, and gestured that he would lower himself.

"Okay. As long as you're coming," Adam said in partial jest and sat at the edge of the opening. Twisting onto his stomach as he had seen the woman do, he grasped the rope with both gloved hands and wriggled backward, trusting his weight to the tree and the tough old Hungarian.

At the bottom, Emese stood in a cavern the size of a large bedroom and while Vilmos descended, the two cast their lights around the rock chamber. Streaks of caramel and vivid lemon flowed down the limestone walls where ground water seeped into the cave and washed minerals over the smooth cream-colored stone. The cavern had seen few visitors and the ceiling hung heavy with mineral straws as thick as Adam's fingers. As he probed the darkness with his lamp, aside from the pit down which he had come, Adam could see no other way out of the chamber.

"There," Emese said, directing her beam at a dark spot no larger than an oven door at the base of the far wall. "We will go through there. I will again go first and you can follow. It is not far."

With Vilmos on the cave floor, Emese crossed to the opening and wriggled into the passage. Adam swallowed hard, drew in a deep breath and snaked after her, arms stretched in front as the tunnel closed around him. A few feet in front of his face, Emese's booted toes scraped at the wet limestone as she slithered forward, then stopped for an instant as she knelt, then rose to her feet. They had been in the passage for only two or three minutes.

"Not as bad as I expected," he said as he stood beside her and cast his lamp about a chamber that was five or six times the size of the first. A larger passage entered the cavern to his left and he could feel slight movement in the heavy air that smelled faintly of mold and sulfur. He gestured toward the head-high tunnel. "And that one looks much easier."

Vilmos struggled to his feet beside him and took his arm, redirecting their lights to the far side of the cavern where the beams reflected with an emerald glow off the surface of a small pool.

"We will go out through the passage—but first, you go there," he said. "If your friend is in the room of the Russian, you must go through the water."

They gathered beside the pool, Adam kneeling to stick a hand into the steaming green liquid. Their lights showed it to be about the width and depth of a large Jacuzzi and the water was Jacuzzi hot, barely tolerable to his bare hand. A passage the size of the tunnel through which he had just crawled appearing as a dark hole where the pool met the limestone wall.

"The water is forty degrees," the old man said. "Do you wish to do this? From now, it will be very dangerous. I have not been into the cave but can only tell you what I have been told."

Adam quickly ran the temperature conversion in his head. Forty times nine, divided by five. Seventy-two…plus thirty-two. The water was one hundred four degrees. His mind flooded with alternatives, suggesting reasons not to plunge into a dark hole in a steaming subterranean pool. No one seemed sure how far he would have to swim, or what awaited him at the other end. He was certain Dreu had disappeared from the church through some entrance into the underground system of caves, but Katalin and the guard may have taken her through to a hillside exit and out into the city. If she had been free to do what she wished, he would have heard from her by now—so she was being held. But on the other side of that hot tub? She could be anywhere in the city by now, or on her way to another part of the country. But instinct told him she was there. And if in the cave of the Russian, she may not have much time.

"Tell me how to do this," he said to Vilmos and the old man gestured for him to undress. When stripped to a pair of tight boxers, he was fitted with goggles, the short fins, and a headlamp removed from his helmet.

"The fins make you move," Emese said. "We will tie both ends of the rope to you—one to your waist and one to your leg." She pointed at his ankle. "You will carry the air bottle. If the cave is closed except for the water, there will be much gas. When you get there, take a little breath. If you are choking, turn on the bottle and breathe with the tube."

"And if I find her?"

"We will keep the rope tight. When you want to come out, pull three times—very fast—and we pull you back. If she is there, tie the rope around her feet, make her take a large breath from the bottle, close her eyes and hold nose. We will pull her by her feet. Then you, the same way with the other end of the rope."

Vilmos raised his hands in front of his chest, dipping them downward in a forward scooping motion, his voice animated as he looked directly at Adam.

"The man who went to the cave of Russian said the passage is not far. But it goes down, then up. So do not be afraid if you are going down."

Adam smiled thinly. Swimming in hot water, tight places, not knowing what was at the other end—if there was another end? What was there to be afraid of?

He wished he were the kind of agent he read about in novels who relished danger and shrugged off the prospect of looming death. But he had found himself to be one who recognized fear when it came and had to crush it with his will. He had learned when the crane came through the canopy of his jet trainer, killing the student in the front seat and taking his eye, that he was motivated less by courage than by shame. He had instinctively reached for the handles of the ejection seat, pulled his knees together and thrust his head back firmly against the headrest. But before he could squeeze, he realized he couldn't leave the plane and let the student's body plummet to the desert floor and be incinerated by the inevitable explosion. If he ejected, facing his squadron commander would be difficult enough—the young man's family, impossible. Dreu may not be at the other end of that passage. But if he made no attempt—and if she didn't show up again—he knew the shame of failing to try would be more than he could bear. He remembered his father's favorite John Wayne expression. "Courage is being scared to death, but saddling up anyway."

The insistent voice of Emese pushed its way into his thoughts. "Sit in the water first," she advised. "When you are not so hot, you can go."

The heat bit sharply as he slid into the pool, reddening his skin and quickening his pulse as his heart fought to pump cooling blood to his extremities. He settled in up to his neck, gradually adjusting to the temperature. Pulling the goggles tight across his eyes, he pushed across the pool to the entrance of the passage and gulped a deep breath. Giving the Hungarians a quick nod, he plunged into the dark opening, kicking forward with the fins and clasping the air bottle in both hands in front of him.

The light was surprisingly bright against the limestone walls of the tunnel and he had no difficulty sinking downward along the sloping floor. Almost immediately it began to flatten but the water became thick with floating particles and he found himself pushed blindly forward, counting the seconds. Without warning, the air bottle hit something solid and his right hand slipped past it into what felt like a small cloth sack. His pulse quickened and he fumbled blindly at the obstructing object.

With a jarring thump, his heart skipped a beat and most of the trapped air in his lungs exploded from his nostrils in a burst of bubbles. His hand had wrapped around what he knew to be a swollen foot and ankle wrapped in a floating pant leg.

THIRTY-TWO

The news team at NBS was grouped around its own conference table selecting and sequencing the evening news when the lead story suddenly changed. As if on cue, four cell phones went off simultaneously and as each was answered, pieces of the headline spilled into the room.

"There's been a bombing at PAX News!" one of the editors with a close friend at the rival network exclaimed.

"Most of the news staff are dead!" another choked, barely able to get the sentence out through a hand that was tightly pressed over her mouth.

"Chase Rayborn was one of them," a feature reporter who dated a cameraman at PAX added. "It just happened.... Just now!"

Grant Huston started toward the outer newsroom as two plain-clothes officers from the NYPD pushed into the news complex and made their way to the conference room. They flashed their badges, asked the staff to leave everything where it was, and began to usher the team out onto the news floor. Huston stopped the first of the officers.

"You got here fast! What the hell's going on?"

"We were doing weapons training at John Jay on West 58th when dispatch called," the tall Latino who introduced himself as Lieutenant Ramirez said. "About a block away. Any packages been delivered to this room this morning?"

The team glanced around and shook their heads.

"Then step out please and we'll be with you in a minute," Ramirez said.

As he led his team into the outer room where rows of partitioned cubicles surrounded an open area with four wide layout tables, Huston noted two other uniforms guarding the doors from the corridor. Another plainclothes team was escorting people from the glass offices around the perimeter. Ramirez followed him from the conference room, checked with his colleagues to ensure everyone was gathered in the main room, and glanced at his watch.

"About ten minutes ago there was an explosion in the offices of PAX News," he announced loudly, pausing briefly as the ripple of exclamations and questions passed across the room.

"All we know so far is that there are seven reported dead and about twice that number injured. The cause of the explosion is uncertain, but it may have been one or more packages delivered to the newsroom during the morning or lunch hour. First of all, is anyone aware of any unopened packages that came in yesterday or this morning?"

An arm rose near the back of the assembled workers. "We had a couple of cartons of paper delivered this morning that haven't been opened," a male voice said.

Ramirez signaled one of the uniforms over to the employee. "Show Sergeant Bentz where the boxes are and the rest of you, please vacate the floor until we can do a thorough walk-through. If you want to go to the cafeteria on seven, we'll give you the all clear when we've swept the area."

"Terrorists going after the media," an assistant editor beside Grant muttered as they moved with the group toward the elevators. "Sounds like Charlie Hebdo all over again."

"We've all been covering those attacks," Huston said. "So why PAX?" He knew the answer, and knew that the attack had not come from WIS. While the others crowded toward the elevators, he walked to the end of the corridor and into the stairwell, moving up the concrete steps instead of down. He had a small office in the executive suite on eleven—a symbolic gesture from management. Anyone from outside asking to see Grant Huston was directed to his working office on the news floor on eight, but the space on eleven provided an escape from the constant pandemonium of the newsroom.

If the police weren't clearing the executive offices, he needed to find a quiet place to think—and get to a locked drawer in his private desk. The corridor and offices on eleven were empty, but it seemed to be only precautionary while the police scoured the eighth floor and assembled the staff on seven. He entered his small office, closed the door quietly, and dropped heavily into the plush leather desk chair.

The moment he had heard about the blast, he knew what it meant. That psychopath Triplett had gone after Rayborn. But what did the Idaho rancher know? Had the PAX anchor told him about Grant's role in finding the tattooed hacker? And was he next? The questions had been eating at Huston like an aggressive cancer since he'd contacted Gio Levanzo about setting up another target. Chase had sworn on his mother's grave that no one else knew about the wager—that if they could extort Triplett into giving up his mad crusade, no one could trace any of this back to Huston.

"He'll believe it's me," Rayborn had said during their meeting at the Rum House. "But he knows he can't do anything to me because I'll make it clear the videos go public if I should have some surprise accident." But for some reason Triplett believed Rayborn was no longer a threat and could be eliminated with impunity. Grant's best guess was that Rayborn had been honest about not talking about the wager. No one else knew he was involved. In which case, he needed to silence the crazed Triplett before this went further.

He unlocked the bottom left-hand drawer of his desk and fished in the back for an envelope that held two small thumb drives and a mailing address for Sandra Triplett. He had already planned what he would do if it came to this. Generic envelopes with no finger prints on the packaging or on the drives. The woman Levanzo had hired was told to stream the video to a computer Rayborn had purchased specifically for that purpose, then destroyed. There should be nothing in the videos that could be traced back to either of them. After his broadcast tonight Grant would drive the hundred miles north to Hartford and mail the packages from Connecticut. One to Triplett's wife, and one that included the recorded meeting of the Order of King's Mountain. That one would go anonymously to the FBI's Washington offices. He knew the revelation that Triplett and his Order had planned domestic terrorist attacks to frighten the public into supporting the candidacy of Carter Graves would torpedo the Graves campaign. But if Rayborn had been killed, all bets were off anyway. Huston owed Chase Rayborn at least this much. And by Wednesday or Thursday evening's broadcast, he should have one helluva headline.

* * *

When Adam's mind registered that his hand was wrapped around the pulpy limb of a corpse, he jerked the hand back along his chest to the rope on his waist and tugged frantically. The liquid that surrounded him felt suddenly like warm syrup, thick and heavy against his sides and face.

For a paralyzing moment, the ropes remained slack. The thought flashed through his mind that out of fear or complicity, the Hungarians had simply done what they knew the Russian wanted—eliminated the American man as the Russian had disposed of the woman by taking them to the place where the troublesome disappear. Adam reached desperately for the sides of the passage and struggled to push himself backward, but the fins now became water brakes and his hands slipped uselessly against the polished limestone. Then the ropes tightened and he felt the warm flow of water as he was dragged backward out of the flooded passage.

When his back broke the surface, he struggled to his feet in the hot pool, gulped a deep breath, and tore the goggles from his eyes. As he shook the water from his face, he turned until his lamp illuminated the startled faces of Vilmos and Emese.

"There's a body in the passage," he panted, pointing toward the dark opening. "I ran into the foot."

Emese raised a hand across her mouth. "*Hulla!*" she gasped, turning her light on Vilmos. The old man's creased face furrowed even more deeply, his dark eyes narrowing to black slits in the shadows cast by the lamps. He replied with two quick words.

"Your friend?"

Adam shook his head. The instant he had touched the ankle, his thoughts had collapsed into a single question. Is this her? And equally quickly, he knew it wasn't. The ankle was wrapped in a stocking and was heavy-boned. Probably male. And had been in the water more than a few hours.

"I think it's a man," he said. "Been in the water a day or more."

"We must get the police," Emese said, turning her headlamp to illuminate the passage on the far side of the cavern.

Adam shook his head. "We don't have time. That would mean hours—and if she's in the cave, she may not have much time."

"What can we do?" she said, her voice becoming frantic.

Adam looked at Vilmos who stood staring at the murky tunnel with the rope still dangling from his rough hands. The old Hungarian raised his eyes to Adam's, waiting for him to suggest what Vilmos was not willing to commit to on his behalf.

"Let's pull the body out," Adam said, his heart again rattling his chest as he crushed the fear that came with the words.

"Will it come?" the old man wanted to know.

"I think it moved forward when I bumped it," Adam said. "If we can get it out, I can see if I can get to the other cave while Emese goes for the police."

"If you go back, we will pull you out," Vilmos said. "If it comes out, we can wait until you try again for your friend. If she is there, then we will have more to tell the police." Emese began to protest but he silenced her with a raised hand.

"If this is the Russian," Vilmos said darkly, "we must know what we are going to do before we do it." He scanned Adam quickly with his light and tossed him a pair of the gloves. "Where is the bottle?" he asked in Hungarian, holding his hands in front of him as if wrapped around the canister.

In what Adam knew had been a moment of panic, he had released the air bottle when he grasped for the pull rope.

"I'll get it," he said and pushed through the heavy water to the mouth of the passage. "Be ready. It will be only a few seconds before I get to it. When I pull, wait for one second. I will need to get my hands on both the bottle and the leg before you pull me out." He looked back and both were standing grim-faced with ropes in hand, braced at the edge of the pool.

The water in the tunnel had become thick with floating particles and he felt his way back to the bottom of the sump. His gloved hands met the bottle and the bloated ankle at the same instant and he pulled the canister back beside his face, reached for the rope at his waist and, with three sharp tugs, grasped both the canister and the soft pulp of the leg. Immediately he felt the pull against his hips and ankle. The body moved with him, then seemed to bind until he feared he would pull the leg free and leave the rest of the body blocking the passage. His lungs screamed for release as the tension on the ropes stretched him against the top of the tunnel. Then he was moving again, but uncertain how much of the corpse was coming with him.

Adam remained submerged until the Hungarians had pulled him most of the way across the pool. He released the ankle and fought to his feet, looking down at what floated in front of him in the pit. The body was intact and fully clothed in a dark suit that stretched under the pressure of the bloated corpse. The head and face were an unrecognizable mass of pasty gray, a trail of dark hair floating back toward the passage.

With a shudder that rippled from his shoulders into the soles of his feet, he steered the body to the edge where Vilmos grasped the ankles with gloved hands and pulled it onto the limestone floor. Emese turned and took a few steps back into the darkness. Vilmos called her back.

"Elek Goda," he said. Emese glanced down at the corpse, then again turned quickly away.

"Elek Goda?" Adam asked.

"He was the minister for finance," Emese said from back in the darkness. "He was very loud against crime in Budapest. He talked against corruption and was a very big enemy of the Russian."

"The man who disappeared?"

"Three days ago," Emese said.

"I'm going back," Adam said, moving again across the pool. "You decide what you want to do but be ready on the ropes." He crouched until neck deep in the hot bath, drew a deep breath, and plunged again into the dark opening.

THIRTY-THREE

The air sucked through the keyhole provided just enough stale oxygen to keep Dreu lucid and she was determined that she would not die in the black hellhole. Somehow, she believed, she could persuade the Russian to let her go. Or Adam would find her before the man returned. She had no idea how—or what he was doing to learn where she was. But she had witnessed his knowing exactly what to do when things seemed beyond salvage, and had been the beneficiary of his uncanny ability to show up at exactly the right moment. And the emotion that surged through her as she clung with her fingernails to the pulpy wood of the door was not fear. It was anger. She was *not* going to allow him to find her dead—to spend the rest of his life punishing himself for allowing her to take on a job he thought he should have done himself. She would not let him believe that she hadn't been equal to it. Because she *had* been! She had learned what he would never have been able to tease out of Reka or Katalin—that Gio Levanzo arranged the blackmailing and had eliminated the girls he feared might talk. They also now knew that Levanzo had used a Hungarian connection called the Russian to manage Budapest during the NATO meeting.

"Don't let the fear of what hasn't yet happened keep you from preparing for what will," he drilled into her, and two things hadn't yet happened. She wasn't dead, and the Russian hadn't come back. Aside from being sealed in an inky pit full of stinging insects and poison gas, she had done just what they had planned, and done it well. His job was to be the body guard and she was going to survive until he took care of his part of the assignment.

If the Russian came back first? What might convince the man to let her go? As soon as she heard the key in the door she would stand and face him as he entered, looking as calm and undamaged as she could manage and protecting the life-saving secret of the key hole. If he decided the cave wasn't going to kill her, he might take her out to where she could scream for help or try to make a break for it.

She was running that thought through her head when the rock cell began to glow, first with a faint greenish light, then more brightly in hazy white. Despite her commitment to live, Dreu's first thought was that this was what death must be like—the light she had heard described and a feeling of drifting somewhere beyond her body. Her eyes had been closed, every bit of her ebbing strength focused on pulling air through the hole in the steel plate, holding it as long as she could, and exhaling through her nose. The burning in her leg fought for her attention, vying with a deep bruise on her right thigh. As she clung in the blackness to the wooden door, another of the crawling creatures had wriggled onto her leg. She had smashed it with the heel of her hand, struck in the same spot where the other had died with such force that she had killed the second centipede before it could sting. But the blow left a bone-deep bruise that amplified the aching cramps as she struggled to remain still and braced upright on her knees.

The light first glowed against her closed lids and when she cracked her eyes open to the sulfurous air, remained a soft green shimmer until it appeared to burst from the floor behind her in a white flash. The voice too seemed to be a summons into the next world—a soft, echoing "Dreu" that begged her to turn, but not so convincingly that she was willing to pull away from her source of life. Then she felt his hand on her shoulder, the light right beside her face, and his voice in her ear.

"You're going to be okay," he said and she heard the sucking sound of him pulling air through a tube.

"Here, breathe this." She felt the tube first against her cheek, then her lips. She sucked in a deep breath and the oxygen coursed through her body like a shot of adrenalin.

"We'll have to share the air," he said, lifting her to her feet. "And we need to hurry. There isn't much left in this thing. Listen to what I say." He pulled the tube back to his own mouth and drew another breath.

"I'm going to lead you to the pool and tie a rope around one of your ankles. Keep your feet tight together. I'll sit you in the pool and give you some air. Then, when I tell you, close your eyes and hold your nose. Keep your elbows to your sides and they'll pull you through. It will take about ten seconds. When they stop pulling, stand up. You'll be okay." He took the tube again for another breath as he eased her across the cave room. She sat beside the steaming water while he lashed a rope to her ankle, then gave her another draw on the air bottle while he repeated the instruction.

"The water's hot but you'll be okay. Keep your feet together and just slide into the pool. Hold your nose, arms tight against your sides, and they'll pull you through." She cringed as he lowered her into the hot water, holding the rope out of the pool while he gave her a final gulp of air. Then with three quick jerks on the rope, she felt it tighten and in that second, pulled her arms against her chest, pinched her nose and was underwater, sliding feet-first along the slippery bottom of the tube.

It happened so quickly and so strangely that Dreu still feared she might be passing into the afterlife—being drawn through a warm, watery canal to a new birth. Then the pressure on her ankle stopped and she lay motionless, immersed in the hot bath and struggling to remember what she had been told to do next.

"I've died and forgotten the instructions!" She found the thought strangely amusing, but she continued to squeeze her eyes shut and trap the air in her nose. There was splashing beside her and hands reached around her and pulled her upwards into cool air. As she opened her eyes, she stared again into a white beam. The arms wrapped her tightly and led her to the edge of the pool where she was eased into a sitting position. Hands gently eased her fingers away from her nose and a woman's voice said, "You are safe."

She risked a gulp of the air and found it moist but fresh, and she again closed her eyes and drew in a long, cleansing breath. The light shone brightly on the pool from which she had just emerged and as she watched in hazy confusion, a long form slid beneath the surface, then slowly stood to face her.

Adam pulled a set of goggles from his eyes and smiled a smile that could only be part of heaven, eyes that dripped more water than drained from his soaked face. He waded to her and lifted her up, wrapping her against his bare chest and kissing her neck.

A voice above and behind her spoke gruffly in Hungarian and the woman's voice followed.

"Vilmos says we must hurry. We will all leave the cave, then he will bring back the police. He says you should first be gone. He will say he found the body while he was exploring. Now—get on the clothes and we must go."

Adam's arms and the voices of the Hungarians jarred Dreu back into the world of the living. He released her and climbed from the pool, untied the rope that bound his own ankle and lifted her from the water. As he bent to untie her tether, he ran a gentle hand down her swollen calf.

"What happened?" he asked, tracking a red streak with his fingers to below her anklebone.

"Something bit me," she said, taking a limping step forward.

One of the other lamps turned to throw its circle of light against her leg. "It is very painful, but you will be better," the woman said. "Now, we must go."

As Adam hurriedly pulled on his clothes, shoes and coveralls, she glanced about the large cavern, gasping and shuddering involuntarily at the bloated form that lay a few yards away beside the pool. Adam took her arm. "I'll tell you about it as we go," he said. "And you can tell us all that happened in the church."

Across the cavern she could see the shadowy form of the woman moving toward a dark passageway. Adam turned her in front of him and followed, his own lamp lighting the floor ahead. Behind them where the old man remained, they heard the splash of the body being rolled back into the pool.

"I know who hired the girls in the U.S.," Dreu whispered to Adam. "And who killed them."

"You did a great job," he said as they followed the woman into a head-high cleft that descended deeper into the hillside. "Scared the life out of me, but you were perfect. Now it's time for us to go home. But we're going to need a new exit plan."

THIRTY-FOUR

The town hall format had been Clayton Mehrens' idea. Let the people say what was on their minds and have an open conversation about issues that really matter. But his staff insisted questions be screened in advance with no opportunity for follow-up. Though the campaign stop in Bettendorf, Iowa, wasn't being broadcast, media from all of the major news outlets followed the candidate like rats after the Pied Piper. Any little comment that fell outside of the Mehrens' norm would become the sound bite of the week. The staff wanted to give their candidate no opportunity to ad lib.

The senator had re-written his speech to address the bombing of PAX News, reminding his faithful, and the curious who had come to see what the man from Delaware was all about, that the attack simply placed an exclamation point after his consistent assertion that extremism in all of its manifestation could not be tolerated. But the answer was not to lash out blindly at an enemy that was impossible to separate from the innocents in the cities it occupied. Or to throw more American lives at a problem that hadn't changed in over a thousand years and was so culturally embedded that it probably wouldn't in another thousand. "The entire world now sees itself as victims of WIS," he said. "We must bring that world together to find a solution that doesn't exact such a price."

But his screeners hadn't accounted for the new level of fear and anger generated by this latest attack on American soil. The first approved questioner, a nineteen-year-old woman from Augustana College across the river in Illinois, chose not to ask about the growing disparity in income that had been the basis of her submission. Instead, she stepped to the mic and nervously asked what was foremost on everyone's minds.

"I'm a college sophomore and I'm concerned about the growing disparity in income and how wealth seems to be accumulating in the top one percent," she began, sticking with her original question. She then left it to say, "but more than anything, I'm frightened. And the money thing doesn't matter that much if you can't feel safe at home. I hear you say that we have to seek some international solution to WIS. But those people aren't a nation and don't care about sanctions or closed borders or tighter airport security. They're playground bullies who just love to beat up other kids and steal their lunch money. What will you do as president that will make a difference, beyond just talking about global cooperation?"

Having moved off script, the senator had no choice but to follow the question.

"Tell me," he said. "We've been involved in these wars for over a decade. Has that made you feel safer?"

"Right now, *nothing's* making me feel safer," the young woman said. "I don't even dare go to a college pep rally!"

"Fighting back at least makes us feel like we're doing *something*," someone shouted from elsewhere in the audience, followed by a smattering of applause.

"But does that something make any difference at all?" Mehrens answered. "Does it really make us safer?"

"Do we wait until they destroy an entire city?" another person called out. "We're losing lives anyway. I'd rather do it standing up instead of lying down." Heavier applause and some shouts of affirmation.

Mehrens held up his hands in an effort to quiet the crowd. "Let's give our people who have questions a chance to ask them."

"These *are* our questions!" a woman shouted from a few rows in front of him. "It's time we heard what you'll do about these attacks. What you'll do to stop the terrorists."

The crowd erupted with shouts of "Answer the question!" and "Let's get tough on WIS!"

An aide stepped to the senator's side and leaned into the mic. "If we can't have a civil discussion here, we'll have to bring this to a close," he said to a chorus of boos and shouts of "Answer the question!"

"I'm sorry then…," the aide said and Mehrens waved uneasily to the jeering crowd as he was ushered off the stage, imagining the headline on the ten o'clock news. "Terrorists strike PAX

News—Mehrens booed from stage for offering no solution."

THIRTY-FIVE

In her plush new lair in the Shenandoah Mountains, the Badger, in a loose T-shirt and panties, was snuggled in the inviting embrace of Gabriella Marzilli watching a talk show on afternoon television when a ribbon at the bottom of the screen announced the bombing of PAX News. She pulled away from her lover, sat stiffly on the edge of the sofa while a brief description of the carnage trailed across the screen, then swore under her breath. Without a word to Gabriella, she padded into a rear bedroom where her laptop sat on a bedside table.

Gabbi had missed the bulletin and scrambled after her. "I missed that," she said. "What did it say?"

"That sonofabitch Triplett did it," the Badger snarled back over her shoulder.

"Did what? I didn't read it."

"Killed that guy from PAX News. That Chase Rayborn." She yanked open the top drawer of a dresser and fumbled among the loose jumble of bras and panties, pulling out a small thumb drive.

"So what did it say?" Gabbi said from the doorway.

"Seven killed in a blast at PAX News, including evening anchor Chase Rayborn."

"So what makes you think it was Triplett?"

The Badger carried the drive to the bed where she flopped with her back against the headboard and opened the computer across her lap. "One of the other women in the Order—the one named LeAnn that I told you was doing the old guy when his wife was away? She told me Rayborn had been to the ranch about the time the Order got started. She thought maybe he had something to do with it."

"You haven't said anything about this before…."

"Didn't think about it. We never watch PAX and I didn't think of it 'til now. But this was Triplett. I'm sure of it."

Gabbi came over and flopped beside her on the bed. "What you gonna do?"

"I'm gonna scare the shit out of the old bastard. He's one

crazy sonofabitch and needs to know Rayborn wasn't the only one who's got his number. Makes me sick that I did what I did, and this has gotta stop."

"Do you think it was this Rayborn that got Gio and Tony to send you out there? They never said so."

The Badger shrugged. "Don't know. But I think Rayborn must have been the one who got the video. And Triplett had to get rid of him. That's what I'm thinking."

"Then he'll come after you...."

The Badger looked up at her and grinned. "Hell yes, he'll come after me. But first of all, he'll never find me. And second, I'll kill his sorry ass if he does. But he's gotta stop and that will only happen if he knows the video's still alive."

"How you gonna let him know?"

"Same way I let the news people know about the store bombings. I'm gonna send him a copy and bounce it off a WIS site in Syria and right into his lap. The guy's a stupid turd when it comes to technology. He'll never trace it and if he hires someone to try, they won't be able to trail it back to me."

"Maybe we oughta talk to Tony about this first."

The Badger sneered. "You gonna tell him you've been living out here with me while he's running his rackets in D.C.?"

Gabbi was silent as the Badger tapped aggressively at the keyboard, finishing with a sharp jab at the send button. "There, you maniac," she said. "You liked me enough the first time. Let's see how this feels the second time around!"

* * *

As soon as they were above ground, Adam stepped away from the Hungarians and placed an encrypted call to Fisher.

"I'm still handling things here," the woman said when she answered, her voice edged with strain and what Adam heard as worry.

"Any information about the Russian?" he asked.

"As you suspected, he has close ties with the Levanzo family here in Washington. Gio Levanzo keeps a yacht in Dubrovnik in

Croatia and the Russian often meets him there. They spend a week in various port cities in the Adriatic and no one knows exactly what they do. But they're obviously closely connected."

"When was Levanzo there last?" Adam asked.

"It's been nearly a year for Gio. But his son Tony was with the Russian on the yacht just a few months ago."

"Thanks," Adam said. "Now I need another favor. Mrs. Russell and I need to leave Hungary without crossing a border. And as soon as possible. I suspect by late tomorrow morning the Russian will be making a country-wide search for us and it sounds as though he has people everywhere, including with local and state police."

"Give me an hour," she said. "We've handled extractions from Hungary before and I think I know what we can do. As soon as you're able, drive toward the city of Pápa."

"Toward Pápa," he repeated.

"I'll call within an hour."

Vilmos had a cab waiting when he hung up and ten minutes later they were back in the locked shop near the Gellert Hotel. While Emese treated Dreu's leg with an antihistamine tablet and ice pack, Adam returned the car. From the rental agency, he walked ten blocks until certain he wasn't being followed, then returned by cab to Hamli's Cave Tours.

"We need to get to Pápa," he told the old Hungarian. "Do you know how I can get a car that we can leave there?"

"I will take you," Emese said. "It is two hours. I can be there, then here again tonight."

"What about the body in the cave?"

"Vilmos has a different plan," she said. "Tomorrow Andris takes two Swiss into the caves. They will find the body for the first time and will call police."

* * *

Twenty minutes west of Budapest on the E66 with the sun no more than a pale glow below the horizon in front of them, Adam received the call.

“Can you get to Pápa?” the woman asked.

“Yes. We’re on our way.”

“There’s an air base north of the city with an International Heavy Airlift Wing. The unit supports strategic airlift operations throughout Europe, with personnel from half a dozen countries. They fly C-17 Globemasters and have a maintenance unit of fifty Boeing personnel. The unit leader is a man named David Sanders. He will meet you at the main gates of the base. Are you getting this?”

“Sanders at the main gates of the airbase north of Pápa.”

“Right. When do you expect to be there?”

He turned to Emese. “How long to Pápa?”

“Maybe one hour,” she said and Adam relayed the message.

“Very good. We have a C-37 on its way down from Ramstein. It’s bringing in a change of seven personnel for the maintenance unit, plus two people who will sign off the base in your places tomorrow, then drive out of the country. We’ll fly you out as soon as the C-37 can refuel and though you’ll have to stop again for fuel at Lakenheath in England, you’ll be back here late tonight.”

“Perfect,” Adam said. “By the time I get there, I need all of the information you can give me on Giordano Levanzo.”

“Anything specific?”

“Yes. I want to know everyone he’s met with over the past six months.”

THIRTY-SIX

The Gmail address on the message was "RatCatcher" and the attached file replayed for Dan Triplett in vivid detail his armchair calisthenics with the voracious Badger. The file and how it was received had her vicious claws all over them. He reached for the mouse to delete and close, but his hand froze above the pad as the screen again brightened and he saw himself standing in front of the assembled members of the Order. Wade Sumler stood beside him and was outlining the plan of attack for the BestMart bombings. Triplett swore through gritted teeth and spun in his chair toward the door of the study where, only months before, he had met with the late Chase Rayborn.

"*Dwayne*!" he shouted through the quiet of the empty lodge.

A moment later his former Special Forces teammate stood leaning against the door frame.

"Look at this," Triplett muttered, swinging away from the desk to give Cargile a clear view of the screen.

Dwayne pushed away from the frame. "Where'd that come from?"

"The Badger must have taken it. And I'd bet all of Sandy's damned fortune that she kept a copy of everything."

"*Jesus*! She's got us all on that thing!"

"Time to close up shop here," Triplett said. "We've got to find the bitch and get rid of her and this video."

"Who else'll have it?" Dwayne asked. "We thought we had all of Rayborn's copies but maybe someone else is in this with them. You think Rayborn found that little whore on his own?"

"That's what we've gotta find out. But if it's been sent anywhere else, the Feds could be swarming all over the camp any time now. We'll use your place over by Judith Gap 'til we figure out where we need to go. Anybody else know about your cabin?"

"No—bought it under another name, just for something like this. How're you going to find the Badger?"

Triplett leaned back in his chair. "Been thinking about that since we got the copies from Rayborn. I was afraid we might have reason to track her down. I think I may have what we need here." He pulled open a file drawer in the desk and lifted out a thin green folder. "Amber Nims" was scrawled across the tab with a black marker.

"She leave a forwarding address?" Dwayne smirked.

"Gabriella Marzilli," Triplett said.

"Who the hell's that?"

"The Badger's cellmate at Aliceville. Word is they got pretty close, and Marzilli picked her up when she got out of prison."

"You think they're together?"

"I'd put money on it."

"And you know where this Marzilli is?"

"No. But I think I know who does. You go start pulling our stuff together and get the best of the salvaged cars we have out there. Gather up what weapons we can hide pretty well and meet me at the car in twenty minutes. We'll drop our things off at your place in Montana. Then we're headed east."

* * *

Adam asked Emese to stop a quarter mile from the gate of the Hungarian airbase and, much to her discomfort, he and Dreu embraced and thanked the woman. Moments later when she dropped them at the guard station, he handed her what remained of the ten thousand dollars he had carried into the country to allow them to work in cash. She pushed it back across the seat.

"We were pleased to help you," she said. "We all want what is good." Adam and Dreu slid from the car, leaving the money on the seat.

A fiftyish man in tan slacks and a green windbreaker stood beside the guard shack, hands thrust deep in his pockets. As they approached the gate, he came forward to introduce himself as David Sanders. He had them stand outside the small building while he signed them in with the guard as Brian and Tanvi Russell and guided them to a parking area off the main drive where they squeezed into a tiny white Opel.

"The top selling car in Hungary," he said glancing over at his tall passengers with their knees tucked beneath their chins. They turned beside a grass field where a static display of four Russian Migs sat on concrete blocks. "I could have purchased a Fiat," he said with an apologetic smile, "but this car had more room."

Sanders knew his assignment and was silent as he drove them directly to a primitive base operations building and ushered them inside. A woman he introduced as his wife Becky met them with a bag of clothing for Dreu. She smiled as she gave her guest a quick once-over.

"We were told size eight," she said. "But they forgot to tell us you were an eight-long. The skirt's going to be short."

While Dreu changed in the single bathroom, Adam stepped with Sanders out onto the concrete apron that backed the operations center. Down a wide taxiway to his right, two giant C-17s sat near what he judged to be a crew ready room, a plain block building just off the edge of the apron with a wide walk to the ramp. Just above the horizon, landing lights flashed on and he heard the distant whine of jet engines throttling back on approach.

"That will be your plane," Sanders said. "We tried to get a couple of replacements that look something like you. We'll take them out in the morning when a new set of guards is on duty."

"Warn them to be careful," Adam cautioned. "We may have people looking for us," then added, "Nothing criminal. So they can afford to challenge any officials if they're stopped."

He watched the nine passengers disembark from the Air Force commuter jet and identified their replacements: a thin man of roughly his height and age with a brown ponytail that was probably a wig, and an Indian woman who would have a hard time passing for Dreu. She was shorter by six inches with a fuller figure. But her long black hair was woven into a loose braid and her skin was the same smooth brown. He hoped he wasn't putting them at risk, but guessed risk was part of their job.

* * *

On the plane, with the first chance to speak privately since leaving the caverns, Dreu was finally able to detail her encounter with the Russian.

"I'm sure he thought I'd never get out of there alive so he talked pretty freely," she said. "He admitted he's connected with Levanzo and I'm certain Levanzo both hired the girls in the States and eliminated the two who talked. He's our man."

"I don't think he's the brains behind this," Adam said. "Not that the old man isn't smart and devious enough. But what's he got to gain from this? I can't see that it's had any effect that would benefit a crime boss."

"Money?" Dreu suggested.

"Maybe. But the politicians aren't being extorted for money. So someone would have to be paying Levanzo to get those men into compromising situations for political reasons. It's that person we need to find."

They talked quietly, curled together in two seats with the armrest retracted until they landed for fuel at Lakenheath. She described the Russian's torture chamber and his slow process of execution and he told her about discovering the result of that process lodged in the watery passage. Neither mentioned how desperately they had feared or longed for the other, but by the time they fell asleep over the Atlantic, they both understood.

Their flight into Andrews Air Force Base southeast of the District of Columbia landed just after 11:00 p.m.—not many hours after the time it had departed Pápa.

THIRTY-SEVEN

Adam had expected a driver to meet them at Andrews but was instead handed a sealed envelope and keys to a car that sat in Operations parking. While he steered out through the main gates onto Allentown Road and access to the Washington Beltway, Dreu opened the envelope and read the brief message.

Welcome back. Rather than send the information you requested, would like to show you some video. Will be simpler if you come to me. Will also help with another issue.

Put Harris Teeters, Ashburn, VA in your GPS. When you arrive at Teeters, call this number. I'll guide you in. Don't worry about time. Will be up and waiting.

The message ended with a ten-digit phone number.

"Sounds like you might be about to meet your maker," Dreu said. But when Adam called from the lot beside the Teeters Supermarket, the phone was again answered by the Latina. She directed them onto Sycolin Road and across Goose Creek, down a dark narrow lane to the front of an ordinary fifties-vintage ranch style with ramps leading to each door. The lot behind was heavily fenced and lighted by four high-wattage halogen floods, mounted on sturdy black poles at each of the corners.

As they climbed from the car, a plump, round-faced woman with brown and gray-streaked hair stepped out into the yellow lamplight of the low porch. Adam remembered her from a brief encounter months before at a service station in Remington, Virginia.

"I didn't expect to ever come here," he said as he approached the steps that climbed beside the ramp. "This was Oz and we weren't supposed to see the man behind the curtain."

"You were close when I met you with the listening equipment for the Compton house during that Weavers mess," she said. "But we never bring anyone here." She turned to Dreu. "Welcome! My name's Nita—well, *Anita*—and I've wanted so much to meet you." She ushered them into a sparse living room that appeared to be completely closed from the rest of the house, each doorway leading from it blocked by wood-grained metal doors.

"Please—come in here." She led them through a door in the rear center of the room. The back of the house was a single large space divided between a wall of elaborate electronic equipment to their left and an open kitchen to the right. A rectangular island filled the center of the room in front of them, covered with computers, keyboards, monitors and digital readouts of every description. An elaborate motorized wheelchair with a semi-circular tray displaying its own array of computer gear stood empty near the windows that filled most of the back wall. Beyond the windows was the brightly lit fenced yard, and across the fence a field that stretched for a hundred yards to another chain link fence. The space between fences was filled with low concrete basins and also lit up like a ball field on game night. Adam noticed that folded shutters of what appeared to be finely perforated metal were pushed back along both sides of the windows, ready to be pulled across to shield the interior if anyone approached the house from the rear.

Nita stopped in the center of the room beside the island and rested an arm against its polished hardwood top.

"Believe it or not, you are the first two people other than Fisher and me to enter this room in over fifty years," she said. "We moved in here in 1961. Bud—the man you know as Fisher—had been pulled out of Norway at the end of World War II and had been managing the Baltic Desk at the CIA. When Washington began getting too concerned about covert operations following the Bay of Pigs, the Director secretly moved him out here and assigned me to join him." She looked nostalgically around the strangely arranged room, then back at her guests. "I was eighteen...a casualty from Miami of the Bay of Pigs. Because of study I had done pretty much on my own, I knew about as much about the new field of transistor technology as any person living."

She directed her attention to Dreu. "You might remember from your classes that integrated circuits were just coming on the market about then, and IBM had released its 1400 series machines. The year I came out here, Fairchild started producing commercially available circuits and FORTRAN IV was created. I'd been trained in all of what was current and they put me here with Bud to see how we could apply this new technology. This little room has been at the cutting edge of digital technology and applications ever since."

"All of that information you ask for," she said, turning to Adam. "All of that data comes from here. We're linked to every satellite, every CIA, NSA, and Interpol database. What we can't access directly, we're a message away from being able to get from Langley. The Director knows we're here—or I should say, he knows we exist. And the president knows in a removed sort of way. No one knows exactly where we are—until today. Welcome to Unit I."

Adam walked to the windows and surveyed the fenced yard. "Doesn't all this light attract attention?" he asked.

"It's intended to. People around here think we're some kind of rural sewage treatment plant," she said with a light laugh. "There's a certain irony in that, don't you think? But it seems to keep them away."

"Where's Fisher? I gather from the chair that he's been disabled."

"For over seventy years," Anita said. "He joined the RAF in the early years of the war and crashed a plane on an ice field in Norway, escaping a German attack on his squadron. It broke his back and he's been chair-bound ever since."

"And…?" Adam asked. She was standing beside the mechanized chair, her hand running affectionately across the top of its back.

"He had a massive stroke a few days after you talked to him last. He didn't make it through the night." Though her face remained perfectly calm and she straightened stoically beside the chair as she spoke, a tear welled in her eye and ran down a round cheek to her chin where she brushed it quickly away.

Adam looked around at the banks of equipment, then back to the proud figure of the Latina.

"And you've been taking care of all this yourself since then?"

She nodded abruptly, lifting her chin an inch higher.

"The Director didn't send any assistance?"

"He doesn't know," she said.

"*Doesn't know*?" Adam's voice was incredulous. "But you can't continue to do this by yourself. How do you get food and the other things you need?"

"I have them delivered. People bring things to the front and don't know any of this is here. There are no close neighbors, and those who are aware of the house know it as 'the place where the old handicapped man and the Mexican woman run the sewage plant.'" She smiled affectionately at the chair. "He wasn't handicapped. And I'm not Mexican."

"And Fisher? How did you take care of…?"

She waved an arm in the general direction of the front of the house. "He died in the bedroom, just off the living room. I had him cremated and his ashes are in the bedroom. He was from Lindsborg, Kansas, and left there to join the RAF before we entered the war. He wants me to take him back there sometime…."

Dreu inserted herself back into the scene. "You need to get help," she said. "No one can manage this alone."

Anita's tone instantly changed from nostalgic to resolved. "He'll shut us down," she said sharply. "This director doesn't value us like some of the others did. If he knows Fisher's gone, he'll close the operation."

"But if he calls…."

"He doesn't call. All our exchanges are by encrypted message."

"He must have some sense of Fisher's age…."

"Possibly. But I'm not sure he knows the full Fisher story, or that there's only been one. And as long as we're functioning and sending results, I doubt he thinks about it."

"So what do you plan to do?"

The Latina seemed to straighten even more, looking from Adam to Dreu and back. "When he knew he was losing his strength, we talked about this," she said. "He knew about you,

Dreu, because of the Weavers affair. He saw what you could do with this kind of equipment and…" she turned to Adam, "…he admired your operational ability. Wanted the two of you to take over."

Adam stood in silence for a moment, then turned to Dreu who was looking around the open, equipment-filled room with what he knew was the same thought. "We could never live out here in this isolation like you have," he said. "You've obviously been two very special people and unique to this kind of responsibility. We couldn't do it."

Anita nodded. "We knew you would say that. But this doesn't need to be here. Since no one knows where it is, it can be anywhere. Even in the middle of a city if it remains secure. In fact," she added, "that might make it even less visible in today's world."

"How do you get your funding?" Adam asked, ignoring a glance from Dreu that said "Surely you aren't considering this!"

"We're part of Langley's black ops budget and receive more every year than we can spend, now that there are just five of you. But they keep adding funds and no one seems to check. Let me just say that support is more than adequate for whatever you need to get done." She again looked seriously at each of them. "Think about it at least. You're right. I can't do this anymore and really don't want to without Bud. But if I notify the director, I'm certain it will be the end."

Adam nodded, again ignoring a withering glance from Dreu. "There are five of us?"

"There were six, but you know we lost one. The agent you took this extortion case from. There are four men and a woman."

"All working independently?"

"Just like you," she said, "…but without a friend like Dreu. That made you right for the replacement."

Adam looked at her in silence for a long moment, over at Dreu who stood staring at the floor with a tight frown creasing her face, then back to Anita. "We'll give it some thought," he said. "Now—let's see what you have to tell us about Gio Levanzo."

Anita reluctantly released the back of the chair and pulled a seat up in front of a set of monitors on the island while Dreu and Adam bent over her.

"He's become pretty solitary," she said, typing a series of commands into the keyboard. "We think most of his coordination work is done now by his son. I was going to go back and track Tony's movements also, but thought you might want to begin with what I have here."

She pulled up a camera shot of a parking area on one of the screens. "When Gio Levanzo meets with anyone, they come by car to the school his grandchildren attend in Bethesda." As she spoke, a black Chrysler pulled into view in the lot and an elderly man, casually dressed in gray twill pants and a light jacket, climbed into the car.

"That's Gio Levanzo," she said. "He owns a limo service called DCLimo and has one of the cars bring his guests. They drive around while they meet, then the car drops him off again at the school and the limo takes the visitor to wherever he's staying."

"Does anyone follow them?" Dreu asked.

"If they can. The driver's pretty good at losing a tail and a couple of times whoever's supposed to be monitoring Levanzo has missed the pickup. But of the five we have on film in the time period you asked about, we were able to identify three of the visitors." A second screen showed the limos as they pulled up to a curb and unloaded their passengers.

"One of these visits was after the liaisons with the prostitutes occurred, so we've concentrated more on the other two. The first was pretty easy to identify." She cued a clip of a video and they watched another older man in a knee-length cashmere coat, dark glasses and hat climb from the car.

"This was out at Dulles. The man is Matteo D'Onofrio. He's the major crime boss in Philadelphia and went from his meeting with Gio to San Francisco for a meeting with some Chinese businessmen. But the FBI thinks he met with Levanzo about a turf war they've been having over the area between Philly and Baltimore."

"None of our girls come from Philly," Adam said. "And none went there after their jobs were over."

"Exactly. And he's not the most interesting one anyway," Anita said, enjoying a bit of drama. "See if you can identify this man."

They watched as a tall, mustached man in dark glasses, plaid cap, and olive trench coat climbed from a Levanzo limo and walked into what appeared to be another airport terminal door.

"This is out at Reagan National," Anita said. "Any idea who this is?" Both leaned closer to the screen and watched the man walk through a sliding glass door.

"No idea," Dreu said and Adam muttered his agreement.

An inside camera picked the man up as he entered a restroom, remaining on the entryway while another dozen men entered or left. Then it froze on a figure as he exited the curved access of the airport men's toilets. There was no cap and no mustache, but the same trench coat was draped over his arm.

"My God," Dreu whispered. "It's Grant Huston."

Adam straightened and folded his arms tightly over his chest. "What's the date on this?"

Anita typed in a command and a date stamp appeared on the frame. It was three weeks before the first affair had taken place.

"But why Grant Huston?" Dreu wondered aloud.

"I'm starting to have a very bad feeling about this," Adam murmured.

"Like what?" she said.

"Like I know that from all reports, Huston and Chase Rayborn loathed each other."

"What would that have to do with our call girls?" Dreu asked.

"No idea," he said. "But can you get me a copy of this video?" he asked Anita. "Dreu, why don't you stay here and keep Anita company. I think I'll take a trip to New York and visit NBS News."

THIRTY-EIGHT

Getting to Grant Huston was as difficult as Adam imagined it would be to get to Gio Levanzo—layers of faithful foot soldiers blocking access at every turn. Adam had hoped to be able to sit down with the news anchor without having to explain to anyone what he wanted. But that reduced his chances to nil. He finally told a tightlipped assistant-to-an-assistant that either she was going to get a sealed note directly into Huston's hands or he was going down the street to the other networks with a major scoop about the PAX bombing. He assured her that the entire NBS team would be fired when it was discovered she had turned him and the story away.

The note played a hunch and informed Huston that Adam needed to talk to him privately about the death of Chase Rayborn. That, and the threat of being scooped, seemed to do the trick. The assistant-to-the-assistant returned minutes later with word that Huston would meet him in twenty minutes at 11:00 a.m. at the Rum House on West 47th Street.

It took Adam ten minutes to get to the bar and order a draft Guinness. He didn't generally drink stout but wasn't certain Huston would show and wanted something he could nurse for a long time. But mention of Rayborn's death brought the NBS newsman through the door precisely at 11:00. He nodded stiffly toward the morning bartenders and walked to a small, two-chair table at the back without looking around. Adam waited until he was seated, then ambled back to the corner and slid into the second chair.

"Can I get you something to drink?" he asked, looking directly into the uninviting eyes of the face of America's news.

"I have a lot to get done today," Huston said coldly. "Tell me what you have to say."

Adam pulled a small tablet computer out of a canvas bag he'd been carrying over his shoulder and turned it on. He punched in his security code and inserted a thumb drive. The stick contained only one file and he opened it, selected "play" on the task bar, and turned the screen to face Huston. From the shadows, he watched across the table as the iconic face saw himself climb with his disguise from the car at Reagan National, disappear into the men's room, and reappear moments later without cap, glasses, and mustache. Huston's mouth turned down slightly and his lips tightened, but he said nothing.

"Why did you go see Gio Levanzo?" Adam asked at a level only Huston could hear in the quiet of the dark bar.

Huston looked up at him over the top of the tablet. "Who are you?" he said, equally softly.

"I'm a man who's trying to figure out why high-priced prostitutes are being killed and politicians are changing their minds—and how that relates to the bombing at PAX," Adam said.

"FBI or NYPD?" Huston asked.

"Neither. But with immediate access to both. Why did you meet with Gio Levanzo?"

Huston closed the tablet and pushed it back toward Adam. "I'm a newsman. I wanted to see if I could get an interview with him on a couple of stories about crime in the District."

"Your idea, or assigned to you?"

"A combination. We've been toying with trying to talk to him for quite a while."

"Then you wouldn't mind my asking your news director about the visit with Levanzo…?"

"It was largely my idea. He may not recall." The man was remarkably unruffled by what Adam knew must be a series of lies.

"You seemed to be immediately interested when I mentioned the death of Chase Rayborn."

"You talked about a scoop. I thought you might have a story."

Adam leaned his elbows on the table. "I think I have. I'm just trying to decide who I'm going to share it with. Let me give you the generalities and you can help me with the specifics." Huston remained unmoved.

"You went to see Gio Levanzo because for some reason you wanted him to arrange for prostitutes to compromise key conservative politicians. My guess is that it had something to do with embarrassing your rival, Chase Rayborn. And possibly something to do with Senator Mehrens. All the changes seem to be in his direction. I think Rayborn figured this out and was going to expose you and Levanzo, and the Capo had him capped, so to speak."

For the first time Huston's breathing picked up and he blinked nervously. "That *would* be a scoop," he said, smiling thinly. "But it sounds to me more like the delusions of a conspiracy theorist."

"Hmmm," Adam mused, rubbing an index finger along his chin. "I'd hate to have to pass these delusions along to the don. You've seen how he reacts when he thinks someone might be about to expose him."

Huston tried to stop the reflex but couldn't stifle a hard swallow. "I've got nothing to say to you and nothing to worry about," he said.

Adam sat back and looked hard at the newsman. "Look," he said finally, "I'm going to give this to you straight. I'm not a lawman or fed or news hound of some kind. I'm a problem solver. I don't arrest people and I don't necessarily expose them. My job is to make problems go away and when they're gone, I'm gone." He stared hard at Huston.

"I'm going to solve this problem, even if I have to do it by hauling Gio Levanzo in and giving him a Guantanamo-style grilling. I just came back from Budapest where I talked to some of the women who were involved there. A friend of Levanzo's—a man they call the Russian—tried to kill my partner. We know he helped arrange to have a group of politicians blackmailed using escorts they met there at a NATO conference. You're in this, and are going to be on one team or the other. You want to be on my team or the one that loses?"

Huston blinked at him thoughtfully for a moment. "What if I told you there will be no more blackmail. No more politicians pressured and no more girls being hurt."

"I'd say if you're going to be on my team, I need to know how you know what the opposition is going to do."

"If you're the problem solver and it stops, what do you care?"

"I have no confidence in a solution I don't understand," Adam said.

"How do I know this isn't all being recorded—and isn't some kind of a setup for me?"

"Let's go into the men's room and you can check me over," Adam volunteered.

"Unbutton your shirt," Huston demanded and Adam complied.

"Okay. Let's take your tablet over and leave it with Kelly at the bar."

Adam re-buttoned his shirt, walked the tablet to the barkeep and checked it, returning to the table.

"If we're playing on the same team, I need to know what my captain really does for a living," Huston said, extending the metaphor. "Where does your playbook come from?"

"Let's just say I'm with an unofficial group that solves problems that are too messy or personal to hand over to the federal agencies. Will that do?"

"Who authorizes this group?"

"I can't comment on that, other than to say we have all the authorization we could ever need."

Huston thought silently. "Fair enough," he said finally. "This is all going to come to a head in the next day or two anyway." He ran a nervous hand through his perfectly arranged hair. "Are you ready for a story that will be almost beyond belief?"

"I've heard some pretty unbelievable stories," Adam smiled.

Huston drew a deep breath. "Well, sometime late last year I was sitting in a place called the NoMad on West 28th when Chase came in and made one of his smart comments about NBS News. I don't remember exactly what he said…."

For the next half hour Adam listened without interrupting, thinking occasionally that this may, in fact, be the most unbelievable story he'd heard.

"…so when I learned about the bombing at PAX, I knew who was behind it and got my copies of the drives. I anonymously sent one of Triplett and the tattooed woman to his wife two days ago. A copy of the meeting of Triplett's Order went to the FBI. I figure we'll learn any minute now about a raid on a compound in

Idaho, the arrest of the members of this Order, and our terrorist group will be gone. Rayborn will probably be implicated by Triplett, but he's beyond reach...." Huston slouched back in his chair and looked grimly at his new solver of problems. "There you have it in a nutshell."

Adam stared silently across the table at Grant Huston, mentally sorting through the loose ends that trailed the story like litter-filled wind gusts after a thunderstorm.

"You contacted Levanzo again—about finding someone to seduce Triplett?"

Huston nodded. "I just sent another order to the same PO box."

"And you think Triplett doesn't know that?"

"I don't think he knows about the wager," Huston said. "His connection was only with Rayborn. I may be wrong. Fatally wrong. But I don't believe Rayborn told him about me, and I had to do what I could to stop the man."

"Have you considered the possibility that he won't be there when the authorities raid the camp?"

"I don't know what would tip him off."

"This situation is too complicated," Adam said. "Too many players. When you two brought Triplett and Levanzo in, they had to let their soldiers know at least part of what was going on. That's a lot of people. And the woman who seduced him—where's she?"

"I've no idea," Huston shrugged. "I figured Levanzo would get her out of the way."

"Maybe for good," Adam muttered. "But if not, when this blows Triplett will believe it's her. He's been pretty successful at getting to people."

Huston's phone buzzed in his breast pocket and he pulled it out and punched in his access code, quickly scanning a text. As he read, his face tightened.

"Well, coach," he said, frowning darkly at Adam. "Better decide on your next play. They just raided King's Mountain and it was empty. Completely cleaned out."

"That shouldn't surprise you. But if I were in your shoes, it would make me pretty damned nervous."

"I need to get back to the station," Huston said.

"And I," Adam said, rising as Huston pushed back from the table. "I need to find the Badger."

THIRTY-NINE

Their only saving grace was that Dwayne Cargile hadn't had his picture taken since he entered the service—at least not in any recognizable form. There were a couple of group shots of him with his Special Forces unit, their faces half covered by helmets and goggles. The single photo that flashed on television screens across the country and was spit out of fax machines in every law enforcement office from coast to coast showed an eighteen-year-old kid with a tight crewcut and cheeks marred by a bad case of acne. The Dwayne who was now doing all of the shopping, checking into cheap motels, and stepping out of the faded red Corolla to get gas would not have been recognized as the same soldier. He wore the camouflage of a shoulder-length thatch of dirty blond hair, a short, ragged beard, and pockmarks he had earned from being too close to an IED on a dusty road in Iraq's Anbar Province.

Hourly reports that the FBI had identified the group responsible for the rash of terrorist attacks now flashed across every television set in America. A stunned and outraged public now knew that the perpetrators were not WIS jihadists, but misguided 'patriots.' Photos of the group's leader, Dan Triplett, were both current and unmistakable.

As Dwayne drove east, Triplett sat low in the passenger seat of the Corolla with a straw cowboy hat pulled low over his forehead and heavy dark glasses. When they passed another car he raised his hand to his jaw to further hide the news-bulletin face and insisted they stay only in motels with outside, ground-level room access. He was limiting his public exposure to the five steps it took to slide from the car and reach the motel door that Dwayne had open and held ready.

At a place that called itself the Ducum Inn just outside Marshall, Virginia, he waited until Dwayne checked them in, then carried a duffle across his left shoulder as he took the five steps, shielding his face from the office window. He threw the bag on one of the queen beds and flipped on the TV as the nine o'clock evening news began its broadcast. The stern face of

Grant Huston looked back at him from the flat screen, the anchor leaning forward across the news desk on one elbow.

"Now for the day's top story," he was saying. "In a stunning revelation, the FBI announced today that it has acquired video footage of the actual planning of one of the horrendous acts that have been terrorizing the country in recent weeks. The video, secretly recorded by an unidentified source at a meeting of an ultra-conservative group that calls itself the Order of King's Mountain, indicates that the group was motivated by a desire to swing public support to presidential hopeful Carter Graves. Their acts of terrorism, attributed to foreign jihadists, were designed to create an atmosphere of fear in the country that would lead people to Graves' get-tough stance on our relationship with groups and countries unfriendly to the United States."

The screen switched to a picture of Graves as Huston continued. "Governor Graves has emphatically denied any affiliation with the Idaho-based Order. But records of financial contributions to his campaign reveal that the leader of the Order, billionaire rancher Dan Triplett, has been a major donor to the Graves coffers."

"Damned whore," Triplett swore as the screen moved through a series of pictures of Order members, beginning with his own. He grabbed the remote and was pointing it at the screen when a familiar face filled the frame.

"In a late breaking story," the news anchor said, glancing down at the papers on his desk, "the FBI has informed NBS News that one of the group's members, a former CIA analyst who left the Agency with a medical discharge, has been arrested in the Uinta Mountains of eastern Utah. Wade Sumler was taken into custody without resistance late this afternoon at a cabin in the Uintas north of Vernal by federal investigators. Authorities were following up on tips from several Vernal residents who had seen Sumler in a grocery store in the Utah community and recognized him from televised photos."

"They already got Wade," Dwayne muttered as Huston moved on to a story about a commuter aircraft accident in West Virginia. "Thought he'd be hard to find."

"Every damned person in the country will be on the lookout for us," Triplett said. "That's why you're going to have to contact Tony Levanzo yourself and sell him on our story. If we don't get to the Badger, they'll have a witness at every trial for one of our people who can point the finger and say 'He bombed one of the stores.' Right now, they got pictures of those who were at the meeting, but that doesn't put them at the scene of the crime."

"Levanzo might put two-and-two together and know who we are," Dwayne said. "The Badger hasn't been out long enough to have been involved in too much shit."

"If we sell our story right, she could have done what we're telling him she did from about anywhere," Triplett said. "We've just got to hope he'll be pissed enough to want to get rid of her."

"Guess we'll find out tomorrow," Dwayne said. "If I can get to see the guy…."

* * *

Adam had accompanied Grant Huston back to NBS Headquarters and picked up copies of the drives the newsman had mailed to Sandra Triplett and to the FBI. He was now back in Virginia at the ranch-style west of Ashburn, watching the beginning of the Triplett-Badger sex tape.

"Adam, I know that woman!" Dreu exclaimed as the Badger turned her naked front to the camera. "She was on a team we competed against when I was at Stanford."

Adam looked critically at the snarling animal bursting from the woman's chest. "You sure? She hardly looks NCAA."

"It was an intercollegiate computer analytics competition. They gave each team a series of complex problems and we got points for how quickly and completely we were able to find solutions. She was on the Virginia team."

"And you remember her specifically? Did she have that tattoo?"

"We didn't get that well acquainted," Dreu said coolly. "We were all kind of nerdy, but she was a real loner. Just a freshman—and didn't work well with her team. But she was amazing. Possibly the best person there."

Adam smiled over his shoulder. "Better than the spectacular Dreu Sason?"

"We beat them," Dreu said. "But mainly because we had a great team and she wouldn't work with hers."

Adam watched the Badger buck wildly on Triplett's lap but his thoughts were elsewhere. "I have an idea," he said. "It may be a longshot, but we can see if the star of the Stanford team can still come out on top."

Dreu looked at him suspiciously. "You think she's left some kind of trail?"

"When the FBI raided the camp, it was deserted," Adam said. "The video copies Grant Huston sent might have reached Triplett's wife, but not in enough time for her to raise hell and force him to clear the camp out. Something warned him earlier that they might be raided."

"Surely the Badger wouldn't have tipped him off…."

"Not tipped him off," Adam suggested. "But let him know after he killed Rayborn and the PAX crew that he hadn't destroyed all the evidence. And the only other person who had copies was this woman."

"Her and your friend Huston…."

"He said he didn't send anything directly to Triplett. But if she…."

"…sent him a copy and we can find out from where, we might find her," Dreu finished the thought.

"Right. That assumes it went to a computer Triplett checked regularly. The FBI might have that now."

"Assuming it wasn't destroyed when the camp was abandoned," Anita said, joining the conversation.

"I'd guess it was at his home rather than at the camp," Adam said. "Won't know 'til we ask."

"If Triplett wasn't too sophisticated with computers, he may have thought deleting the messages would get rid of them," Dreu suggested. "Happens all the time."

"If the FBI has them, I think we can get to those machines,"

Anita said, turning to Adam. "In fact, while you were in New York, I showed Dreu how it could be done. Why don't you lay out the problem for her, and let's see how well she's mastered our little setup."

"If we find there was a message to Triplett, we try to track it backward to its source," Adam said. "That won't tell us where she is, but it might give us a chance to let her know she's in danger."

Dreu was already at one of the keyboards. "This equipment and its connections are incredible," she said, referencing a series of codes in a book beside the keyboard. "Okay—this should send a coded message to the Director…." She typed a brief message and sent it into the ether.

"What did you ask for?"

"Immediate connection to any computers taken from Triplett's home. While they work on that, I need to find an email address for the man. He was quite a financial figure so there are probably several published addresses he used. If I can find one and access the computers the FBI picked up, I'll send him a message and follow it to his account. I can find out what computers have received messages sent to that email address and if I can work my way into them, I should be able to access their memory and deleted files."

"She's very good," Anita whispered to Adam. "While I was trying to show her how all this worked, she was three steps ahead of me."

"One of the curses of working with her," Adam said with a grin.

It took the Director twenty minutes to send confirmation that two computers located in Triplett's lodge had been recovered during the raid. Both were now connected to the web and turned on.

"I have Triplett's standard business email address," Dreu said. "He has it listed all over the internet. Now—let's see what he left in his trash basket."

FORTY

Dwayne started with the youngest-looking hooker he could find on 14th Street at 2:00 in the morning, a kid who couldn't have been more than fourteen. She wore her skimpy black top, skirt and heels like she was trying them on for the first time. The night was cold but she seemed to believe a jacket would ruin her appeal and stood shivering against the wall of a closed flower shop. He figured someone that fresh to the streets wouldn't give him much lip and would be happy to turn him over to her pimp.

He was wrong. She was a smart-ass little whelp who claimed she worked alone. Plus, she insisted he looked like a cop.

"I ain't no cop and I ain't askin' you for sex—so how can I arrest you? I just want to talk to a guy here in the city, and your pimp might be able to help me find him."

"Yeah? Who you wanna talk to?"

"A guy named Tony Levanzo."

"Never heard of him."

"Your pimp's heard of him. Listen—I'll give you fifty right now if you just call him and tell him there's some guy here trying to find Tony Levanzo. I don't even need to see your man. Just talk to him on the phone."

She stayed against the bare section of wall and inspected him in the shadows cast over the car by the streetlight, arms folded tightly across her youthful chest. "You're gonna give me fifty bucks to call my pimp? What if he don't wanna talk to you?"

"Just call him and give me the phone. You don't need to say nothin'. Just give me the phone."

"Lemme see the money," she said.

He lifted a fifty from his wallet and leaned across the seat, waving it in front of her through the passenger window. She stepped forward to grab the note and he pulled it back.

"*Nah*…you make the call and hand me the phone and I'll give you the bill." He could see the watery eyes and runny nose, the swollen track marks that ran up the inside of her left forearm. The girl was desperate for the money.

"Tell you what," he said. "You call and I give you this when you give me the phone. Then I give you another if it's your man and he can give me the right information."

She frowned, eyeing the fifty, then reached into her small black purse and autodialed a number on her cell. "I got some guy here who wants to ask you about a Tony Levanzo," she said when the phone was answered. "Says he ain't no cop and don't want nothin' from me. Just to talk to you."

She listened for a brief moment. "I'm on 14th just west of the Circle. Just past the Studio," she said and again listened, then disconnected and dropped the phone back in her purse.

"He'll call back," she said. "That's fifty bucks."

"Fifty bucks when you hand me the phone to talk to him," Dwayne said. "I don't even know there was anyone talkin' to you."

She pressed against the bricks with a childish pout that made him want to climb from the car and whup the living daylights out of her for being such a stupid kid. She glanced to her left and in his mirror Dwayne saw a long white Lincoln with deeply tinted windows pull up to the curb in the shadows three car-lengths behind. Her phone rang immediately and she pulled it from her bag as she teetered over to his passenger window on the narrow heels.

"You wanna talk to him?" she said into the phone, then handed it through the window and swiped the bill from Dwayne's hand, palming it before the arm was out of the car.

"What you want with my girl?" a deep voice asked. Dwayne tried to picture the man in the white Lincoln but nothing came. The only accent in the voice was one of menace.

"Don't want nothing from your girl," he said. "I have business with Tony Levanzo and need to know how to get ahold of him."

"How come you have business with him and don't know where he's at?"

"He doesn't know about the business. But he'll be interested. It involves his friend Gabriella Marzilli."

There was silence for a moment. Then, "He won't be taking calls this early in the morning. But if I can get a message to him, how does he get to you without you bothering one of my girls?

They're supposed to be working."

Dwayne gave him a cell number.

"I'll make some calls," the voice said. "What was his friend's name?"

"Marzilli. Gabriella Marzilli."

"How you spell that?"

Dwayne spelled it out from the note Triplett had given him.

"If he calls, he calls," the man said. "Now, leave the girl alone and get outta here."

Dwayne leaned across the seat and waved the girl back over, handing her the cell and another fifty. "Go back to Kansas," he said. She dropped the phone and bill into her bag.

"Yeah, sure," she said. "Like, there's no place like home. You can shove Kansas up your ass."

As he pulled from the curb the Lincoln trailed him, breaking away when he turned left on U Street. He followed U until it became Florida, then 22rd Street and skirted Rock Creek Park. He turned into the park and found a small lot beside one of the walking trails, curled up on the seat and tried to sleep while he waited for the Levanzo network to do its business.

The call awakened him a few minutes after 6:00 a.m. and his "hello" was thick with sleep.

"You the person who wants to talk about Gabbi Marzilli?" the caller asked.

Dwayne straightened on the seat and stretched his jaw to get the cobwebs out of his head.

"Is this Tony?"

"We're not using names. But this is someone you can talk to about Marzilli." The voice sounded young. Confident, with an edge of irritation. "What's this you're saying about her?"

"I'm not really calling about her, but about a friend she had when she was in lockup. A special friend, from what I been told."

"What do you mean? Special friend?"

Dwayne stepped out of the car to let the cool morning slap him more widely awake. "Let me tell you what I'm calling about. Then you can decide."

"Just don't be bullshitting me," the voice said. "It's early, and I don't really do early."

"When your friend was doin' time, she had a cellmate they called the Badger," Dwayne said. "Called her that 'cause she's got this badger tattooed all over her tits. Anyway, she's a real computer genius. Sent up for hacking the government. But now she's out, she's turned to making her money through what they call 'hackmail.' You heard of that?"

"Yeah. I know what it is. But what's this got to do with Marzilli?"

"Well, my partner and me's got a little operation out west. Nothing bigtime, but big enough to make us comfortable. Then this Badger—she gets into our system and freezes our computers. Does this encryption thing and tells us it will cost us two hundred grand to unlock everything." Dwayne paced around the car, hoping he was sounding convincing. "We had way too much on there to just let it go. So we paid the bitch. Been chasing her down since."

"You're wasting my time here. I'm still not hearing anything about what this has to do with Gabbi—except they were in lockup at the same time."

"Cellmates," Dwayne corrected. "And the way we hear it, Marzilli picked her up when she left prison and they've got back together. Word is, the Badger's living with your friend. So I thought you might know where that could be."

"Let me get this straight," the voice said, the edge sharpening. "You're saying this Badger woman got close to Gabbi when they were at Alice, and now they're living together?"

"That's the way I hear it."

"That's a load of shit," the voice said. "I can tell you firsthand, Gabbi's no dyke."

"I'm just tellin' you the way we heard it," Dwayne said, slipping back into the Corolla as another car parked in the lot and two morning joggers climbed out. "And we don't care about your girl anyway. We just want to get to the Badger. You know for a fact your friend's not got someone stayin' with her?"

There was a long silence at the other end. "What makes you

think this Badger hacked your computer?" Levanzo said finally.

"We got some inside sources at Alice… at the prison, and they told us she was asking around before she left. Looking for good targets."

"And if you find her, what are you planning to do?"

"Get our money if we can. But one way or another, she pays."

"You planning to burn the bitch?"

"Let me put it this way. We won't be risking a repeat performance."

There was again a long silence and Dwayne thought he could hear a woman's voice in the background. Then Levanzo said, "I'm not telling you I know where she is. But if she's with Gabbi, suppose I tell you where you might find her. What do you plan to do—and when?"

"Clean things up and leave you out of it," Dwayne said. "If they're together, we might scare the shit out of both of them, but we won't hurt Marzilli."

"Not my concern what happens to Marzilli. She's past history. When would this be?"

"Depends on where it is. As soon as we can get there."

"I mean, like today?"

"If we can get to them today."

Silence, then, "I don't have any idea who you are. How do I know you're not just shittin' me?"

"You don't know who I am. I don't know who I'm talking to for sure. I'd think you'd want it that way. We just go take care of business, and nobody knows nothin'. Best for all of us."

More silence, then, "I've got to think about this. I know where you're sitting right now and I'm told you don't look like a cop. You just sit tight and I'll call you back. Maybe thirty minutes. You got that?"

"I got it," Dwayne said, glancing about at the largely empty parking area and wondering if it was a smart place to be at 6:15 in the morning.

* * *

Tony Levanzo kept a home on the family cul de sac in Bethesda but spent most of his time in Baltimore where he knew all the neighborhoods and where had become a nightly regular at Larry Flynt's Hustler Club on the Baltimore Block. He loved the women, reveled in the throbbing energy of the club, and enjoyed being Tony Levanzo in a place where everyone knew who he was and what that meant. Early mornings were now shared with Marci Madison, a strawberry blond who he kept in a top floor apartment at the Munsey on North Calvert, a few blocks from the club. Marci had been the previous year's Hustler Honey of the Year, a title earned partially because of her centerfold face and figure and partly through an unbridled enthusiasm for all things Hustler, an enthusiasm she shared willingly with the club's most notorious patron.

When the text from the capo who managed prostitution in Washington buzzed on his cell, Tony was sleeping soundly beside the naked Marci but snapped instantly awake. Though he thrived on the club's party atmosphere, he never allowed himself to drink too much, always mindful of his father's counsel that in their line of work, being alert may mean being alive.

He slid to the edge of the bed and snatched the phone from the bedside table, read the lengthy text and scowled. His day usually began at ten, and not with a reminder that he still had Gabbi Marzilli holed up at the family's summer home in Virginia. He twisted into a sitting position on the edge of the mattress, stared irritably into the carpet for several minutes, then dialed the number in the text message.

"You the person who wants to talk about Gabbi Marzilli?" he said when a sleepy voice answered. The text told him that the man was parked at a trailhead in Washington's Rock Creek Park.

Marci stirred behind him, pushed herself upright against the headboard, and listened to the exchange. She waited for a pause, then complained, "You said you'd gotten rid of that woman."

Tony's arm swung back to silence her but slapped harmlessly against the pillows.

"I've got to think about this," he said finally to the man on the phone. "I know where you're sitting right now and I'm told you don't look like a cop. You just sit tight and I'll call you back. Maybe thirty minutes. You got that?" He listened, then disconnected.

"That was about that woman who was in prison," Marci muttered, easing toward the far side of the bed. "I thought she was long gone."

"Shut up," he snapped. "You don't need to be worrying about her." Tony stared again for a long moment at nothing in particular, then walked into the bathroom and closed the door. Perched on the closed lid of the toilet, he dialed another number.

"Mike," he said quietly when the phone was answered. "I've got something I need you to do. Can you be on the road in ten minutes?"

"I'm on my way," Mike said. "Where to?"

"I need you to get out to the family's summer place in the Shenandoahs. Gabbi Marzilli's out there, and it sounds like she's got a woman with her that we sent out to do a job for us in Idaho. A couple of guys are going to be heading out there in about an hour to burn the bitch. I think they may be part of that Order bunch that's been doing this terrorist shit. I want you waiting for them when they get there. Out of sight where you can watch them. Let them take care of the woman, then ice the bastards. They can't leave the place alive. You got that?"

"Got it," Mike said and Tony could hear him descending the stairs of his Alexandria apartment as they spoke.

"What do you want me to do with Marzilli?" Mike asked.

"If the guys from the Order don't take care of her, kill her with one of their guns. We can't have anybody around who can link us to that crazy bunch."

"It's going to take me a couple of hours to get there," Mike said.

"I'll give you half an hour before I give the guy the address," Tony said. "That give you time?"

"Yeah. I'm headed out now. I'll call when it's done."

"Just send a note," Tony said.

"Gottcha," Mike said and Tony heard his soldier's pickup rumble to life.

He walked back through the bedroom to the walk-in closet and sorted through the clothes he kept in a dresser beside Marci's racks of shoes. She came to the door and leaned loosely against the frame, still naked, arms folded across her ample breasts.

"You told me that Marzilli woman was gone," she said again, watching him pull on a pair of gray jeans and a tight black pullover shirt.

"She's gone," he said, "and you'd be smart to remember she was right where you are a couple of years ago." He pushed past her back into the bedroom, glancing at the digital clock beside the bed. He made another quick call, then re-dialed the number of the man in Rock Creek Park.

"In about ten minutes, a jogger's going to run up beside your car and hand you an address," he told the man. "It's a place you can reach today. And you need to make it today. If the woman you're looking for is there, she's all yours. Do what you want with Marzilli. But if this Badger's not there, we're through talking. No more of this tracking me down shit."

"You got my word."

"Okay then—you stay where you are until you get the note, then get the hell out of my town."

FORTY-ONE

While Dwayne Cargile was waiting in Rock Creek Park for the first call from Tony Levanzo, Adam was driving west on Virginia Highway 55 toward the Shenandoah Valley. He, Dreu and Anita had also worked through the night. Dreu was back-tracking an emailed file of the video of Triplett with the Badger that she had dug up among the deleted files in one of his computers. Adam sifted through the tangle of information that had come from his meeting with Grant Huston, making sure he understood the sequence of events. Nita chased down questions that were coming at her rapid fire from both. Their activities all collided when Dreu was able to trace the email to a transmission tower near Luray, Virginia.

"You can hide these transmissions pretty effectively if you know what you're doing," she said. "And the Badger knows what she's doing. But there's always a trace. A partial fingerprint. If you have enough computer power, you can find it. And this place has got computer power!"

"Luray rings a bell," Nita said from a keyboard on the opposite side of the island, running a quick search through the data she had been amassing on the Levanzo family.

"Ah, here it is. The Levanzos have a summer place in the mountains south of Luray."

"And Huston was certain the Badger was hired by the Levanzos to set Triplett up," Adam said. "I'll bet dollars to donuts they've got her hidden away up there."

Nita drummed on her keyboard. "I'll get you an exact location…."

"I think I'd better head in that direction," Adam said, looking at his cell. "This shows Luray is a little under two hours from here."

"And what should I be doing?" Dreu asked.

"See if you can send a message to the Badger back through that channel—or more directly, if you know how. Tell her Triplett's on the loose and we think she may be in immediate danger. If you can make contact and do it safely, explain that some girls involved in the same scheme, but with different targets, were probably killed by the Levanzos. She needs to know that she might be a target from both sides. Tell her to keep her head down and stay where she is until we can figure out how to help her."

"She'll want to know who the message is coming from," Dreu said.

"If you think she'll remember you, tell her. Right now you're just a hired computer hack working with some people who are trying to help."

"Right. Thanks," Dreu muttered.

"You know what I mean. I wouldn't give her a name. Just the college competition connection—and no current affiliation. You're pretty creative about that kind of thing."

"Will she be able to trace my message to a transmission station near here?" Dreu asked Nita. "I'm sure she'll try."

"No. All of our communication goes through a discreet tower that only we use. It has no location identifier."

"Very slick," Dreu said, turning to Adam. "We'll do what we can,"

"You have any weapons in the place?" he asked.

Anita rose from the counter and led him to one of the kitchen cabinets, pushing a button inside the top of a drawer frame. The entire unit swung away from the wall, revealing an assortment of handguns and automatic rifles. He selected a Glock 19 and three fifteen-round clips.

"You may want to take this," Nita said, pulling a Remington 700 with a Leupold 3-9X40 mm scope from the rack. "I suspect you might not want to be as close as that Glock requires."

Adam held up the rifle for Dreu to see. "Look familiar?" he asked with a wry smile.

"I'm glad I'm not at the other end this time," she said.

"Inside joke," Adam said to Anita. "During that last assignment you helped us with, Dreu got saved by one of these." He slipped the Glock into the side pocket of his khaki cargo pants, tucked the Remington under his arm, and headed for the car.

As he now turned south on Virginia 340 along the edge of Shenandoah State Park, he was sorting through what he knew about the Badger and what he should do with her if he found her. The road followed the Shenandoah River, occasionally skirting its banks as it meandered across farmland dotted by neatly kept white-frame houses and classic, high-pitched barns. In the cool morning, a ribbon of mist hung over the river, lifting above the warmer green of the pastures but shrouding the two-lane road where the river flowed beside the highway. Adam switched on his lights as he entered a thin patch of fog that glowed pale yellow as the sun edged above the horizon to the east. He eased his speed back to forty, allowing his thoughts to remain partially on the problem ahead.

According to Huston, Chase Rayborn admitted that he'd approached Triplett about putting a scare into the American public but balked when it turned violent. He'd asked Huston to help him stop the guy, and the NBS newsman had again contacted Gio Levanzo who was setting up the call girls. Huston assumed from seeing the Triplett sex video that the Badger had been the answer, but the film of the meeting at King's Mountain suggested more. Even though the copy sent to Huston showed Triplett and his man Wade making specific assignments for the BestMart attacks to eight members of the Order, there had been nine bombings. So either Triplett or Sumler had carried out one of the attacks, or whoever was recording the meeting had been bomber number nine. If she wanted to maintain her cover with Triplett, the Badger hadn't been able to duck an assignment.

Adam had told Grant Huston that he was a problem solver, not law enforcement. And that's pretty much how he saw himself. He was on his way to Luray because he guessed Triplett was coming after the Badger and sooner or later—probably soon—would be able to find her. Adam's job was to stop him and end this thing. Problem solved. But if he could get his hands on one of the bombers, did he just slap her hand and let her go? Turning her in would mean going public, and he couldn't afford to do that.

His cell rang in the cup holder beside his seat and he swiped it on. "This is Zak," he said.

Dreu sounded like the proverbial kid in a candy store. "I've just got to say—before I tell you what we've got for you—that this is one incredible setup! Amazing stuff!"

Adam chuckled. "So what's this amazing setup given you?"

"Real time view of the Levanzo place south of Luray. There's a geosynchronous satellite that sits over D.C. and provides a continuous hundred miles scan. The house is just inside that radius and we have the capability to drop right down on it. Like Google Earth in real time."

"Any signs of life?"

"Two women sitting on a back deck that looks out over the valley. I'd say they're having morning coffee."

"Can you ID?"

"Interestingly enough, the satellite must be right over D.C. and we're getting some slant range imaging. I'd say one is definitely our girl."

"I'm about thirty miles out according to this GPS. I'm thinking I might find some vantage point to watch the place for a while instead of just barging in the front door. Any suggestions?"

"We've been tracking your progress. I can pull back pretty easily and see where you are on the road up the valley.... Ah! Got you! Pretty cool."

"Okay, Big Brother. Back on task. Can you see any good observation points?"

There was silence while Dreu played with her new toys. "You leave Luray going west, then turn off into the foothills. When you reach Levanzo's place, a drive goes off to your right and looks like it might wind down the hill through the trees to the front of the house. Maybe a hundred yards. If you continue past that drive, the next one is shorter and takes you to a house that appears to overlook it. Has a big back deck just like Levanzo's. I don't see any cars there, but they could be in the garage."

"Your equipment can't penetrate the roof?" Adam joked.

"Just a minute. I'll ask," Dreu quipped.

"I'll go up to the house above and see if I can get onto the deck," Adam said. "See what you can learn about the owners and the place's security. Any response from your message to the Badger?"

"None yet—but she has her cell out. And she just got up and went inside. I'll call if I get anything. And just to be safe, when you get out of the car, wear a hat. If these images are being recorded somewhere, you'll want your face covered."

* * *

Had Dreu known what other images of importance were visible to her satellite, she would have been tracking a white Ford F-150 pickup that trailed Adam by twenty minutes and a red Corolla that left the Ducum Inn fifty minutes after Adam passed the town of Marshall, following the same route south on 340 along the edge of the state park. Dwayne drove while Triplett tried to follow the hastily scribbled directions.

"What the hell is this place?" he asked.

"Some kind of family summer retreat. That's all I know."

"And he said the woman would be there?"

"No. Just said if she was with Marzilli, that's where they'd be."

"So he doesn't know where she is. Is that right?"

"That's right. He don't know. But if she's there, we can get rid of her."

"And the Marzilli woman?"

"He said he didn't care, but I couldn't tell. I think we'd be smart to let her alone if we can keep her out of it."

"I'd be getting rid of that bitch if she's gone queer on him. And it's hard for me to imagine the Badger going both ways. She really seemed to like riding a stallion."

"Can't see what difference it makes," Dwayne said. "If I was Levanzo, I'd just be happy she wasn't gettin' porked by some other dude."

Triplett sniffed. "If I was Levanzo, it'd make a difference. Don't like my women hanging out with *anyone* else!"

"That different than you hanging out with a lot of other women?" Dwayne wondered.

"Helluva lot different," Triplett said and Dwayne let it go.

"What're we gonna do when we get there," he asked.

"She'll know us, so we've got to break in and catch them by surprise. We got the masks, but she'll know our voices. And they may not be alone. You ever consider that we might be getting set up?"

"Yeah. After it took so long for him to call me back, I started to wonder. I wonder too what else is around the place."

"We got suppressers," Triplett said. "We can keep the noise down. And I think we should stop short of the target, divide up, and one of us run recon for the other. I'd like to get to the Badger and see what she's done with the videos before we kill her. If you think we should leave Marzilli alone, we can tie her up somewhere else in the place before we say anything—someplace far enough away that she can't hear us. Make it look like a robbery that went bad."

"They'll know it's us—whether we leave the Badger's body there or dump it somewhere else. That video's gonna be with the cops everywhere. And why would some robber come in and kill one woman and leave the other just tied up? Maybe we better do Marzilli, too. He didn't sound like he'd care much."

"I don't want him having that on us. And hell," Triplett said. "So what if they figure it out? They're looking for us both anyway. Before the Marzilli woman gets loose, we just got to get far enough away to make it back to Montana without being stopped."

"Simple as that," Dwayne muttered.

FORTY-TWO

The text first showed up on her smart phone and said simply "*You're in immediate danger. Contact me.*" She hated to read mail on that little screen, especially when the message was one she had to think about. And what the hell was this?

Back in front of her computer she ran a trace on the text but came up empty. Nothing that showed where it originated. She typed out a quick "*Who is this*?" and hit "send."

The response was almost immediate. *"Someone who's trying to keep you alive."*

"Who is this?" she asked again.

"Remember the computer games at Penn? I was the woman on the team you lost to."

"The tall face from Stanford?"

"That's me."

"What do you want?"

"I'm working with a group that's trying to resolve this mess you're in. We think the people from the Order are trying to find you and we want to get to them before they get to you."

"How do I know you aren't just trying to get to me?"

"We already got to you. Now we want to keep you safe."

"You have no idea where I am."

"Wrong. I just watched you go into the house from the deck. Your friend is still sitting out there with her coffee. Still a little fog in the valley over the river...."

Shit! The Badger pushed her chair back from the desk until she could see through the sliding French doors to where Gabbi sat curled around her cup. And there was still haze over parts of the valley floor. She listened for the sound of rotors overhead but heard nothing.

Back at the computer she typed, "*Where are you and what do you want me to do?*"

"I'm where I can have help to you very soon. Just sit tight for now. Who else is at the house—other than your friend?"

"How come you don't know that if you think you can see everything?"

"I can't see inside the house."

The Badger paused before sending. What were they trying to do to her? "*I got all the protection I need,*" she typed.

"If Triplett comes after you, you won't be safe. Let us help."

"I don't need your help."

"Just stay connected," the message said. *"I'll let you know what to do."*

"Leave me alone," the Badger typed and again pushed away from the desk. "Shit!" she muttered aloud. Now what?

* * *

For the first time since she and Adam left for Budapest, Dreu felt like she was completely in her element, and she liked the feeling. The screen in front of her showed an aerial view of the Levanzo property in the Shenandoah Valley. Nita sat across from her searching for information related to the security system for the house on the hillside above. Adam stood at the door of that home telling her through a headset that no one was there. On a second screen to her left, the email exchange with the Badger sat idle, waiting for someone to make the next move. She sat at the center of a small digital community and she was enjoying being its mayor.

She backed the satellite feed off to the point that she could see both homes and the surrounding thick canopy of mixed hardwoods. Adam's car was in the drive of the upper house and she had him listening in while she talked to a service agent at PHS Home Security, with Anita's information spread on the desk in front of her.

"Yes. This is Mrs. Baughman. We're at our home on Red Oak Drive in the Shenandoah Valley. I'm afraid my husband and I have both forgotten our security code for the alarm system. It's in the little booklet by the bed, but we haven't been out here since June and neither of us remembers it."

The woman asked for her birthday and Dreu glanced at Anita's neatly written note.

"September 23, 1953."

"I'll need to ask you some of your security questions," the woman said.

"Certainly—though I don't remember which of us filled out your form. Let me get Harold." She cupped her hand loosely around the mouthpiece of her headset and shouted across the room. "*Harold*! I need you back here for a minute."

"Okay," she said after a brief pause. "We're ready."

"Where did you go on your first date?"

"That one we agree on," she said, looking at Nita's note. "Cub's game. Wrigley Field."

"And what was your first pet's name?"

"If I filled that out, it was 'Trudy.' If he filled it—just a second. Harold, what would you put for first pet?" Anita mumbled something in a deep baritone.

"Patches," she said to the woman. "Trudy or Patches."

"Thank you. One more. Where did you go to elementary school?"

"Parchman Elementary for me and...Harold—elementary school?" Anita mumbled again. "Hillcrest for Harold."

"Thank you," the woman said again. "And just for your records, you filled out the form. Are you at the door now?"

"I am, but Harold keeps wandering away. *Harold*!"

"We're going to give you our pre-coded backup setting for your system, Mrs. Baughman. As soon as you are inside, enter seven-seven-four-nine and it will turn off the system. Then either check your code or reprogram the master unit with a new code before you leave. Do you understand the directions?"

"Yes, Ma'am. I think so."

"Would you like me to stay on the line while you try?"

"No. I've got it."

"Is there anything else I can help you with?"

"No, thank you. That should be all... *Harold*...it's seven-seven-four-nine. Be ready when you get inside."

The woman hung up and Dreu imagined she was turning to the woman at the call station next to her and telling her what an airhead she had just spoken to.

"Did you follow that?" she said to Adam.

"Seven-seven-four-nine," he repeated. "I'm in and it worked. And that was quite a performance! Where did you get all that personal security information?"

"Anita got it from the company's files. In her words, 'There are no secrets.'"

"Can't say I find that comforting.... I'm out on the back deck now and have a pretty good view of the Levanzo house below. Some of the deck is hidden by the house, but there's a pretty good-sized paved area in front of the house and garage and I can see most of the drive. I'll be able to see anyone who comes or goes."

Beside her Anita was calling up photos of women who were known to have connections with the Levanzo family. "This may be our friend," she said, pointing to a picture of a woman with large dark eyes, full wavy brown hair, and a thin pretty face. "She's a longtime girlfriend of Gio's son, Tony. And ahhh...look at this. Did time at Aliceville that coincided with the time the Badger was there. That's our connection—and I'd guess that's our friend-in-residence."

Dreu turned back to her view of the house. "Adam, I think we've identified the woman that's with the Badger. Name's Gabriella Marzilli. A friend of Tony Levanzo who did some time at...." She stopped and leaned into the screen, watching a white pickup turn up Red Oak Drive toward the houses. Only one other home was on the road above the Baughman place and it also looked vacant.

"Adam, you might have company," she said sharply. "A white truck just turned up your way...and it pulled into the trees to the left of the road just before it reached the drive. Can't see it now.... *Wait.* There's a man walking up to the drive...and turning down it."

"I've got him," Adam whispered through her headset. "I'm on my belly on the deck with the Remington and—just a minute. Let me get the scope on him." There was a pause, then, "I don't recognize the man. Don't think it's one of Triplett's people."

"I can see him on the drive," she said. "It looks like he's climbing up into the bushes on the uphill side. Can you see him?" She could hear Adam sliding along the floor of the deck.

"I can just see part of his back from up here," he whispered. "It looks like he's found a place to sit and wait."

"Do you think someone knows you're out there, or that Triplett might be coming for the Badger?" Dreu asked.

"Or he's waiting for the women to come out," Adam suggested.

"What do you plan to do?" she asked.

"Wait with him," he said.

For twenty minutes Dreu sat silently, her eyes roamed methodically across the array of screens. No response from the Badger. No movement from the man perched above the drive. No whispers from Adam. Nita had taken a frozen image of the white pickup and was trying to refine a steep, slant-angle shot of the plate to try to identify a driver.

"It's Virginia," she said. "And I think I have three of the...."

Dreu raised a silencing hand and again leaned into the screen displaying the overview of the houses.

"Another car's turning up toward you," she said to Adam. "Red—and its stopping at the end of the Levanzo drive. Two men are getting out...."

"I see them," he whispered. There was a pause in her headphone. Then, "One of 'em's Triplett. And I think the other's one of the men who was in the video of the Order's meeting. Both armed. Better see if you can get word to the Badger."

Dreu was already typing a message into the email chain. "*Badger. Triplett is at the house. You and Gabriella get somewhere safe!*"

Within seconds an answer came back from the Badger's smart phone. "*What do you mean—Triplett's at the house?*"

"He and another man just pulled up at the end of your drive. They're headed for the house."

"I'll kill the son of a bitch!"

"They're both armed. Stay out of sight. Is there a safe room in the house?"

A pause, then, "*Yes. But what's going to stop him?"*

"We'll stop him. Will your phone work in the room?"

"Don't know."

"If I can't talk to you, we'll pound eight times on the door when it's clear--twice. Two series of eight. Now, get in there."

FORTY-THREE

Adam heard the car before Dreu's warning reached him and he flattened against the Trex decking with the rifle barrel sticking through the railing. His cell was in the breast pocket of his jacket with a wireless earbud and mic looped over one ear. At the mouth of the drive the two men pulled on masks and silently separated, Triplett using hand signals to direct his partner farther up the road. Each had a pistol strapped to his waist and Triplett carried a short-barreled shotgun. The other man had what looked like a SIG 516 assault rifle tucked under his arm. Adam was no match for them in firepower—nor was the man hidden midway up the drive.

"The Badger's headed for a safe room," Dreu whispered into his ear as if the men fifty yards below might hear her if she spoke normally. "Want me to call in backup?"

"Not yet," he whispered. "Let's see what happens. And I need to get out of here before anyone comes. Going silent for a minute."

Triplett stood at the end of the drive until his partner was midway up the hill toward the Baughman house. The man stopped and studied the trees to his right, signaled that he was heading into the woods, and turned along what looked to Adam like a faint deer trail.

The leader of the Order stooped into a crouch and eased up the drive, staying tight in against the uphill side where he passed in and out of view as he moved toward the hidden figure. Adam moved the scope to his uphill partner who also slipped in and out of view, moving with surprising silence. Well-trained soldiers, Adam thought, and swung the scope to pick up the man hiding along the drive. He hadn't moved, suggesting that he didn't know there had been more than one man in the car and was focusing all of his attention on the figure moving toward him up the drive.

Like a general seeing a battle unfold below him through the eye of a drone camera, Adam watched the three men maneuver. Triplett passed the hidden figure unmolested but when ten yards beyond him, the man rose quietly from his hiding place. On the hillside fifty feet above and to his right, Triplett's partner froze. Slowly he raised the SIG and fired a single, muffled shot—*thump*—and the man pitched forward through the bushes onto the concrete surface.

Triplett spun, shotgun swinging up into firing position, and held the weapon at the ready while his partner moved silently down to stand beside him. They rolled the man onto his back, removed his weapons, then divided again and one scanned the hillside above while the other swept the slope that dropped off on the downhill side of the drive.

"I need to take out one of these men," Adam whispered into his mic. "I'm going to go for the other guy first, then I'll probably have to go down after Triplett."

"Be smart," she said, and he smiled that she hadn't said, "Be careful."

His first thought was to cripple the man—shatter a hip or blow out the lower part of his spine so he couldn't move, but could still talk. But then Adam would have to make his way past him in the open area in front of the house. If conscious and able to move at all, the man had the SIG and another weapon strapped to his side and could still be dangerous. Adam would either have to disarm him while Triplett was loose with that blaster, or finish him then. Might as well do it now. And it looked like they were both wearing body armor.

The pair remained twenty feet apart in a semi-crouch and slowly started again up the pavement, disappearing behind a screen of overhanging trees. Adam moved his sights to where they would emerge—Triplett first against the hill closest to him, then the man with the SIG. As they came into view, Adam sighted just above and in front of the man's left ear and squeezed off a shot. The bullet took the killer over the edge of the slope that dropped away from the drive on the far side. As Adam threw the bolt on the Remington, Triplett took two steps to his right and dove down the incline after the fallen man, turning as he went to scan the house above.

Adam rolled back against the glass doors of the Baughman

house to where he could rise into a crouch without being seen from below. To the left of the doors, a set of stairs descended to a small walled patio notched into the hillside. He sprinted toward them in a crouch, jumping the first five steps as automatic rifle fire sprayed the wall behind him. He vaulted the railing where the stairs turned, dropping the six feet to the terra cotta tiles of the patio. Triplett had recovered the SIG.

The wall was only waist high but he was again far enough from the patio's edge to be out of sight. Adam dropped to his knees and crawled to the brick barrier.

"Can you see them?" he whispered to Dreu.

"They're lying just off the drive—almost to the parking area in front of the house. No sign of life in the one you hit. I think you'll be below the tree line now if you need to move. But I'm looking pretty much straight down on things and it's hard to get perspective."

Adam rose quickly and glanced over the wall, then dropped back into a crouch. The brush on the other side was thick enough to screen the patio from the drive below and he was able to stand and study the slope more carefully.

"Nita's just called up a profile on Triplett," Dreu whispered. "He was Special Forces."

"Heard it on the news," Adam said, already aware that he was facing an experienced soldier with an assault rifle. And now, no element of surprise. But at least that gave Adam a better sense for what the man might do. And he had Dreu and the sky cam.

Immediately below the patio to his left a steep ravine cut into the slope, angling down along the side of the Levanzo house.

"Can you make out the ravine on your satellite image?" he asked.

"Yes. Let me get in a little closer.... It starts just below you and goes down by the north side of the house—that's to your left. The deck comes around that side and extends over the ravine when you get down there."

"Has Triplett moved?"

"No. He looks like he's trying to gather up the weapons."

"He'll find a place to wait where he thinks I'll have to come.

When two people are hunting each other, you want to be the one who's hiding and stationary."

"If he gets under the trees, I'll lose him," she said. "The leaves are thinning, but I can't see through in most places."

"Just watch. And when he starts to move, tell me which way." Adam slipped silently over the wall, made his way to the edge of the ravine, and started slowly downward. Brown leaves covered most of the ground with a dry, brittle carpet and he picked his way carefully along a series of small outcroppings where erosion had uncovered the bedrock. Recent rains had flooded the ravine, leaving the same gray stone exposed along its bottom.

From the Baughman deck, Adam had been able to see that on the back of the Levanzo place the hillside dropped away steeply enough that the ground floor was accessible only from the front. A paved walk led from the main door to the garage, then from the garage to a deck extension. If Triplett planned to get into the house, he had to cross the open parking area unless there was a basement entrance in the rear—or steps up the back like he had just used at the Baughman's. Adam glanced back at the house behind him. No basement doors there and he guessed that for security, Levanzo's wouldn't have one either. He also doubted that they had rear stairs to the deck. The house would have been designed to minimize access.

"Any steps going down from the Levanzo deck?" he whispered to Dreu.

"No. Railing all the way around to where the deck joins the drive by the garage."

What was Triplett thinking? Now that he knew he was being hunted, he would either find a place to burrow in and wait for the enemy to come to him or get into position to cover the front of the house. Levanzo's girlfriend may have called for help and have others on the way. Until he knew, a trained soldier wouldn't want to be trapped inside, even with hostages. He'd want plenty of room to maneuver.

"Any contact with the Badger?" Adam whispered.

"No. I hope that means they're locked in a safe room."

"Going dark for a while," he said. "Let me know if he

moves." He edged down the stone bed, moving a slow step at a time, scanning the brush at the upper edges of the wash. Ahead, the pillars that supported the deck extended almost to the bottom of the ravine.

As he neared them, a dirt trail climbed both sides of the wash where he guessed some of the Levanzo children had slid down to play under the overhanging decking and scrambled up the opposite slope.

"He's moving!" Dreu said sharply into his ear. "Down the other side of the house."

Now—what would he do? Find a central position below the house where he had a view of both corners and the deck above, or work his way around to where he had a clear view across the front? If it were him, Adam thought, he'd want control of access points to the house.

He moved as quickly as stealth allowed, climbing the side of the ravine away from the basement wall. Near its top, a thick clump of rhododendron partly obscured the trail and he burrowed through it to a patch of bare ground, twisting on his stomach until he could see both down and across the cut in the hillside. He was now north of, and slightly below, the edge of the deck. Across from him was a bare stretch of concrete wall. He drew a deep, silent breath through his nose and waited.

"I've lost him," Dreu whispered. "He went under the deck in back."

The woods surrounding Adam also seemed to be holding its breath—nothing stirring on the crisp leafy floor or fluttering in the branches overhead. He could hear and feel his heart against the cold earth, suddenly aware as he had been in the cave beneath Budapest of the unnerving darkness on his blind side. He knew he hadn't been completely silent as he'd moved down the wash and Triplett wouldn't be either. He focused every sensory impulse on sound and eased the rifle into position, the end of the barrel still hidden in the dense brush. Silently he reached to his waist, released the safety on the Glock and moved it up beside his shoulder.

To his left, a cascade of small stones trickled down the slope, dislodged by a foot edging along the exposed bottom of the foundation. Adam remained frozen, watching Triplet first glance quickly around the corner of the basement, then slowly ease across the base of the wall. The man edged forward a quiet step at a time, the SIG held ready and his back against the concrete, scanning up and down the wash and peering up through the slats in the deck overhead.

When he reached the end of the foundation where the faint trail climbed to the front of the house, he stopped, crouched lower, and looked up the path in both directions. His eyes fell for a brief moment directly on Adam's hiding place. Adam tightened his finger on the trigger, then relaxed as the man shifted his gaze back up the ravine.

Easing slowly around the end of the basement, Triplett started up the opposite slope, the SIG pointed ahead of him. Adam knew he would stop just below the crest and stretch out, surveying the area in front of the house and looking for a strategic vantage point. Right on cue, Triplett lowered himself silently to the ground at the top of the path and edged slowly to his right behind a row of azaleas that bordered the parking area. Adam had to act before the man decided to run for cover somewhere else along the front of the house.

"*Freeze*!" he barked sharply, pulling the rifle snug against his shoulder.

Instead, Triplett rolled hard to his right, bringing the SIG around and spraying the opposite side of the ravine with automatic fire. The branches above Adam's head shredded under the hail of bullets and he swung the Remington after Triplett and fired, throwing up a blast of dirt just beside the moving figure. Adam reached for the Glock and extended it with both hands, keeping his body as flat against the ground as physics allowed. His first shot hit Triplett's vest and he saw his body jerk under the blow but knew it hadn't been a kill shot. The head was too small to target with the pistol from this position so he moved downward, firing at Triplett's groin. What came from the man was more an agonized groan than a scream and he doubled forward but kept the SIG firing in Adam's direction until the clip emptied.

Adam edged into a crouch, the Glock still trained on the wounded man. Triplett was fumbling for another clip.

"Hands out where I can see them," Adam barked, stepping out of the brush to the edge of the ravine.

The leader of the Order of King's Mountain glared at him, his face twisted in agony. He dropped the assault rifle and his right hand groped for the pistol at his hip.

"*Don't!*" Adam ordered and fired a round into the padding covering Triplett's right shoulder, pitching him again onto his back. He lay for a moment without moving, then struggled again toward a sitting position, his hand feeling for the weapon.

Adam fired at the uncovered arm but only grazed it as Triplett's hand found the grip and pulled the weapon free. Adam raised the Glock and fired and Triplett collapsed backward, the pistol still gripped in his hand.

Edging downward with the Glock trained on the still figure, Adam climbed the opposite bank until he could see where the shot had pierced Triplett's forehead. He eased carefully around him, leaving the SIG where it lay and the pistol in the dead man's grip, and walked out onto the apron in front of the Levanzo garage. Immediately Dreu's voice was in his ear.

"I can see you," she said breathlessly. "What's happened?"

"Both men down," He said. "Both dead."

"The French doors to the deck are still open in back," Dreu said. "The women went in fast when I texted them and left them open. You should be able to get in there. I told the Badger you'd pound eight times on the door of the safe room, pause, then pound eight more as an 'all clear.'"

"I'll find them and give her the signal, then I'm out of here. Send her a message to have some of Levanzo's men come clean this up. I need to be gone."

"Sending it now," she said.

He followed the walk around the side of the deck, Glock still at the ready, and slipped through the sliding doors into a casually furnished sitting room. A quick walk-through of the main floor didn't turn up a safe room and seemed to account for all the floor space. Nothing hidden behind a false wall.

In a central hallway he found a door that opened onto basement stairs. He flipped the light switch and inched downward, stopping with each step and hearing nothing. The safe room was a concrete box with a heavy metal door tucked into one corner of the bottom floor. No effort to hide the thing. He walked to the door and pounded eight times, paused, then pounded again. A few seconds later a voice came through a small speaker beside the steel frame. "This Mike?"

"No. Who's Mike?"

"Who is this then?"

"I'm with the person who's been sending the texts. All's clear outside. Triplett's dead."

"How do we know it's safe?"

"I gave the eight knocks, right? She told you that would mean you could come out."

"I don't know that I can trust her either. I don't even know who sent those messages."

"Stay in there then. But if you have a way to get ahold of Levanzo, tell him there are three bodies outside. Triplett and some guy who was with him—and maybe one of Levanzo's people. One's on the drive. One's just off the edge before you get to the house, and the other's beside the walk that comes around onto the deck. Someone might have reported all the shooting and he'll probably want to get rid of the bodies before the cops show up."

He turned and climbed the stairs, exiting through the open French doors. Dreu was back in his ear as he scrambled back up through the woods toward the wall that surrounded Baughman's patio.

"Where are the women?"

"The Badger didn't seem to want to leave the room. Asked if I was 'Mike.' Might be our man on the drive. I'm on my way up the hill to close up the house. I'll punch in the code before I leave. Should be no sign of entry, but there are bullet holes all over the back wall. Do you show any traffic coming our way?"

"Nothing. But you may not want to come back on Highway

340. If Levanzo's sending more people from Washington or Bethesda, they'll be coming from the north."

"Pick a route and call me."

"Nita's got one already. When you get to the main road, turn west about ten miles and you'll hit Highway 11 going north to Winchester. Then you can take 7 back across to Ashburn."

Adam scrambled over the low brick wall, checked to make sure the Glock was still in his waistband, and climbed the stairs to the Baughman's deck. The one casing from the Remington lay near the far end and he retrieved it, locked the sliding doors as he re-entered the house, and re-armed the alarm system. Five minutes later, he turned west on Virginia 221 toward New Market, wondering if the Badger and her friend were still holed up in their concrete box.

FORTY-FOUR

Gabbi Marzilli called Tony Levanzo from the safe room phone as soon as they locked themselves in.

"What the hell do you mean, someone sent a text and told you some guy was coming to kill you?" he said. "Why would anyone be coming to kill you?"

She told him she was staying there with a friend who'd just come out of Aliceville. The one they'd sent to do the computer job in Idaho. "They're after her," she said.

"What're you doing there with this friend?"

"Givin' her a place to lay low for a few days. Nothin' to get all bent outta shape over…."

"So what the hell did she do to have people hunting her down?" Tony asked.

"I think it has something to do with that bunch that's actin' like terrorists and killin' all the people."

"Christ!" Tony Levanzo swore. "You getting us mixed up in that mess?" He turned from the phone to talk as if he had someone on another line. "You stay put," he said when he came back to her. "I've got a guy coming out. His name's Mike. He'll tell you who he is when everything's clear."

"Okay," she said. "We're not leaving 'til Mike gets here."

* * *

After the man gave the eight knock signal and left them, Gabbi again called Tony.

"Some guy was here at the safe room. Said he killed three people outside—someone named Triplett and two other guys. I think they might be some of the terrorist people who's been on TV. The guy knew this was your place and said you might want to send out someone to clean up."

"Where's this guy now? Mike should be there."

"I think the guy left, but I'm not goin' out 'til I know Mike's here."

"Listen. Have you got the cameras on? Go to that box below

the screens and turn the cameras on. You can look at every room and see if anyone's walking around. Do it now. If the guy's gone, I need you to do something."

Marzilli handed the wall receiver to the Badger. "Here. Hold this a minute," she said and messed with the switches in the box until the screens lit up, showing three different rooms.

"I got it," she said, returning to the phone. "I can see three of the rooms."

"Flip the switches for each screen and you can see the whole house."

"I'll look at it. What if it's clear?"

"Then there's something I need you to do." She listened without interruption for three or four minutes.

"I can't do that," she said when he'd finished, then listened for another minute.

"I know, Tony, but…." His voice was loud enough against her ear that the Badger looked over.

"Okay. Okay. I understand," she said and hung up.

She looked grimly at her tattooed lover. "Tony wants us to check the house with the cameras and if we don't see no one, go out and see if that guy was telling the truth. See if there's three bodies outside."

"We can do that," the Badger said calmly. "How do we check the rooms?"

Gabbi led her to the control panel. "Switch these settings for each screen from one room to another. Here—they're all labeled." She moved from room to room with the cameras while both watched the screens. "If the bodies aren't dead, we need to finish them off," she said without looking at her partner.

"If they're bodies, they'll be dead," the Badger grinned. "And we can do that, too. If it's Triplett and some of his men, I'll do it myself. But with what?"

Gabbi walked to a heavily padded bench seat and lifted the lid. The base held four handguns, a shotgun and two assault rifles. "Pick what you want," she said. The Badger selected a light Beretta and slammed a clip into its grip.

"This will do just fine," she said. They worked their way

through the rest of the house, scanning each room with the sweep feature of the cameras.

"Looks clear," Gabbi said and they threw the heavy steel lever on the door and edged it open. With the Badger leading with the Beretta gripped in both hands, they made a quick sweep of the house and around the end of the deck to where it joined the walk beside the garage. The Badger leaned cautiously over the rail and looked into the ravine.

"Here's one. And the guy was right. It's Triplett. And there's no need to check him. Bullet through the head."

Gabbi looked over the edge and shuddered. "Just where he said he'd be. I hope the others are just as dead." She followed the Badger across the front of the house.

"Dwayne Cargile," the Badger said as they stared down at the second body, crumpled beside the drive. "He was Triplett's main guy. Former Army buddy."

"Pretty dead too," Gabbi said. "Whoever got 'em was good."

The Badger stood over the body for a moment, pointing the Beretta down at the pale corpse. Then she stepped back up onto the drive and looked toward the road where the third body lay face-up a hundred feet away. Marzilli trailed her until they both stood over the dead man.

"Not one of Triplett's," the Badger said.

"No. I've seen this guy before," Marzilli said. "This is Mike."

The Badger turned slowly, studying the trees that climbed the hill in front of the house and what could be seen of the overhanging deck above.

"Come on," Gabbi said, pulling at her arm. "The guy's gone and Tony's sending more people out here. They'll be here in an hour. I'm feeling all dirty. Let's go get cleaned up."

The Badger looked over at her. "This stuff does that to you, too?" she said with a suggestive smile.

Back in the house Gabbi led her into the master bedroom where the shower was a large walk-in in rose-colored marble.

"Get the water hot and I'll be right in," she said as the Badger stripped off her clothes. Gabbi undressed slowly and waited until she could hear the water running, then took the Beretta from the bed and stepped into the shower. The Badger turned and looked at her, her eyes immediately understanding and her mouth curling into a cynical smile.

"So it's going to be Cypher," she said cryptically as the bullet shattered her chest between the outstretched paws of the badger.

FORTY-FIVE

They met again at a back table at the Rum House, Adam arriving early and waiting near the door nursing a Guinness until Grant Huston was seated at his customary table. Adam ambled to the dim corner and before he was even comfortably in the other chair, the newsman spoke.

"They've been able to catch five more members of the Order. But not Triplett—though we did get a report his wife's filed for divorce."

"Triplett's dead," Adam said.

Huston's brows arched and his mouth tightened into a downward bow. "You sound certain."

"I am certain. And another member of the Order with him. A man named Dwayne Cargile."

"And you know this because…?"

"I learned from a very reliable source."

"One you'll share?"

"No. But I know it's accurate information."

"We can't go public with it without verification," Huston said.

Adam shrugged. "My guess is you'll never get it. But it might be a good thing for you to know. The Order's pretty well history. Eight dead or in custody."

"What happened to the woman who was in the video with Triplett?"

'No idea. But I doubt she knew you were part of the wager—or that there ever was a wager."

"Probably right. Is that why you wanted to meet? To tell me Triplett's dead?"

"Partly," Adam said, taking a sip of his Guinness. "And partly to tell you it's time for you to step down at NBS. I'll give you until the end of the year."

Huston's face relaxed into an expressionless mask. "I thought you said you were a problem solver—not law enforcement."

"Exactly right," Adam said. "I'm not turning you in—though I do think you're responsible for a number of deaths. But you're a problem. And your leaving the newsroom will be a big step toward the solution."

Huston sniffed. "What's to be gained by that? Both the candidates are toast. Graves is scrambling to try to prove he didn't have any direct ties with the Order and his numbers have dropped to zilch. During the crisis, people saw Mehrens as milquetoast—with no real solution to a terrorist threat if one were to come onto our soil. The man's not able to make the tough decisions. The public's better off with both men gone."

"That's beside the point," Adam said. "We expect politicians to lie, cheat and steal. We hate it about them, but that seems to have become life in Capital City. But newsmen? They're supposed to be above all that. The place we go to find out what's really going on. You've pretty well shown you can't be trusted to do that."

"You think I haven't learned my lesson?"

"Not if there's no consequence."

"*No consequence*? I've been scared shitless the last two months. How's that no consequence?"

"Poor you," Adam muttered. "But I'll make you a deal. I can turn over all the information about your wager with Rayborn and everything that happened as a result and let you sort that out with the authorities—and with your network people. Or you can step down by the end of the year. If you think you've done your penance, we can see what they all think."

"I'll have to give this some thought."

"You've only got a few weeks. I have the file ready to go if I see you on the news in any capacity after January first. And don't start toying with the idea of sending some of your Bethesda associates after me. For one thing, they won't find me. And for another, if I get wind of it—and I will—you'll go the way of Triplett and Dwayne Cargile."

"Don't threaten me," Huston hissed as Adam pushed back from the table and stood.

"As Eastwood would say," Adam said, leaning back over the table, "'That's not a threat. It's a promise.' I've learned from all this that you're something of a gambling man. I sure as hell wouldn't bet on this one."

FORTY-SIX

By the time the transition was complete, Grant Huston had announced that he was stepping down at NBS News to allow more time to complete a memoir. The final member of the Order of King's Mountain had been taken into custody, though no one had ever found Dan Triplett or Dwayne Cargile. In the Iowa caucuses neither Carter Graves nor Clayton Mehrens drew enough support to be considered serious contenders and both formally withdrew from the primaries, Graves under the cloud of an ongoing investigation.

Dreu read the details of the investigation in an online edition of the *Washington Post* and turned to Adam, who sat with his long legs stretched across a brown leather ottoman, a thick notebook cradled in his lap.

"Do you think Graves even knew about the Order and Triplett's activities?" she wondered.

Adam looked up and considered the question for a moment. "My guess would be no. I think both of our newsmen were trying to keep the people involved in their manipulations to an absolute minimum—and tell even those few as little as possible."

"Are you surprised nothing's turned up about Triplett and Cargile?"

"No. I suspect the Levanzos took care of them in whatever way they dispose of those who get crosswise with them. They probably have something equivalent to the cave of the Russian. We'll never know what happened to them."

"The Levanzos. They're the only ones who really came out of this unscathed. Them and the Russian, I guess...."

"And it appears he's under investigation for the death of that minister. What was his name?"

"Elek Goda. But they won't be able to pin it on him."

He nodded absently. "You missing your business?" he asked.

Dreu shrugged. "Not really. The employees collectively bought me out and will do a great job. Smart bunch and really creative." She laughed softly to herself. "My mother's having a fit—not knowing exactly what I'm doing and whether it's an acceptable profession. I mean, what does one tell one's friends?"

"What *did* you tell her?"

"That I'm now involved in high level security consulting with the government. She reads that as meaning my business failed."

"And how are you feeling about that?" he asked.

She thought for a brief moment. "Not too bad, actually," she said finally. "I should have followed Arun's example years ago and gone off to race with my own team. What about you? Are you going to miss being out on assignment?"

"Who said I'd stop being out on assignment?"

She frowned over at him. "Maybe I should have read through the 'terms and conditions' a little more carefully."

A small black communication console on the table beside Adam buzzed loudly, echoing from four other speakers in strategic places throughout the Scottsdale apartment. Dreu stood quickly and started for a new circular staircase in one corner of the living room that led up into the top floor apartment they had acquired after returning from Virginia.

"I'd better get up with Nita and the equipment," she said. "She only agreed to help for a couple of days and may need to talk me through this one. Put it on speaker."

Adam glanced at the digital readout on the console. Jeffrey Lyons. He waited until Dreu had climbed to the data center and punched the answer button.

"This is Fisher," he said.

There was a long moment of silence. "This doesn't sound like Fisher," the man said finally as the voice recognition program in the console confirmed his identity as Lyons.

"Different voice," Adam said. "But everything else is the same."

Author's Notes

In the Acknowledgments I thanked my friend Lori Marble for initially suggesting the central idea of this plot. During a drive home from a work assignment that had taken us to the state capitol, she said that she had always thought there would be a great novel in a story about two network news anchors who make a wager that they can shape the outcome of an upcoming presidential election. That was probably twenty-five years before this novel was written – but I did ask her permission to use the idea before I started this work. I suspect she was thinking of a contest that was much more above board, not one involving blackmail using expensive call girls and domestic terrorism. But that's the risk you take when you turn over an idea!

Part of my own academic background is in media studies and political theory and I've been particularly intrigued over the years by the way the media shape public perception. I agree that news organizations aren't completely successful at telling us what to think, but they are quite successful at telling us what to think about. I continue to believe that the "mainstream media" do work at maintaining some semblance of balance. It is a balance that is strongly shaped by commercial pressures to satisfy various public interests, but in a broad sense, there is reasonable balance. Advocates on both sides of the political spectrum like to imagine that there is not – because we tend to interpret "balance' as meaning "largely supportive of our particular point of view" and I admit that each news organization has its leaning. The most accurate news presentation comes from exposure to a number of sources with disparate points of view.

At the risk of becoming preachy, I hope that this novel has served to some degree to get readers to think about the complexities of the issues we face in the world, and how unlikely it is that one political perspective is completely right while another is completely wrong. We should all be seeking solutions to complex problems through some complexity of thought – not through endorsement of one simplistic set of tenets.

As with all of my novels, I have attempted to take the reader to some new part of the world, to acquaint you with interesting peoples and places. It is always some place I have visited myself and I try to recreate it as accurately as possible, within the limitations of the story. This time it was Budapest – a beautiful, historic, romantic city on the Hungarian Danube. The Liszt Academy, Gellert Hotel, Gellert Hill, and Cave Church are all actual places and I hope, effectively described. The hill is honeycombed with caverns, and though as far as I know there is no secret passage behind the alcove with the chi rho cross that stands at the end of one of the side chapels in the Cave Church, it wouldn't surprise me at all if one were discovered. Hungary is a productive member of the European Union and does support an international heavy airlift wing at Pápa, with a large Boeing maintenance support group. To my knowledge, none of its employees is affiliated with the CIA.

All characters in this novel are purely fictional and creations of my imagination. Any similarity to public figures is coincidental – the result of writing about a political climate in which someone is likely to be similar to virtually any created character.

Unfortunately, information reviewing a threat assessment study of the BART system, how to make an M183 military demolition kit, and where to acquire a stinger missile is all available online to anyone willing to look hard enough. One of the great ironies of living in a society in which one of our inalienable rights is free expression is that it seriously compromises both our personal and national security.

Finally, readers have occasionally criticized my books for outlining attack strategies against the United States that seem too plausible. Why, they ask, would you even want to make a potential enemy aware of such a vulnerability? My answer is pretty simple. If I can think of it, some warped mind much brighter than mine probably already has. And I hope someone in our own security and defense organizations has as well and is doing something about it. My greatest wish as a writer of thrillers is that nothing I write about will ever happen.

Other Allen Kent Novels

Unit 1 Series

The Shield of Darius

The Weavers of Meanchey

Domestic Mystery

Backwater

Historical Fiction - The Whitlock Saga

River of Light and Shadow

Wild Whistling Blackbirds

International Mystery

Guardians of the Second Son

71136917R00190

Made in the USA
San Bernardino, CA
11 March 2018